RANSOMED PEACE

BAY TOWN BOOK FOUR

KATHLEEN J ROBISON

ISBN: 978-1-962377-16-4

Celebrate Lit Publishing

304 S. Jones Blvd #754

Las Vegas, NV, 89107

http://www.celebratelitpublishing.com/

Thou dost keep him in perfect peace,
whose mind is stayed on thee,
because he trusts in thee.
Isaiah 26:3 (RSV)

PROLOGUE

Roxanne Cook held her breath. Waiting, hoping, watching. What were they thinking? She sighed and walked to the bay window, looking out on Main Street. Sucking in a breath, she drank in the florist shop's sweet floral perfumes and fresh-cut greenery.

The Pink Rosette. Her haven. She'd worked here part-time throughout high school and on college breaks, sitting on a stool at the large table. Green smudges covered the well-worn butcher block. Cuts and slices marred the wood, telling tales of beauty, sorrow, and gaiety. Now, just out of college, here she stood again.

She looked back at Miz Philippa Tippet, whose eyes darted across the lines of Roxanne's manuscript. A crisp wind blew through the half-open Dutch door, and Roxanne drew her knit tunic around herself. Max, Miz Philippa's husband, hovered over his wife. The couple owned the Pink Rosette, the award-winning florist in Bay Town.

Max glanced at Roxanne and winked. The rock of assurance. Well, Mama and her church taught her that Jesus was the rock, but Max held a close second. The old soul, yet only ten years her senior.

Miz Philippa took the stack of pages in both hands and

shuffled them. "It's good," she said. "Of course, it needs a thorough edits, but you wrote this very well." A smile barely graced her lips, but her eyes shone with approval. "Roxanne, you are a gifted writer."

Roxanne rushed to the worktable with outstretched arms but stopped short. Miz Philippa's back straightened. The prim and proper British lady didn't hug. Roxanne politely extended her hand, and the woman gave it one firm shake.

Turning to Max, Roxanne smiled, and he flung his arms wide. She rushed into them, practically knocking Phillipa off her stool. The story papers flew everywhere. Roxanne gasped. It wasn't her scattered pages now soaking dampness from the concrete floor which horrified her, but that she'd inadvertently assaulted Miz Philippa.

"Well, that's a fine way to end my critique." Miz Philippa righted herself.

"And a fine critique it 'tis, my dear." Max winked.

Roxanne stooped to gather the limp pages. Some dripping, others tearing as she lifted them off the floor.

Miz Philippa huffed. "Oh, it's all right. I have it saved on my computer."

A rising panic gripped Roxanne. "You didn't mark these pages yet, did you?"

"Of course not. Why would I do that if it weren't worth reading first?"

Max laughed and kissed his petite wife smack on her pink lips. Philippa blushed. Like Max, she was a decade older than Roxanne. Though sometimes it felt like more years hovered between them. Max and Philippa had no children, and they'd become like an aunt and uncle to her. They'd been her writing mentors through her high school and college years. They chattered about the characters and plot lines in her book with Philippa already giving advice about searching for agents and sending out queries.

"Ladies, shall we celebrate?" Max exited to the backroom

and promptly returned. He held three glasses by their stems in one hand and a bottle of sparkling cider in the other.

"Did you really like it, Miz Philippa? Not too sappy? I mean, I've always liked romance books, but to write one myself..." She took a glass from Max. "What about you? Did you get a chance to read it?" She shrugged. "Oh, probably not, huh? You're so busy."

"Hold on, there. First things first. And by the way, yes. I already read it."

He poured the cider and raised his glass. "To you, Roxanne, for finishing the book. To my lovely Philippa for her critiques. But most important to God for giving the gift of words, for His glory. Cheers."

"You read it? Really, Max?"

"I did, and it's lovely. Sure, a little sappy, but that's romance, eh?"

A chuckle escaped Miz Philippa's lips as she sipped.

Warmth flooded Roxanne. Having their approval felt as good as when she'd won first place in the local jr. high writing contest. Philippa Tippet, Bay Town's famous local author, had been the judge for the competition, and they'd become friends ever since.

"Now, Roxy, don't go quitting your teaching job just yet, but you must promise me you'll keep writing. After you get these pages cleaned up and make this the very best your story can be, Max will help me with a first edit. When it's ready, we'll ask my agent to take a look. Agree?"

"Yes, of course. Agreed!"

Roxanne wanted to hug them both, but with restrained joy, she smiled. *I'm going to be an author.*

CHAPTER 1

Present Day, fifteen years later

R oxanne held her breath and typed *The End.*
       Backspace, backspace, backspace...*maybe not.* The movement caused her to wince as she rubbed the ace bandage on her wrist.

It is The End. She sighed and pulled a flash drive from her desk drawer. Inserting it into the hub, she hit save and crossed her fingers, hoping her old computer wouldn't fail her now. Unprompted, she twisted the opal ring on her right hand. Pushing it round and round till the one bent prong scraped.

Ouch. She glanced at the flecks of purple flashing through the pure white stone. Ignoring the poke, she thought of her mother and smiled. The ring had been a gift when she'd graduated from college. A long time ago. The tiny blue sapphires surrounding the opal set in the shape of a dove still brought a smile to her face. She rubbed the light lines, cupping the corner of her eyes. The gem signified inner peace and joy, and the bird symbolized hope. Her smile faded.

Her mama's prayers for her all these years. Inner peace. Joy. Hope. Roxanne sighed. The blue circle on the computer screen continued to scroll as she twisted her braided hair in both hands, wincing at the pain in her wrist. How did she get here? Trapped in her own house in Meridian, Mississippi, hours away from her childhood home. How she missed Bay Town by the gulf.

"Come on. Save." She pleaded with the ancient PC as if begging an old friend but simultaneously berating herself for not purchasing a new one long ago. Gazing at the light screen, she glanced at the time on the bottom corner. Her heart sunk. *Oh, no.*

The front door slammed, and Roxanne's body stiffened.

"What's for dinner?" a deep voice bellowed.

Roxanne glared at her screen threatening it to hurry. The still-scrolling, little blue circle only angered her, but she looked up and forced a smile.

"Hey, Dwayne. It's five already? Wow, I lost track of time. How about some sandwiches?"

Dwayne Payton, her boyfriend, strode to where she sat. Baggy basketball shorts fell just below his muscled thighs, and a sweaty tank top stretched across his formed chest. His six-foot, three-inch frame towered over her. She pushed her chair to stand, but he pressed her down. His large hands squeezed both her shoulders and her body ached under his pressure. Still, she held her tongue until he nuzzled her neck, and his stubbled cheek scraped her skin.

"That hurts," she said.

"Come on, Roxy. You love it, and you know it."

His hot breath on her neck caused a revulsion, and she hunched down out of his grip. Scooting off the chair, she stood. "Turkey or ham?"

"Dinner isn't ready?"

Sometimes, he promised to come for dinner, and stood her up. Not this time.

Dwayne blocked her path, and she spotted the cast-iron skillet sitting on the stove, then glanced at him. No, but she'd thought about using it before. A weapon if needed. Her mind sputtered in all directions, trying to decide the best course of action. *Diffuse, deflect, or run?*

She smiled, hoping he'd return the gesture. She never knew what would trigger his rage. But a hungry stomach guaranteed it. He glared back at her.

Dwayne grabbed her wrist and yanked hard, pulling her to him. She stared back. Perhaps she shouldn't have. The submissive glance downward might have been the better choice. It didn't always work, but sometimes it calmed him. Other times, it fueled him.

She waited and a grin inched it's way to the corner of his mouth.

"Listen, babe, let's go out," he said.

Roxanne allowed a smile to form while holding a breath of relief.

He bent over and kissed her. Stroking her cheek, he held her face in his hands.

Roxanne released a breathy sigh. She never knew how long this mood would last, and she hated that she welcomed the change. When his dark eyes softened, she remembered his softer side. She stroked his forearm.

"I can make a quick dinner. Just a quiet evening for the two of us. Besides, we've eaten out a lot this week," Roxanne cooed.

His biceps bulged, and he dropped his hands, balling them into fists.

Roxanne stepped back, holding onto the computer chair behind her.

"Always watching that budget thing, aren't you?" He pushed her away.

Decisions. Argue? Defend? Submit? Roxanne pushed aside the inappropriate timing and chose to press it. She was tired of him dampening her dream.

"I have to. I'm planning to quit my job at the end of the

semester. Remember I told you?" Roxanne glanced at her computer.

His eyes followed, and he smirked. "Yeah, right. So you can be a writer." His fingers mimicked quotation marks. He peered at the computer screen, and a hollow laugh rolled out. "The End? You finished something?"

Roxanne drew her shoulders back and twisted her ring again. "Yes. I did. And others too." Tipping her chin up, she crossed her arms. "I've been working on those books for years. Long before I met you."

"Yeah, and they're all useless. You'll never do anything with them, and you know it."

"What's that supposed to mean?" Roxanne asked.

He definitely hit a nerve. This is where she usually cowered. Giving in to her insecurities. Yet, somehow, finishing this book renewed her resolve. Her resolve to pursue her writing career. It had been too long. Discontent with her life, the longing for a dream, and getting older fueled her perseverance to see this through. She hoped as she glared back.

"You're too afraid of rejection. Besides, you got me now." With splayed fingers he thumped his chest and grinned. "You don't have to live in that fantasy world."

Confidence ebbed out of her like a leaky hose. The partial truth of that statement stung. After years of being alone and unsuccessful as a writer, an emptiness weakened her, and when she met Dwayne, she thought she'd hit the jackpot, at least until recently. He didn't seem like such a catch anymore. She lowered her arms, clasping one hand in the other, and glanced at the flash drive. Her stories. All there, waiting. Dwayne followed her gaze, and his fingers reached for it.

Roxanne gasped and grabbed his arm. "No, Dwayne. Don't."

He shoved her, and she stumbled banging her head on the desk. Her eyebrow hit the corner. She didn't feel the pain and she grabbed him again, but he yanked out the precious memory stick containing all her stories. She watched as the blue dot continued to circle. The connection severed.

Dwayne walked to the kitchen sink.

"No!" she yelled.

He threw the flash drive in the garbage disposal and flipped the switch. A sickening, grinding sound blared briefly, then stopped short.

"Oops. Looks like you have to get your disposal fixed. Come on, babe. Quit wasting your time."

"No. I'm not going anywhere with you." A warm trickle slithered down the side of her face.

Dwayne's eyes widened. "Oh man, I'm sorry." He pointed. "Are you all right?"

Roxanne touched her temple and pulled back her fingertips covered in scarlet.

"Let me buy you dinner. Seriously. Go get cleaned up." He waved a hand at her. "I didn't mean to, Roxanne."

Good thing he hadn't been drinking. It could have been worse. Then again, she might not have stood up to him. Now that his drunken rages had escalated, she gauged his outbursts better.

He reached forward with a napkin trying to wipe the blood, but she stepped back. He snarled and waited until she took the crumpled napkin from him.

Roxanne pressed the napkin to the cut. "You should just go."

"Oh, come on, baby."

"I mean it, Dwayne."

"Okay, calm down." He kissed her cheek and smiled.

She swiped it off, and her eyes narrowed.

"I said I'm sorry." His tone went cold. "What else do you want me to do?"

"Go." She sucked in a breath. "Please, go now. I don't feel so good." Leaning against the wall, she played the weakness.

"Fine."

The front door slammed, but before she could turn the lock, he pushed it back open, crushing her against the wall. *Get out.* She wanted to scream, but her silent voice took over.

"Forgot my keys." Grabbing them from the table, he spun them around his finger. "I'm going to hang out with the guys tonight. Looks like you won't be any fun anyway."

Good, and don't come back. She hoped he'd stay at his own apartment.

His dark eyes were cold, and he reached for her chin and squeezed.

Roxanne yanked her face away, but flinched when he grabbed for the door, slamming it as he left. She leaned against the wall and touched her face. Blood slid down her cheek again. Add to that, her stomach hurt where the doorknob had pressed in. Her shoulders slumped, and she wanted to cry. She couldn't. She just stood.

Faint music rang from the living room. Her cellphone.

"Hello, Mama." She grabbed a clean napkin and dabbed the cut.

"Hey, sweetie. You sound tired?"

"How can you tell? I just said hello."

"I called to see how you're doing? I worry about you, you know. Almost time for summer break, eh?"

"Another few weeks, and I can't wait." Roxanne checked the blood-streaked napkin. She couldn't seem to stop the stream.

"So, do you think you'll come out this summer? You haven't been back to Bay Town in ages." Bethie Cook's voice lilted with hope.

Roxanne hadn't told her mama about her plans to leave her teaching job to pursue writing. She'd been saving for years and had been frugal with her money, but keeping this news from her sweet mother roiled her stomach.

"Probably not, Mama." She grabbed another napkin. "I need to stay put and write. Besides Dwayne—"

"You're still with him? I thought y'all broke up after my last visit?"

Me too. But as always, Dwayne had charmed her again, making promises she knew he wouldn't keep, and her loneliness made excuses to take him back. She'd tried to blame her current situation on her past experiences with men. A woman scorned made foolish choices. Spencer, her ex-fiancé in particular. But first, there was Gregory. Although, he'd never scorned her. God had taken him from her life.

"Mama, please. We had a rough patch, that's all. We worked it out."

"He's not good for you."

The silence that followed made Roxanne's stomach churn, and she couldn't think of anything to say.

"He's no good for anyone," finished her mother.

The damp napkin laced between her fingers. She threw it down and grabbed another, dabbing at her head.

"Listen, Mama. I need to run."

"Roxanne, you are precious in God's sight. You belong to Him, and He loves you so much."

"Mama, please. Can I call you later?"

"Why don't you come back to Bay Town? There's going to be a wedding. Lacey Thompson is getting married this summer."

"Who is that?" *And why on earth would I want to come back for a wedding?*

"My Pastor and his wife Melanie, it's their daughter, and I'd love for you to meet her. It would be a nice break for you."

"We'll see. I'll call you later this week. Love you, Mama." *Like a wedding would be a nice break.* Had her mom forgotten already?

Roxanne clicked off. She stood, but dizziness dropped her to sitting again. She couldn't remember how long since she'd been to Bay Town. Actually, she could. It had been for

Miz Philippa's funeral. Gathering her keys and purse, she left for the urgent care.

CHAPTER 2

In the Meridian Urgent Care, Roxanne's blood splattered shirt and napkin pressed to her temple gained her immediate priority. A younger man in scrubs with longish hair brushing his shoulders and wearing wire-framed glasses attended her. His resemblance to Max jarred her. Though she hadn't thought of him in a very long time, intense feelings for her old friend stirred within her.

"Hi, I'll be your nurse today. I'm Travis." He pulled out a sterile pack. "Hurts, doesn't it? Looks like you might need stitches, but we'll see what the doctor says." He handed her some thick compresses and grasped her hand. "Hold it there. So, who did you get in a fight with?" He chuckled.

Roxanne blinked. Too much truth to that question. "Oh, stupid me. Finishing up a story on my computer I'd been writing for hours, and I stood up too fast and got all dizzy. I fell and hit my head." She raised her wrapped wrist and brushed back a strand of hair.

The nurse seemed to take notice and glanced at her wrist. "Did you hurt that at the same time?"

Roxanne nodded. "Oh, yes. I did," she lied. Remembering just a few weeks ago when Dwayne had twisted her arm so hard she thought he'd broken it.

He smiled. "So, you're a writer?"

Thankful that someone had acknowledged that, she answered. "Well, sort of—"

"Stop right there and repeat after me," he said. "Yes. I am a writer."

Roxanne giggled. "Yes, I'm a writer, but I have nothing published."

"Nope. No buts. You are a writer. So, what do you write?"

Heat rose from her neck, and her fair skin flushed. He gazed at her eyes. People often complimented her on her interesting eyes. Gray-green with gold flecks. She smiled, wishing she'd colored her hair roots this morning. Although the sparse gray contrasted well with her light brown hair with natural blonde highlights. Still, she hated it when the gray roots showed.

"I write…" she shrugged, "I guess it's sweet romance." Roxanne waited for the sarcasm.

"Great. Are you in a critique group?" His question sounded genuine.

Roxanne shook her head as memories of her critique partners from many years ago flooded her mind. "I had some friends in college that read my work." She paused. "Wait? Do you write?"

He grabbed a blood-pressure cuff and placed it on her arm. He put a finger to his lips as he finished taking her blood pressure. "It's a little elevated. Is it always high?"

She shrugged.

He squeezed her hand, and warmth flooded her once more.

"I'll check again in a few minutes, don't you worry." He replaced the equipment, pulled out a digital thermometer, and pointed it to her forehead. "Good. Temp is fine, and yes, I'm a writer. I'd love to quit my job here and just write."

"Me too. I'm planning on it." Her eyes widened.

"Really? Well, you should come to my critique group. It's a

great bunch of people. They get new writers all the time. It's through the library, and everyone is welcome."

"What library?" Roxanne asked. Not the county library, she hoped. Dwayne worked out at the gym across the street, and she couldn't chance him catching her outside their regular hangouts, especially with another man.

"Not too far from here. Meridian County Library. We meet on Tuesday nights. You should come."

"No thanks, I'm busy then," she lied.

"Okay, but if you change your mind, we meet from five-thirty to seven o'clock."

Roxanne nodded.

"You should come sometime." He patted her shoulder and grinned.

The curtain swung open, and a small older woman walked in. Her dark, graying hair, pulled back, exposed creases on her neck. Her spotted hands gave evidence of her age.

"I think you're done here." The woman raised a chin at Travis. "They need you out front."

How rude.

Yet Travis smiled, waved, and exited without a word.

"Hello, I'm Dr. Rashid." Her eyes narrowed. "You look familiar. Weren't you in here recently?" She glanced at Roxanne's wrist and removed the compress from her head. "Tell me what happened."

Roxanne made up her story as the doctor stitched her wound and then prescribed an antibiotic.

"Can I look at that wrist?" asked Dr. Rashid.

"It's fine, really." She refused to look at the doctor.

Doctor Rashid picked up her tablet and searched. "So, you have been here recently?"

Roxanne looked up. "Oh, yes. I'm a little clumsy." She tried to laugh.

"You're saying no one did this to you?"

Roxanne glanced down. *Don't say anything.*

Dr. Rashid leaned in closer and laid a hand on Roxanne's arm. A gentler voice took over. "I can help you. I run a foundation, you know? I know the signs of abuse. You should heed the feelings they bring on."

Heat rose in Roxanne. How dare this doctor talk to her this way. She sounded like her mother. Roxanne's eyes darted at the door, but she forced a smile. "You're mistaken, Doctor. Like I said, I'm a little clumsy. I'll be fine."

"Okay, then. You can go." Pulling a card from her pocket, she handed it to Roxanne. "There are all kinds of abuse. And all kinds of signs. We educate too."

Roxanne sucked in a breath. Travis peeked in and winked, but as Dr. Rashid turned in his direction, he pulled the curtain closed, and his footsteps retreated.

Dr. Rashid tilted her head in Travis's direction. "Like I said, we educate. You might learn something about men." She smiled. "All women should know these things, and you might be able to share them with someone who needs to know. Take care, Ms. Cook. I hope not to see you here again. But come by the Refuge House anytime." She smiled and left.

After a restless night's sleep, Roxanne awoke early and showered. She stepped out, toweled down, and wiped the condensation from the mirror. Leaning forward, she frowned. The mirror didn't lie. She had a black eye, and the cut above her brow created an ugly Frankenstein-type scar. Her students would be horrified. Middle school kids held nothing back, and she knew she'd face a battering of questions.

Roxanne pulled out a simple bandage, but it didn't cover the wound. She needed the white gauze. *Why couldn't this have happened on a Friday night instead of Thursday?* At least she'd have the weekend to recover, and the bruises might have faded.

Taking another look in the mirror, she forced a smile that

quickly disappeared. She couldn't hide anything, and she was tired of making excuses. She reached for her phone. Calling in sick would buy her time to heal, but she quelled that idea and set down the phone. She'd done that too many times.

Roxanne swished through her hanging dresses and tops. Nothing to draw attention to herself. Something so she could just blend into the classroom and especially the teachers' lounge. No, she'd avoid the teachers' lounge today. She'd bag lunch and eat in her car.

Choosing taupe slacks and a pale, pink long-sleeved tunic, she dressed and checked her image in the mirror. Her bandaged wrist glared back at her. Unwinding the wrap, she rubbed her skin. She'd go without the support today. Just today, but she'd have to be careful.

One final check and she smoothed back some loose strands of hair but frowned. The tightly pulled-back ponytail emphasized the bandage on her face. She walked to the bathroom sink and pulled out the elastic that held back her hair. She shook her head and winced. The movement hurt her head, and doing everything with her uninjured wrist slowed her down. Still, she parted her hair across the top of her forehead and held scissors with the other. Holding the thin bunch of hanging locks, she snipped. The new bangs covered the bandage somewhat, but the length she chose made it a little hard to see. Still, she could finger part an opening.

Throwing down the comb, she sighed. Burning eyes threatened tears, but she held back. No. No whining. She had no one to blame but herself. If she'd just kept quiet. Roxanne's shoulders drooped.

~

Keeping her head down, she'd hoped to avoid the morning greetings of the other teachers. But it didn't lessen the looks and stares. She almost wished they'd ask, knowing what they were thinking.

The children couldn't be ignored and asked about her injuries. Making up a story about tripping over something amused them, and even Kimi, the shy girl who never talked, giggled in the back of the room. Alaina, the girl sitting next to her, reached over, and Kimi let out a soft squeal.

Roxanne clipped down the aisle. "What's going on?"

"She laughs like my weird aunt. Mama says it sounds like a hyena," Alaina said.

The room exploded in laughter. Roxanne spun around.

"Class, that's enough." Before she could dismiss them for recess, the bell rang.

Books slammed, and everyone ran outside. Roxanne huffed. She had to maintain better control. "Walk," she called out.

Kimi remained, holding her arm. Roxanne reached out. "May I?" She removed Kimi's hand, exposing a red welt.

Roxanne's lips pursed. "Did she pinch you?"

The girl shook her head. "May I be excused?"

"Of course," Roxanne said.

Kimi ran out, and tears welled in Roxanne's eyes. Why? Why that sweet little girl? And why wouldn't she fight back? It seemed they shared the same curse. Meek and victimized. Yet this little one was so young. Roxanne hadn't succumbed to abuse until much later in life.

She glanced out the windows overlooking the playground. Within minutes, girls surrounded Kimi. Alaina stood tall in the middle of the circle. Roxanne wanted to run outside and help but looked around for a yard monitor instead. There were two of them, chatting it up by the basketball courts.

Grabbing her sunglasses, Roxanne ran. Reaching the circle, she found Kimi sitting on the ground. The others taunted her. Roxanne grabbed the perpetrator. "Alaina, what did you do?"

She spun around and glared. "You can't touch me. I'll tell my mama, and she'll get you fired."

Roxanne ignored her and offered her good hand to Kimi. She took it and stood, but the bully grabbed Roxanne's injured wrist, and Roxanne screamed. Pulling her arm in close to her side, she glared at Alaina, but with her good hand, she protected Kimi.

"Go to the principal's office. Now," Roxanne shouted, surprising herself. "And don't you ever touch her again."

The yard monitors rushed over. "What happened?" one asked.

Everyone remained quiet except for the bully. Alaina pointed at Kimi. "She fell."

All the kids laughed, but the other yard monitor pointed to the main building. "Go, young lady, now."

Her eyes widened. "Why me? I didn't do anything."

"I saw you grab Miss Cook's arm. Hard enough to hurt her."

"She grabbed me first," Alaina yelled back.

"You can tell it to the principal. Let's go." She marched the girl to a far building.

"Girls, you'll need to tell us what happened but for now, go play." The remaining monitor turned to Roxanne. "Miss Cook, are you hurt?"

Heat flooded her body, and Roxanne lowered the wrist she'd been favoring. She shook her head but turned her attention to Kimi. She stroked Kimi's slick hair. Silky like her own, only black and shiny.

"We won't let her hurt you again. I promise." She didn't know how, but she wouldn't let it happen again. Roxanne reached into her pocket and pulled out some trendy, oversized stickers. "Here, put these on your notebook."

The girl wrapped her arms around Roxanne's neck and hugged her. Roxanne never wanted the hug to end. So full of love, it felt like a desperate need missing in her life right now.

But the thought of God's love flashed before her. Authentic love, just like this little one.

"Summer vacation is just two weeks away. Maybe we can get that bully expelled for the remainder of the year," the yard proctor said, interrupting Roxanne's thoughts.

Roxanne looked up. "Can you take care of Kimi? Make sure she gets back to class okay? I'm sure I'm needed at the principal's office."

"Sure thing. I'm sorry. We were focused on trying to keep the boys playing a fair game. I forgot about our local bully."

"Sure, I understand. Can you take my class for a few minutes if I'm not back in time?"

The woman nodded as Kimi stuck close to her side.

Roxanne's rapid footsteps led her to the principal's office. Before entering, she lowered her injured wrist, trying to let it hang naturally. She removed her sunglasses and fingered her bangs to cover the bandage. The secretary smiled. A miserable smile. How Roxanne hated that sympathetic look.

"Mrs. Franklin said you can come back after school. She's already called the parent, and she'll hold the student till then."

Roxanne nodded and turned. *Not again.* She'd had a few confrontations with this parent. No wonder her daughter picked on others. And the mother always had excuses for her child's behavior. It often resulted in the child returning to school with no punishment after she attended the required counseling.

CHAPTER 3

R oxanne's heel tapped the ground. Her knee bumped up and down. Out the window, she watched parents arriving and students leaving. The day had finally come to an end. But not for her. She sat in a chair across from Principal Franklin. Alaina sat between her and her mother on the other side. A large, imposing woman dressed flashy with a lot of bling. Her platinum-dyed hair hung down her back in dull, heavy curls. She clicked her gold-sparkly nails together and threw disgusted looks at Roxanne.

Principal Franklin began. "Mrs. Nichols, I understand from the Yard Proctor and the other students, that this is another case of your daughter's over-aggressiveness."

"Oh, give me a break. If you and your staff can't control the students, don't blame it on them," Mrs. Nichols said.

"Miss Cook, I understand this student grabbed you hard enough to inflict pain," Principal Franklin said.

The mother's glare caused Roxanne to shift in her seat. "I'm fine. My concerns are for Kimi."

"She tripped. She's always getting hurt." Alaina pointed at Roxanne and giggled. "Like you."

Mrs. Nichols patted her daughter's arm and accompanied it with a smirking approval.

Principal Franklin's lips formed a tight, straight line. She glanced at Roxanne. Roxanne cringed. *Oh, no. Please don't go there.*

"That's enough, Alaina. You will respect our teachers."

"Respect? They have to earn it. You know darn well that my daughter couldn't have hurt Miss Cook with a friendly little tap. That woman is always coming to school with bruises. Look at her face, now."

Roxanne resisted the temptation to touch her cut eye. Instead, she gazed straight ahead. A common tactic, hoping people would ignore her battered face. Although she hated the sympathetic looks, as long as they kept their comments to themselves, she could deal with it. It also helped her deny that the episodes with Dwayne were escalating. Thankfully, people like this woman were few and far between. Still, the words signaled a wake-up call.

"That's enough. Your daughter has enough aggressive behavior for me to suspend her indefinitely," Mrs. Franklin said.

The mother tipped her head and pasted on a sickeningly sweet smile. "Listen, it's the weekend. Let's all cool off, and everything will be fine on Monday." The mother raised her brows. "Hmmm? How about it?"

"Alaina is not to return to school until I evaluate the situation," Principal Franklin said.

"Are you kidding me? And what do you expect me to do with her?" The mother's voice escalated. "I have to work, you know."

"That is your dilemma. We're finished here. You may leave now."

Grabbing her child by the arm, Mrs. Nichols pulled her to her side and jabbed a finger at the principal's face. "I'm reporting you to the school board. Alaina isn't the problem." Her finger wagged at Roxanne. "She is. She's weak, and she favors other children. She doesn't like my daughter, and she plays favorites."

Principal Franklin stood. "Miss Cook is one of our finest teachers, and if you say another word against her, I'll file a report of verbal abuse against you."

Mrs. Nichols glared and moved towards the door. "Like heck, you will."

As the woman slammed the door, Roxanne melted in her seat. She glanced up through the fringed bangs. Mrs. Franklin sat but said nothing, and the heavy silence made it hard to breathe.

Roxanne's knees bounced. "Mrs. Franklin, I apologize for putting you in this predicament. I did touch Alaina first. I shouldn't have."

Mrs. Franklin raised a hand. "Yes, you should have. It breaks my heart when bullying goes on. We just can't seem to catch it all. I believe parent education would prevent this, but sometimes they are the problem." She looked at Roxanne's wrist. "I will say, I don't think she could have grabbed you hard enough for you to scream unless it was a prior injury. But I'm thankful for the excuse. We can't have the students accosting our teachers."

Roxanne nodded, but a knot formed in her throat. She couldn't swallow or speak.

"Miss Cook, I'm a mandatory reporter."

Oh no, not again. "I appreciate your concern. But I assure you, I'm not in any trouble."

"So you've confirmed to me before. Out of respect for you, and because of your denials, I haven't reported my suspicions. But if you are in an abusive situation at home, please seek help. Not only for your sake but the students' as well. Home life affects everything. In this case, your teaching, and your students. You did a good thing today. That little girl needs a protector, and she'll remember this day. But she also needs a strong role model."

A tear fell as Roxanne felt the stinging words of truth. She nodded.

"Miss Cook, if I can help in any way, I have resources."

Resources. How many times had she heard those words? Shame and guilt conflicted within. "Thank you. I'll heed your advice. But please don't worry about me. I can handle this. It's not as bad as you think."

Mrs. Franklin pulled a tissue from a box on her desk and shook it in Roxanne's direction. "I'm afraid I've heard that too many times," she said softly. "Please, get help. You're a valuable teacher here, and some students need more than just your academic instruction."

She continued to warn her, but Roxanne listened with half an ear. She'd heard it all before. Why did she stay in the relationship? Her value held more worth. People like him are no good. They're sick or just plain evil. Monsters. But no one really knew Dwayne. He hadn't always been like this. Roxanne hated being lumped into the battered women group.

Glancing out the window, she watched the sun dip lower in the sky. Had she been here that long? She stood. "Thank you," she managed. The walls felt like they were closing in, and her heart beat faster. Closing the door, she could physically feel the sympathetic sadness emitting from the principal behind her.

The weight burdened her once again. When her phone rang, her pulse quickened, and she realized why. *Oh, God, no.*

She didn't answer but asked the secretary, "What day is it?"

"Friday. Short day. But it turns out not so short for you."

"You're right there." Roxanne reached for the door.

"Hey, your phone is ringing?" the secretary called after her.

Roxanne picked it up outside the office. An explosion of cursing assaulted her ears.

"Where the heck are you? You told me you were off early today, and I've been sitting at your house, waiting for you." Dwayne shouted through the phone.

Great. That meant he'd been drinking too. She contemplated not going home. Maybe if she stayed away, he'd just blow off steam. Maybe. Or she could try to calm him down. She knew the tricks, a good meal or... The choices made her stomach churn. But nothing guaranteed her safety. His unpredictability gripped her.

"I'm sorry, Dwayne. I had a meeting with the principal, and I had to stay late. I'm on my way. How about I take you out to eat?"

"I'd planned on it, but I wanted to go to the gym tonight too. You know what? Just forget it. I'm out of here. The guys are going dirt bike riding for the weekend. You can stay all by your lonesome."

She smiled. "Okay, Dwayne. Have fun." The words came out too cheery, so she added. "I'll miss you."

"You better."

Roxanne walked a little lighter. She envisioned a hot bath and a quiet evening alone. Once home, that's exactly what she got, and she relished every moment. And it didn't end there. On Saturday, she stayed in her pajamas all day. Grabbing a snack here and there, she sat at her computer and wrote until the sun went down. A peaceful silence filled her house, and she fell into bed exhausted. Another night of calm. Dwayne hadn't returned, and she slept soundly.

Sunday morning, Roxanne slept in. Dwayne must have been having fun. She hadn't heard from him all weekend. She smiled, snuggling in, scrunching the covers under her chin. Breathing effortlessly, she rested like she always did when he went away.

Hopefully, he'd come back happy after a weekend with the guys. Sometimes, he just needed to get all that energy out. His hovering angst that she couldn't figure out. Roxanne shook her head, trying to clear all thoughts of Dwayne. Leaving the comfort of her unshared bed, she showered.

When she finished, she couldn't pass the mirror but stared once again at her reflection. A creeping shiver of humiliation enveloped her. Her empty stomach churned, and bile rose. How could she let someone do this to her? She picked up a comb and started to run it through her hair. "Never again," she said out loud. "Never again," she repeated. The firm sound of her voice grew more assertive.

Another voice spoke. Her mother's words. A soft, gentle impression. *You are precious in God's sight. You belong to Him.* Dropping the comb, she frowned. *Precious?* The guilt of her life with Dwayne this last year made her skin crawl. But she couldn't blame it all on him. It started earlier than that.

Little by little, Roxanne had walked away from God, and it all started with Gregory. Her first love. Her only real love. She forced herself to recall her past. She'd never really gotten over him, and God had taken him away. She shook her head, moving on to Spencer.

How could she have almost married him? Like Dwayne, Spencer changed. Or she had misjudged his character from the start. Sorrow turned to anger. The biggest mistake of her life. Hot, angry tears formed. She could never think of Spencer without tying him to the death of her father.

She grabbed a towel and rubbed her eyes. Her life played out in rejection and tragedy. Yet, Roxanne knew. Deep inside, she knew the choices she'd made in response to those things were her fault, and God wasn't pleased with her. Precious in His sight? How could that be?

The doorbell rang, jarring Roxanne to the present. It couldn't be Dwayne. He had a key. She threw a robe on and ran to the entryway. Her wet hair dripped on the floor mat as she swung open the front door. Her heart lifted, and she smiled. The adorable little girl from next door stood holding a single rose wrapped in foil. Her slick, straight, dark bob with bangs framed a sweet, round face.

"Hey, Miss Cook." Her high voice sang out as she stuck out a red rose with curling, yellow edges.

Roxanne knelt down. "Hey, Kayla. Why thank you." She stuck her nose in the flower and breathed deeply. "Mmm, is it the Double Delight we've been waiting for to bloom?"

"Yup. Mama cut it so I could bring it to you."

Reaching out for a hug, Roxanne embraced the girl, then pulled back. "Don't you look pretty? Is that a new dress?"

Kayla's head dipped up and down, and she pointed to her feet. "New boots too."

Roxanne laughed. A warm wind blew through the door. It was a sandals type of day, but this little girl didn't care. Her sweet smile lit up Roxanne's life. She took another deep breath and sighed. She wished a new dress and boots would fill her with the same joy. "Well, thank you, sweetie pie. I'll take it to school and put it on my desk tomorrow." Roxanne's drawl dripped with southern sweetness.

Kayla nodded and turned to leave but spun back around. "Want to come to church with us? Mama told me to ask."

The question caught Roxanne off guard. Not just an invitation from the neighbor, but she'd been thinking about God since her mother called. As much as she'd been avoiding church, she missed it. She blinked long then gazed back at the girl. "I'm sorry. I can't. I'm not dressed."

"Kayla, come back, please." Her mother called. "We have to eat breakfast, and you need to practice your song before we leave for church." Mrs. Ishida, Kayla's mother, stood at the end of Roxanne's driveway and waved.

"I'm singing today. Bye!" The little girl skipped away, singing, "Jesus Paid it All."

In a split-second, Roxanne knew this second chance came

from God. She'd have plenty of time to get dressed. "Kayla? I'll be there." She waved to the mother, taking her daughter's hand. Roxanne called out, "What time does service start?"

They exchanged information, and Roxanne agreed to meet them there. She thought of her own mother and wanted to call. To tell her she would attend church today. *No. Mama will call this afternoon.* She always did on Sundays.

Roxanne dried her shoulder-length brown hair and loosely waved it, ensuring her bangs covered her eyes. She began to apply her makeup but decided against a heavy hand with the eyeliner and dark lipstick. That's what Dwayne liked. Instead, she moisturized with lip gloss and applied blush and a little mascara. Smacking her lips together, she smiled but fingered her bangs again. She sighed and covered her cut with a small band-aid.

She pulled out a floral peasant dress. It didn't do much to show off her shape, but she needn't please Dwayne this morning. Loose, fashionable, and cute. Perfect for church. Roxanne hummed, remembering the words to that old hymn Kayla had sung. Tears filled her eyes, but they felt good, and she sang out loud.

Digging through the bottom of her closet, she hunted for boots. The neighbor girl would love it. Little girls loved to match. She found them, pulled them on, looked at herself, and spun around. She hadn't felt this free in forever. Roxanne sprayed on a light floral scent, grabbed her purse, and started for the door. She stopped and frowned.

Her Bible. When had she read it last? Rummaging around the house where she thought she might have left it, she wondered if Dwayne had taken it. A vise-like feeling squeezed her heart, and her pulse sped up. She hadn't thought of him in the last thirty minutes. How refreshing. But, about out of time, she gave up looking and headed for the door.

She started to hum again when a key in the lock turned.

Sweat popped up on her brow and upper lip. A lump formed in her throat that almost choked her. *No. Please no.*

The door flung open.

"Hey, baby. I'm home." Dwayne grinned. His eyelids were rimmed in red, and his hair looked like he hadn't washed it all weekend. He pulled her close and kissed her hard.

She wrenched herself from his grasp.

"Wow. What are you all gussied up for?" He raised a brow.

"Church," she said. The tune she'd been singing rose inside, giving her strength. "I'm going to church, Dwayne." She reached for the doorknob.

"Seriously?" He laughed. "I bet you want me to come too. I might think about it, but I'm real tired."

He must have had a good weekend. "That would be nice but go ahead and rest up. I'll be back soon."

He smiled and stroked her arm. "Stay home and rest up with me?" He whispered while fingering the soft fabric of her dress. But his eyes moved past her and rested on the rose on the entry table. "So, someone bringing you flowers while I'm gone?"

Before she could answer, he grabbed the rose and crumpled the bloom. Red and yellow petals fell to the tile floor.

Her lips pursed. "The little neighbor girl brought it. She invited me to church."

"Well, ain't that sweet."

The doorbell rang, and Dwayne yanked the door open. His imposing figure filled the door frame.

The neighbor girl scrambled behind her mother's skirt, peeking out. Mrs. Ishida held her daughter protectively behind her back. "Miss Roxanne, I just came to tell you we have room in our car if you'd like to ride with us?"

"Sorry, she ain't going." Dwayne slammed the door and took Roxanne's hand.

Her stomach knotted like she'd been punched, and she gasped. She reached for the door against her better judgment.

Dwayne shoved her back against the wall. His face drew close to hers.

Her breathing sped up, and she couldn't catch a breath. "Dwayne, please."

"Come on, sugar. I missed you." He opened his mouth, covering hers, and kissed her long and hard.

Roxanne pulled back and gasped for air.

He laughed. "Besides, we'll meet the gang for pizza and beer. I'm playing pool, and you know you wanna watch me. Now go get out of that sack dress and put on your tight jeans." He stepped back, twirled her around, and smacked her behind.

For a single moment, she clenched her fists but retreated down the hall. Any last notes of "Jesus Paid It All" left her brain and her heart, and she trudged to her bedroom. Her second chance had slipped away. No. It had been snatched away.

CHAPTER 4

Roxanne stroked her wrist as Dwayne drove to Leroy's Sports Bar. He kept glancing over, but she remained silent. He acted like he didn't have a care in the world. Like a mood lamp changed color, so did his demeanor.

He blew out an exaggerated sigh. "Take that stupid wrap off your wrist and pull off that bandage over your eye."

"I have stitches." Her words were curt. Stuck behind the wheel, he couldn't hurt her. She felt a little safer as long as he wasn't drinking. And since they were meeting up with friends, she trusted him not to hit her in public.

"Just keep your sunglasses on when we get to Leroy's. I don't want people asking questions." He squeezed her hand a little too hard.

They often went to the bar on Sundays for lunch. Roxanne never minded. When Dwayne played pool all afternoon, he left her alone to hang out with the girlfriends of the other guys. They were nice enough, and so were the men. What they saw in Dwayne, she didn't know. Probably the same thing she did at first. He could be funny and charming, but his selfish ego-maniac soon took over and alienated everyone. But these were his old buddies, who hadn't given up on him.

Roxanne pulled her hand away.

"Come on, babe. You'll have fun. I'll hit all the pockets, just for you."

Like he didn't always do that when playing pool, and not necessarily for her. If he weren't that good, she'd have thought his friends just let him win. No one wanted to deal with his foul temper. Not worth it when he lost. Thankfully, that wasn't often.

Roxanne pressed her lips into a frown. It hadn't always been that way. Dwayne's attractive demeanor caught her eye when she first met him at the gym. A fluke. She didn't regularly work out, and honestly, she only went when a writer's slump hit. Changing her routine often jarred her back. The first time she saw him, she ogled his good looks, just like all the other girls. He turned on the friendly charm with all of them. Even her.

When he found out she had a steady job and owned her own house, he took more of an interest. That should have been her first clue. She made a decent income, but her father had left a nest egg when he died years before, and she'd bought the little house in Meridian, Mississippi. Just short of a three-hour drive from where she'd grown up in Bay Town.

Her phone buzzed. After checking the screen, she ignored it and stuffed the phone back into her purse

"Aren't you going to get that?" Dwayne sped up a little.

"No."

He reached for her purse. "Let me see that." The car swerved as he grabbed again but failed. "What? Is it an old boyfriend or something?" His voice gruff.

"No, Dwayne. It's my mother."

Dwayne rolled his eyes. "What's she want?"

Roxanne ignored his question and turned up the radio. His favorite old song, "Wild Thing," played. He slammed the steering wheel to the beat and screamed out the lyrics. Roxanne's head began to throb.

He pulled into the parking lot, and the music pounding

from the sports bar energized Dwayne. He parked the car and jumped out, not bothering to open Roxanne's door, or even wait for her. Reaching the entrance, he turned. "Ya' comin'?"

"In a minute."

Roxanne adjusted the sunglasses and got out. She maneuvered the car door with her uninjured wrist, repeating the maneuver when reaching for the heavy door to the bar. Dwayne hadn't bothered to hold it open.

A sweet barbecue aroma floated throughout the noisy, dimly lit restaurant. Baseball, golf, and all manner of sports games played on the giant screens covering the walls. Cheers and yells accompanied the televised games. Pizzas and pitchers of beer covered the plastic, red-checked tables. Roxanne ordered a diet cola and made small talk with the girl-friends of Dwayne's friends. The country music playing almost soothed her.

"Hi, Roxy." A smiling woman scooted in next to her.

"Hey, Lucy."

Lucy wore a short, tiered skirt and cowboy boots. Her wavy hair fell below her shoulders, and dangling earrings shined under the overhead lights. Lucy always dressed young for her age, but she carried it off nicely with her sweet spirit. The friendliest of the bunch, Lucy claimed Jason as her boyfriend. Dwayne's closest friend.

Interestingly, they shared the same features. Tall, dark, and handsome. Though Jason's build was less defined and muscular, and his face was much friendlier.

"I just got out of church," Lucy said.

Roxanne's eyes widened.

Lucy giggled. "Weird, huh?"

"What's weird?" Roxanne peered at Lucy over the top of her sunglasses, wanting desperately to remove them.

"Going to church, then coming here." Lucy giggled again and waved a hand at a waitress.

"I'll take a diet cola." She smiled at Roxanne. "I'm always asking my boyfriend to go with me to church, but he won't."

"Well, at least you went. I missed this morning." Not really a lie, but not the whole truth. She'd been missing church for too long. Ever since she'd met Dwayne.

"What happened to your eye?" Lucy pointed.

Pushing her glasses up, Roxanne shrugged. "I opened the cupboard into my face. Stupid, huh?" She smiled weakly.

Lucy's eyes saddened, and her lips pouted. "Oh, honey, why do you even stay with him? Dwayne is such a hothead. Even my Jason says he's getting worse."

Roxanne's shoulders slumped. *Did everyone know?* If anyone knew Dwayne, Jason knew him best. They'd been best friends since high school. And although Jason didn't exactly ignore Dwayne's outbursts, he didn't confront him, either. No one did. It seemed like everyone just put up with him.

"Jason said Dwayne's always been kind of a jerk, but not as bad as lately. What's a nice girl like you doing with him, anyway?" Lucy sipped her drink.

Roxanne said nothing. Some of the other women had asked her the same thing. Roxanne glanced over. They'd all left to hang with the guys near the pool tables. Roxanne turned, and Lucy stared at her face.

"Dwayne did that to you, didn't he?" Lucy's voice rose.

Roxanne's eyes widened as Dwayne sauntered up behind Lucy. His large hands gripped her shoulders, and he squeezed. Lucy jumped.

"Dwayne!" Lucy yelled. "You about scared the living daylights out of me."

"Did what? What did I do?" He glared at Roxanne. His white-knuckle squeeze gripping Lucy made Roxanne wince.

Lucy grabbed his fingers, ripping them off. "Get your hands off me." She glanced at Roxanne.

Roxanne gave an almost invisible shake of her head, and Lucy nodded.

"The ring." Lucy pointed. "I, uh... I wondered if you gave that to Roxanne. It's gorgeous. Opal, right? I love opal." She rattled on. "I think it's my birthstone. October, right?"

Dwayne pulled up a chair, spun it around, and straddled it. "Nah. I wouldn't give her an old lady ring like that. When I give her a ring, it's gonna be a big one."

Something inside Roxanne lifted, and she smiled at Dwayne, even if he meant nothing by it, the thought that he cared enough about her to imply marriage. Roxanne blinked slowly. *But I'm not going there again. That's stupid.*

She held up her hand. "My mother gave it to me."

"Does she live around here?" Lucy asked.

"No." Roxanne's body stiffened.

Dwayne didn't know where her mother lived. He'd never bothered to ask about her family. At first, it bothered her, but since he'd become increasingly unstable, she was grateful she'd never told him. He didn't care about them. Still, she feared Lucy might ask more.

"She's in my hometown. After I graduated from college here in Meridian, I went home and got a local teaching job, but things happened." Roxanne looked away. "My dad passed, and I needed to get away, so I came back here. Anyway, Daddy left me a little inheritance, so I bought a house, and this is my home now."

Dwayne walked over and grabbed her chin. Tilting her head up, he kissed her. "You got that right. This is home." He left to join his friends.

"Where's your real home?" Lucy asked but didn't wait for an answer. "You don't want Dwayne to know, do you?"

"He's never asked."

Lucy sighed. "I can't believe you've been with him for a year, and he doesn't know."

"He's got so much on his mind." Truthfully, he'd been brooding for months. "It's okay." Roxanne tried to smile.

"Oh honey, why don't you go back there?" Lucy narrowed her eyes at Dwayne.

"Too many expectations." *Too many bad memories.* "Everyone at home thought I'd be a published author by now, but it never happened." She crumpled a napkin. "After graduating from college, I got my teaching credential and took a job as a fallback."

Lucy frowned. "A fallback for what?"

"Writing."

"But that's a hobby, right? Not a job."

"Yes. My teaching is my job, my career. And I love the kids." Roxanne didn't dare tell anyone she planned to quit her job and write full-time.

"But you can teach back home. Start over, right?"

"I did teach there. But, no, I'm not going back."

Lucy's wide eyes begged her to continue.

"I had a bad relationship there." Roxanne sighed, and her shoulders relaxed. She hadn't shared that with anyone in Meridian, but Lucy put her at ease.

"Oh, honey, there too?" Lucy pointed at Roxanne's eye. "I mean, back home."

"No. Not like that. Not even close. But bad in a different way. Here is home now."

"How could anywhere be worse than with him?" Lucy covered her mouth. "Oh, I'm sorry. I guess we all get caught up after a rebound, huh? Heck, I've had my share." She glanced over at Jason. "But I think I finally got a good one. If only I could get him to church." Lucy giggled.

There was too much truth to Lucy's rebound statement. Roxanne still hurt over lost relationships and regretted that she fell for Dwayne so quickly. She'd been desperate, and he'd been available.

"Hey, don't I know you?" A man approached Roxanne.

Her pulse quickened, and her eyes darted to Dwayne, who was laughing but not looking in her direction.

Roxanne pushed up her dark glasses once again. "No, I don't think so."

"Remember me? Travis? I treated you at the urgent care."

"Urgent care?" Lucy's eyes widened.

"Oh, man. I'm sorry. I shouldn't have said that. Patient confidentiality," Travis said.

"Right. Thanks." Roxanne didn't invite him to sit, and an awkward silence followed. She hoped he'd take the hint and leave.

"All right then. Cheers, and keep writing." He raised his drink. "Hey, wait a minute." He set the glass down and pulled a crumpled paper from his jeans. "I forgot I had this. I grabbed it from the meeting last week."

She stared up at him.

"The writers' group. Remember? I told you about it." He smiled.

She didn't.

"It's at the library? I invited you."

Roxanne ignored him and said nothing.

Leaving the wrinkled yellow paper on the table, Travis took a few steps before turning back. "Hey, you should come." His voice rang loud. Too loud. Roxanne couldn't help but glance at Dwayne. He stood like a statue. More like an ugly stone gargoyle.

"You should go. Go now, please?" Roxanne begged.

"Yeah, listen to her. Her boyfriend is really jealous." Lucy nodded towards the pool tables.

Dwayne stomped to their table, but Travis raised his hands and left.

"Yeah, you better leave," Dwayne yelled. His fiery eyes glared at Roxanne. "Who the heck is that?"

"Oh, Dwayne, come on. You know the guys here. They can't resist a couple pretty ladies." Lucy gathered a hank of her hair and threw it back over her shoulder. She laughed.

"Let me refill your glass." As she reached for the pitcher, she slid the paper to the ground and poured. "Here, sweetie. Now go beat them boys at your game. Jason is dying for a rematch." She wiggled her fingers toward the pool tables.

"You sure you don't know him?" Dwayne narrowed his eyes at Roxanne.

"Yes. I'm sure."

He grabbed the mug, downed the drink, and slammed the empty glass on the table. "My turn," he yelled.

She waited for his turn to shoot, then grabbed the yellow paper, stuffing it into her purse.

"Oh, honey. Do you really think it's worth it?" Lucy asked.

"What?" Roxanne said, but she knew what Lucy meant.

"If he finds that paper...honey, I'm scared for you."

CHAPTER 5

Tuesday came, and Roxanne decided to attend the critique group, although she suffered with anxious nausea for days. But it was all for naught when she remembered that Dwayne always played basketball in a local park at an outdoor court on Tuesdays. There would be no chance of running into him. Still, her stomach reacted.

After teaching, she stayed after school making lesson plans, then drove to the library. She brought a printed copy of her manuscript just in case. Roxanne walked into the building, asked about the group, and followed a kind woman to a conference room. People of all ages sat at a table, and everyone smiled when she walked in.

Travis, the nurse, gave her a puzzled look. "Hey, there. Didn't expect to see you." He looked around her. "Did you bring your boyfriend?"

"No, of course not. He doesn't write."

"I didn't think so." Travis chuckled. "He probably doesn't read either."

Roxanne raised her brows to show her surprise at the snide comment.

"I mean, not everyone reads books, and he doesn't look the type."

Contemplating a response, she stopped herself. Why should she defend Dwayne?

"Travis, would you like to introduce your friend?" A woman at the head of the table spoke.

"Sure. Everyone, this is Roxanne." He looked at her and winked. "Roxanne is a writer."

The seven seated people exchanged names, and the woman in charge spoke. "Welcome, Roxanne. I'm glad you could join us. We're about to get started."

Roxanne sat and listened as the woman called on two people to read. Apparently, they'd been assigned for this week. As Roxanne listened, her heart blossomed. Astonished by their works, she marveled even more as the discussion and critique went around the table. Everyone gave encouraging tips.

By the time the evening ended, Roxanne felt like crying. Happy tears, again, like when the neighbor girl invited her to church. Just being here gave her courage, and she felt good about her writing. Inspired, even.

She said her goodbyes, and Travis accompanied her to the parking lot.

"Hey, if you'd like, I'd be happy to look at your manuscript," he said.

"Are you serious? You would do that?" Roxanne immediately thought again of Max and how he had kindly edited her work.

"Sure. We're all in this together."

"But, in the meeting, the readers shared a scene or chapter." She glanced at her tote, slipping her hand in.

Travis smiled. "Do you have some pages in there? Let me take a look."

She pulled out the entire manuscript.

His eyes widened, and a grin spread across his face. "Wow. You *are* a writer." He reached for the folder. "May I?" Flipping through the three-inch stack of paper, he asked, "You have a copy on your laptop, correct?"

"Maybe. My computer has difficulty saving, and my backup is iffy." She cringed, hearing the metal grinding of the garbage disposal in her head. "I printed this before my last edit."

"Good. I'll read this as fast as I can." He pulled out a business card. "Here, you can call me if you get anxious."

She glanced at his simple card with his name, Travis Howard, in a flourished script with the word "Author" printed in bold letters underneath. She smiled and hid the card in a zipped compartment of her purse. Roxanne had mixed feelings about handing her book over to a stranger. Yet, his friendly manner made him appear trustworthy, and his genuine interest convinced her.

The week crawled by, and the elation of the critique group kept Roxanne humming, unless Dwayne appeared. She hated that she walked on eggshells in his presence. She heeded the warning, though, since he'd been complaining of headaches and drank more, which escalated his anger issues. She compensated by fixing elaborate meals for him, and it calmed him, but it took up all her spare time. Couple that with lesson planning and grading papers, writing took a backseat to everything.

The following Sunday at Leroy's Sports Bar, Roxanne told Lucy about the writers' group, pulling out Travis's business card. Sharing her writing with Lucy made Roxanne flush with renewed excitement, especially as Lucy expressed her admiration. Roxanne felt a little lighter, the constant fear faded, and something that felt like hope replaced it.

"That's amazing. And you've finished more books? I could never do that."

"Well, they're all in rough drafts."

"Why don't you publish any of them?"

"I tried. After college, I intended to get serious about submitting to agents or publishers." Roxanne shrugged. "I'm not a good enough writer. Years ago, my mentor pitched it to her publisher. And they rejected it."

Her mentor. The thought of Miz Philippa made her sigh. She missed the woman she admired. Although Miz Philippa had passed away, Roxanne felt relieved she wasn't here to witness her failings. She'd wanted so much for the woman to be proud of her.

"Anyway." Roxanne waved a hand. "Ancient history."

"So try again. You've been writing all this time, why not? Oh, Roxy. Take your books and get out of here. Dwayne's holding you back, honey. If God gave you a gift, use it."

That's what Max had told her. But the way she lived her life now, God couldn't be much interested in her, not after all that had happened.

"Whoo hoo!"

Roxanne turned to see Dwayne pumping his fists in the air.

"Yeah, baby. Who's the man?"

Dwayne had beat everyone in pool... again. The men returned to the table along with the other women. And Dwayne bent over and nuzzled Roxanne's neck. She shivered.

"What's the matter with you?" He growled.

"Hey, Dwayne, so how'd you get so good at shooting pool?" Lucy interrupted.

Roxanne appreciated Lucy's rescue. Not one to resist any attention to his prowess, Dwayne let go of her hair and leered at Lucy.

"Well, baby, if you want, I can teach you?" He winked.

Lucy grabbed her boyfriend's arm. "No thanks, I got my own private teacher here."

"Yeah, Dwayne. Lay off my woman," Jason said.

"I ain't nobody's woman," Lucy teased.

A little rough around the edges, Lucy had her wits about

her. But most importantly, she genuinely cared about others. Maybe church taught her that. If Dwayne would let her, Roxanne would go. Wouldn't she?

The thought warmed her, and she glanced down, but froze. The white business card lay on the table. Dwayne's hand slammed down over it.

He picked it up. "Travis Howard, Author?" He narrowed his eyes at Roxanne. "You two-timing me with some kind of a book geek?"

Dwayne wound his hands through Roxanne's hair and yanked her head back.

"Whoa there, buddy." Jason stepped forward.

Roxanne slightly shook her head at Jason. Dwayne wouldn't do much here, and she didn't want a scene. Perspiration dripped down her back. "Of course not, Dwayne."

He grunted and let go, but then his eyes went wild. "Wait a minute. Was that the guy here last week?"

"I don't know what you're talking about." Roxanne clenched her hands tightly. "Look, Dwayne, I'm a little tired. Can we leave?"

"No," Lucy shouted. Her voice trembled. "I mean, we haven't eaten yet. Have some pizza, Roxy."

Roxanne saw panic in Lucy's eyes as she shot a pleading look at Jason.

"Yeah, come on, Dwayne. Besides, I need another chance to beat you at your own game."

Stupid me. Leaving now, with Dwayne so angry, would leave her defenseless. At least in public, he couldn't do that much damage.

"Okay, sure. Maybe I should eat first. That's probably why I'm so tired. I haven't eaten all day," Roxanne said.

Dwayne picked up the card and shoved it in his pocket. His friends tugged at him and led him to the dart boards. "I'll deal with you later." He glared.

Lucy whispered, "Honey, please don't go home with him. Come with me now. I'll take you to my place."

"No. But thank you. We'll stay a little, and he'll cool down."

But he didn't. In fact, many hours, and many beers later, after his reckless driving and near miss accidents, they arrived home. Driving drunk with him didn't compare to what she anticipated if she couldn't get herself locked into a bathroom for the night.

The alcohol had caught up with him, and his coordination lacked stability. He parked haphazardly and fell from the car.

She scrambled out and ran into the house as he cursed after her. If she could just get into her bathroom. He'd pound on the door for a while then hopefully pass out. Better yet, he might leave and return to his own apartment. She heard his stumbling footsteps just as she locked herself in. Backing up, she tripped and slid to the floor.

"Roxy!" He yelled. Then silence.

If he fell into a dead sleep, she could leave the restroom and go to a hotel. She'd have to grab some clothes for work, and her classroom would be her safe place once again. But exhausted, Roxanne lay on the bathroom rug and awoke when it was still dark.

Shoot. She glanced at the bathroom clock and moved quickly. Stepping out quietly, Roxanne never looked back at the bed as she grabbed a bell-sleeved peasant dress and tiptoed to the entrance. She reached for the knob.

Gushing water sounded from the kitchen. A glass clinked. Roxanne's fingers went numb as she fumbled to open the front door. Dwayne's large hand planted above hers, and he shoved the door shut.

"So where ya' going, Roxy?"

CHAPTER 6

Strange sounds clicked. Beeping and whooshing followed a rhythmic pattern, and this didn't feel like her bed. The unfamiliar antiseptic smells confused her, but her mind couldn't think straight anyway. Try as she might, she couldn't force her eyes open, and she lapsed in and out of consciousness.

Roxanne finally awoke and once again tried opening her eyes. Only one eyelid cooperated, and with it, she looked around.

Dr. Rashid stood over her. "You're lucky to be alive."

"Where am I?" Roxanne asked.

"You're in Meridian General Hospital."

"What day is it? I have to work."

"It's Monday but you won't be working today." Dr. Rashid looked at the clock on the wall. "The ambulance brought you in a couple hours ago. Is this the worst?" the doctor asked.

Roxanne turned her head sideways. Embarrassed and ashamed, she tried not to cry, but nodded.

"The next time, he may kill you. You need to get away from him, and you need to get help." Dr. Rashid patted her arm. "Rest now. I'll be back soon."

Roxanne's head pounded as she tried to recall the morning. Her uninjured eye weighed heavy, but she forced it to stay open. Where was Dwayne now? Other than being kicked and beaten till she blacked out, she didn't remember anything. Glancing down at her battered body, she stared at her casted wrist.

She tried to turn but winced at the pain coming from her back and abdomen. She glanced at the tray table and decided against looking for a mirror. She could almost feel how bad she looked. One eye so puffy it swelled shut. Her lips cracked, cut, and dried. She reached up and touched the swelling on her forehead. She tried to swallow, but the lump in her throat caused her to moan, "God, please." *Please what?* Finally blocking the questions, she managed to fall asleep. When she awoke, as promised, there stood Dr. Rashid.

Roxanne forced herself to face the doctor. Her lips parted, but she didn't speak. As if knowing that she would ask about Dwayne, Dr. Rashid gave a report.

"The police are still looking for him. Some neighbors heard the ruckus and called the authorities. Paramedics brought you here. Your boyfriend —"

Roxanne shuddered. "No, not anymore."

"He got away, so he's still out there. Do you have some-place to go? You cannot go home. He'll be back."

"I can go to my mother's house in Bay Town," Roxanne said.

"Does your mother know?"

"Yes. I'm sure she does. But it would kill her to see me like this."

"Does he know where she lives?"

"No." Roxanne explained how Dwayne had never even asked about her past. Yet, she knew much of his. As sad as she felt about her former life, his read like a tragic novel.

"We'll run a few more tests to ensure there are no internal injuries, and I may release you after that. But you cannot go home."

"She can stay with me." A sweet voice spoke from the doorway. Lucy and Jason walked toward the bed.

Lucy extended her hand to the doctor. "Hi, I'm Lucy Lovell. Roxanne's friend, and this is Jason Dean, my boyfriend."

Lucy grasped the doctor's hand with both of hers. Dropping her large tote in a nearby chair, Lucy rushed to Roxanne's side.

"Oh, Roxy. We've been waiting for you to wake up. I'm so sorry. We left the bar right after you guys did, but Dwayne drove so fast we couldn't keep up, and I didn't know where you lived. Heck, I don't even have your cell number." She choked with a sob, and Jason wrapped an arm around her shoulders, pulling her close.

Dr. Rashid patted Lucy's arm. "You tried, dear, and thank heaven for the neighbors. If not for them, Roxanne might have died."

Lucy's body went rigid. "Why, that's a terrible thing to say."

"But it's true, and you women need to realize that dangerous men out there will take advantage of you any chance they get."

Jason nodded. "I'm real sorry, Roxy. I had no idea he would do something like this."

Lucy touched Roxanne's face. "Honey, I'm so sorry."

"It's not your fault, Lucy. I'm an idiot. I'm so stupid, I just —"

"Don't do that. We don't berate ourselves for being abused. You had nothing to do with him doing this to you. You will find that out when we get you some help," Dr. Rashid said.

Roxanne pressed her lips together. Still trying to figure out the getting help thing but blaming it all on Dwayne somehow helped her feel better. Yet, a niggling of something cut her heart. "Thank you, Doctor."

"Promise me you'll call me?"

"Sure," she said weakly.

"All right then. Lucy, is your place safe?" Dr. Rashid raised a brow.

"Yes. Of course. I have a little one-bedroom apartment, but it's in a good neighborhood."

"I can stay there too, to make sure they're safe. I'm done with Dwayne. I can't believe he did this," Jason said.

"Well, just be sure that no one knows Roxanne is staying there," Dr. Rashid said.

"But my work. I only have a week before summer break."

"It'll take that long at home to recover. At least. Please call your employer."

Principal Franklin will definitely understand. "But I have to get some things. My clothes, my car, everything is at my house," Roxanne said.

"I must keep you for observation at least one more night. When I discharge you tomorrow, I'll call the police for an escort. They'll help you get whatever you need. Then go to your friend's house and stay there," Dr. Rashid said.

"How long?"

"As long as it takes to be sure you are safe." Dr. Rashid looked at her watch. "Where do you work? I can write you a note."

"At Lauderdale Elementary School," Roxanne said.

"She's a writer, also." Lucy smiled.

Roxanne gasped. "My computer! It has all my writing on it. At least all that I've been able to save. But it's a lot. If Dwayne goes back to the house, he might damage it."

"Right now, your life is more important than anything else. Some things you cannot handle all by yourself. Whether you believe or not, there's a God up there looking out for you."

"Are you a Christian, Doctor?" Lucy squealed.

Dr. Rashid smiled. "I'm a believer in Jesus Christ, yes. But we'll have to continue this conversation later. I have other patients to tend to. Lucy, you pray with Roxanne. Pray for God's safety and protection and I will too." She turned to leave but stopped and gazed at Roxanne. "Pray for the strength to leave this toxic relationship."

Roxanne nodded. Dr. Rashid said her goodbyes, and Jason went to get coffee for the girls.

Lucy looked at Roxanne. Tears formed again. "Oh, Roxy. We're too old for this. How can we let a man terrorize us like this?"

"He's not a man, he's a monster." Roxanne closed the open eye. "But he didn't used to be."

"You can't make excuses for him," Lucy said.

"I'm not, but he came across as a decent guy when I met him. Really." She sighed. "But I'm done with him, and he won't do this again. Whatever I have to do."

"Let's not go that far. Start with getting away," Lucy said.

"He's not going to terrorize us anymore." Roxanne blinked long but continued. "I didn't tell you, but I'm quitting my job and going to write full-time."

"That's wonderful. Go to your mama's house. It'll be peaceful there."

"No, I'm staying here. I have a home here, and I'm not letting Dwayne chase me away."

"Honey, you better think about it. Maybe just go home for a bit, then? Until they get him. Even then, he won't be locked away forever."

Roxanne's brain muddled, but the ringing cell phone jarred her. Without thinking, she answered it.

"Hey, baby. It's me. I'm so sorry. Are you okay?"

She couldn't speak.

"Sweetie, come on. Talk to me. I'll quit drinking. It won't happen ag —"

She hung up, put the phone down, and shook uncontrollably.

"It was him, wasn't it?" Lucy hugged her friend and cried.

CHAPTER 7

The phone went dead. He didn't think for a minute that the battery died. Roxanne had hung up on him. Dwayne threw his cell on the seat. She'd never done that before. He'd really blown it this time. After he'd fled Roxy's house, he got more beer, drove to the woods, and drank till he passed out again. He hadn't slept long with the morning heat and the annoying mosquitos. Dwayne slapped his neck.

That stupid neighbor. He knew she'd called the police. Over his own yelling and Roxy's screams he'd heard banging on the front door. He ignored it as he continued pounding Roxy. Dwayne slammed the steering wheel. How could he have done that to her. He loved her. Dwayne grabbed another can of beer and guzzled it. Then three more.

Groaning, he choked back a sob. Mama warned him. *Mama!* He had to go see her. What if he got caught and they locked him up? *I better go now*

Dwayne glanced at his watch. He had a three-hour drive ahead of him, but his head pounded, and his vision blurred. With all the alcohol he'd consumed, he knew he couldn't manage it. *Just a quick nap, that will help.* As the blackness enveloped his car, it also seeped into his brain, his past terrorizing him.

Later that day, the sun barely shone through the dark forest, but perspiration dripping down Dwayne's face awoke him. That and the intense itching from the bug bites swarming in the thicket where he'd parked. Waking with a worse headache than when he'd fallen asleep, he righted himself and lifted the hem of his t-shirt. He wiped his face, started the engine, and focused on the dashboard's LED lights. Two o'clock! He'd slept all day. Cursing himself, he drove frantically. If he didn't hurry, he'd miss visiting hours. He groaned. Roxanne's fault again.

Three hours later, he peeled into the prison driveway and parked. Checking the rearview mirror, Dwayne wiped his sweaty face and combed his hair. He glanced at his watch just as the siren blared. Slamming a fist on the steering wheel, he groaned. *Why that little...* Dwayne gazed at the stark white building. Visiting hours were almost over, and he'd wasted the whole day.

If not for all the bars on the windows and barbed wire rolling across the tops of the chain link fences, the main offices of the Women's Facility looked like a big, white house. A home. A home to nine hundred and eighty-five incarcerated women housed in the concrete structures behind the main building. Some of the prisoners were on death row. The facility was under investigation by the Department of Justice. Staff abuse against the inmates had been exposed and reported. This was Dwayne's mother's home.

Dwayne chewed his fingernails, his eyes riveted on the building. As a registered visitor on file, he visited his mama often. And he never missed a week after he started dating Roxy. He'd brag about his girlfriend every visit, and Mama loved hearing about her. The little joy she savored for his happiness. She always asked to hear more about this Roxy girl.

But the first time he hit Roxy, he skipped his weekly sojourn to the prison. One miss turned into a month, and when he finally came to see her, somehow Mama knew. Every time he'd hurt Roxy, his mama knew. And the last time he came, his mother told him never to come back if he hurt her again. This time, he'd done it.

But if Roxy hadn't been fooling around with that book geek none of this would have happened. *Mama would understand. Wouldn't she?* Dwayne glanced down at the card in his cup holder. He crushed the white business card with black lettering but stopped and opened his palm.

Travis Howard, Author. *Idiot is more like it.* Had he put all the ideas of her being a writer in her head? Dwayne's throat tightened. Nah, she'd been writing when he met her, but had she known the geek before? Maybe they were just friends. But he never bothered to ask, and she'd lied to him. She knew the guy.

I should have listened to Mama and quit drinking a long time ago. The booze always did it. Dwayne pressed a fist to his forehead. Then pounded. Roxy was the best thing that ever happened to him. They'd been happy together in the beginning. He loved her and couldn't get enough. But then she tried to pull away. And he only wanted her more. To be with her night and day.

He stared through his streaked windshield.

"Hey."

Dwayne jumped at the rapping on his raised window. Sweat ran down his temples.

"You can't loiter in this parking lot. It's not allowed, and you know it." A heavy, pale-skinned, uniformed officer met him eye-to-eye.

Dwayne's jaw clenched. His grinding teeth grated in his ears. He should have known better. His neon-green, lifted truck was a dead giveaway, and he'd forgotten they knew him here. If he went in, the penitentiary would log in his name, license plate, and arrival time. By now, his truck and his pictures might even be spread around about the assault.

"Hey. I said you can't just sit here."

"I'm leaving." Dwayne started the car.

"Stop. Just a minute." The officer spoke into a radio on his shoulder. "Uh-huh." He looked up at the guard station over-looking the parking lot and nodded. "Park it, buddy. Come in with me."

But he didn't. Dwayne threw the truck in reverse and peeled from the parking lot. He drove as fast as he could from the Alabama Women's Penitentiary and kept checking his rearview mirror. Driving down the interstate, he swerved around cars, knowing the police would be after him. If he could just make it to the exit. He knew the back roads well enough.

An hour later, he disappeared into the rural woods of Alabama, where streetlights were absent. With dusk encroach-ing, he could spot any headlights that might rise up behind him.

He glanced at the cupholder where the business card lay, and his breathing stepped up to a rapid pace. The darkness outside matched the black in his mind. He'd blown it. If they caught him, he might end up in jail. And if his dad still lived, he'd be laughing at Dwayne. All the beatings the man had given Dwayne's mama, and he never landed in jail. Instead, his father ended up dead, and Dwayne wouldn't let that be his fate. He'd get Roxanne first.

He just needed a place to lie low for a while, and they'd never find him out here. He zipped past the trees. They all looked the same, but over one hundred varieties grew tall in these parts. He didn't know one of them, and he didn't care, but they guarded him. He'd hidden from his father in the deepest part of the woods, and the thick forest protected him sometimes.

Dwayne had been fortunate enough to earn an athletic college scholarship and escape the poor community where he'd grown up. He had brains, too, and he wasn't dumb.

Dwayne rubbed his chin. Stupid sometimes, but not dumb. If only he could control his temper.

He slowed the truck and turned down an unmarked dirt drive. Narrow enough for just one vehicle. His monster truck knocked tree branches as it passed. He slowed. There, up ahead. His sister's house. He stopped in front of a white clapboard structure. The clearing around the house enclosed by a white picket fence. No white trash out here. A weed-free thriving garden, even a wooden swing set. Nothing like the broken-down ramshackle house where he grew up.

Dwayne parked and hopped out. An addition had been built onto one side since he'd last been here, and it even looked like they had added a room upstairs. About time with the passel of kids they kept having.

Iris stormed out of the house, letting the screen door slam. "You go on, Dwayne. Git." She stood on the top of the three steps that constituted the front porch. Small in stature and build, but strong in spirit. Strong enough to boss anyone. Her dark hair was piled high on her head, with wisps hanging down, sticking to her face. She wore a breezy sundress. Something Roxanne couldn't wear because of the bruises he always left on her arms. Dwayne shook his head, trying to rattle out the image.

"Place looks nice, sis."

"You can't be here. The kids will be home from youth group soon, and Billy needs his sleep for his graveyard shift."

Dwayne ran a hand through his drenched hair. He slapped his arms. "What the heck, sis? These bugs are eating me alive. Let's go inside."

"You should be used to it. Now, get back in your truck and leave."

He rubbed his chin, and his eye started to twitch as he glared. "I got no place to go."

"And it's your own fault. I saw the local news. Your picture is everywhere. You blew it big time. You had a nice girl there, Dwayne. How could you?"

"I know, I know. I just had too much to drink."

"You can't blame it all on that. It's that temper of yours. Everyone tried to help you, but you're just like Dad."

"Don't say that." He lunged for the porch.

Before Iris reached for the knob, the door swung open. Dwayne stopped just short of the bottom step. A man, even larger than him, pulled Iris inside, taking her place. He trudged down the steps and grabbed hold of Dwayne's tee shirt. He half-dragged him to the truck, opened the driver's side, and shoved Dwayne in. He didn't struggle.

"You heard your sister. Get out of here. We don't want you around our kids." A man of few words, Billy, Iris' husband, shoved again. Not prone to violence, but decisive to act. "If I catch you back here, I'll drag you to the police myself."

"Yeah, that ain't happening." Dwayne swung hard, but not hard enough. Billy wobbled.

A siren wailed in the distance. Dwayne shoved the key into the ignition, but Billy's reach cut him off. He grabbed Dwayne's wrist, yanking away the keychain.

"Looks like you ain't getting away with it this time."

Billy walked to the edge of the clearing and heaved the keys into the dense forest. Dwayne cursed him as he ran from the truck.

The siren faded and Dwayne kept running. He ran so long that the dark night took over, but it didn't clear his mind. He slapped at another mosquito. Then another. Why his sister continued to live out here, he had no idea. Nothing but bad memories and bugs. But she'd met Billy, and they married young. Billy grew up in the Alabama woods, and he told Iris he'd never leave. He protected her from Dad, and Iris couldn't ask for a better man. Billy treated her good. Real good. For a quick second, Dwayne wished he would have treated Roxanne like that.

But he cleared his mind and continued running. The thick ferns and shrubbery whipped at his bare legs and arms, not slowing him down. It was a good thing he'd stayed in shape playing basketball all these years. Even still, the physical exertion paled compared to the bugs that came out full force at nightfall. But they were the least of his problems.

He ran parallel to the main road, hidden by the trees, and finally reached the next community. He broke into the clearing where a faint neon sign blinked, but no cars were parked out front. Nothing more than a gas station, a market, and a bar next door.

Dwayne walked towards the familiar establishment. In high school, he and his friends went to Charlie's Bar after Friday night games. If they won, Charlie treated them to soda and let them play pool as long as they wanted. Most of the kids went home before midnight, but Dwayne usually stayed until his dad showed up.

Good mood, and Dad played all night with Dwayne. In a bad mood, Dad gave Dwayne a beating outside. Charlie always felt sorry for him, and sometimes intervened. Dwayne hoped he still owned the bar.

Opening the heavy door, Dwayne peered in. His eyes needed no adjustment. It was as dark inside as out. On weeknights, the bar drew only a few people. This Monday evening, it remained empty. He gazed toward the wooden bar where a young guy wiped down the counters.

"Who are you?" Dwayne asked.

"I'm new here. What can I get you?"

"Where's Charlie?"

The bartender waved a towel toward the screen mounted on a wall. A white-haired man slumped in a chair, his back to

Dwayne. The news station flashed Dwayne's picture on the screen, and Dwayne swallowed hard.

The bartender stared from the TV to Dwayne. He picked up a cell phone.

"Don't do it," Dwayne yelled. Reaching over the counter, he grabbed it from the guy's hands and threw it. The bartender stepped back.

"That's a good-looking picture they got of you," Charlie called from his seat, not turning. "Ya' need help, don't ya, son?"

"Yes, sir," said Dwayne. He breathed deeply. Hope replaced angst, and Dwayne walked over and shook Charlie's hand. The old man nodded.

"Sit down." Charlie waved at a wooden club chair.

"But Charlie, we gotta call the police," called the bartender.

"You do that, and you can leave now without pay."

Dwayne glared at the bartender.

Charlie's voice lowered. "Why'd ya' do it?"

"Too many beers, and —"

Charlie raised his hand. "I'd a thought you knew better by now." He sighed. "I got a car behind the building. It's registered in my brother-in-law's name, but he's dead. Keys are in the visor."

"I got no place to go." Dwayne sighed. Exhaustion hit him. "I've had a really bad day."

"Haven't we all, son? Go find someplace. You're not a kid anymore. Too bad you squandered your talent and your brains. Lay low for a long while. Maybe the girl will drop the charges. Go on, get out of here. I never saw ya'."

"Thank you, sir."

"Go out the back door." Charlie paused. "Say, Dwayne? How's your mama?"

Dwayne gulped. "I tried to see her today but didn't make it in time."

"Your mama did right by killing your daddy. But you better change your ways, boy. You're gonna land up just like him, and you're gonna break your mama's heart."

I already done that.

The front door swung open, and Dwayne turned just enough to see a uniformed man enter.

"That's him," yelled the bartender, pointing toward the hallway.

Dwayne raced toward the back exit but stopped when he heard laughter.

"That's who?" A voice boomed out, laughing again. "Whoever he is, it's his lucky day 'cause I'm off duty. Besides, I ain't no cop. I'm just a paid security guard for the Quick Stop next door. Now, give me a beer."

"But it's the guy on TV."

"You're fired," Charlie said to the bartender. He stood and waved at Dwayne. The old man took his place behind the bar.

CHAPTER 8

The hospital monitored Roxanne for head injuries, and Dr. Rashid kept her an extra day, releasing her on Wednesday. Jason drove the women straight to Lucy's home. Roxanne, Lucy, and Jason sat on the couch remaining awkwardly silent until Jason cleared his throat.

"I'm sleeping on the couch tonight." He nodded.

Lucy patted his shoulder and snuggled in close to him. "Thanks, sweetie. That's right nice of you."

He turned to face Roxy. "I'm so sorry. I never thought Dwayne would hurt you. Otherwise, I would have warned you. Honest, I would have."

"It's not your fault." Roxanne spoke just above a whisper. "I've been with him enough to see the signs."

"Yeah, I think when his mama didn't make parole, it did a number on him," Jason said.

"Parole?" Lucy squeaked.

"It's a long story, sweetheart," Jason pulled Lucy in for a hug. "I'll tell you later."

"I think you're right. Just before the State denied parole, Dwayne wanted me to meet her, but he couldn't get me clearance," Roxanne said.

"Yeah, he said she'd be pretty happy that he got himself a nice girl like you. I can imagine it upset him that he couldn't show you off."

"Really, Jason. We're not trophies, you know." Lucy glared.

He laughed. "I know, I know. You keep telling me that you're precious in God's sight, even if you're not in mine. But you are, sweetie. If you just agreed to marry me, I'd show you how precious you are."

"I told you. If you'd start coming to church, I just might consider it." Lucy gave him a playful shove.

Roxanne listened to them banter. It hurt her face to smile, but the laughter made her heart feel good. She'd always thought she'd return to church one day but didn't consider inviting Dwayne. She wondered if it would have made a difference.

Lucy turned to Roxanne. "So, what's the plan? You should really move back to your mama's. Don't you think?"

Roxanne gave her a sad sideways glance.

Lucy's eyes widened. "Oh, come on. You're not taking Dwayne back?"

"Of course not. But I have a house here I need to tend to. It's my home." Her cell rang.

"Don't answer it!" Lucy yelled.

Too late.

"Roxanne, this is Dr. Rashid."

Roxanne whispered her name to Lucy and stepped outside.

"Hello, Doctor."

"I hope you don't mind, but I called the police to see if Dwayne Payton has been caught. I'm very concerned for your safety. He hasn't been seen. It's like he's disappeared. The police visited you at the hospital, correct?"

Roxanne's hand started to shake. She held the phone tightly to her ear. "Yes, I told them what I knew. I gave them a description of his truck. They said my neighbor made a report too."

"Most likely, he switched cars or left town. But I doubt it."

Why did she have to say that? Roxanne had tried not to think about Dwayne.

"I believe he's hiding in plain sight. When are you leaving town?"

Roxanne cleared her throat. "I'm not sure. I need to pick up my things at the school."

"Do you think that's wise? Does Dwayne know where you work? Leaving tomorrow will not be too soon."

"I understand." Roxanne had no other response.

"It's your decision. Make a wise one, and please keep in touch. If you decide to leave, I have contacts everywhere."

"Thank you, Doctor."

"And Miss Cook, please file charges as soon as possible."

Roxanne gulped. She didn't want to think about that right now. She saved Dr. Rashid's number in her contacts. It seemed everyone wanted to help. No one seemed to trust her to overcome this on her own. She straightened and reached for the door. Once inside, she grabbed her purse.

"Hey, Lucy, could I borrow a hoodie and some sunglasses? I'm running errands, and I don't want to scare anyone with this face." Roxanne tried to chuckle. She hadn't looked in the mirror since she'd left the hospital. She couldn't.

"I'll go for you. What do you need?" Jason offered.

Roxanne didn't want to reveal that she'd planned to go to her house. Right now she had the courage to take care of business, hoping Dwayne was far away. "I'll be fine."

"Lucy?" Roxanne said.

"Oh! Sure thing, honey. Are you sure we can't join you?"

"I'm fine."

Lucy retrieved the items and reluctantly handed them to Roxanne. "Watch out for yourself, girl."

Roxanne nodded. "I'll be back later. Don't worry."

"Easy for you to say," Lucy called.

"Call if you need anything," Jason said as the door closed.

Driving away, Roxanne warmed at the thought of sweet Jason.

He cared so much for Lucy. He respected her values, and Roxanne recalled him offering to sleep on the couch. It probably meant that Lucy wasn't sleeping with him.

Like she had been with Dwayne. Roxanne shivered, loathing inside making her stomach churn. When had life turned into this? Not just the abusive relationship but getting involved intimately outside of marriage. She never in a million years thought she'd do it. But she met Dwayne at a low point in her life and sank even lower. She'd let herself slip away from her values and her God. *For what?*

Roxanne pinched the bridge of her nose as she drove. You'd think his explosive outbursts would have scared her away. She winced as she looked over her shoulder.

But Dwayne's anger issues were not noticeable in the beginning of their relationship, at least not the rage. He seemed somewhat responsible. He even had his lifelong friends. Why would they stick by him, a dangerous man? Still, the drinking and fury escalated, and she stuck around too long. Why hadn't she listened? Listened to everybody except that weak inner voice. Although she feared him, she never believed his rages would result in this.

Roxanne arrived at her house, and her heart pounded, ready to burst. She couldn't believe her eyes as she scanned the yard. Stepping from her car, she stared at her garden. Ripped apart, succulents lay strewn about. Blooms from her rose bushes crushed into the ground, and broken terra cotta pots scattered all across the driveway. Something made her gaze down the street. An older, black vehicle parked on the street, several houses down. One she didn't recognize.

"Roxanne?"

"What?" Roxanne answered abruptly. Seeing her neighbor, she toned down her voice. "Oh, hey there, Mrs. Ishida."

The petite woman cleared her throat. "He came back. I saw him in the driveway when I drove up."

"He? You mean, Dwayne? When?" Roxanne hated saying his name.

"Yesterday."

"Did he go in?"

Mrs. Ishida pushed back her dark hair. "I don't know, but I yelled at him to stop when he started smashing things outside. He acted so crazy I ran back into my house and called the police. He must have known because he left quickly. He was gone when they got here."

"I'm so sorry you had to experience that."

"That's what neighbors are for. I would have cleaned up, but I had to pick up Kayla and we've been busy."

"Oh, I wouldn't expect you to do that. But thank you." Roxanne gazed at her house.

"If you want, I'll get my son to go in with you. He just got home from college, and I asked him to clean up your driveway, anyway."

No, thank you perched on her lips, but fearful caution prompted her otherwise. "Yes, would you mind asking him?"

"Of course not."

Within seconds, Mrs. Ishida and her son, a good-looking, muscled man, much like Dwayne, returned. Roxanne trembled and walked to the front door.

"Give me your keys," he said.

Roxanne bristled. His forceful voice commanded rather than asked.

Mrs. Ishida gave her son a playful shove. "This is Toby. Toby this is Miss Cook."

"Hey, nice to meet you," he said. He pointed to the house, then raised his palm and barged ahead. "I'll go in first. Make sure you're safe. Is that all right with you?"

The request calmed her. "Of course."

Toby unlocked the door and pushed it open. His deep voice bellowed. "Anybody home? We're coming in, and the police are right here too." He looked at his mother and winked, stepping inside.

The eerie silence rocked her, but Roxanne followed, hiding behind him. She peered into the living room. Broken lamps and smashed glass end tables were scattered everywhere. Shattered potted plants, dirt, and destruction met her all around. She closed her eyes. Every room seemed worse than the previous. Dwayne had even thrown dry concrete mix down the toilets. The empty bags were scattered in the shower and tub.

"Wow. That guy is bad news." Toby whistled. "I'd say you dodged a bullet, but it doesn't look like it."

Roxanne looked up. She tried to laugh.

Mrs. Ishida frowned and whispered for him to pipe down.

"No, he's right," Roxanne said.

"Thank God that you're alive, but can we do anything to help?" Mrs. Ishida asked.

"No. Thank you. You've already done so much." Roxanne stood and walked into the hallway, stepping over debris.

"I can help. See what we can salvage," Toby offered.

"No, thanks. It's all just stuff. I'm unsure if my homeowner's will cover it, but it can be replaced." Her eyes widened as a thought popped into her head. "My computer!"

Roxanne climbed over debris heading toward her computer desk just outside her kitchen in the TV room. Mrs. Ishida warned her to be careful as she stumbled across the wreckage. But at this moment, nothing mattered but her computer. Too late. A hollow space her PC had occupied gaped before her. Her monitor lay cracked, the keyboard was smashed on the ground, but the hard drive was gone. Roxanne slumped.

"I'm so sorry. Anything on there that can't be replaced?"

"My writing," Roxanne whispered.

"Oh my. Are you an author? I had no idea," Mrs. Ishida said.

Not yet, she wanted to say. "I wanted to be one. Always have."

Mrs. Ishida squeezed Roxanne's shoulder. "Don't let this stop you. I tell my little Kayla that with the Lord, the sky is the limit. Just put Him first."

That's my problem, she wanted to say. "Thank you," Roxanne said weakly.

"Say, would you like to stay for dinner? I always have plenty."

"Oh, no. But thanks. I'm staying with a friend, and she'll be worried about me."

"We all are." Mrs. Ishida smiled. "Would you mind if I gave you a hug?"

Roxanne swallowed, but a lump formed in her throat. "Of course not. I could use one."

Wrapping her arms around Roxanne, Mrs. Ishida hugged her gently. "I wasn't raised in a hugging family." She laughed. "My Japanese culture you know."

"Well, I sure appreciate it. Thank you again. For everything."

Roxanne had barely said more than good morning to the neighbor since she'd moved in a couple years back, and now the woman helped in the best way possible with love and encouragement. Looking around, Roxanne resolved to get this place cleaned up and then head for Bay Town. But not today. Once in the car, she sat and stared at the broken pots again. She grit her teeth. *No more.* Her cell rang, and she grabbed it, angry enough to scream at Dwayne this time.

"Hello," she demanded.

"Hey, baby. It's me. Are you okay?"

She didn't answer.

"Sweetie, come on."

"We're done, Dwayne."

"Talk to me. I'll quit drinking. I'll never hurt you again. I promise."

"You're right. You won't. We're done." Roxanne clicked off.

CHAPTER 9

Roxanne drove back to Lucy's and burst into her home. Jason lay sleeping on the couch, and Lucy lay awake next to him watching TV.

"I did it!" Roxanne called out.

Lucy untangled herself from Jason's embrace, careful not to wake him. "Did what?" she asked.

"I told Dwayne we're through." Roxanne's chest swelled.

"He called you again?"

"He did. He apologized, but I told him he'd never hurt me again."

Lucy raised her hand for a high five. "You go, girl! So you're leaving, right?"

Roxanne sighed heavily. "I don't know, yet. I guess I'm undecided."

She'd had the courage to take this step. She needed time to think, not just run. Feeling proud and empowered, she basked in the excitement.

"Roxy, you're crazy. Just go. God will take care of it. You've really ticked Dwayne off now."

"I don't care." She fisted her hand. "I won't let him run me off."

"But you wouldn't be running. You'd be making a smart

decision to move on. Seriously, Roxy. Listen, let's talk over dinner. I made some taco fixings."

"You didn't eat yet?"

"We did, but you didn't. Eat, get a good night's sleep, and I'll kick you out in the morning." Lucy's lips pouted. "Go home, Roxy. Please go home to your mama."

Roxanne hugged her friend. "In time, Lucy." She wouldn't make promises. She had responsibilities here.

"But what about your writing?"

Roxanne huffed. "Dwayne took my PC and destroyed my flash drive."

"But I thought you said that Travis guy took a copy."

Roxanne's eyes widened. "That's right!"

She reached into her purse, searching for Travis' business card.

"Dwayne took it. He took the business card, remember?" Lucy bit her lip.

Roxanne closed her eyes. "That's right. I forgot. Listen, I'm not very hungry. I think I'll go lay down."

"Sure, sweetie. You do that. I'll have the tacos ready whenever you are. Oh, hey? Have you called your mama?"

Guilt gripped her heart. She hadn't talked to Mama in a week. How could she tell her?

"Right now." Roxanne held up her cell.

She slipped into Lucy's bedroom and placed the call.

"Hello, Bethie Cook's phone," a man with a familiar British accent answered.

"Max? Max Tippet? Max in Bay Town?"

"Yes. Roxy, it's you, isn't it?"

She smiled. His proper British accent was such a contrast to the southern drawl of most Mississippians. She hadn't spoken to him in years and smiled, remembering her school-girl crush. Married back then, Max reminded Roxanne of Edward Ferris, played by Hugh Grant as the proper clergyman in the Hollywood rendition of Jane Austen's *Sense and Sensibility*.

"Roxy?"

"Yes. Hello, Max."

She smiled, remembering him. She hadn't seen him since Philippa's funeral. Although Roxanne drove into Bay Town to attend the memorial, she never spoke with him. At the funeral, Max's quiet demeanor couldn't cover his anguish over the loss of his beloved wife. Wiping tears the entire way home, Roxanne drove straight back to Meridian. There, she mourned for her mentor, and the hope of becoming an author faltered.

"Yes, Roxy. How have you been?"

Roxanne drifted off. How disappointed Miz Philippa would be if she'd known of Roxanne's life today. Remembering calmer days, she thought of the Pink Rosette. The quaint red brick building with baskets of hanging flowers cascading from the balconies of their second story. All their vibrant colors complemented the artistic center of town. Bay Town, her home.

"I'm fine. How are you?"

Max paused. "I'm well, but it's your mum."

She opened her mouth, but no words emitted.

"Listen, love, I need you to sit down. Your mum is all right. She had a bit of a setback last weekend."

Roxanne's head spun, and guilt heaped upon her already battered psyche. Why had she let a week go by? She felt something amiss. Dwayne, *it's his fault*. The jerk had incapacitated her. She rubbed her wrist and touched her swollen brow, but remembering how she neglected to call her mother, she shook her head. *No. No one's fault but my own.*

"Set back? What happened?"

"Right after church, your mother took one bite of her jelly donut and dropped it." He stopped. "Roxanne, your mother suffered a mild stroke."

"A stroke?" Roxanne whispered. "But she's been taking medication."

"Just a slight episode. Not to worry. She's able to converse quite nicely now."

"Oh, thank God," Roxanne gasped.

"She had difficulty walking and using her left arm, but we rushed her to the hospital in time. She needs some rehabilitation."

"I'm coming."

"Excuse me?"

"I'm coming now. I'm just three hours away."

"She'll be so happy to see you. But she is in a facility, so there is no need to rush."

"Why didn't she call?" Roxanne knew it had something to do with the stroke. It had to have, but she needed to hear it.

"I wanted to, but she made me promise not to. And had she not been so rapidly improving, I would have called anyway. Her speech slurred a little at first, and she wanted to improve before she spoke with you. Can you stay awhile?"

"Yes, of course." Perfect timing, she thought but winced. Was tragedy what it took to move her?

"Roxy? Are you okay?"

She nodded.

"Roxy?"

"Yes. Yes. I will be. I'm coming home."

"That will be nice. Your mum needs someone to care for her until she's back on her feet. I offered, but I can only be there in the evenings."

Sweet Max. "Oh, no. After working all day, that's the last thing you must do. I'll be staying indefinitely."

"Well, do what you must, but the church ladies are stepping in, too, so take care of your business first."

"I need to be with Mama."

"Right, oh, then. When you make your plans, call me, and I'll meet you at her house. I have the keys. Be safe then, love."

"I will, thank you, Max."

Roxanne hung up. *I should have called her.* Guilt churned her stomach, and she flopped on the bed and cried. Tears came in gushes, and regret tore through her. *Sweet Mama, how could I ignore her like that?* She gripped the pillow but winced at the ache in her cast wrist. Rubbing it, she wondered how she could face her mother like this.

Lucy walked in. "Oh, honey. What's wrong?" She sat beside Roxanne and grabbed a Kleenex, shoving it into Roxanne's hand.

"I'm leaving." Roxanne blew her nose. "I'm leaving for Bay Town."

"Yeah!" Lucy clapped. "I'm glad to hear it. But wait. What happened?"

"My mother had a stroke," Roxanne said.

"Oh dear. Is she all right?"

"Sounds like it." Roxanne sniffled. "But I still need to see her."

"Of course, you do. Now, don't worry about a thing. Just tell me what you need, and Jason and I can take care of everything on this end."

"Would you mind going by the school and picking up my things before the end of the week?"

"Yes. Do I need a note from you?"

"I'll call Principal Franklin. She knows. I'll go to the bank in the morning and head out. But this is my home. I'll come back when Mama's better and get the house fixed up and go from there." She wouldn't let Dwayne steal her life. What was left of it.

"Just go home and write. Get your book published. The timing is perfect."

Roxanne swiped her tears. "We'll see."

Lucy sighed. "Honey, maybe you should get some counseling. I mean, Dwayne messed you up pretty good. What if you have nightmares and stuff?"

Closing her eyes, Roxanne tried to blot those out. The night terrors of Dwayne attacking her. She never told anyone about them. Not even Dr. Rashid, when she called, trying to convince Roxanne to get counseling.

"My aunt had an abusive husband." Lucy continued, "Four of them. My mama kept telling her she didn't have a good picker. She picked bad men. Really bad."

Afraid to ask, Roxanne forced the question. "What happened to her?"

Lucy cleared her throat. "The last one killed her. An accident, kind of. He drove drunk with her in the car. They'd had a fight, and she called my mama to come pick her up, but before Mama got there, her husband had thrown my aunt into his car and screeched off. He crashed and walked out pretty much unharmed, but apparently, her body flew out of the car. They found her yards away."

"That's terrible." Roxanne straightened. "But that's not me," she said firmly. But she convinced neither Lucy nor herself.

The following day, Roxanne drove to the bank and parked. She drummed her fingers on the steering wheel and searched the parking lot before exiting. *Would Dwayne still be driving the same truck?* The police said they hadn't spotted it.

Breathing deeply, she grabbed her purse and walked in. She approached a teller with her transaction request.

"What do you mean, only fifty dollars in that account?" Her voice escalated. "I had over five thousand dollars in there."

The young teller stared back wide-eyed.

Roxanne sighed, pressing a hand to her forehead. Dwayne had a debit card to her checking account. *How could I be so stupid?* His beatings had taken a toll on her, and she'd forgotten all about that. "My savings. Please, check my savings."

The teller wrote down the amount and slid the paper to Roxanne. "There haven't been any withdrawals in quite a while."

Roxanne blew out a sigh. The bulk of her money safely stashed. "I'll withdraw all of it, please. A cashier's check and a few hundred in cash."

CHAPTER 10

Roxanne closed both accounts and suddenly felt free. Driving southeast, Roxanne had plenty of time to contemplate her future and think about her past. No. She wouldn't think about that now. *Writing. That's my future. Hopefully, Mama will be fine. Then, I can concentrate on my writing career.*

Approaching the Bayou La Croix Bridge, crossing over into Hancock County, only thirty more minutes and she'd be in Bay Town. Her heart skipped a beat, and she took another glance in her rearview mirror for the hundredth time since she started the drive two and a half hours ago. She patted the puffiness around her eyes. A fluttered breath escaped as she pushed the mirror back in place and glanced instead at the scenery unfolding.

This part of the road soothed her almost as much as the gulf. The Bayou La Croix Preserve flourished with lush green trees rising behind dirt patches closer to the highway. Marshy riverways lay hidden in the backcountry. Though some houses dotted the landscape, this part of the road held natural beauty. Tempted to take the turn-off to the preserve, Roxanne thumbed her steering wheel. Seconds from the exit, a small black car swerved beside her, forcing her to exit.

Cars screeched, and metal crunched around her. She

couldn't see what happened, yet sure of a collision involving other cars, she yanked the wheel, struggling to maintain control. Veering down the ramp, she eased on the brakes and pulled off the road.

"Whoa!" Roxanne yelled, still gripping the wheel. She drew a deep breath, and wiped perspiration from her brow. *Crazy driver*, she thought, but a shiver ran up her spine when an old black car pulled up behind her. She stared into the rearview mirror. Her eyes widened and her heart pounded. Dwayne stepped out of the vehicle.

Roxanne threw her car in gear and peeled back onto the road, entering the Preserve. Questions flooded her brain. How did he find her? Where did he come from? Suddenly she remembered seeing it. The car, the one parked on her street. He'd been following her.

She searched for a Ranger Station as she drove too fast down the narrow two-lane road. Her roaring engine disturbed the quiet bayou, but Dwayne followed close behind. So close, she feared he'd ram her bumper. She sped up, driving deeper into a secluded section of swamps. Not knowing where it led, she feared she'd get stuck. Sunlight flickered through the trees, but the farther she drove, the darker it became. Her stomach flipped, and she felt nausea coming on.

No! No! Not again. He can't do this to me. She gripped the steering wheel with white knuckles. Almost home. Why? So close, yet she still couldn't escape him. She twisted the opal ring on her finger. *Oh God, please.* She blinked and blinked again. A clearing up ahead. A turnout. If she could make a U-turn and get back to the main highway, she'd stand a better chance of escape. In the middle of nowhere, no one could hear her scream. And this time, she'd scream.

She slowed, waiting for Dwayne to follow, then she planned on a quick turnaround. But he thwarted her plan.

Pulling alongside, he blocked her in and stepped out of his

vehicle. Leaving it idling, he walked over laughing as he approached.

"Did you really think you'd get away that easy?" he yelled. "Get out, now."

She looked around. There's no way she'd take her chances with him or the alligators living out here. She'd heard too many stories, and half-hoped one would show up now while Dwayne stood outside.

Although the doors were locked securely, she didn't put it past him to try and break the windows. He pounded, and Roxanne closed her eyes, trying to think. *Don't freeze. Don't cower.* She reached for her phone. Before she could dial 9-1-1, she heard sirens. "Thank you, Jesus," she said, surprising herself.

Dwayne slammed the top of her car with his fist. He ran to his trunk. She saw it pop open, and he returned with a crowbar. He raised his arm, and she bounded to the passenger side and jumped out. Running to the street, she waved her arms, hoping to hail the patrol cars accompanying the sirens. One came into view. At the same time, she heard a low growl. Frozen, she shifted her eyes to the swamp. An alligator, maybe six feet in length, peeked up the bank.

Dwayne laughed. "Honey, you can take your chances with me or him." He pointed at the slow-moving animal. "You better hope he's not hungry."

Roxanne screamed as he grabbed her, but she kicked and scratched. Dwayne had never experienced her fighting back, and she could tell it caught him off guard. The alligator climbed out of the bank as Dwayne dragged her to his car. The gator moved forward as if curious.

The patrol cars approached, only yards away. Dwayne reached for the back door. It wouldn't open. He cursed and grabbed for the driver's door, but she elbowed him hard enough to hurt him. He shoved her to the ground.

"I'll find you, Roxy," he said. "Unless the gator gets you first."

Jumping in his car, he roared off, slipping and sliding on the slick road.

Roxy scooted backward, staring at the strange animal as it ambled toward her. Scrambling for her car, she yanked at the doors, forgetting that all but the one passenger side remained locked. The gator drew closer. Finally, she scrambled on top of her hood. She pulled off her shoes and threw them at the alligator, who had continued its crawl to the opposite bank from which it surfaced. She watched as it slithered into the swamp.

The highway patrol car screeched to a stop. The last pierce of the siren made her cover her ears. Roxanne slumped on the hood, shaking, waiting. Two cars. Lights still flashing, sirens silenced.

"Are you all right, ma'am?" He stared. "Oh, it doesn't look like it."

Roxanne lowered her head and touched her face. She'd forgotten her bruises.

The officer looked around, picked up her shoes, and offered them. "Lucky you were armed." He chuckled. "May I help you down from there."

Roxanne shook her head and stayed put. She didn't trust that the alligator wouldn't return. Retrieving her shoes from the officer, she glanced at the mud-splattered ballet flats, then gazed down the road. "He took off that way."

"Who, ma'am? The gator?"

She pointed. "Of course not. He swerved me off the highway and chased me down here." Trying not to cry, she gulped.

"Yes, ma'am. That's the report we got back at the scene. Officers are investigating there now. Are you okay? Do you know the man?" He narrowed his eyes. "Did he do that to you?"

"Yes, I just got out of the hospital yesterday, but I'm fine." She didn't fool him or herself. She was a wreck. "His name is Dwayne Payton. He's from Meridian."

As the officer took notes, he nodded to the other, who got in his car and headed down the stretch of the mud-covered two-lane road.

The officer took Roxanne's complete report, wrote down her personal information, and gave her his card.

"If he's out here, we'll find him if the mosquitos don't eat him alive. I'll call the rangers for help. Do you have someplace safe to go?"

She nodded, not able to speak.

"All right then, ma'am. Do you need help getting down from there?" He asked again.

Roxanne glanced back at the dark green waters. "Would you mind unlocking my car? From the passenger side?" She pointed.

"Yes, ma'am. You sit tight."

He unlocked all the doors, walked around the car, hand on his gun, searching. "You're safe. That critter's gone."

She knew what critter he meant, but it wasn't the one she feared most.

"Be careful, drive slow, and report this incident to the Chief of Police wherever you're headed."

He cleared the way for her to U-turn. Heading back to the main highway, she tried to drive calmly. Her breathing finally slowed, but her stomach remained unsettled. She entered the onramp, and seeing no ambulances, gratefulness filled her heart. No one seemed to have been hurt by Dwayne's crazy driving antics. No one but her. Again.

She glanced again in her rearview mirror. The highway patrol cars offered a little solace. Could they be sure to find him? She switched on the radio and searched until she found a Christian station. How long had it been since she'd listened to that? The lyrics of each song spoke of hope and peace in trials. The playlist matched her life somewhat. A mess, but instead of trusting God, she ran from him. Just like she ran from Dwayne.

Crossing over the Bay Bridge, Roxanne squinted at the glistening sun shining off the water. She glanced at her watch. She had to see her mama. And she had to distance herself from Dwayne.

The main highway between Meridian and Bay Town emptied right into the city's heart, and Roxanne took a turn onto Highway 90. It ran through the business district, which housed the rehab facility where her mama resided. She glanced in the mirror again and flushed. A panic came over her, urging her to find a place to freshen up, but what she really wanted to do was hide. Roxanne pulled into a shopping center and parked.

The buildings looked much different than years before, and Roxanne saddened at the chain shops in the strip mall. She hoped that Main Street hadn't changed that much. She could use familiarity and security. She could use home. But first things first. She needed large sunglasses. No amount of makeup could possibly cover her battered face.

She entered a drugstore and found the sunglasses. A meager selection, but she tried on every oversized large pair on the rack. The largest was a blinging set of frames that covered her eyebrows down to the tops of her cheekbones. Not her style, but it would suffice. She paid for the frames, avoiding the mature checker's gaze.

"Do y'all have a restroom available?" Roxanne asked.

"Yes, ma'am." The checker pointed.

"Thank you so much. Oh, and could you cut the tags off these frames for me, please?"

"My pleasure. These are some big frames." She looked up over her own reader glasses attached to a colorful chain. "But they'll look lovely on you, I'm sure."

"I have sensitive eyes. I need all the coverage I can get." Roxanne winced. *Well, I do*, she reasoned to herself.

The woman raised her brows but nodded. Her smile was warm, sad, and sympathetic.

These better work. Roxanne headed toward the Ladies Room. Safely inside and in front of a mirror, she removed her old sunglasses and replaced them with her new purchase. Perfect. They covered almost the top half of her face. If not for her high cheekbones, they might slide off her slender nose. Removing them, she laid them aside and turned on the water. Wet paper towels served as cold compresses, and she patted each eye and the area below. Holding a fresh towel across both, she tilted her head back and breathed. *Home, at last.*

"Are you okay?"

The voice startled her, and the towel fell as her head straightened. She stared at a pretty, fresh-looking woman in the doorway. Her light brown hair pulled back into a high ponytail, made her look a little younger than what Roxanne guessed she might be. She wore a pair of wide, flowing white pants, wedge sandals, and a simple taupe tank. A light floral scent wafted around her.

"I'm fine." Roxanne grabbed the new glasses and slipped them on.

The woman smiled. The same sympathetic smile the checker gave her. Would she forever be receiving looks of pity from everyone? Even when her bruises healed, could she be rid of the victim mentality that might shout, *poor me*. Roxanne straightened, but before she could speak, the woman approached the sink next to her.

"It's sure hot out there, isn't it? It's always too humid for me too. Sometimes, I wonder why God made it this way. I can't seem to get used to it." She smiled again and reached for a paper towel, wetting it, and patting her face like Roxanne had done.

Roxanne's instincts told her to ignore the woman, but she

warmed at her friendliness. And why did she mention God? "Are you not from around here?" Roxanne asked.

The woman chuckled. "Well, this is my home now, but I guess I haven't mastered that southern drawl yet." She winked. "I'm from California, but I've been here for a few years. You'd think I'd be used to it by now."

Roxanne looked at her watch.

As if on cue, the woman washed her hands and turned to leave. Opening the door, she turned. "Have a nice day." The smile again, but not a condescending one. "By the way, I like your sunglasses. They remind me of home." And with that, she left.

Turning back to the mirror, Roxanne chuckled. The sunglasses sure would do the trick if she lived in Hollywood.

CHAPTER 11

Back in the car, Roxanne looked at herself once more. The rearview mirror and harsh sunlight didn't lie. She still needed help. The oversized glasses had to come off at some point, She scrunched her brow, reached for her phone, and scrolled for a salon with an esthetician and five stars. She tapped the one that indicated just one minute away and looked around. Helena's Hair, Face, and Nails sat between a beauty supply and a coffee shop. All in the same shopping center where she'd parked. Roxanne stepped out and walked into the salon. She held back a chuckle. The tasteful arrangement of the gaudy décor caught her eye. A white sculpted bust of a beautiful woman rested atop a white pillar, and ivy garlands hung around the room, creating a soothing ambiance.

"Welcome to Helena's. The face that launched a thousand ships." A bouncy teen with too much makeup, though aptly applied, smiled back at her. "What can we do for you today?"

"I'd like a facial." Roxanne hesitated. "And do you have a makeup artist here as well?"

The girl laughed. "An artist? Why we have the best." She looked around and lifted a finger to her lips. "But she prefers to be called a Beautician. She just started, but she's great. A real natural."

"Brittney." A voice cooed from the back. "I'm taking lunch, now. Block me off, please."

A gorgeous African-American woman walked to the front of the salon. She wore black leggings and a belted tunic that fell just above her knees. As she untied it, a bright floral kimono wrap fluttered. She smiled at Roxanne.

"Okay." Brittney wrote in the schedule log and looked up. "I'm sorry, ma'am. Can you come back in an hour?"

"Oh, I really needed to get that facial now."

"You need a facial? Well, you're just in time. I'm the beautician, honey." The striking woman with ombre-dark bouncy curls pulled off her shoulder bag and threw the black tunic at Brittney. Much like Meryl Streep in *The Devil Wears Prada*.

"Well, let's go, sweetie, follow me." She tugged at Roxanne's arm and sauntered to a small, portioned-off corner in the back.

Roxanne stared at the dimly lit room. LED candles flickered on a table in one corner, and a large potted fern poised aside them. The scent of lemon grass and citrus smelled heavenly, and Roxanne tipped her head. She spotted a small Bible and a stack of little books resting on a round table. Large shutter doors separated the space from the rest of the shop, and a colorful, floral fabric tri-fold screen portioned off a corner.

"Go behind that screen and remove your top." Neon-orange nails sparkled as she waved her fingers. "There's a fresh gown. Just slip into it. It's not very flattering, but comfortable. By the way, I'm Tina." Her cooing voice settled Roxanne's rising anxiety.

Would this work? She hoped Tina wouldn't ask any questions. Roxanne stepped out, and Tina pointed to a chair. She adjusted the shutters to a slightly opened position, removed Roxanne's sunglasses, and then flicked on the overhead lights.

The room brightened so that Roxanne blinked, her eyes adjusting.

Tina gasped. "Oh dear. What happened to you, sweetie?"

Looking down, Roxanne contemplated leaving, but inquiring minds would be the same everywhere she went if she didn't do something to remedy her battered face. She looked straight into Tina's eyes. "Can you cover my bruises?"

The corners of Tina's lips lifted, and Roxanne thought if she saw that sickening, sweet, sympathetic smile one more time, she'd scream. Instead, Tina's grin broadened and lit up her face. Her eyes sparkled.

"Oh honey, do you see any bags under my eyes? Or wrinkles up here?" She grazed fingers across her forehead. "Or here?" She tapped the corners of her mouth. "Leave it to me, I can work miracles." Tina shrugged. "Well, God works miracles, but I can do wonders. Sit down, sweetie." Tina laid the chair back into a reclining position.

Her fingers massaged Roxanne's face, and her gentle touch avoided the painful areas. She patted the cut over Roxanne's eye, and her light touch and circular motions lulled her to sleep. After what seemed like hours, Roxanne lay refreshed and renewed. It helped that Tina played soothing instrumental music and dimmed the lights as she finished the facial and put another warm cloth over Roxanne's face.

"Now honey, you just lay there and relax. I'm going to read my devotional for a minute or two." Tina paused. "Would you like me to read it aloud?"

Roxanne tensed. Why would she do that? Her ears tuned in to the music playing. As violin strings wafted out, Roxanne realized it was a hymn. She'd been listening to hymns all this time and never knew it. The calming presence extended beyond Tina's touch and the warm compresses.

"Yes, please do."

"*Thou dost keep him in perfect peace whose mind is stayed on Thee because he trusts in Thee.*" As Tina read, the words breathed life into Roxanne. Between the scriptures and the excerpts from various authors, her heart swelled with joy. But not just joy, hope. Roxanne also felt like crying but knew the tears would undo the work Tina had done in the last half-hour.

Tina stopped reading, and Roxanne heard the book close with a snap. "Well, we have work to do now."

"What were you reading from?" Roxanne asked.

As Tina removed the cloth and raised Roxanne's chair to a more upright position, she smiled. "Joy for the Journey. It's my favorite little go-to book. Not too deep." Tina giggled and waved her hand in the air. "I'm not that deep like some of the women in a Bible Study I go to."

Roxanne tensed. Her mother went to a women's Bible study. She'd forgotten how small Bay Town was. Roxanne stared up as Tina prepped her face for makeup.

"What church do you go to?"

Never stopping the application, Tina drawled. "Bay Town Community?" She stopped and stepped back. "Wait a minute, are you?" Her face scrunched as she stared at Roxanne. "No, you can't be?"

If she intended to lie, now would be the time. But if her mother knew Tina, she'd be caught. Wait. She recognized this woman and now she had no way out.

"I'm Roxanne Cook. Bethie Cook's daughter."

"Yes. Yes. I remember. We were in high school together, just barely. Not that we knew each other, but since I met your mama years ago, I feel like I know you. She talks about you all the time. You went to college in Meridian, and you're an author, right?"

"No. Not really."

Tina ignored her and gushed. "Your mother is so proud of you. Winning that contest here in town."

"You remember that?"

"Not really. You were just a kid, right? So your mama says." Tina pulled up a stool. "I'm so sorry about your mother's stroke. But we've been praying for her and taking turns visiting her." Tina slapped Roxanne's arm playfully. "Why, she's doing wonderful. God's healing her right up. Does she know you're here?" Tina's smile faded, and her eyes looked sad.

Roxanne's mind went blank, and she had nothing to say. *How do you tell this story?* Wetness pooled in her lids, and Roxanne closed her eyes hoping to hold the tears back but one by one, they escaped.

Tina grabbed a cucumber wipe and dabbed at Roxanne's face. "Oh, now, none of that. You'll be undoing my work here." She stopped. "Sweetheart, may I pray for you?"

Roxanne nodded, and Tina's sweet drawl asked Jesus to heal Roxanne inside and out. Her prayer remained short, sweet, and to the point. At the end, she yelled, "Hallelujah" and Roxanne's tears stopped as she flinched.

"Honey, you're going to be fine. I don't know what's going on in your life, but you give it to Jesus, and somehow, He'll make it right." Tina gave a firm nod as if her words were final. "I can promise you that. Now let's get back to work."

As Tina got down to business, she asked no questions, but Roxanne knew that she had a friend here and, in time, perhaps a confidant. At last, Tina applied the lipstick and motioned for Roxanne to squish her lips together. Roxanne laughed at Tina's exaggerated motion. Her lips were so full and beautiful and bright. She hoped her own weren't quite that orange.

Tina spun her around to face her reflection in the lighted mirror. She also handed her a hand mirror, and Roxanne stared back.

Sucking in a breath, she uttered, "Oh, my." She tapped her face. No sign of bruises or cuts, yet she looked so natural, and her lips were a neutral shade of nude.

"I told you I work wonders. Now, let's get you out of here. If I know Bethie Cook—" Tina winked, "—and do I know

Bethie Cook. She's wondering where you are right about now."

"She doesn't know I'm coming. Only Max Tippet knows." Roxanne couldn't stop staring at herself.

"Max? He's a doll."

Roxanne smiled. "Yes, he is. How is he doing?"

Tina frowned. "So sad about his wife. I guess you know she passed away years back? It's good he has the shop. It's kept him busy, that and helping everyone in town. Some of the single ladies have an eye on him now that some time has passed." She gave a sideways glance at Roxanne. "Say, you don't have a boyfriend, do you?" Tina's hand flew up to her mouth. "I'm so sorry. I didn't mean to say the 'b' word. I mean… Oh, my. I've never been good at bridling my tongue. Actually, it's my brain, not so much my tongue."

"It's fine. No, thank goodness, I don't have a boyfriend anymore."

"Good for you, girl." She stopped and took a step back. "You know we have a home for abused women, and they have great counseling."

Roxanne's shoulders dropped.

"I'm so sorry. Me and my big mouth. I just wanted to help … not that you need my help, right?"

A fake smile twitched at Roxanne's lips, and she waved her hand but thought of Dr. Rashid and Lucy. She stared back at Tina. And now her. Everyone wanted to help. Maybe she should look into counseling or some resources. She tucked the thought away. "So, you were saying? Max is the most eligible bachelor in town?" At the thought of her old friend, a bubbling laugh felt so natural.

"Yes. Ever since Pastor Brooks married my neighbor, Melanie, Max is the man." Tina's sly smile returned. "Say, you two would make a nice couple."

Roxanne pulled her shoulders back. "Excuse me? He's much older than me."

"Ouch." Tina pouted. "But he's only a few years beyond me, and I'm not much older than you, honey."

Her mouth gaped. "I didn't mean anything. It's just that I've known him since junior high school." Roxanne couldn't finish. She'd stuck her foot in her mouth and insulted two people in one sentence.

"Honey, I'm kidding. You'll be our age before you know it." Tina stepped back and crossed her arms. "Age is a mind-set, my dear. What counts is living a joyful life." She offered a hand, helping to pull Roxanne from the chair. "Now go live yours."

CHAPTER 12

Go live yours? Is that what Tina said? But not just that, she said to live life joyfully. Roxanne fluttered out a breath and touched the radio button. The song, *You Say*, floated out, and the words lifted her. It spoke about being enough in God's eyes. The DJ credited the music to the artist Lauren Daigle, and the lyrics resonated in Roxanne's heart. Maybe with God, she could pull this off, and instead of driving to her childhood home, she decided to face her mama now.

Gripping the steering wheel, her knuckles whitened, and her confidence waned as Dwayne and his beatings, and this last altercation flooded her mind. "Stop," she told herself quietly, Then drove to the rehab facility.

Sitting in her car, Roxanne glanced at her watch. She couldn't believe it was still Thursday. So much had happened, and suddenly exhaustion threatened to paralyze her, but Roxanne stepped out and faced the one-story concrete building. She shook her head, imagining the pungent odor of disinfectant trying to mask the human scent that would assault her nostrils once she entered the building. These places always smelled like that, but as she approached the entrance, freshly planted white petunias lined the walkway. Healthy green plants potted in large blue planters flanked the entrance. The windows were still framed with old metal but clean, and the steel-framed double front doors screeched a little as they slid open.

Elderly people sat in wheelchairs outside the entrance, soaking up the sunshine. Family members smiled, trying to communicate with their loved ones. Roxanne's heart sank a little. A nice place, but it looked more like a nursing home than a rehabilitation facility. She planned to move Mama home today.

Trudging through the double doors, Roxanne breathed deeply. A clean citrus scent greeted her, and fresh flowers graced the lobby. Her heavy footsteps lightened as she approached the smiling receptionist. She hesitated but removed her sunglasses.

"Well, good day to you, ma'am. Are you here to visit a loved one?" the receptionist said.

No sad, sympathetic look or a shock of horror. Tina did wonders.

Relieved, she welcomed the sweet greeting. With formalities quickly over, she retrieved her mother's room number and clipped down the hallway. Pleasantly surprised at how fresh and clean everything appeared, she smiled at the friendly employees. A few wheelchairs with apathetic souls sat about, but nurses and aids lent a soft touch or kind words as they passed.

Roxanne arrived at her mother's room, and a cheerful voice emitted. Her mother sat in a chair wearing a faded summer Mumu, her favorite lounging attire. Roxanne had brought it back for her from Hawaii years ago when she'd gone on a getaway by herself. After Gregory. Roxanne shook her head, banishing all thoughts of him.

"Hey, Mama." Roxanne beamed as she rushed to her mother's side. She squeezed her tightly, and when Roxanne pulled back her mother stared.

Holding her daughter's hands, Bethie Cook responded, "Why, Roxanne, you look so lovely." She glanced down at Roxanne's cast wrist but quickly averted her eyes.

Roxanne felt the blood rise and stepped back, dropping her mother's hands. Tina did work wonders, but Roxanne had forgotten to cover her cast. She placed her arm behind her back.

"Oh, Mama. You always say that."

Roxanne hadn't even done anything with her hair this morning, and the clothes she wore were thrown on in her rush to leave. Fitted jeans covered her too-thin frame, but the tight t-shirt she'd pulled on made her feel uncomfortable. She pushed back her disheveled hair.

"Oh, it's not just me that thinks that." Her mother cocked her head to the corner.

Roxanne felt as if eyes bored into her back, and she turned.

"Wouldn't you say so, Max?" Bethie Cook chuckled.

His eyes were as blue as Roxanne remembered. His hair had turned a beautiful white, but contrasted nicely with his smooth, tanned face. She recalled he'd been prematurely gray in his thirties many years ago. The length of it rested atop his shoulders. He smiled back at her, staring.

"Max?" Bethie Cook said again as she waved her wood-carved cane at him.

He broke his gaze on Roxanne for a moment. "Oh yes. What did you say?"

Max wore blue jeans and a blue cotton chambray button-up shirt, though he wore it casually without the top button closed and the sleeves rolled. His familiar scent of Old Spice lent a nostalgic air, and Roxanne warmed. She couldn't help but stare back. Giddy feelings of her school-girl crush made the heat rise within. She stuck out her uncasted hand.

"Hey, Max. It's so good to see you." Roxanne hadn't anticipated the giddy euphoria upon seeing him again.

He nodded and flexed his fingers. She waited for his signature arms flung wide, give me a hug stance, but it didn't come.

"Hello, Roxy." Max nodded.

Roxy. No one in Bay Town ever called her Roxy except Max. He had nicknamed her that when he used to read her manuscripts. Her brow furrowed. *What if he asks about my writing?* What would she say? Dismissing the thought, she smiled.

To her surprise, he moved forward, took her hand in both his, and squeezed. Roxanne's fingers tingled at his warm touch. He held the clasp slightly longer than appropriate until they both let go and looked down. The electric touch lingered and coursed through her body. *This is ridiculous.* She couldn't possibly be falling for another man already. But then again, this was Max. *No,* she silently told herself and spun on her heel back to her mother.

"So, are you ready to blow this place?" She clapped her hands.

"Now?" Bethie asked.

"Yes. I'm here. Let's go home."

"Not yet. I have a therapy session today. Can you check me out tomorrow? Max, do you think they'll let me leave?"

His gaze lingered on Roxanne. So much so, that a flush heated her cheeks.

"Oh, for goodness sakes, Max." Bethie laughed. "It's not like you haven't seen the grown-up Roxanne before."

He breathed deep, shoving his hands in his front pockets. "Indeed," he said. Rocking back on his heels, he chuckled. "I guess she grew up a long time ago and I hadn't noticed. Philippa would have loved to have seen you again." He sighed and finally flung out his arms as if his deceased wife had given him permission.

Roxanne leaned in and hugged him back. As strange as the cozy embrace felt, the familiarity and the security of his arms filled her with a sentimental joy of better times. With her head against his chest, she said, "I wish I could have seen Philippa again too. I miss her." His arms squeezed her tighter.

Max released first, and Roxanne let go, stepping back. His clear eyes and friendly smile somehow made her feel like everything would be okay. Funny, how a good man could make you feel like that. At least, that's what all the Hallmark movies portrayed.

"Well, Philippa is rejoicing now. Has been for quite a few years." He twisted a plain gold band on his finger.

Taking a deep breath, Roxanne whooshed out. "Max, I'm so sorry I didn't speak to you at the funeral, but I came. I was there."

"Not to worry. I saw you, and if Philippa could, she felt your presence."

"She's in heaven. I doubt she felt anything from down here," Bethie Cook said.

Max winked. "Right then. Shall I see to your discharge tomorrow?"

"I thought you two had forgotten about me." Bethie chuckled.

Max blushed. "Right, oh. I'm off then. I'll check at the nurse's station and leave you two." He strolled to the door and turned. "Roxy, I left a key for you under the mat at your mum's house. Please call me if you need anything."

"Thank you, Max. I will."

"Very well, then. Welcome home, Roxy."

Home. It already felt like home, and she'd almost forgotten why she'd left in the first place. If only she could. But so much had transpired. Could it really be home again?

"Mama, how'd you find this place? It's so old, but it's different."

"It's a happy spot, isn't it?" Bethie reached for her daughter's hand. "It's a Christian, non-profit facility. It's well-supported, and I'm on the board of directors." Tears misted in her eyes. "Your daddy did good by us, didn't he? Leaving that nice inheritance. I'm able to contribute financially."

Roxanne looked up and noticed an old audio speaker in the ceiling. Soothing instrumental hymns floated out. So subtle she hadn't noticed it but experienced it when she arrived.

"It's a lovely facility, Mama. No wonder you don't want to leave."

"Who said that? I'm ready to go, dear. I can't wait to catch up."

Catch up? A rush of heat rose, and Roxanne felt the sweat on her brow. Her face must have shown it, too, because her mother's aura took on that look of sympathy. Roxanne closed her eyes. *Not her too.* She dropped into a chair beside her mother.

"Honey, you can't hide from God, and you can't hide things from me." Bethie reached out and touched her face. "You are beautiful, with and without all this makeup. I don't know what that man did to you, but I'm glad your daddy's no longer here."

"Mama, please."

"No, Roxanne, hear me out. I'm your mama. You owe me that. While you're here, I pray that you'll turn back to God. That you'll put Him first."

Roxanne opened her mouth, but her mother silenced her with a finger. "We have plenty of time for discussion, and I'll do my best not to bring this up again unless you do. But there is one thing. I'd like for you to attend church with me while you're home."

Roxanne nodded. That was something that had nagged at her. But the thought of attending her old church didn't bring much comfort.

"And Ladies' Bible Study, and the Prayer Meetings. Oh, and we can't forget the monthly potlucks. Wait till you meet Pastor Brooks. You'll love him. Too bad he's not the most eligible bachelor in town anymore."

"Mama. I did not come back here to find a man. And I'll go to church with you but give me some time for all the other activities." She wouldn't tell her mother that her future plans were to return to Meridian.

"They aren't just activities, sweetheart. They are a sacrifice of praise."

Roxanne recalled how prominent church had been in her young life growing up. Her father had been an elder, and her mother had served many years in the Women's Ministry. She smiled, remembering the Bible studies both her father and mother hosted in her home. She would even sit on the stairs and listen. Until the time she reached the age to attend.

Oh God, what happened? How had she wandered so far? What had become so crucial that she neglected the one who brought such joy? But she knew exactly what happened. Bitterness from her past reared its ugly head. Roxanne fought it and allowed the feeling of joy bubbling up inside to win. It filled her once more, and she liked this euphoria that had been fleeting in her life for quite some time. It felt so good.

"Sweetheart?" Bethie squeezed her daughter's hand. "May I pray for you, my dear? I've prayed so long for you to come home."

Roxanne gulped. She still had the house in Meridian. And what about Dwayne? She closed her eyes tightly. *One day at a time.* "Yes, Mama, please pray for me. God knows I need it." Tears welled as she swallowed her words.

"God, you are all that is mighty and good. You give, and you take away, and I thank you today for giving. Thank you, Jesus, for bringing my baby girl home. Guide her on this renewed journey back to you. Protect her, God. Amen."

The tears flowed, and Roxanne dabbed her face. Her eyes widened at the amount of makeup that colored the white tissue. All of Tina's work wiped out in an instant. She laughed. *I'll get through this. I know I will.*

The peace she felt fled as her cell buzzed.

She looked at the screen, and blood rushed from her face.

"What's wrong, Roxanne?" her mother asked.

She couldn't believe it was him. The Highway Patrol said he wouldn't make it out of the Bayou. She stood, but her knees wobbled, and she braced herself on her mother's bedside rail. Leaning over, she kissed her mother.

"Nothing, Mama. I better go. See you tomorrow."

Roxanne clipped through the hallways and the peace she'd experienced on her way in fled. Bursting through the automatic doors, she stepped into the dimming afternoon sunlight. This time, some of the patients in wheelchairs looked up, but she didn't acknowledge them. On her way to the car, she searched for Dwayne's number and blocked it.

Her heart raced. What good would that do? This only meant the authorities hadn't caught him. Roxanne searched her purse for the highway patrol officer's card. He told her to report the incident. She didn't ask why but surmised she needed to leave a paper trail of the assault and attempted abduction. Laying aside the card, she drove to the local police station on Main Street. Roxanne stared at the small, brick building reminiscent of the old days, like the Mayberry Police Station in *The Andy Griffith Show*.

She parked and called the number on the card before exiting. It took minutes to connect to the officer. Identifying herself, she waited as he told her they'd blocked the entrance to the Bayou and were searching for him. She told them he'd contacted her and gave them his number. He assured her that she was safe. They'd get the guy.

Taking a deep breath. She reached for her car door handle but stopped when a large Hispanic man in uniform exited the station. He nodded at her, and she nodded back. She glanced at the gold and black lettering on the window. Chief Bert Hidalgo. When did the old chief retire?

Starting her car, she backed out. She hadn't even met the guy. In time, she'd work up the courage to tell the Chief of

Police, a stranger, that she may be bringing trouble to Bay Town. Not confident that she had done the right thing, she left and checked into a hotel. Going home to an empty house didn't feel comforting.

~

The early evening sun barely filtered through the thick growth. The aluminum, flat-bottom boat hummed along the tributary, snaking through the swamps. With dusk fast approaching, the bugs were out in full force. Dwayne slapped his neck too many times, smashing mosquitos in his palms. He couldn't believe Roxanne had escaped him this afternoon. If it hadn't been for the Highway Patrol, they'd both been on the road again. He just didn't know where.

"That's why we wear long sleeves and jeans down here. Ain't too smart being in the Bayou wearing them shorts." The boat driver spit brown spittle into the brackish water.

Dwayne hadn't planned on getting stuck out here, but sheer luck brought him a swamp rat like this old guy. After he'd ditched his car and run up the dirt trail where no squad car or ranger truck would fit, he took his chances. It panned out when he ran into this guy.

"How much further?" Dwayne asked.

"Not too much. The creek narrows down too much for me to slither through. You'll have to hike up to the road from there. If you go East, you be reaching the Pearl River."

"Where are we?"

"Still in Hancock County. Bay Town is south." The man pointed back over his shoulder.

Dwayne wondered where Roxanne was headed when he shoved her off the road. He repeatedly gripped his pocket, assuring himself he still had his phone. A lot of good it did him. He couldn't call her anymore. She must have felt safe cutting him off like that.

"What did you say that town south of here was?"

"Bay Town. A real nice community," the man said.

It sounded like it might be Roxy's destination. If only he'd paid attention, he might know where she came from. Dwayne shoved a hand through his damp, sweaty hair. No. It wouldn't have made a difference. He had to get a car so he could find her.

"Jump out, fella. This is it. Watch out for the gators." The man let the engine idle.

Dwayne stepped out of the boat and waved a hand, not bothering to thank the man. His expensive athletic shoes sunk in the mud. He didn't care. They were already ruined. He began a jog and kept the pace for quite a while. He didn't know how far, but he ran along the creek, high enough off the bank to avoid any creatures. Without warning, the trees parted, and a road lay in front of him. It separated the swampy forest, which continued on the other side. He stuck out his thumb.

He hitched a ride pretty quickly. Of course, the newer cars and family vans sped right past him. But there were plenty of good old boys driving trucks down the road. One picked him up and drove him as far as a main highway. Now, he had a decision to make. North or South? Take a chance in Bay Town or back to Meridian? Dwayne stuck his thumb out once more.

CHAPTER 13

"Did you sleep well?" the hotel clerk asked.

Of course not, Roxanne wanted to snap. After yesterday's harrowing day, sleep eluded her, but she answered politely. "Thank you. Everything suited me fine."

"Sure you don't need to book another night? It's Friday and we fill up fast for the weekend."

"No, thank you." Roxanne smiled as she paid the bill.

She drove to her mama's house and parked her car along the street. Standing on the sidewalk, she gazed at the aged, two-story, red-brick house. She took in a deep breath, savoring the sweet fragrance of the rose bushes that bordered the path leading to the front porch. A feature that had been present as far back as she could remember. When a gentle breeze swept by, she instinctively shielded her hair, attempting to manage her swirling locks. Her eyes then fixed on the imposing pecan tree in the front yard, evoking fond recollections of swinging on a sizeable black tire suspended from its lowest branch. She smiled. Another gust of wind offered relief to her heavy heart.

She walked up to the front door and found the key lying hidden under the doormat as Max had instructed. Once inside, Roxanne's soul settled even more. Home at last. She felt safe, but an emptiness lingered. It wasn't the same without her mother or her father. Dropping her purse, she walked to the kitchen, recognizing the gnawing grumble in her stomach. The free continental breakfast at the hotel didn't sound like such a bad idea now. Too bad she skipped it.

Opening the refrigerator, she scrunched her nose. A stale smell lingered, but she looked for eggs. None. Roxanne concluded that breakfast wouldn't be found here. Going out in public didn't sound appealing, but a drive-thru would suffice. She reached for her purse again. Out fell a few business cards.

She picked up the Meridian County Police card, along with another plain white card. Travis Howard, Author. Had he given her two cards? She gulped. Dwayne had the other. Should she warn Travis? Pulling out her cell, she tapped Travis' number.

"Travis. Hi, this is Roxanne." Her voice wavered.

He cleared his throat. "Whoa? What time is it? Who is this?"

Roxanne glanced at her watch. Too early to call someone. She hadn't realized she'd checked out of the hotel before seven. "I'm so sorry. This is Roxanne. I'll call you later."

"No, that's fine." His voice graveled. "I'm glad you called. I missed you at the last meeting."

Missed me? How nice to be missed. "Well, yes. I had a family emergency."

"A family emergency? I ran into your girlfriend at Leroy's and that hulky boyfriend of yours wasn't there, so I asked her about you. She said you were in the hospital. Are you okay?"

Why would Lucy tell him?

"Lucy?"

"Yeah, I think so. What happened?"

Roxanne quelled a rising angst. *What else had Lucy said?* She forced a chuckle. "Oh, I'm fine. I took a bad stumble and..."

"Yeah, you seem to be a little clumsy." He laughed. "Like the time you came into the ER after you banged your head."

Roxanne winced. How many lies had she made up to

cover Dwayne's battering? But not this time. "Well, my mama took ill, and I came home."

"Where's that?"

"It's in Bay…" Something made her stop. He didn't need to know. "Where I grew up. Say, how did the critique group go. Did you read? I'm sorry I never got a chance to hear one of your stories." She'd hope he'd take the bait and talk about his writing.

"Oh, no worries. But I did skim your manuscript."

"The whole thing?"

"Yes, ma'am. The whole thing," he drawled.

Roxanne stood straighter, and her stomach fluttered. No one but her mama and Miz Philippa and Max had ever read her entire manuscript. But she felt relieved that giving it to him now seemed right.

"What did you think?" Roxanne closed her eyes.

Not sure if she could take the rejection right now. Still, to be talking about her writing, her dreams. It felt so good. Not quite good enough to take away her fears, but good enough to let excitement filter in. But his pause caused her to fidget. She clicked speaker, looking for a place to lay the phone down, as if it could hurt her.

"Well, it's got some good bones, but it needs work."

Roxanne slumped in the nearest chair.

"I can help you if you'd like?"

She went from deflated to inflated in a nano-second. "You'd do that?"

"Sure, just give me a few months and I'll get back with you."

Months? She hoped to work on that book while home. Hoped to submit queries. "Oh, that's okay. I'll be home indefinitely, so I can work on it some more. Maybe you can help me on a second edit."

"No, no. I mean it. The characters are great. It just needs a little structure. I'd be happy to help."

Roxanne bit her lip. Her manuscript. Her baby. And she didn't want to let it go. But maybe it needed more work than she thought. "Oh, that's so kind of you. But will it really take a few months?"

"Give me two at least. In the meantime, just write. Every day, write something. I better go. I have the night shift at the ER, and Dr. Rashid is on tonight. I'll keep in touch. Bye."

Roxanne breathed deep. Two months. She hadn't really planned on staying in Bay Town for two months. She planned to get back to Meridian to fix up her house and get serious about writing. But Dwayne. Roxanne's eyes flew open. *Shoot! I forgot to warn Travis.* She called, but this time she reached his voicemail. She opened her mouth but couldn't leave a message. He'd been so encouraging about her writing. Why spoil their partnership?

And Travis was right. She needed to write. But how she wished she could continue working on her manuscript. Without a lap top and no access to her story she was sunk for the time being. Thanks to Dwayne. He had destroyed everything. She pressed a hand to her forehead and stepped outside.

The hot, orange sun glared, even this early in the day. She glanced up and down the street, hating what she feared. Across the street, a figure stepped out from beneath an old pecan tree and approached. Fumbling for her keys, she didn't know whether to rush back inside or jump into her car.

"Good morning, Roxy," Max called, crossing the street.

She wanted to laugh at herself. Her feet tickled, and a lightness floated up within her. She smiled back and waved. He trotted over.

"What are you doing here?" She smiled so big, a slight pain reminded her of her bruises, and she touched the spot above her eye. Thankful that she'd taken the time to apply makeup, though not as perfectly as Tina had, she pulled her sunglasses on.

Max waved and pointed to the well-manicured lawn and perfect shrubbery across the street. "That's my house, now."

"But you and Philippa? What happened to your house on Second Street?"

"Oh, yes. I sold it."

As a younger man, Max had been the groundskeeper at Cedar Rest, the local cemetery. Years before he opened his florist shop on Main Street, he and Philippa lived in a house adjacent to the graveyard. He'd purchased the dilapidated French colonial house that had deteriorated for too many years. No offers had been made on the property, so he bought it for a pittance. With grants and hard work, he turned it into a pristine historic landmark, and Roxanne loved it. It saddened her now to think he sold it.

"Sold it? But why?"

"Well, when Philippa passed, God rest her soul, I didn't need, nor did I want to stay in that large old drafty mansion. Besides, when the city started the Halloween Graveyard Haunt years ago, I wanted no part. I sold it for a good price and picked up this little beauty just for me." Max's eyes shined with more than a little wetness.

"You miss her, don't you?" Roxanne touched his shoulder.

"Every day, my dear." His hair blew in the breeze, and he pushed it back. "Now, where are you off to?"

"I'm starving. I need a bite to eat."

"Why, so do I. How about I take you down to Bubba's at Pier One?"

"Never heard of it."

"Of course, you have. The nostalgic little shack near the far end of Beach Road?"

Roxanne laughed. "Are you serious? The old Crab Shack or Snack Shack? The greasy spoon?" Everyone called it something different.

"But great food." Max gave her a sly smile that just about

melted her. "You most likely remember it when Bubba's father served as the chef."

"Chef?"

"Well, I guess more of a cook. But his son Bubba runs it now, and he's soon to become a bona fide chef. He's been taking cooking classes at the Culinary Arts School in New Orleans."

The nearness of Max's presence swirled around, calming her. He'd always done that to her. He and Miz Philippa. But somehow, this felt unlike that. "Okay, then. How can I say no to that? Jump in, I'll drive."

～

Roxanne breathed the fishy, morning gulf aroma as she drove and forgot her troubles. The dancing waters glistened. "I'd forgotten the beauty of Bay Town."

"That it 'tis. Especially on the water."

Roxanne felt his gaze on her, and she trembled a little. Not a frightening feeling, but soothing and euphoric. The same feeling continued when she parked at Pier One, and they approached the familiar little shack.

"May I order for you?" Max asked as they stood at the window.

"Sure. I like everything," Roxanne answered before she could think. Did she like everything? She never expressed her likes and dislikes much with Dwayne.

"Well, what is it that you feel like eating this morning? Your choice, love."

Roxanne loved the way he said love. It warmed her and she smiled, raising a hand to swipe back her bangs. She stopped and instead, fingered the lines around her eyes. Time seemed to have closed the age gap between them.

"Hey, Roxanne?" A large round man with a bushy red

beard and red bandana stood in the pass-through window of the shack. "Long time no see."

Roxanne frowned.

A wide grin spread across his lips, and he chuckled, patting his stomach. "I've gained a few pounds. It's Hank, we had high school Creative Writing class together?"

Her eyes widened. "Seriously?" She squinted and tried to imagine him without his beard. "Oh, there you are. How are you?" Roxanne extended a hand. "So, Hank, are you still writing those—" she searched for words that fled her brain, "—those interesting stories?"

He laughed. "Call me Bubba. Those awful stories is what you mean. Nah, but I heard that sci-fi fantasy stuff is pretty popular now. The kids love it."

"Do you have kids?"

Bubba looked down. "We uh ... we lost our only daughter couple years back."

Roxanne's jaw dropped. "Oh my. I'm so sorry, Bubba."

"Thanks. Me and the wife have been on an adoption list, but not sure if we're ever gonna get picked."

Max reached out and touched his hand. "We're praying, Bubba. We're trusting in God's good timing, we are."

Bubba's face brightened. "Yes, we are, and I know that. I keep telling the wife, but she's getting a little discouraged."

At a loss for words, again. It seemed everyone had troubles and disappointments, but this didn't seem to be of his own making. She cringed. *Like mine.*

"So, the special today is a Mississippi hometown dish. Fried Catfish, fried okra and my homemade biscuits and gravy. Only on the menu for the weekend."

"For breakfast?" Roxanne asked.

"I can throw in some fried eggs." Bubba laughed.

Fried, again? Eating all that rich food could kill a person, Roxanne thought, but didn't voice it.

Max smiled. "Well, Roxy? What do you think? It's up to you."

There again. The kind, calm assurance that she mattered. Like her writing, Max and his wife had always cared about her.

"Why not, let's have that special."

While waiting, they occupied the metal tables on the boardwalk. Seagulls swooped overhead prompting Roxanne to duck, much to Max's amusement. They shared stories of bygone days until the conversation dwindled into a comfortable silence which Roxanne found soothing. The tranquility of sitting beside a man who didn't fidget, or tap his legs, as if racing against time, felt refreshing.

"Order up!" Bubba called.

Picking up their food, Max set it down and prayed a blessing. They ate quietly, and the food pleased her palette. Bubba really could cook. She giggled.

Max turned his gaze toward her, and his piercing pale blue eyes sparkled causing Roxanne to shiver. He reached around placing a hand on her shoulder with a gentle pressure. Roxanne flinched.

"I didn't mean to alarm you I'm so sorry." He pointed to the closed umbrella above. "Just wanted to give you some shade."

How could she even compare his touch to Dwayne's? "I'm just a little jumpy." She cleared her throat. "It's a bit strange being back here."

"I imagine so. But I'm so glad you came. So, how is your writing?" Max asked.

Sweat beaded on her forehead. She'd hoped he wouldn't ask. But of course, he would.

Roxanne waved a hand. "I haven't done much. With teaching and all, I haven't had much time." She hated that she lied.

"Oh, I don't believe that," Max said kindly. "You've always made time, even when you had your finals in college."

Roxanne huffed. "You're right. I did have time." She gazed up at the seagulls and blinked. A move to stop the tears welling in her eyes.

"But life got in the way? Took lots of turns you didn't expect?" Max said softly.

How like him to assure her of non-judgement. She nodded. "A big turn, and not at all like I expected."

"Yes, well those are the Lord's unexpected ways, aren't they?"

If you only knew, she wanted to say.

"Roxy, I'm here for you. Whatever you need, whenever you need it."

"Thank you," she whispered.

"Not just me. Many of us are. Your mum asked for prayer for you." Max's kind eyes searched hers.

She gulped, but a knot in her throat made it hard to swallow. "What did she tell you?"

His hand covered hers on the table and he patted. "Nothing, she just asked for prayer. God knows all, I don't."

The tears fell and Roxanne dabbed her face, wishing her sunglasses were even bigger. But the shame of her past overshadowed the embarrassment she'd felt over her battered appearance. "I had a boyfriend, and he…" She couldn't finish. Heavy sobs racked her body.

Max moved next to her. Tenderly, he pulled her close, and she melted into his chest. His wiry arms exuded strength, and comfort. Not the passionate embrace of a man in love, but a man who cared. One who cared for a very long time. Roxanne pressed into his shoulder and let the tears flow until she had no more.

She didn't say anything more but knew Max must have wondered. The bruises, the cast. But the gentle man asked nothing. He simply ate, while commenting on the harbor, the boats, and the wildlife, appreciating God's surroundings. Exactly what she needed.

"Well then, what's the plan today?" He picked up their red, plastic baskets.

Roxanne had barely eaten.

"Would you like a to go box?"

She chuckled. "No thanks." Fried Catfish leftovers didn't sound too appetizing.

"I didn't think so." Tossing the trash, he replaced the baskets on the counter.

"I'm going to check Mama out of rehab today."

"Right, oh. Would you mind dropping me off at my shop?"

"Sure. I'm heading home to freshen up a bit before I see Mama. I can take you by the shop first."

"No need. Home is perfect. That way I can get my van and head to the shop myself."

Arriving home, Roxanne stepped once more inside her house. She didn't like the eerie silence, but at least it wasn't destroyed like her house in Meridian.

In the bathroom, she pulled out the makeup she'd bought from Tina and applied a bit more the best she could. Perhaps a little too thick and not as professional as Tina had done, but it covered. The amazing product worked wonders. Packing up to head out the front door, she opened it, and a uniformed officer filled the doorway.

CHAPTER 14

"Miss Cook?"

"Yes, that's me." Leaning out, she peeked around him.

"Just checking on you. Have you seen Dwayne Payton?"

"No. I haven't, but the Highway Patrol said they were sure they'd find him."

"I'm with the Hancock County Sheriff's, and we got the report about the assault and attempted abduction."

"So, you don't have him in custody?" She leaned against the door jamb. It was only Friday, but what a way to start the weekend.

"No. I'm sorry. They called off the search in the bayou. They did find a car. But not registered to him."

"An older, black vehicle with peeling paint?"

"Yes. The rangers found it abandoned in the swamp."

"But not him?" Her voice cracked.

"Unfortunately, or fortunately, he probably didn't exit the bayou alive. The rangers searched all known exits out of the preserve. We're doubtful that we'll find him now."

Relief and fear teetered in her brain. He'd escaped the authorities twice now. Something warned her that he wasn't finished.

"All right then." She shrugged.

"I suggest you ask the local police for a patrol as a precaution. I'm sorry, ma'am. You can call us for updates, and we'll contact you if there's any imminent danger."

Roxanne's eyes widened. She'd never made a report with Chief Hidalgo. He didn't even know her, but soon he would. "Yes. Thank you for coming out." She closed the door.

Throwing her purse on the chair, she trudged up the stairs and closed her door quietly. Sitting on the bed, she wanted to cry, but couldn't. Or wouldn't.

Glancing at her nightstand, she eyed her old Bible. The cover worn half off. She'd had it since girlhood and abandoned it for a newer study Bible in high school, and that one, she had abandoned altogether years later. She pulled out a bookmark and read the marked page. *"Fear not, for I am with you."* Isaiah 41:10. Her mother's favorite verse. Roxanne leaned back against the pillows and read the entire passage. Time to fill her well, once again.

The resolve lightened her somewhat, but the disturbing, unfinished business about Dwayne haunted her. Shaking it off, she hopped into her car and drove toward town. Stopping at the donut shop, picking up a treat for Mama, then off to the facility. She checked in, ready to bring her mother home.

"I'm sorry," said the nurse. "You'll have to speak with the doctor. Your mother has had a little setback."

Not waiting for an answer, she rushed to the room and found her mother lying in bed, still in her nightgown. Roxanne placed a small box containing a gourmet jelly donut on the tray. Her mother's eyes fluttered open.

"Oh, hello, dear. I had a rough night. I'm afraid I tried to use the bathroom alone and fell. At least, I think I did. I don't remember." She touched her head.

Roxanne peered closer. "Mama, you have a good-sized bump there."

"Yes, she took a nasty fall." A man in a white coat walked in, extending his hand. "I'm Dr. Marquis."

"Don't you monitor the patients?" Roxanne glanced at his hand and took it. "I'm sorry. I don't understand how this could happen here."

"We monitor all our patients from the nurse's station cameras. One of our aides saw her getting out of bed, so he hurried to her assistance. Had she pushed the button, he would've been there quicker."

"Sugar, I'm fine. Wayne helped me up." Bethie Cook opened her eyes.

Roxanne gasped. "What did you say?"

Bethie chuckled and babbled on. Something about not needing to use the restroom but sleepwalking.

"Dwayne, who? Who is Dwayne?" Roxanne's voice shook, and she gripped her mother's bed rail.

"It's Wayne. He's the nursing assistant," Dr. Marquis said. "He's new here. Just hired but comes highly recommended."

"Are you sure his name is Wayne, not Dwayne?" Roxanne lifted her hair off her shoulders and fanned her neck. This couldn't be happening. He couldn't possibly know where she lived, but what lengths would he go to find her? The blood drained from her face, and a wooziness came over her.

"Miss? What's wrong?" The doctor didn't wait for a reply but pushed over a chair and took her elbow.

"What does he look like?" Roxanne pleaded as she dropped down.

"Who?"

"Wayne, the nursing assistant."

"He's a short man. Asian descent, I believe," the doctor said.

Roxanne huffed loudly and long. More like a gush of air escaping.

"He's Filipino," Bethie Cook said. "They're the best caretakers. God has a special place for them in heaven."

"Mama," Roxanne reprimanded in a hushed tone. Her lightheadedness left her, and she planted her feet before standing. "You can't say things like that."

"I can too. It's true. All the Filipino workers here are amazing." She glanced at the doctor. "Sorry, Doctor, but they're better than all the other workers you got here."

He chuckled. "I'm inclined to agree, but let's keep that between us, shall we?" He winked and turned his gaze to Roxanne. "I'm afraid, besides the head injury, she's got a slight sprained ankle. We want to monitor and ensure your mother is not a fall risk. It might be another week before she can put weight on her ankle, so we'd like to keep her."

"Another week?" Bethie rose up but fell back. "Oh well, as long as you feed me good and get me walking, I'll cooperate."

He wrote something on a chart and flipped it shut. "That's what I like to hear." He turned toward Roxanne. "And you, miss? How are you feeling? Do you get lightheaded often?"

"Only at the mention of her ex-boyfriend," Bethie mumbled.

"Excuse me?"

"Nothing." Roxanne rolled her eyes. "I'm fine, Doctor. I just moved back into town and haven't quite settled in yet."

Fabricating falsehoods and trying to hide the circumstances that put her back in Bay Town were taking their toll. How long could she keep up the deception? After the doctor left, she looked at her mother.

Bethie gazed back. "Sugar, we need to formulate a dialogue."

"A dialogue?" Roxanne asked.

"Yes. You know, when people ask, you can tell the truth without pouring out your heart. People don't need to know everything. Just tell them you're leaving a... what do they call it?" She scrunched her face. "Toxic. You've just left a toxic relationship, and you're trusting the Almighty to get you back on track." She smiled. "That will silence anyone that's not a nosey busybody gossip."

"Dialogue? Toxic? Where is this new language coming from?"

"Our Ladies Bible Study. Our facilitator, Miz Melanie, brought in a speaker from The Refuge, the home for abused women and human trafficking victims. She taught us some communication tools in case we needed to help a woman in trouble. So they wouldn't feel put off and run from us."

The Refuge. Where had Roxanne heard of that before? Her eyes widened. Dr. Rashid in Meridian had mentioned such a home. "Is it here in Bay Town?"

"One is, but I hear they're popping up everywhere. It's about time. I've known too many women in my lifetime that would have had a better life if places like that had been around to help." Her sad eyes gazed at Roxanne, and tears welled. "Roxanne, I believe you should get some counseling at the Refuge."

Roxanne knew her mother would bring this up sometime. She just didn't figure it would be "counseling." Prayer and strength, yes. But counseling? When had her thinking changed? What happened to hiding and denying problems existed? She almost wished that's the way things still were.

Knock, knock.

Roxanne turned toward the door as Bethie called out, "Hey. Pastor. Come meet my daughter, Roxanne."

A tall, dark-haired man stepped into the room. Stunningly handsome, he looked much like Superman. Roxanne's mouth gaped, and she flushed with embarrassment, and even more so when she noticed the slender woman with light brown hair pulled back in a ponytail holding his hand. Roxanne's eyes widened. Her. The one in the drug store who had seen her battered face in the restroom. The woman smiled back at Roxanne but didn't say a word.

Pastor Brooks dropped her hand and stepped forward. "Hello, I'm Desmond, and this is my wife, Melanie."

"Hello, Roxanne. It's so nice to meet you."

Her sweet voice didn't have that familiar southern drawl, and Roxanne remembered she had transplanted from California. Roxanne held her breath, waiting for a battery of questions. They didn't come. Instead, Pastor Brooks and Melanie directed all their attention to Bethie. Melanie slipped around Roxanne and placed a white bag on the tray table. She winked.

Bethie laughed. "I'm getting so many jelly donuts. The staff and I are getting fat. But thank you, dear."

Pastor Brooks offered a chair to Melanie, but she waved it off and walked to the end of the bed. He showed it to Roxanne, but she shook her head, so he pulled it up next to Bethie and sat.

"So, Mrs. Cook, let's discuss my sermon for Sunday."

"Well, if you're still in the book of Jerimiah, I don't have much more to add. That book goes on and on and on." She patted his hand. "So, tell me, how will you encourage us in that message of pain and suffering to come?"

"There's always hope and encouragement. You know what the Bible says, 'All scripture is God-breathed and useful for ___'"

"Teaching, rebuking, correcting, and training in righteousness, so the servant of God may be thoroughly equipped for every good work. 2 Timothy 3:16." Bethie finished his words.

Roxanne stared at the two of them and listened as they discussed spiritual things. She realized how far she'd strayed away from God. It had been so subtle. Missing church, just one Sunday here or there. Instead of rising early to read and do a quiet time, she'd skip her Bible reading and write her stories.

No wonder she got depressed and despaired over her life.

And then she started dating Dwayne. The worst decision of all. Even her friends seemed to give up when she began refusing their invitations and quit Bible study.

Melanie leaned toward Roxanne and whispered. "This is one of my favorite parts of the week. I love to hear these two go at it."

"So, you and the Pastor? How long have you been married?"

"Going on two years." Melanie's eyes glistened as she gazed at him.

"Newlyweds, huh?"

She laughed. "Yes, but we had a long engagement."

"I guess that could be a good thing." Roxanne didn't guess anything.

Melanie nodded. "Well, I had a lot of baggage to work through." She smiled at Roxanne. "So did he."

Roxanne's eyes widened. "The pastor?"

Melanie laughed. "Oh, yeah. Even the pastor. For a time there, I didn't think we'd make it. But God pulled us through." She chuckled some more. "Literally pulled us through, and He used the whole community to do so. God's love is so incredible." She looked at Roxanne. "We just need to trust Him, don't we?"

Before Roxanne could answer, her mother spoke out.

"I understand the interpretation, pastor. But what application are you going to use?" Again, Bethie glanced at her daughter.

Roxanne bristled and turned to leave, already thinking of an excuse, but Melanie touched her arm.

"Your mother is amazing. She reminds me of my dad. She loves the Lord so much and wants everyone to live her joy. She exudes such peace."

Joy and peace, again. The room took on a misty glow, and the conversation between her mother and the pastor infused her thoughts about joy, rejoicing, and suffering. She couldn't help but think they were talking about her. She turned to Melanie.

"Would you like to grab a cup of coffee?"

Melanie checked her watch. "I'd love to, but I have an appointment with a photographer and have to leave in a few minutes. Maybe another time?" She pulled out a business card that read "Quaint Affairs". "Please. Give me a call."

Disappointment registered, but Roxanne forced a smile.

"I'm a wedding planner and event consultant. I have a little shop on Main Street. You should come by sometime."

"Mama told me about a wedding coming up. A local girl, I think?"

"Yes, that's my daughter, Lacey. The day is coming up soon." Her eyes misted. "Don't get me started."

Roxanne pocketed the card, and a few moments later, the pastor prayed for her mother, and the sweet couple left.

"You best get on home now too. I need a little nap before my physical therapy session."

"Yes, ma'am. I'll be back for dinner."

The thought reminded her of the meal she shared with Max last evening.

"What's that silly grin you're wearing?"

Roxanne felt heat flooding her face. She pecked a kiss on her mama's cheek.

"See you later, Mama."

She strolled to her car and smiled at the butterflies flitting about. That's how her stomach felt, thinking about Max. Roxanne had every intention of visiting The Pink Rosette until she spotted an old, muddy, black vehicle.

CHAPTER 15

A s she tried not to stare at the familiar looking older vehicle, the panic returned, and Roxanne peeled from the rehab facility parking lot as fast as she could. *It couldn't be Dwayne's car, could it?* Someone yelled for her to slow down, but she had to escape, just in case. After checking in her rearview mirror numerous times, she assured herself that no one followed, and she pulled over to the side of the road.

Scrambling to find her phone, she searched her purse and berated herself for a bag with too many pockets and all the junk she packed. Giving up, she rechecked the mirror. Her eyes widened. The vehicle approached. She slunk down into the seat, shaking with the stupidity of the move. She closed her eyes tightly and waited. Minutes dragged by, and no one approached her car.

Sitting up, she looked around. No black car. No vehicle was parked behind or in front of her. Sitting for a few more minutes, she noticed every shape and size of a black automobile whizzing by her. With each one, she started to giggle. Paranoia. *Crazy. I'm going crazy.* She closed her eyes and tried to remember her conversation with Melanie Thompson. She recalled her mother and Pastor Brooks discussing the sermon, and the picture of her worn Bible on the nightstand floated in her head. Her resolve returned.

Wiping sweat from her brow, she drove to Main Street. Slowing the car and her brain to a crawl, she reminisced at her familiar high school hangouts. The Old Book Shoppe and Second Chance should both be up ahead. Gone were many of the old shops, replaced by newer upscale boutiques, yet the charm still remained. She saw Melanie's wedding shop, Quaint Affairs. Roxanne pulled in and parked.

Standing before Quaint Affairs, she smiled at the elegant storefront but glanced back at Second Chance, just a few doors down. The door to the upscale vintage boutique rested wide open, flanked by wicker chairs, a tea cart, and a dress form covered with a nostalgic apron. Carol's shop. The landmark establishment sent a warm feeling through her, and she stepped in.

An electronic ding-dong sounded when she entered, and she frowned. But glancing back, the old familiar bells still dangling over the back of the door welcomed her too.

"Hey, there. Welcome to Second Chance." A young, beautiful platinum blonde wearing tight jeans and a loosely knit tunic stood with her hands on her hips. She waved. "I'm Virginia, the shop owner. What can I help you with?" She swept her arms around the colorfully decorated boho-chic store.

"Carol? Is she still here?"

"Do you know her? Why, she's my best friend." The sweet girl squealed.

Roxanne imagined the girl to be in her early twenties. Carol had to be at least fifty by now. Virginia exuded youthful joy. Looking around, Roxanne spotted a pile of vintage books stacked on a glass table.

"Carol moved." The voice lilted at the end, her accent perfectly southern. "I sure miss her, but after what happened to her here, she needed to go home and settle some unfinished business." Virginia nodded. "She moved back to New Mexico."

Home to settle unfinished business? Is that what I'm doing here? "But I always thought Carol hailed from Bay Town." Roxanne frowned. "Wait. What happened to her?"

"Oh, my." Virginia lowered her voice. "Awful. Just terrible. We don't even talk about it no more." She looked around. "She saved me from my uncle. Not really, my uncle. He's more like a second cousin or something. But I always knew him as my Uncle Will, Will Boudreaux."

"The man who died in that fiery crash? My mama told me about that." And she'd never forget it. A warning about evil men that she'd heeded too late. "And he abducted Carol?" Roxanne had been so wrapped up in her problems that she didn't remember.

"Yes. And he got me too, once."

Roxanne stared at this sweet young thing. She appeared so innocent. What had she lived in her short life? "Oh my. I'm so sorry."

"Yeah, me too. But this town saved me. Have you ever heard of the Refuge? I lived there for a while."

The Refuge. How many times would she keep hearing that name? It must be a coincidence. But the thought didn't sit well.

"Yes, I've heard of The Refuge. Sounds like a good place." She shrugged and didn't know what else to say. Something in her stomach churned. Once again, she didn't want to have to identify herself with those kinds of women. Broken, battered women. Yet, one stood before her. Vibrant, so full of life, not at all damaged. At least not on the outside.

"Well, I better run." She didn't know why. She had no place to go but then asked, "Say, do you know if the Old Book Shoppe is still around?"

Virginia shook her head so vigorously that wavy locks fell on her forehead, and she swiped them back. "I think it's down the way. But I never looked in." She giggled. "I don't read much, and I'm not from around here." Yet her sweet southern drawl told otherwise.

"You're not from Mississippi?"

"Of course, I am! I can't hide that. But not Bay Town." Her eyes brightened. "But my husband is, and he reads a lot." She raised her ring finger. "I still can't believe we're married. Miz Melanie planned my whole wedding, and Pastor Brooks did the ceremony. I even got married in the church. I always thought I'd like a park wedding. You know, church weddings are kinda stuffy. But those people from Bay Town Community? They rescued me. They said God did, but I know they helped."

She bubbled on and on, and Roxanne wanted to catch her joy, but weddings didn't do that to her anymore. Still, she smiled while trying to make an exit. "That's wonderful. I'm so happy for you. I'll be back."

"Okay, you do that." Virginia followed her to the door, smiling, waving to all passing by. "Hey, there, y'all!"

Roxanne walked down the street a few more doors and stopped. The day sweltered hot and sticky by the minute, but her temperature rose a notch more when she stood in front of the little floral shop. She reached for the bottom half of the open double Dutch door and pushed. Bells rang. Every little shop on Main Street had bells, so she'd remembered.

"I'll be right there," Max called from the back.

Roxanne breathed deep the fresh scent of cut, green stems. Floral wisps lifted her spirits as she waited.

Max strolled from the back of the store, wiping his hands on a stained white apron. Roxanne chuckled at the pink, single rosette embroidered on the bib. He stopped. A smile spread across his face, and he stepped forward with his signature hands spread wide for a hug. *Just like old times.* She melted into his arms, but he squeezed only once and let go.

Stepping back, he rocked up on his toes. "So, my dear.

What can I do for you? A welcome home bouquet for your mum?" Those pale blue eyes twinkled.

Roxanne blinked. How could she think of him as anything but Philippa's husband? Fluttering her lips, she berated herself with the foolish obsession.

"Roxy?" He stared at her over his wire-rimmed glasses. "Hello? Are you okay?"

Shaking her head, she laughed. "I'm fine. But no, no bouquet. Mama's not coming home. She fell last night."

"Oh, my? Is she all right?" He reached out and touched her shoulder. "Anything I can do?"

Sweet Max, always the gentleman, the servant, the knight in shining armor. How appropriate it was that the only proper British gentleman in town would be the knight.

"No, the doctor said it's just precautionary to keep her one more week. I'm joining her for dinner tonight." She stared back at him. "Hey, would you like to join us? I thought I'd make something and take it to eat with her."

"Sounds awfully tempting. I'm sorry, love, I must pass. I have a Men's Bible Study tonight. But give me a rain check? A widower like me gets tired of frozen dinners." He winked.

"Oh, Max. I know you better than that. You're a great cook." But she pondered on the word widower. He didn't say bachelor or even single.

"Is that so? If that's how you remember me, I'll have to fire up the grill and have you and your mum over."

"Sounds like a deal. But I'll give you the rain check. We'll see who's the better chef."

"Right, oh. You're on. Now, go on with you. I have plenty of work to do here. I've been looking for an assistant so I can take a break once in a while." He gave her a sideways glance. "You're not looking for some part-time work, are you?"

Her heart fluttered a little, and Roxanne bit her lip. "I'd love to help, but I better wait and see how much care Mama needs. Besides, I'm hoping to write a little while I'm here, remember?"

"Perfect. I'd hoped you'd be on it. Let me know how I can help. Remember, I used to edit as much as Philippa did."

Pointing a finger, Roxanne smiled. "Okay, I'll hold you to it." She said goodbye and turned to exit. His phone rang, and he waved to her before answering.

Roxanne walked a little lighter and stopped by the galvanized buckets placed all around the store. One particular pail sat on the counter, filled with single-stem pink rosettes. Max's signature flower. She heard Max's voice behind her.

Not interrupting his phone conversations, he reached around her, plucking a single stem, and handed it to her. He continued his call, leaving her to exit by herself. She felt at home, and the euphoria of being in The Pink Rosette with Max melted when she stepped out.

The hot, humid Mississippi June assaulted her. She pulled the thin tank tee away from her stomach, hoping to cool her skin as she walked. After a few more boutiques, she should be approaching the Old Book Shoppe. She picked up her pace when she spotted a shingle hanging above a doorway. The shingle looked lopsided, but its familiarity made her heart beat faster.

Years ago, she'd always imagined her book in the window one day. With a quickened step, she resolved that it would. New town, new goals, and renewed dreams, but when she reached the shop, a paper sign taped inside read, "Out of business". Roxanne peeked in, and the empty, dust-laden shelves saddened her.

She'd gotten her first job here. Sally Trotman, the owner and her mother's feisty best friend, hired her in high school. Cupping her hands, Roxanne peered in. The wooden shelves, the checkout counter. Even the old cash register sat there. Drawer open. Everything but the books remained. She tipped her head and squinted at a sign on the floor. "All books donated to the Friends of the Public Library. Go there, not the big box store."

Roxanne chuckled. It sounded like Miz Trotman. A hot wind blew, and Roxanne lifted the hair off her neck, allowing the air to cool her. She turned and sat on a bench across from the abandoned shop. The benches hadn't been here in her younger days. The magnolia trees, with glossy green leaves and large white blossoms, were new to her too. Mama told her that the city had renovated after the big hurricane. Now, years after they'd been planted they provided the well-needed shade.

Roxanne sat and stared at the abandoned store. She imagined Miz Sally boxing up all those books to take to the public library. She recalled spending hours there, writing, perusing books, walking the aisles. She smiled at the happy memories, and a gnawing in her stomach reminded her it was almost lunch time.

Her phone rang. Realizing she had it all along, she rifled through her purse again. She hadn't been able to find it earlier when she needed it. Finally, she slapped her back pants pocket. She'd forgotten it there and pulled it out. She didn't recognize the number and let it go to voicemail before checking.

"Please, Roxanne. I need help!"

CHAPTER 16

Roxanne sucked in a breath and punched buttons. "Lucy? Is that you?"

Sniffles muffled through the phone line. "Yes," Lucy cried.

Roxanne's pulse quickened and sweat beaded on her brow; her stomach churned in knots. The nightmares that Roxanne had lived with every waking and sleeping moment with Dwayne returned. She stood.

"Lucy, what happened?"

"I'm so sorry to call you. I don't know what to do. Dwayne came to the Sports Bar last night. He looked awful. Dirty, and he stunk like all get up."

Roxanne glanced up, shading her eyes from the overhead sun. She stepped back under the tree. How did he get back to terrorize Lucy so quickly? It didn't matter. He got out. Dwayne escaped the Bayou.

"Roxy? Did you hear me?"

"Yes, I'm so sorry."

"He grabbed me and wanted to know where you were. He twisted my arm, but Jason and the guys at the bar pulled him off. They called the police, but he screamed at me and ran." Lucy choked back a sob. "He said he'd get me."

"What did the police say?"

"They said I could put a restraining order on him. But they couldn't guarantee that he'd abide by it. Roxy, I'm scared."

Breathe. Just breathe. Roxanne didn't know for a moment if she expressed that aloud to Lucy or silently to herself. "Did you tell him where? Did you tell him about Bay Town?"

"Of course not. But I know he'll be back. He asked about that guy too. The nurse. I was so scared. I went to a hotel last night. Jason stayed with me, but he slept on the floor."

Roxanne's stomach lurched. Dwayne had turned psychotic. She had to warn Travis. Bile rose, and as tears filled her eyes, her nose clogged, and she couldn't breathe. How many more people were in danger because of her?

"Lucy, do you have any place to go?"

"No. My parents are missionaries in India, and my sister lives in Idaho. She's got a pile of kids. I can't get her involved. I don't know what to do."

Stuck on the missionaries in India reveal, Roxanne stuttered. "Missionaries?"

"I know, I know. My parents raised us right, but I chose a different path. I think God is punishing me."

Roxanne felt victimized and unjustly abused, but she knew in her heart that God hadn't given up on her. She thought so once, but not anymore, and he wasn't punishing Lucy. She couldn't explain it, but no more blaming God.

"No, Lucy. You know God better than that. Maybe we both need to get our act together again, but Dwayne is crazy."

"Okay. Yes. You're right. But what do I do?"

"Come to Bay Town," Roxanne said.

The crying stopped, and Lucy blew her nose hard.

"Really? Are you sure?"

"Yes, I'm positive. Don't tell Jason or anyone else. Make sure no one follows you. I'll text you the address."

"All right. How far are ya'?" asked Lucy.

"Just three hours southeast. Call me when you get here but come straight to the address. It's my mama's house."

"Okay, I'll be there tonight. Thanks, Roxy. I sure appreciate it."

"I'm so sorry, Lucy. This is all my fault."

"No, it's not. It's Dwayne's. Let's just pray the police get him."

Lucy clicked off, and Roxanne gazed back at the empty book store. She searched up and down Main Street aware of her surroundings once more. She slumped on the bench. *Think. Think. What do I do now?* If only she had someone to talk to. Yet, who could she tell? *Pray. Just pray. Yes. Please, God, help us.*

Her throat suddenly parched, but lunch no longer filled her thoughts. She headed for the Mockingbird Café, the local coffee shop hangout. Turning the corner, and walking another block, she approached the yellow house with the wrap-around porch. She remembered it long ago, but not as a business. Back then a family resided there. Roxanne trotted up the front steps, and once inside, she ordered a sweet tea. She sucked in a breath. The cool air-conditioning and the smell of dark roasted coffee beans energized her. Finding a seat, she plopped in an overstuffed chair and closed her eyes. A few minutes of rest.

"Mind if I join you?"

She recognized Pastor Desmond's voice and her eyes fluttered open. Uncrossing her legs, she sat up straight.

"I'm sorry. I didn't mean to disturb you," he said.

"Oh, no. I'd love the company." Roxanne waved to a chair. "I've had a pretty crazy morning." She winced, wishing she hadn't shared that already.

"Melanie says I'm a good listener." He smiled, sipped his coffee, and took a seat.

"I'm afraid it's a long story, and I don't know where to start." She looked back at him. *Did God send him to her?* "Did your wife tell you she saw me at the drugstore the other day?" *All beat up*, she wanted to add.

"Yes. She did. Although she didn't know who you were then. I'm sure your mother is glad to have you back."

"She is. But I'm not sure how long I'll stay. I left a bad relationship in Meridian."

"Are you safe here?"

"I hope so. But I'm not sure." Roxanne crumpled the napkin in her lap. "I met a guy, Dwayne, about a year ago. After that, my life went downhill."

"I'm sorry. Sometimes people aren't who we think they are."

"I'm to blame too. I'd been in a slump for years before meeting him. You know, unhappy with my life." She glanced up wondering why she spilled her guts. "Do you always do this to people?"

"Do what?"

"It's like you're a priest, and I'm confessing or something."

Pastor Brooks laughed. "Jesus is your confessor, not me. But I'm all ears."

She shrugged. "I grew up here and loved it. My parents were great. But then real life happened."

"Life can be tough. Just read the Old Testament," he said.

"That's putting it mildly. I went to college in Meridian and met..." Roxanne gulped. "Anyway, I graduated and returned here to teach school at Bay Town Elementary. Then my dad died." Roxanne frowned. She hadn't meant to go there. She never talked about the details of his death.

"I'm sorry. I know what it's like to lose someone so close." Pastor Desmond patted her hand.

"You do? You lost a loved one too?"

He nodded. "I did. My first wife. She died of cancer."

"Oh, my. So you're a widower." *Like Max.*

"I was, and I'll always love her, but I couldn't be happier with Melanie. God works miracles when we submit to him.

And He really pulled out the stops with Melanie." His eyes shone.

"Yes, but I'm not expecting a miracle from God in my life. I lost more than just my dad," Roxanne whispered.

"Excuse me?" He leaned forward.

"I lost someone else too, when I was in college, and it still hurts." Roxanne swiped her eyes. "Anyway, stuff happened and after Daddy died, I moved to Meridian and bought a house with the money he left me. I knew everyone would care for Mama. Besides, she wouldn't leave here anyway. She had all her friends and neighbors and the church. But I just couldn't stay."

"So you left because of your father's death?"

"Sort of. There's a bit more to it." *Oh, so much more.* "But I left, and I didn't want to come home again." Roxanne waited, expecting him to interrupt. He didn't. "Then, too many years went by, and I couldn't return because I felt like I failed as a writer." She tapped her foot, and her knee bounced.

"Are you still writing?"

Roxanne nodded.

"Then you didn't fail. Failing is quitting."

She chuckled. "I always dreamed of bringing notoriety to Bay Town. Did you know Bay Town's claim to fame is Hemmingway taking vacations here?"

"I didn't know that. But I heard that Philippa Tippet brought the town some author renown here. But that was long before I came."

"Yes. She and Max were my mentors. I always thought I'd be a published author by now and married." Another reveal she hadn't meant to disclose.

Roxanne's eyes shifted around the room. She pulled back her hair and quickly twisted it, securing it in a messy bun. "Listen, I probably should go. I have a guest coming this evening."

Pastor Brooks looked at his watch. "Sure. Me too. But

listen, if you ever need to talk, both Melanie and I are available."

"Thanks." Roxanne nodded but never intended on spilling her guts again.

"Will I see you at church on Sunday?" Pastor Brooks asked.

Roxanne shifted in her seat. "If Mama had her way, but she's still in the rehab facility."

"You could come without her. We don't bite." Pastor Desmond grinned.

"Bay Town Community Church has some harsh memories for me." There, she did it again.

"Wow. I'm so sorry. I hope we've changed."

"No. It's not the church. Just a person, and he's not there anymore." She reached out her hand. "Thank you, Pastor."

"My pleasure, Roxanne. I'll be praying for you." He turned to leave but didn't get far before more than one resident stopped him and chatted. They had to be residents. They all knew each other.

She wished she hadn't shared that much about her life. Perhaps everyone did that to him. Roxanne glanced at people leaving and the exit looked more inviting by the minute.

She walked directly to her car and didn't stop by the Pink Rosette to say bye to Max. She also avoided the exuberant Virginia standing outside Second Chance. While driving home, a fast-motion video of her life rolled out before her, and she let loneliness and disappointment grab hold and wrench her heart.

CHAPTER 17

Friday evening, Dwayne drove to a motel.

"*Dumb move, Dwayne,*" he said to himself thinking about his altercation with his friends over his attack on Lucy. His temper had got the best of him, and he shouldn't have gone after her last night. But after making it out of the Bayou yesterday, all he thought about was finding Roxy, and Lucy had to know. He should have never gone to Leroy's. It got him nowhere, and now he needed to sleep so he could think clearly.

But he couldn't stop thinking about last night. He'd hitched a ride back to Meridian straight to Leroy's. He needed familiar surroundings, and Leroy's Bar and Grill called his name. It was like home, and he longed for the comfort, and a beer or two always helped. It wasn't quite the same as Charlie's but close, and he already missed shooting pool with his buddies, with Roxy watching. So he got a ride straight there but with Lucy on his agenda, and he blew it again.

After sleeping off the alcohol behind a dumpster all night, he awoke this morning and returned to his apartment. He showered, ate three bowls of cereal, and took a nap. Sleeping fitfully, but better than he had in the hot back alley. Luckily, he hadn't encountered any cops, and surprisingly he hadn't noticed any surveillance on his apartment. Heck, he hadn't killed anyone. Why would they waste manpower on him? Still, he didn't feel safe staying in town.

He counted out the cash he'd taken from Roxy's bank account. A tinge of guilt pricked his conscience. He'd never stolen anything from her. As if that would be the worst thing he could ever do to her. He growled and reasoned that he needed it and left to purchase an old clunker automobile. Remorse also hit him over the fact that he'd had to ditch the car that Charlie had given him. Disappointing those he loved most, his mother, Roxy, and Charlie weighed heavy on his mind. But he'd get used to it. It had all started with his Dad anyway.

After waking late and finally purchasing an automobile, he drove a little ways out of town checking his mirrors the whole way. Yet, even with no one following, he couldn't rest. It hadn't been wise to return to Meridian, but he had to find Roxy.

Dwayne hung his wrist over the steering wheel as he drove to a cheap motel. He'd stay the night and continue heading south toward the gulf. He just had a hunch. Roxy had mentioned growing up near the water a few times. *Why hadn't he paid more attention?*

He parked, got a room, and headed up the stairs. He passed an open door jammed with sorry looking souls and peeked in. Most of the men were shabbily dressed and unshaven. The room smelled of body odor and stale beer. *Must be a drug rehab group*, he thought. A man with a bible on his lap seemed to be preaching to them. He looked up.

"Come on in. Everyone's welcome, just sharing some hope here." the man smiled at Dwayne.

Dwayne walked by. *Losers.*

He unlocked his room and flung himself on the bed. Before he got comfortable, sirens blared, and tires screeched outside. He jumped up and pulled aside the curtains. Tweakers and druggies flew out of the rooms. It was a drug bust. But why did the police even bother? The druggies always hung out there and landed up back on the streets anyway. Still, he couldn't stay.

Grabbing his backpack, he shoved a ball cap on his head and left his room. Panic almost got the best of him until he heard the preacher next door. *Thank the Lord*, he mocked as he slipped into the open door. The room had about ten guys sitting around. Some on the bed, others on the floor. They listened to the man with the Bible lying open in his lap. None paid any attention to Dwayne's entrance.

He took a seat on the floor and hunched down while the preacher spoke. Sweat dripped down Dwayne's face as he listened. Although he anticipated the cops busting in, the preacher's words registered in his brain.

One officer stepped in, but Dwayne lowered his head and folded his hands, still watching with a sideways glance.

"I'll take responsibility for them," the preacher said.

The uniformed man nodded and left him and the hopeless losers alone.

With the police gone, Dwayne didn't feel settled. The haunting Bible verse the preacher spoke about hung in his brain. He quoted that verse that everyone knew. John 3:16. The preacher talked about peace and making it with God. *Right. Like that would ever happen.* What did God ever do for him? For a second, the faces of his sister, his mom, and the college scholarship streaked through his mind. But, like the preacher's words, those things weren't enough to make a difference.

Dwayne's thoughts faded back. He enjoyed peace once. When he went to youth group growing up. The singing, not so much the preaching. But he always wondered why his mom had sent him and his sister to church. She never went. Maybe if she had, they wouldn't have found her beat up when they came home.

Wait. Like a lightbulb switched on, he figured it out. His mom never went to church because Dad wouldn't let her.

That sleaze had sent them weekly so he could be alone with Mom. Dwayne gagged at the thought and no longer listened to the preacher but tried to focus on a plan. After what seemed like forever, he left without a word and drove to the woods.

Dwayne got lucky and spotted a campground. *Lucky? Maybe not so much.* The heat of summer and the tents-only campground remained empty. Dwayne swerved into a secluded, woodsy spot by the river. He fought with the gear to shift it into park, half wishing he still had the black Camry. Those cars ran forever, but this one had to suffice. He had no more cash for another, and he'd burned his bridges with all his friends. Especially Jason.

They'd been buds since high school, but Jason turned on him after Dwayne grabbed Lucy at Leroy's last night. Except for the danger of getting caught, he'd return and take care of her like he did Roxanne. These women were ruining his life. His life. His buds and his bar. He had nobody. Nothing.

Even if he wanted to start over, he couldn't. No one would hire him. His buddies had always recommended him for jobs, and he took no fault that he couldn't stay employed. If not for the other jerky employees, he'd still be working. Dwayne wasn't a team player. His forte lay in winning over customers. Often top in sales with new clients, the others were jealous. At team meetings, they always complained about his methods.

Dwayne's head ached, and he rummaged in his glovebox for aspirin. He grabbed a water bottle from his cup holder. It wasn't quite dusk. Except for a homeless old man who looked like he couldn't afford anything else, the place was empty. Heck, no one in their right brain would stay by a swampy river with one port-a-potty and a single water faucet that ran brown. But he would for one night only.

Dwayne exited the car, and the skinny old man hobbled over. He coughed. The cough turned into hacking.

"Hey, you got any smokes?" he asked.

"I don't smoke. I'm not killing my body like you. Get lost."

The man sneered at him. "They was here, you know."

Sweat ran down Dwayne's temples. The temperature felt hotter with the rising humidity, but more so with what he thought the man meant.

"The cops. They came asking about you."

Standing to his full height, Dwayne towered over the old man. "What are you talking about? I don't know you."

"I told him no one that looked like the picture they showed me was here. But here you are now. That picture was you. That's for certain."

Dwayne's fists clenched, and his arms tensed.

The man held out his palm, rubbing his fingers together, indicating he wanted cash. "I'll bet they'll come again, and I probably shouldn't lie to the cops." He laughed.

Dwayne growled, moving forward.

"They'll be back. You hurt me, and I'll pin it on you."

Dwayne didn't take threats from anyone. He shoved the old man, who toppled over the edge of a rickety picnic table. A sickening thud sounded as he hit a large rock. Blood seeped from his head. His eyes rolled back, and his body went limp.

Dwayne cursed and threw the water bottle at the man lying still on the ground. The water flew out, and the plastic bounced off the man's chest. Dwayne turned and stomped to his car. The old man had it coming, but Dwayne's heart beat recklessly, ready to burst from his chest. Something in his head fluttered, and he held his head and stumbled to the car. Falling into the driver's seat, he started his engine and backed out. He thought for a brief second that he should check on the guy. But it passed. He didn't have time, and he needed a beer, but he didn't dare set foot into a store now.

Instead of driving to the interstate, he pushed deeper into

the woods. He'd chance upon an old mini-mart or something, serving the poor folk squatting in the woods. The trees encroached, and the thick darkness suffocated him, as well as the noisy crickets and the bugs. Sweat trickled down his face. He hit the button for the air conditioner. Nothing. Dwayne slammed the console again and again. He didn't know where to go, and he blamed Roxy for his predicament.

The darkness didn't allow him to drive too fast. The white lines on the two-lane road were visible for only a few feet ahead. He hit his bright lights and rubbed his forehead. He needed aspirin. Badly. He reached for the glovebox and popped it open. Taking his eyes off the road, he spotted the bottle but couldn't get it. He glanced once more back at the road before reaching for the bottle just within his grasp.

Bam. Thud. All went black.

After what seemed like hours, a light shined in his eyes. "Turn that stupid thing off," he yelled.

His head pounded more than it had before, and he didn't know how long he'd been out. He remembered hitting something. Or something hit his car and caused him to swerve into the ditch.

"You're lucky to be alive. Looks like you hit a deer."

Dwayne shoved the flashlight aside. *Just my luck.* This guy wasn't some do-gooder civilian. He wore a uniform. A State Trooper, no less. He could tell by the silhouette of the wide-brimmed hat. The pulsing pain in his head incapacitated any thought of escaping. *This is where it ends.*

He unbuckled and fell out of the car. The soft, dry dirt puffed up when he landed. He coughed and shut his eyes. He tried to stand but couldn't. His ankle twisted under him, and his brain fogged.

"Stay put. I called for help."

Dwayne tried sitting straight and blinked. When his eyes adjusted, he saw a Forest Ranger, not a State Trooper. The brown hat and uniform, as well as the logo on his sleeve, confirmed it. *Better.* Maybe this guy didn't care about crime outside of the woods.

How he caught all that, Dwayne didn't know, but it woke him up all right. "I'm fine. Leave me alone." But between the pain in his head and the throb in his ankle, black dots formed before his eyes.

"Hold on, there. I got an ambulance coming."

"No. I said, I'm fine." Dwayne pressed a palm to his eyes. "Just give me a ride to ..." Dwayne didn't know his whereabouts and found it hard to think. "Uh, I'm going to meet my friends for a camping trip. Some isolated spot up the road." He hoped for a spot like that.

"You passed it." The ranger pointed back the way Dwayne came. "Ain't much more secluded than the campground by the river back there. I was headed to check in on it when I came across you in the ditch here."

"No, I'm sure the one I'm talking about is up ahead," Dwayne said before yelping like a sick puppy. The bugs were eating him alive, but he hadn't the strength to slap them off. He swallowed hard. "Say, you got any aspirin?"

"I do. Hang on." The ranger headed for his vehicle but stopped. "There's nothing up ahead for sixty miles. Just a mini-mart."

Dwayne tried to nod, but his head felt like the heavy bag in the gym. "That's it. That's where I'm meeting the guys. The mini-mart."

"Let me get that aspirin."

A siren screeched in the distance, and without turning, Dwayne could see flashing red lights approaching them. Running wasn't a possibility. The dots in front of his eyes connected, and he slumped to the ground.

∾

What a long day, Roxanne thought, but with evening setting in, she busied herself at home getting the guest room ready for Lucy. Flinging open the door, a fresh lavender scent surprised her as if the room waited for visitors. Although the hot Mississippi humidity hung heavy, the open window let a breeze blow through. Nothing appeared dusty or stale. Sweet Mama. Always ready to invite a missionary, a guest speaker from the church, or just someone who needed a place to stay. She said that God gifted her with hospitality. Roxanne wondered if she even had a gift.

Still, she stripped the bed and washed the sheets. Retrieving fresh towels from the hall closet, she placed them on a side chair. The robin-egg blue matched the coordinated floral print curtains and the patchwork quilt on the bed. She stepped back, admiring the welcoming room.

But Lucy never showed.

CHAPTER 18

Roxanne waited up practically all night and no Lucy. She'd called her a half-dozen times, but no answer. She didn't know when she'd finally fallen asleep, but Saturday morning her phone dinged. The sun shined in the guest room, and the morning birds sang. She reached for her phone on the nightstand

<Hey, there Roxy, the police called me. They picked up Dwayne. He's in jail. I'm not coming. Call you later.>

Lucy's text stared back at her, and Roxanne blew out a huge sigh.

Every range of emotion filled her. First of all, irritation. Why hadn't Lucy called? Still, joy, relief, vindication, even disappointment. She'd looked forward to seeing Lucy. And then fear. The safety net of Dwayne's imprisonment didn't bring total peace. What if he got out? What if they got the wrong guy? Roxanne had never pressed charges, but the police issued a warrant for his arrest. She pushed out second guesses that threatened fear. Time to take the next step.

She called the Meridian Police, and after being redirected numerous times, a detective had information.

"Yes, Miss Cook, Dwayne Payton is in custody. He's awaiting bail now."

"What?" Roxanne asked.

"We haven't quite built a solid case. There were no actual eyewitnesses to the assault." She heard papers shuffle. "Dr. Rashid, an abuse specialist, insisted that we go after him. But I'm not so sure we can keep him. Unless you want to press charges?" He didn't let her answer. "Why didn't you? Is this man your boyfriend, or ex-husband?"

Roxanne wanted to hang up. Here it came again, but instead of cowering, she took a deep breath. "I'd like to press charges now. What do I need to do?"

"You'll have to come to Meridian."

Her confidence deflated. "Why? Can't I do it over the internet?"

"I need to take a report, or at least someone from the Domestic Violence unit does."

He sounded so cold. Her chances would be better with that unit. She'd never heard of such a department, but surely they'd be more sympathetic. She huffed. How often had she shunned sympathy? Walking to the window, she peered out. The blue skies held a few clouds, but the blistering sun fueled courage.

"Fine, how long do I have?" She stroked the sheer curtain.

"For what?"

"How long do I have to file before you release him?" She choked on the words.

"We'll keep him overnight. If the judge rules we don't have a case, he could be out tomorrow afternoon. But if you press charges, bail all depends on his priors." She heard papers rustling again. "Looks like he's formerly been arrested for a bar fight and a drunk driving. His bail won't be too high."

"What about a hit-and-run, and evading the police?" Roxanne's fingers knotted around the sheer curtain, wrinkling it into her fists.

"Hmmm. Hasn't been filed yet. When did all that happen? Are you sure it's the same guy?"

"Of course, I am. He's a dangerous man." Roxanne gripped the phone. "Oh, and theft. He drained my bank account."

"Did he have access to it?"

She sighed. "Yes, but I didn't give him permission."

"Figures. A woman scorned," he said quietly.

"Excuse me? Are you going to help me or not?"

"Okay. Okay. Do you have a restraining order against him?"

Roxanne closed her eyes as she leaned on the window jam. How could the air outside smell so sweet when a sour taste filled her mouth? "I didn't. But I will. Can I do that online?"

"Wouldn't that be nice? If everyone in a domestic dispute filed a restraining order, the system would crash." He chuckled. "Just come down to the station. If you're serious about this case against your boyfriend or ex-husband."

"He's neither." Roxanne's voice rose. "I'm on my way."

"Hold on, lady. The courts are closed today. It's Saturday, so the County Clerk is closed too. You can't do any filing. You'll have to come in on Monday."

Pinching the bridge of her nose, Roxanne sighed. "Fine. I'll be there on Monday."

Roxanne threw her phone on the bed and resolved to do nothing for the rest of the day, or tomorrow for that matter. Since her mama remained in rehab, she didn't have to worry about attending church either. There's no way she'd go alone.

Monday came and Roxanne prepared herself like a woman on a mission and walked out the door. The dawn greeted her. Just a hint of the cool, late-night air remained. She blew out a breath, convincing herself she could do this, but once outside, her resolve waned. A little help would be nice. She stepped out and glanced across the street, hoping to see Max. Not that she'd say anything to him, but he always had an encouraging word. But no. No Max, no deliverance. No support. Aloneness gripped her, and her movements slowed, but she slipped into her car and drove for three hours.

When she arrived at the Meridian Police Precinct, a slight woman in uniform sat at the front desk. Her hair pulled back into a tight little bun framed a thin face, and she officiated over the tall desk. Roxanne cleared her throat, and the woman looked down at her.

"May I help you?"

Her soft voice surprised Roxanne, and she wondered how this officer could defend anyone. "Yes, I'm here to file a restraining order."

"You'll need to do that at the courthouse. It's over on Constitution Avenue. Just a short walk from here."

Roxanne's shoulders slumped. "But the detective said to come here."

"What's his name?"

"I have no idea. I just talked to him on Saturday. I came all the way from Bay Town. It's three hours away."

"I know where it is. What are you doing here?" The woman clasped her hands. "Did the abuse occur in Bay Town or here in Meridian?"

"Does it make a difference?"

"Yes, it does, ma'am. Does he or she live here?"

Roxanne's brows raised. "She?"

"You'd be surprised how many women abusers we get, ma'am."

"He. He lives here."

"Did the abuse take place in Meridian?"

Sucking in air, Roxanne coughed. Her heart rate quickened, and she swiped at her brow. She tried to find words, but they wouldn't come.

The woman looked around the empty station. "Listen, my shift is over in a few minutes. If you wait, I'll walk you over there. What's his name?"

Roxanne gazed back.

"Your abuser, what's his name? I can look him up on the computer."

"Dwayne Payton."

The keyboard clicked for a few seconds before the officer pulled down a fist. "Yes. We got him."

"Excuse me?"

The woman held up a finger as she read the screen. "Yup, back there. Now I remember. They brought him in late the other night." She pointed at a door behind her.

Roxanne searched the room, her eyes fixed on the exit. Her knees wobbled, and she braced an arm on the desk. She stared at the door where the officer directed her, and the thought of him so close made her skin crawl.

"Ma'am? Are you all right?" She looked past Roxanne and yelled. "Hey, my time's up, you're on."

Roxanne turned, and a medium-height man with a short buzz stared back. He glanced at his watch and threw up his arms. "I got five more minutes."

"Well, get over here. It'll take you five minutes to settle in." The female officer glared.

He shook his head and stood. Sauntering over, he nodded to Roxanne and traded places with the woman. She disappeared behind the desk, and Roxanne watched as she stepped off a platform. She stood all of about five foot, nothing. *She had to be taller.* Weren't their height restrictions?

"Let's have a seat." She instructed Roxanne to a bench against the wall. "He can't hurt you." The woman shook her head. "No way, now. I saw them bring him in, and seriously, he can't touch you. He's got a busted-up ankle from a car wreck. Anyway, you do need to take action. The judge will rule soon." She looked around. "Tell me what happened."

Roxanne closed her eyes and then leaned her head against the wall. All strength waned.

"Okay, I know it's hard." The woman's whole demeanor softened. "How bad did he hurt you? Were you hospitalized?"

"Yes."

"How long ago?"

Shrugging, Roxanne's shoulders slumped. "A week or so ago. I think."

The officer shot a quick glance at Roxanne's healing head wound and patted her arm. "I know, honey. I don't like to remember either. But we have to be strong. We want the jerks off the street."

Roxanne's eyes widened. A victim too. She knew what Roxanne felt. Her gut twisted.

"How long has he been beating you?" the woman asked.

"Too long, but soon after I met him," Roxanne whispered.

The woman's eyes widened. "You're lucky to be alive, sweetie. Someone's been watching over you. At least, that's what some people say. Okay. Let's go. I'm taking you to the courthouse to file that restraining order."

"That's so nice of you."

"Hey, I need to get my steps in anyway." She stood. "I'm Officer Chen. The sooner we do this, the better. Did the detective you talked to ask you to file a report too?"

"Yes."

"Did you?"

Roxanne shook her head.

"Well, I suggest you do and do it fast. It'll make a difference in the judge's bail decision. Let's get you started."

Roxanne did everything as instructed and sent a silent prayer of thanks too. So grateful for this feisty woman. First, Officer Chen contacted the Domestic Violence unit and demanded a detective to take Roxanne's report. She sat with Roxanne the whole time while she relived the horrific ordeal.

In moments, unable to continue, Officer Chen's encouraging nods prompted her to finish.

"Good," Officer Chen said, then turned to the detective. "File that right away, please, and she needs a copy to take to the court for an immediate restraining order."

"It'll take a while," the detective said.

Officer Chen glared.

"All right, all right. I'll type it up right now." He shook his head and stood. "I keep telling you, Chen, you should go for the promotion. We need you in this department."

"Not a chance. I want nothing to do with abusers. We'll wait here for that report."

Roxanne gazed at the woman. She didn't look like she could hurt a fly, but Officer Chen sat up straight, and her pulled-back shoulders exuded confidence. Her voice forceful and assured. Roxanne would never guess she'd have let anyone hurt her. *Let.* What a terrible word. Like, who would give another person permission to harm them? Losing herself in memories of how she'd spiraled to this point, she closed her eyes and rested her head against the wall behind her. Neither of the women spoke for a while.

"Here," the detective said, handing an official document to Roxanne.

"Thanks. I owe you." Officer Chen shook the detective's hand. "Now, let's take that report and go to the courthouse."

Roxanne's heart swelled with relief and gratitude for Officer Chen. It took a while, but she got an immediate temporary restraining order, and the women walked outside.

"Make copies of that order and give it to everyone. The police, your place of employment. Let everyone know."

Roxanne's chest tightened, and she gulped air.

"Whoa, there. Take a breath. You can do this. It won't work if no one knows, especially your local police. You have to do this." She removed a card from her front pocket and handed it to Roxanne. "You tell them to call me if they have any questions."

Staring back at her, Roxanne's eyes welled.

"No more of that. You took the first step when you left the bum; now, don't blow it. You're a strong woman." She looked around. "If you believe in God, trust Him. He's the only one that can bring you real peace. No matter what happens. And for now? We got this guy. Don't let him paralyze you. You got away. Now stay away."

With every word, layers of fear shed, and Roxanne felt strength rising. She could do this. With Dwayne locked away, he couldn't hurt her. She breathed deeply. "Thank you. Thank you so much."

Officer Chen waved her off. "You can thank me by not getting into a toxic relationship again. Give yourself a break from men." She rolled her eyes. "They're not all they're cracked up to be."

Roxanne shook her hand but wanted to hug the officer. She'd done more than just help her. She gave her renewed courage and strength. Before Roxanne reached the door, the woman called.

"Roxanne? Get some counseling." She stepped closer. "Biblical counseling is best." The officer put her hands together, indicating prayer, and she smiled for the first time all day. "Promise me?"

Driving home, Roxanne thought about the officer's last words. Maybe. Just maybe she might. But the elation of safety, courage, and strength filled her for now. Tomorrow was a new day. She felt like Scarlett O'Hara. Tomorrow, she'd pick up her mama and begin her new life. Perhaps, here in Bay Town and not Meridian. Roxanne looked forward to a good night's sleep as she crossed the Bayou La Croix once more. A slight shiver shook her, but the thought of home comforted her even more.

CHAPTER 19

After taking action against Dwayne yesterday, Roxanne slept soundly, and woke early on Tuesday morning. She expected to pick up her mother today. Hopefully there wouldn't be any more setbacks, but as anxious as Roxanne was for her mother's return, she appreciated the extra physical rehab her mother had been receiving.

Sipping a cup of coffee, she watched the flittering birds outside the kitchen window. Realizing she wore only a camisole and sleep shorts, she stepped away from the window. Her cell rang.

"Good morning, Mama." Roxanne smiled. "Are you ready to come home?"

"Well, you sound refreshed. I'm glad. Heaven knows you needed a good night's sleep."

Roxanne pressed the speaker button as she walked to the bathroom. Peering into the mirror, she touched her face. The bruises were already healing. Maybe stress did have something to do with wreaking havoc on one's body. Her face appeared better already, and the lethargic heaviness that plagued her body had left her. She stared at herself. *Would it last?*

"Roxanne? Are you still there?"

"Oh, sorry, Mama, yes, and I feel wonderful."

"Good, then come pick me up. The doctor's already been by. He said I'm ready to go."

"Can you give me a few minutes? I still need to shower."

"All right, dear. I'll see you in an hour or so."

She took a quick shower and toweled off. Turning to the mirror, she applied a slight foundation coverage and added a little blush to perk her up, but when she pulled out her lipstick, she stared at the glaring red and threw it in the trash. Instead, she bit her lips a little, adding fresh, natural color to the surface. A few shots of hot air blew dry her tangled mane, and a quick comb through made it shine. She finger-combed her bangs, thinking she might keep them after all. Not something to hide behind, but a new look. A new her.

A gray suitcase still lay on the floor, and she dug out a light sundress, thin straps, loose and free. She slipped it on and swung around in front of the full-length mirror. *It's perfect*, she thought, because *Dwayne hated it.* She laughed but stopped and stared at herself. Fading, purple marks striped her arms in a few places. She stroked the bruising.

Behind her reflection, she caught her Bible on her night-stand and turned. Her concentration persisted on Dwayne, but she needed to focus on God. Walking to her bedside, she picked up the worn turquoise book and let it fall open to the Psalms. Her old friend. As she bowed, she said a prayer of thanks and read. She kept reading.

RING. RING.

Roxanne picked up. "Sorry, Mama. I'm on my way."

"Did you fall asleep or something?"

"No, I got lost in the Psalms." Her voice lilted.

Silence. A sniffle, and Bethie Cook cleared her throat. "Well, sweetheart, take all the time you need. I love you, dear, and welcome home."

Roxanne sniffed a little too. "Thanks, Mama. See you soon."

Running downstairs, Roxanne stopped at the hallway

mirror. A light-weight, knit shawl hung beside it. Her mother loved to knit and had one in every color. This white one matched the sundress, and she grabbed it, covering her shoulders and arms.

After check-out procedures, Roxanne wheeled her mother to the exit. They said their goodbyes, and Bethie promised to bring her sweet potato pie for all the workers at the rehab facility. Some even wiped a tear as she left.

"Well, dear? What's on the agenda? Shall we go out to eat? It's a beautiful day."

"Whatever you'd like, Mama." Roxanne stared at her hands and raised her fingers to look more closely. "Hey, how about a mani-pedi?"

"What's that, dear?"

"Oh, Mama, surely you know."

Her mother waved a hand. "Of course I do. But I do my own nails." She flashed them before Roxanne's eyes. "But I guess I could go for a pedicure and lunch."

"You got it. Shall we go see Tina at her salon?"

"Tina works at a salon? I can't keep up with that woman. I thought she worked for her husband?"

"She's the first person I met when I arrived." Roxanne touched her face, feeling more comfortable without a heavy layer of coverage.

"Well, I'd rather go to my beauty shop on Second Street."

"You still going there?" She glanced at her mother's flattened bouffant hair and chuckled. "Of course. I'll take you there now."

Roxanne reveled in the afternoon of normalcy. First, the beauty shop, and then lunch at a local diner that her mother loved. Everyone knew her mom, and the excitement of little Roxanne returning to Bay Town echoed from the familiar old friends. Although they'd aged, and so had she, the way they fussed over her, she felt like the little freckled face girl with long pigtails. She'd been gone too long.

Arriving home in the early afternoon, Bethie exclaimed exhaustion, and Roxanne helped her to bed for a nap. Roxanne walked to her room and felt like writing but plopped on her bed. She'd have to use pen and paper. Why hadn't she ever invested in a laptop? Because she preferred to write on her PC at home. At least until she'd met Dwayne, and when she considered buying another PC and laptop, he had interfered in her life. Crossing her arms, she felt a familiar ache in one wrist. No. She couldn't blame it all on Dwayne. That old PC brought her comfort. An old friend now gone, and the flash drive she'd saved everything on it too.

She thought of Travis. It hadn't been two months, but he had the single copy of her manuscript, and she was ready to write. Running to the living room, she retrieved her phone from her purse and called Travis. It rang, then went to voicemail.

"Hey, Travis. This is Roxanne. I'd like my manuscript back. I'd really like to work on it, now. Hope you are well. Thanks for your help. Call me, please."

She hung up just as she heard a knock at the front door. Flinging it open, she smiled, her heart lifting, and a flutter wrestling in her stomach.

"Hey, Max."

He grinned back, and his chest rose and fell as he waved a hand and nodded.

They stared a few moments before he spoke. "Sorry to bother you. I came home for lunch and thought I would check on your mum. Did she come home today?"

"She did. Would you like to come in?"

"Only for a moment. Here you go." He held out a rolled newspaper. "I've been collecting the daily rag for your mum."

"Thanks. I miss this old rag."

"Well, it's not the same. They've gone online, so the print copy has fewer events and articles."

"Good to know." She laid it aside. "So, Mama is fine. Just resting."

"Glad to hear it. May I barbecue for you both tonight? Or perhaps you need to think about it."

"That would be wonderful."

"Why, Roxy, what's come over you? You used to be Miss Indecisive."

She hit his arm playfully. "Hey. I made some decisions. I went to college, moved away, got a job. How is that for indecisive?"

"Right, and you chose wisely. Teaching is a good profession. My Philippa did it for years until her writing took off." He winked. "And yours will too."

Roxanne nodded. "It took a long time to make this move to quit my job and dedicate some time to writing." *Just a beating,* she thought, and shivered inside.

"Well, that's decisive. Can I help in any way?"

She shrugged and glanced around. Her eyes rested on her mother's PC in the corner. Walking over to it, she beckoned Max to follow.

"I'd forgotten all about that. Do you know if Mama ever uses it?" she asked, forgetting Max's question.

"Yes. I taught her how to check emails and look at the news. She's showed me your emails with your writing attached."

Roxanne sucked in a breath and coughed. "What?" Dwayne had messed with her head and her writing. "I forgot that I'd done that." She walked to the PC and turned it on.

"No password?"

Max stood behind her. "No, your mum said she couldn't remember it, and no one else here used her computer anyway."

Roxanne stroked the keys. "Oh, Max. This is amazing. Thank you." She felt like kissing him but thought better of it.

"When Mama wakes up, I'll ask if she can retrieve them for me."

Max laughed. "Maybe you should wait till I return this evening. I don't think she can do that."

"Good idea. Thanks."

"Right then. Looking forward to it."

Me too. Roxanne sighed and watched as he strolled back across the street, and for a moment, she felt safe. Perhaps Bay Town might be the place for her to stay. Walking to the kitchen, she laid the paper on the table before the window seat. Birds flitted at the feeder, and the chirping lifted her spirits even more. She opened the fridge and grabbed a bottle of water.

Roxanne stretched out on the window seat, sipping her water. She opened the paper, just four pages long. She enjoyed reading the few editorials about town council meetings and articles highlighting the shops in town. The last page listed HELP WANTED. Her eyes stopped on Bay Town Public Library, Volunteers Needed.

Picking up her phone, she dialed the library but reached a recording. She hung up, grabbed her purse, and left to go apply in person.

"Hi, I'm Roxanne Cook, and I'd like an application for the volunteer position." She·smiled at the librarian and leaned to her right, looking past her, wondering if the sour old librarian from years ago remained. The bright, fresh, younger woman at the desk looked behind her.

"I'm the Head Librarian here. Did you need someone else?"

"Oh. I wondered," she chuckled. "Miz Hancock isn't here anymore, is she?"

The woman smiled. "Well, I'm also Miz or Mrs. Hancock. You're referring to my husband's grandmother. But she passed many years back."

"I'm sorry to hear that." Not the friendliest person, but old

Miz Hancock assured a familiar security like many things in Bay Town. "But I'm glad you're keeping it in the family."

"Yes, well, sometimes I think that's why she approved her grandson to marry me." She winked. "She knew I graduated with a master's degree in library science."

"I've never heard of that discipline of study."

"Most people don't. But we aren't all old spinster school-marm types." She chuckled, but when Roxanne didn't, she winced. "Are you a schoolteacher? Because we love teachers here. I'm sorry. What a thoughtless statement."

"Spinster, yes. School Marm, yes, but I'm ..." she hesitated. "I'm a writer now."

Mrs. Hancock's eyes widened, and a look of admiration covered her face. "That's wonderful. What do you write?"

Roxanne felt a need to explain before more questions arose. "Well, I write romance, but I'm not yet published. Someone's helping me to edit now."

"So, you have a finished manuscript? That's amazing. Please let me know if I can help. I read ARCs for authors, Advanced Reader Copies. I can do some proofing too." Her voice trailed as she looked past Roxanne. A line had formed.

"Here." She pushed an application form forward. "Fill this out. I do the hiring. What's your name again?"

"Roxanne Cook, I grew up here."

"Bethie Cook's your mama?"

Chuckling inside, Roxanne thought Mama should run for mayor. "Yes."

"Why, she attends our weekly book clubs."

Someone's throat cleared behind Roxanne.

"Just fill this out and call me tomorrow. The position is yours." She winked. "We'll talk more later."

Roxanne stepped aside, filled out the application, turned it in, and left. Stepping outside, she fanned her neck but turned her face to the late afternoon sun while relishing her life's new turn.

CHAPTER 20

That night, Max came over, and after dinner, he retrieved Roxanne's manuscript from her mother's computer. He offered to help work on it, and one evening turned into another. Almost every evening except Sundays. Max and her mother frequented Sunday morning and evening services without her, and Roxanne had made excuses not to attend.

But as a month passed, Max came and went just about every night after work, taking time to read each chapter out loud. His clipped British accent brought life to every character. With every intimate scene, butterflies swam in her stomach. Who were these characters she created? She thought she knew them well, but as she listened and gazed at Max, she wondered. Had he been her protagonist's romantic interest all along? She stared, barely noticing that he'd stopped reading.

"Roxy? Helloooo. I'm all finished, dear."

A hand waved in front of her face. It held scars from the beautiful stems that left faint red lines. She admired every one of them until he called her name, and her focus turned to his lips. A friendly, almost permanent smile and a healthy pinkish bit of color smiled back at her.

She took a breath. Had she made him her hero in the book? No, her hero sported youth and vitality. Staring back at

Max, she saw maturity, vibrance, and joy. *Those are still not bad qualities for a hero.* She sighed.

"Roxy?"

"Oh, yes?"

"We're finished. Did my voice bore you into a trance?" He chuckled. "Philippa said it did."

"No. Not at all." *Well, maybe a little. A tender trance.* Perhaps dreaming of a new hero in her books, her life. "Did you read to her often?" The romantic notion made her imagine floating on a cloud.

"All the time." He sighed.

All the time to Philippa and now to her.

"So, my dear, I'll let you have at it then. I best be going." He stood.

"Oh, we can do another chapter, can't we?" She sounded almost too desperate. She didn't want the tender evening to end, or more so, for Max to leave.

He smiled. "Well, you can, but I must get to bed. I'm off to the flower market early in the morning."

Roxanne smiled. *Flower Market?* She envisioned a street lined with baskets of colorful flowers like the scene from the movie, *My Fair Lady.*

"It's my day to go into New Orleans. The market opens at dawn, and if I want the best pick of the bunch, I must be there just before."

"Can I go?" Roxanne asked abruptly.

Max raised his brows. "I don't see why not. It's a lovely sight. I'll be leaving at 4:30 in the morning. If you're still serious about it, meet me then." He held her gaze for a moment, before glancing away. "I'll let myself out, but I'll see you bright and early."

The door closed, and Roxanne whooshed out a held breath. She touched her chest as if calming her fluttering heart. *Yes, bright and early.*

∼

The quiet Wednesday morning car ride lulled Roxanne to sleep. She awoke to Max gently jostling her.

"We've arrived," he whispered.

Roxanne opened her eyes, stretched, and used her sleeve to dab at the side of her mouth. She shrunk down, embarrassed that drool dribbled from her lips while she'd slept. Before she knew it, Max had run around and opened her car door, offering his hand. As she took it, her eyes grew wide as saucers. The hustle, the bustle. Vans and trucks everywhere. And the smell, the colors. An exhilaration of senses bombarded her. Sweet floral, spicy, clean green scents. All shades of lavender and blue. Pops of red and yellow on flowers she'd never seen before.

"Oh my. This should be a mandatory field trip."

"Ah. That's the school teacher in you. Let's see if we can arouse the writer in you. Philippa always brought a notepad. She wrote down everything she felt. Some of what she saw, but mostly how this place aroused her."

Roxanne pulled out her phone. "I can take notes here."

Max reached out. "May I?"

She frowned but handed him her phone. He took it from her and deposited it in his pocket. He retrieved a small, brown notebook from his clipboard and handed it to her. "Now, I hope you have the ancient apparatus to accompany this little booklet." He winked, "A pen? Or even a pencil. Perhaps you can sketch some things."

"What's wrong with using my phone to take notes?"

"You're not taking notes but recording your experiences. Let your heart embrace everything here, Roxy. Seeing an array like this in their natural habitat is the only thing more beautiful." He swept his arms wide.

She followed the motion of his hands, and the covered outdoor market spread out before her. Digging for a pen, she pulled out a crayon. *How long had that been there?* Always the teacher, but now the student.

Roxanne followed Max and listened to every word as he spoke with vendors. Greeting many by their names, giving a friendly pat on the back to some, and hugging others, he appeared well-liked.

Roxanne admired his affection for people.

He picked up a stem and sniffed. He twirled flowers between his fingers. He sometimes flicked the buds, but if the vendors objected, he'd pull out a bill, purchasing the abused stem.

The flower market still bustled with masses of customers, but an hour later Max couldn't fit another flower into the back of his van. It burst with buckets of roses, peonies, gerber daisies, and flowers that Roxanne didn't know the names of. Greens were stuffed in other containers, secured in an apparatus to keep buckets from tumbling over. Max had parked near a water hose, and filled each pail just enough to keep the flowers fresh until they arrived home.

"Shall we go, then?" He opened the van door and ushered her in.

"That was amazing." Roxanne turned, looking at the array behind her. She breathed deeply. "Thank you, Max." Staring down at her notes, she tried deciphering her scribble, surprised that she could read it. Her face must have shown it because Max chuckled.

"May I suggest you transfer those notes to a Word document as quickly as possible before you can't read them anymore?"

Roxanne crinkled her nose.

"Philippa learned that lesson."

Roxanne looked around for her presence, knowing she wouldn't find her. She glanced at him, and suddenly became aware of how much he still grieved his wife's passing.

"It's like God gives you these beautiful thoughts and

images, but you may lose them if you don't preserve them for posterity. Flowers attract us to their beauty and nature. The lovely, seemingly perfect creations."

"I'll do that. Thank you."

The hot sun shone brightly, so much so that Max turned up the air-conditioning, and Roxanne shivered. He reached behind him and grabbed his jacket.

"Here you go. Toss this on, then. Sorry, I must keep the air cool for the flowers back there." He chuckled again. "Do you mind if I drive to the shop and drop these off?"

Roxanne didn't mind and helped him unload at The Pink Rosette. When they'd finished, he looked at his watch and frowned. "Oh, my, later than I thought. Right-O, let's get you home then."

She smiled. "You know, Max, I'll walk to the Mockingbird and get some coffee. I'll call Mama to join me for breakfast, and she can take me home." She gulped in a last whiff of the perfumed air. "Thank you again. I really enjoyed the morning."

His outstretched arms welcomed her, and she leaned in for a hug, just like old times. But different. Just the two of them stood embraced, surrounded by flowers.

"Oh, you two. Caught you." Virginia squealed from the doorway.

The exchange was so quick that Roxanne's flushed face didn't have time to recover.

"Shall I come back later?" Virginia winked.

"No, I'm just leaving," Roxanne said.

Max didn't seem fazed and waved. "I'm sorry, Virginia. I'm running late. I'll have your red roses ready for you in thirty minutes."

Virginia seemed to have forgotten what she'd witnessed, or it didn't matter. "Okey, dokey. I'll be back to pick up my roses in a few. Gotta finish opening up my shop too. See y'all later."

Max began arranging Virginia's flowers, but Roxanne

stood uncomfortably, not wanting to leave his side. She stared while he worked, and he caught her. Their gazes locked. "Thank you, Roxy, for joining me. I relished having someone on that long drive again."

"I wasn't much company. Sorry I fell asleep."

"As did Philippa when she went." His eyes glistened.

Roxanne's shoulders drooped. "You miss her a lot, don't you?"

"I do." He blinked. "But life goes on. And God brought you back. Phillipa would be thrilled that we've reacquainted after all these years. I'm glad you're here, Roxy."

She'd spent so much time with Max since she'd returned she couldn't deny the growing attraction. Even more so with each additional day. Reacquainted. Like old friends. Maybe God's plans included an old friend right now.

Roxanne cleared her throat. "I better be going. But can I bring you a cup of coffee?"

"No, thanks." He bent over a bucket of beauties. "Enjoy your day, and thanks again for joining me. So lovely having you."

A flutter rose in her spirit, and she pressed a hand to her chest. "Thank you, Max. Have a nice day."

Walking the distance of Main Street, Roxanne reached the Mockingbird Café, the morning crowd filled the shop. She walked through the door, and instead of roasted coffee, she smelled the aroma of freshly baked pastries. The rich, buttery sweetness called her name. The last in line, when she finally reached the counter, she couldn't decide.

"You should try one. They're the best." A large, dark-skinned woman greeted her.

"Oh, I don't know. They're probably a million calories." Roxanne stared at the name tag. "Jacquie, did you make them?"

"I'm too busy to bake, but our baker, he's from New Orleans. Mmm. Mmm."

"You sold me. I'll take a chocolate croissant, please, and a small vanilla latte."

"You got it." Jacquie packaged the croissant and rang up the order on an old-fashioned register. "You from around here, ma'am?"

"I used to be. I just returned."

"All by yourself or with family?" Jacquie asked.

Roxanne frowned.

"No worries. I'm all by myself. Except for my daughter."

"Just the two of you?" Roxanne asked.

"Just the two of us. I got rid of my deadbeat ex a long time ago."

Roxanne stared back and wondered what she meant by deadbeat. Dwayne defined deadbeat. A violent one. But Jacquie didn't look like the sort of woman anyone could abuse. *Was there a look? Did she look like it?*

"I'm originally from Northern Mississippi, but we moved here quite some time ago." She handed the bag over. "Here you go, ma'am. I'll call you when your drink is up."

"Thanks, Jacquie."

Roxanne found a comfy club chair by the window and waited for her order. ce4t The bells rang as people came and went. She glanced at the free local paper on the table, read a few pages, and reached for her phone. Missing. A momentary panic rose, and she emptied the contents of her purse before realizing that Max had it. Warmth spread, happy that she'd need to see him again before she left. A deep breath caused an unuttered expression of thankfulness, but a sweet cooing trill interrupted.

"Well, good morning, everyone." Tina stood at the entrance. She smiled and waved like a Mardi Gras parade queen.

All eyes turned toward her, and voices yelled back, "Hey there, Tina."

She wore a white maxi-dress made of simple cotton eyelet

lace. The ruching from the waist to the bustline accentuated her trim waist, and a string tie hung from a peephole. The short, puffed sleeves added sweetness. Tina's signature ombre curls were combed out to a full, wavy mane. Roxanne wished she had the confidence to dress with such flair.

When Tina saw Roxanne, she said, "Save me a seat."

Jacquie called out Roxanne's order, and she picked it up. Tina did the same. Roxanne frowned.

"How'd you get yours so fast? I've been here for more than a few minutes."

"Oh, honey. They know me here. Just wait. When you're a regular, yours will be ready every time you walk in that door."

Tina squinted. "Your bruising is gone. Or else, you're applying that foundation as well as I do. Girl, you're going to put me out of business." She followed Roxanne back to the chairs by the window. "Seriously, how are you, sweetie?"

If she didn't know Tina's compassionate heart, she'd think this could turn into fuel for town gossip. Still, she wasn't ready to talk.

"I'm good. I volunteered at the library and I'm checking out a few critique groups." She might as well spill her life now. She'd already done some of it with Pastor Brooks.

"For what? Is that like a support group? I'm so glad. We all need support. Honey, I hope you're staying away from whoever did that to you." She whispered the last words, stroking the skin around her large, almond-shaped eyes.

Roxanne slumped. "A critique group is for writers."

Tina's mouth gaped. "Oh, my goodness. Silly me. There I go again, sticking my big foot in my mouth. So, are you a writer?" She waved her hand, and her glittery gold nails sparkled. "Of course you are. You won that contest. So, what do you write, dear?"

Sinking further into the chair, she wished she could climb under it. "Romance."

Tina squealed. "I love romance. Oh my, that Hallmark

channel? Why, it drives my Rudy crazy. But what I really love is a good tearjerker. You know those sad, bittersweet endings. Hey, have you ever seen 'Waterloo Bridge'? It's an old black and white with Vivian Leigh and Robert Taylor."

Roxanne gaped, trying to follow the conversation.

Tina's eyes watered. She dabbed at the corners. "You'll have to come watch with me. I've seen it a hundred times and I blubber all over the place every time. Lacey Thompson used to watch those old movies with me. But she's getting married, so my movie nights are over. Rudy doesn't much like those old classics." She touched Roxanne's arm. "So, what's your story about?"

Roxanne didn't know where to start. She taught creative writing to young students but never mastered the synopsis.

"It's about unrequited love, I guess."

"Do tell, but not the ending."

"It's about a young woman who is a writer, in love with a military man." Roxanne sucked in a breath. "They plan to marry, but he dies in a training accident. She's devastated, so she pours everything into her career, and of course, she becomes rich and famous. She falls in love with an older man, a landscaper at a big estate, who happens to be someone she knew when she was young."

"Oh, like her writing professor or something?"

"Not really." *But sort of.* Tina seemed good at guessing. "But her agent plots to tear them apart."

"Wait a minute. I bet the gardener is like a proper English gentleman, right? I mean, why else would she fall for him?"

"Right," Roxanne said.

She fingered the sleeve of her coffee cup. *Perhaps it's too predictable.* She sucked in a breath. Oh no. Max had been reading it aloud. What did he think?

"Don't tell me anymore. I just want a good cry."

"Right. Well, I should be going now. I have to stop by Max's."

"Oooh! Is he the older gentleman in your book?"

Roxanne blushed. "I need to call Mama for a ride."

Tina winked. "Let me take you home. I'm headed to the salon, anyway." She stood, towering over Roxanne in her four-inch espadrilles.

Stepping outside, they stopped short at a shouting couple inside a parked car. Roxanne cringed. The man flung open his door and slammed it. He cursed, and the woman huddled in the car, arms crossed. Loping around to her side, he yanked her door open.

CHAPTER 21

The woman screamed, tumbling into the street. Roxanne shuddered and froze. But Tina shoved her purse at Roxanne and rushed to the woman's aid. The man stuck out his hand, stopping her.

"Get your hand off me, and you get away from her. Roxanne, call the police," Tina yelled.

"Go ahead," The man said. "I'll be gone before you get your phone out." He tried to kick at the girl, but Tina shoved him, and he lost his balance, hitting his head against the car parked beside him. He leaned, stunned.

Tina bent, helping the woman. "Come on, sweetie, come with me."

The man shook his head and stood tall. Just as he reached for Tina, a siren squealed.

"Hold it right there, man," a policeman called out. The Hispanic man in uniform again. This time, in his squad car.

"Chief Bert. Boy, are we glad to see you." Tina gave Roxanne a thumbs up but walked the girl toward the Chief of Police.

"You all right, ma'am?" He kept his eyes on the man. "Sit on the curb."

The man moved to sit but looked back, and his eyes

connected with Roxanne's. She tried to look away, but terror gripped her as he stepped toward the sidewalk. Cringing, Roxanne stepped backward, stumbling into the brick building behind her. She had no place to go.

"Honey?" Tina called out. "You're fine. Nobody's going to hurt you."

"Who are you talking to?" Chief Bert asked.

Tina nodded towards the building. "Roxanne."

Chief Bert turned to the man. "Hands on your head, now. And stay there." He placed the girl in his squad car. "Sit tight, ma'am. Just taking precautions here."

Roxanne stared at the shivering woman and glanced down at her shaking frame. She wrapped her arms around her waist and gripped herself, sliding to the ground. She hated herself for cowering, but flashbacks sparked her brain. She stared at the man on the sidewalk. She didn't trust him.

"I said hands on your head," Chief Bert bellowed.

The man complied but sneered at Roxanne. He broke into a mocking laugh. "You're all the same."

Roxanne closed her burning eyes and dropped her head on her knees.

Tina rushed to her side. "Honey, what's wrong?" Taking her shoulders, Tina nudged her to stand.

Chief Bert cuffed the man and returned him to the curb. He retrieved the woman in the car and brought her out, walking her to Tina and Roxanne. Looking up, Roxanne caught shame in the woman's frightened face. They both glanced away. Like whipped puppies cowering with tails between their legs. Did Dwayne see that in her when he beat her? She glanced at the man sitting on the curb. Noticing his rigid frame forced her to stand.

"Watch her for me, ladies." The chief pulled the man from the curb and planted him in the squad car.

"I didn't do anything. You can't keep me," he yelled.

Chief Bert said something inaudible, and keeping their

conversation subdued. The man quieted as if he knew anything he said might incriminate him. The one-sided conversation continued but the man didn't appear to be listening. Finally, Chief Bert removed the cuffs, led him to the driver's side of his car, and opened the door. The man slid in, still silent.

"Your visit to Bay Town is over. I don't want to see you here again."

"Fine, I didn't want to come in the first place," He said, directing his comment to the huddled woman.

Roxanne forced herself to watch his departing car. Like closure whenever she watched Dwayne leave. Temporary relief. The other woman also gazed toward the retreating driver. *Pathetic*, thought Roxanne. She gulped. *Just like me.*

"Honey, how can we help? Do you have family in town?" asked Tina.

"No, I just met him in Biloxi last night, and we…well, we decided to visit Bay Town this morning."

"Oh, honey, that man is bad news. Stay away from him."

"But he seemed so nice. And he said such sweet things."

Chief Bert took off his hat and hit his legs. "Ma'am, you owe this lady some thanks. She saved you. Don't you go running back to that guy. I see the end result of this too many times."

Roxanne blew out a breath she didn't realize she held. "They're right. It happened to me," she whispered.

The woman's eyes widened. "What?"

A dry throat made it hard to swallow. "He almost killed me," Roxanne said. "He put me in the hospital, and I couldn't even remember the beating. That's when I came back here. I ran away from him."

Tina gasped. She placed a hand over her mouth.

"Did he follow you?" the woman asked.

"He's in jail," Roxanne said.

"Oh, for Pete's sake," Chief Bert blustered. "And you were going to tell me this when? What's your name?"

Tina slapped at his arm. "Give her a minute, Chief. She's Roxanne Cook. Bethie's daughter."

He nodded. "I'll write my report over there. You okay here?" Chief Bert pointed. "Miss Cook, we just met, but I think for your safety, you might come talk to me at the police station when you get a chance."

She stared at him in disbelief. "But my …" she didn't know what to call him. *Ex-boyfriend?* "He's not from Bay Town. He doesn't know I'm here."

"Don't put anything past those kinds of men," the chief said.

Suddenly, she clutched at her purse. The restraining order. She'd been carrying copies around all month. Slipping a hand into her shoulder bag, she pulled out the papers, separated one copy, and handed it to the chief. "Here."

He opened the paper, read it, and looked at the other woman. His eyes bore into her. "This is a restraining order. I suggest you get one too."

"We can help her." Tina jammed fisted hands on her hips. "How do we do it?"

"Go to Hancock Court House and file. The altercation happened here with witnesses, so you can do that. Otherwise, go to the town where you live."

"No. I can't," the woman whispered.

Tina patted her arm. "Honey, Chief Bert, here? Why, he takes good care of us, and he knows what he's talking about."

"I can't because I don't know his last name or where he lives."

Oh my. I'm not that bad, thought Roxanne. But when their eyes connected, the woman immediately looked down and Roxanne felt ashamed for judging.

"I think it's time I introduced both of you to The Refuge," Tina said. "They have some nice women to talk to there."

They shook their heads.

"Just listen. Talk is all. No one will make you do anything you don't want to do. Not like those...those...those monsters." She thrust out her hand, a pointed finger landing in Chief Bert's direction.

"Not me. But she's right. Listen to the smart woman." He slipped into his squad car.

"No. I'm not going to any place like that. I'll be fine," the woman said. She straightened and stood tall.

"Fine, honey." Tina huffed a breath that fluttered her lips. "Let me give you a lift, then. Anywhere but back to him."

She lowered her eyes. "He's not that bad. He just had a hangover. I'm the one who wanted to come here. He just didn't want to, but I nagged him too much."

"Whatever," Tina said, "but he has no business treating you like that."

"I can take care of myself, thank you. You didn't need to help. I'll just take the bus to Biloxi." She threw her shoulders back.

Roxanne's shoulders dropped. She could predict what the poor woman would say next. She'd reasoned the same way too many times. And too many times, she'd refused the help loving people offered. *But what if I go with her?* Together, they could get help. Go to the Refuge, as Tina suggested. Roxanne lingered on the thought but couldn't find her voice.

"Thank you, though." The woman pulled away, and she stepped in the direction of the bus terminal.

"Wait. Can I pray for you?" Tina's soothing southern voice returned.

The young lady stopped, and her quiet voice replied over her shoulder, "No, no, thank you. I'm fine."

Tina stared, and so did Roxanne. Finally, Tina took Roxanne's hand and squeezed. She began to pray, asking God to intervene in the woman's life. She asked for protection, wisdom, and God to draw her close. Tina finished by praying for the man. That God would grab hold and shake him. A forceful but final Amen and she turned to Roxanne.

"And you, my dear." She looked into Roxanne's eyes. Not the pathetic look she often received from those who knew her story. "That is quite a testimony." She raised her hand. "You are a brave soul. Give me five there, sister."

Roxanne tapped Tina's palm. "Brave? I don't think so. I'm just like her." She gazed back at the sad soul.

Tina grabbed her shoulders. "You left him. You walked away. No, you ran. That's brave, that's strong."

A chuckle caught in her throat, and Roxanne wanted to laugh. "No one's ever called me that before. I let him beat me so badly that I landed up in the hospital. Then I ran."

"You didn't let him do anything. He's an abuser, and you were his victim. Now it's time to take the next step, don't you think?"

"Maybe. Soon." She wanted to agree to go check out this Refuge, but not yet. She smiled at Tina. "How do you do that?"

"Do what?"

"Jump in and save people? Pray for strangers?"

Tina giggled. "No. I'm usually a puddle of tears. But my goodness, when he yanked her arm I had to do something. Anyway, I do pray for strangers all the time. Sometimes it's the only thing I can do. I should have been praying when I jumped in to help, but I forgot. It's a good thing you called 911."

"But I didn't."

"What? You mean Chief Bert just showed up?"

"I guess he did," said Roxanne.

"Wow. Well, isn't that just amazing how God works? He delivered the chief to help us."

"Yes. Yes, He did." But something that felt like resentment rose inside her. *But God's never came to my rescue.* Yet it didn't linger as she recalled all those who had. Her neighbor, Lucy, and all the people she'd met and reconnected with in Bay Town.

The women walked to the Pink Rosette before leaving, but Max had a "Be Back Soon" sign on his window, so Tina drove Roxanne home. As they passed the bus terminal, Tina slowed. With the top down on her white Solara convertible, Tina pointed to the young woman sitting on a bench. She held her phone to her ear, giggling as if she didn't have a care in the world. Roxanne stared sympathetically and said a prayer for her.

Tina dropped Roxanne off at her house, and she trudged up the walk with her heart heavy for the woman on the street. She glanced down as she unlocked her door and saw her cell phone hiding behind a potted plant. Thoughtful Max. Picking it up, she entered the house.

"Mama?" No answer.

A flutter stirred inside her. Fearful that her mother could have had another stroke or episode, Roxanne rushed for the refrigerator, hoping there would be a note left for her. She breathed a sigh of relief and grabbed the flower bordered note. A friend had picked up Mama, and they'd gone to the church to help make meals for housebound people in the community. Roxanne chuckled and her chest swelled. Her mama, so active and caring. Always a thought for serving others.

Serving. Roxanne glanced at her watch. She had to get ready for her volunteer work at the library, and today, she looked forward to teaching a memoir writing class for seniors. Changing into a slim navy polka dot skirt and a white tee, she freshened up, and headed to the library, thankful for the distraction from the afternoon's events.

∽

They had a full house for the Senior Writing Group at the library. Though the group was open to everyone, only women were present.

"So, everyone seems to be coming along quite nicely. I think it's time to start reading aloud. I'll pass around the calendar for the next two months. Please choose two dates to read your chapters. We can have two readers per date." Roxanne handed the paper to Sally Trotman on her left.

"I don't need to read." She passed the sign-up sheet.

"Why not?" asked Roxanne.

"I'm just here for posterity's sake. My story will never be published. Besides, it's more about my founding ancestors who settled in Bay Town. It's not really my memoirs."

"But Miz Trotman, that's a valuable contribution. Of course, we should publish it."

"We? Are you in the publishing business? Because I certainly don't have the energy to see this through." Sally Trotman crossed her arms.

Looking at the other women, Roxanne noticed the sheet passing without signatures. Dejected faces stared back at her. Not like the youthful innocence of children who were ready to print their stories after the first draft, wanting all the world to read their scribbled dreams.

"No, I'm not," Roxanne said. "But I'm learning a lot about the publishing industry. I've heard about many writers who self-publish. We could look into that after we complete our manuscripts here."

Smiles and bright eyes lifted on the faces looking back at her, and one person signed the sheet, then another as it went round the table.

"So, what if we do publish them? Who will buy them?" Sally challenged. "All that useless work."

Roxanne's old demons were coming back to haunt her. *What if the editor doesn't like it? And even if she gets published, what if no one buys her book?* The passing of the sign-up stalled again.

All eyes were on her like a losing football team staring at their coach at half-time. She drew back her shoulders.

"Most people never even finish writing their book. That's the first step we'll focus on for now." She waved at the sheet. "Keep signing. And as for publishing, let me worry about that."

"Who will pay for that?" a frowning, white haired woman gripping her pearl necklace asked.

Renewed strength charged through Roxanne as she thought of the small inheritance that her father had left her. She looked at Sally Trotman and winked.

"Oh, no. You're not going to ask your mama. That woman has funded more projects than this town deserves. That's all I need is to be beholden to her again." Sally waved a hand.

"But Bethie Cook is a saint." A quavering voice spoke from a sweet woman with a long gray braid. "She'd never hold anyone in her debt."

"She's my best friend, don't you think I know that?" Sally snapped back.

"Well, if you know that, then maybe it's just your pride that's holding you back." A woman with more wrinkles covering her face than smooth skin spoke. "Maybe you need to confess."

"Maybe I do, but it wouldn't be to you." Sally crossed her arms.

Roxanne held back a chuckle. After spending the last month with these seniors, she enjoyed the fun bantering with the feisty bunch.

"Yes, I do wish you would have taken her help before you closed down The Olde Book Shoppe." The stiff bouffant didn't move, but the head nodded. "Maybe you could have sold all our memoirs there."

"You haven't even written them yet." Sally's voice rose.

"Why, I think that's a wonderful idea," Roxanne said.

All eyes looked back at her.

"We'll have all the shops in Bay Town sell them." She looked at Sally and whispered, "And I wasn't thinking of Mama." Glancing at the clock, she nodded. "Well, ladies, I'll see y'all next week. Sally, could I have a word?"

"Oh, no, you don't. I'm not taking any charity. That bookshop's days are over."

"Why?"

Sally remained quiet for a few moments. "I'm tired, Roxanne, and I just want to enjoy my days. I tired of trying to compete with the big bookstores, not to mention the computer online businesses."

Roxanne smiled. "Online business thing, yes. But Miz. Trotman, will you pray about working with Mama and me to possibly reopen?" Roxanne almost couldn't believe she'd voiced that, and wondered where the idea came from. "I'm not working now, and I have the time. Besides, I grew up in that shop."

Sally's eyes watered a little. "Are you here to stay?"

It caught her off guard, and Roxanne bit her lip. "Perhaps."

Sally threw a wave at Roxanne as she started for the door. "Fine. How can I refuse to pray? I guess I'm afraid the Lord will say, go." She glanced back at Roxanne. "I think he said that back when your mama first offered. Maybe it is time for a little confession."

Roxanne thought how faithful these women were to the word of God. Prayer and confession. She had a lot to learn. It had been too long.

CHAPTER 22

C rackling hymn music filtered up the stairs and Roxanne chuckled. Her mother had always blasted her old FM radio on Sunday mornings. Bethie Cook's sweet voice warbled throughout the house reminding Roxanne that church was in order. She couldn't avoid going back anymore, and why should she?

Bad memories.

"Roxanne, please get up, dear." Bethie's sweet voice called up the stairs. "I won't be late for church."

Church. She promised her mom that she'd attend. It was time. "Yes, Mama." Roxanne forced her feet onto the bare floor.

The bay breeze hadn't cooled down the evening before, and the oscillating fan blew the light sheers in her room. She promised herself to get Mama's air-conditioning unit fixed.

She showered then pulled on a flowery sundress. Roxanne donned a Panama-style straw hat and floated down the stairs with her flat, strappy sandals in hand. Walking into the kitchen, she pecked her mother's cheek with a kiss.

"You keep taking two showers daily, and they'll cut our water off."

Bethie Cook sat sipping her coffee. She posed wearing a

simple, blue A-line sheath, with her handbag hanging on her elbow and white gloves clenched in one hand.

Roxanne poured herself a cup of coffee. "Well, if you'd fix the air-conditioner, we'd save on the water bill."

"And run up the electricity. Besides, I'm perfectly fine with a fan."

"Mama, once the heatwave hits, you'll melt. I'm calling someone tomorrow." Roxanne opened a bag of English muffins and reached for the toaster.

"Humph. We'll see." She stood. "No time for that. We'll have donuts at church."

"Oh yes. A jelly-filled, right?"

"Oh, I don't know. Maybe an old-fashioned today." Her mother grinned slyly.

Roxanne giggled. No one touched the jelly donut on Sunday morning. It had Bethie's name on it. Growing up at Bay Town Community Church with her mama and daddy brought back memories. Sweet ones until a dark cloud crossed her mind. After her dad passed, Roxanne had never gotten used to church without him. His sudden death had crippled her, and Bay Town Church brought painful reminders.

Bethie patted her shoulder. "Come, dear. It will be all right. I promise. Things have changed, you'll see."

Taking the car keys from her mother, she tried to smile, but bitterness crept in.

The closer they got to the church, the faster her heart beat. Roxanne's upper lip and every part of her body perspired. She'd be a dripping mess, even with the air-conditioning.

The white clapboard structure rose before her. Quaint and old, it used to bring her comfort. Not anymore. Thankfully, as they parked and walked to the entrance, the church had changed. First, the younger pastor on the front steps.

"Well, good morning, Mrs. Cook." Pastor Brooks shook

her hand, gave her a side arm hug, and smiled at Roxanne. "Welcome, Roxanne. Good to see you again."

She nodded and wished she could say the same. Stepping into the building, Roxanne welcomed the new sounds. An acoustic guitar backed by a bass guitar, a drummer, and a pianist played upbeat worship music. Roxanne looked around at the faces. Some smiling, some noses buried in the bulletin.

Her mother walked ahead, leading Roxanne to the front row. But the pews were still there, flanking the aisle, and Roxanne couldn't help feeling she should have been walking this aisle with…

"Hey, Roxy. Good to see you." Bubba stood. "You remember Karissa? She's my wife now."

Roxanne's eyes grew wide. "Yes, Karissa. You haven't changed a bit. You look great." The slender, stunning woman stood. A little heavy on the makeup, but still as beautiful as in High School. Roxanne glanced at Bubba. Once the football star, now many pounds heavier, but joyful as ever.

"Well, some of us try and keep it together." She glanced at Bubba while patting his tummy.

A stab hit Roxanne's heart, and she recalled years ago how Karissa, the cheerleader, didn't quite match Bubba's jolly demeanor. In high school nor now, it appeared.

Bubba laughed and stroked his long, red beard. "But you gotta admit, I clean up pretty nice?" He adjusted his bright purple tie.

Karissa did the eye roll thing, but she managed to smile.

"Yes, you do." Roxanne hugged them both. "I better run. Mama's waiting."

She passed Big Joe and met his wife and children. Many others she knew from years ago were still here. Most of whom would have been at her wedding. She turned and looked back up the aisle to the entrance.

"Come, Roxanne," her mother whispered as almost everyone took their seats.

The worship settled her heart, and an older woman stepped up and read the scripture passage. Roxanne listened as the woman read Psalm 30, but verse five hit too close to home, and she didn't hear much more of the passage but dwelt on the verse, "...*Weeping may last for the night, but a shout of joy comes in the morning.*"

Roxanne stared forward as if in a trance. Her mother's warm hand slipped into hers and pulled her down as everyone sat following the reading. Pastor Brooks' sermon spoke of joy. Bittersweet joy. He said you could only find joy in suffering when you anchored yourself in the Lord. He said that God's unchanging character would get you through the darkest valleys and that by drawing close to him in your time of suffering, you could choose joy leading to peace. Our choice, the pastor said. Would she ever find peace again?

He continued. If you chose joy, you could redirect your pain, as difficult as it may be. You could point others who experienced pain and suffering to God through your example, thereby finding joy and peace.

Use her pain to help others like her? Facing it head-on. She preferred burying it. But that hadn't worked. When everyone stood and sang the closing prayer, Roxanne's mind spiraled down. Escape. That had been her choice. She knew she should have focused on the message, but this building held painful visions. Maybe that's why she attended the mega church in Meridian. But even then, she hadn't gone regularly or at all in the last year.

With her head down, Roxanne trudged behind lingering parishioners. As she passed the polished wooden pews, she envisioned the baby's breath and ribbon that she and her bridesmaids had placed there for her wedding. She clenched her purse as she scooted by. "Excuse me. Thank you. Pardon me."

∼

Stepping out on the porch, Roxanne gasped for air. The hot summer morning blasted her face like a hair dryer and didn't bring much relief. She wound her way to the end of the porch and clung to a pillar.

"Roxy?"

She spun around. "Hey, Max." The hurt slipped away but didn't cease the impending waterworks.

Before the dam burst, she hugged him tightly. Not the churchy side arm hug, but a full embrace. She would have held him longer, buying time to gain control of herself, but his body stiffened.

She pulled back and glanced around. "Sorry, I forgot, we're at church."

Max nodded. "Not to worry." He touched her arm. "Are you all right?"

She shook her head.

"Right, then. Let's get coffee and take a seat under the tree."

She nodded and followed him out. They slipped past Pastor Brooks while he greeted everyone on their way out. She waited on the lawn for Max, her head lifted to the sky. Her brow furrowed as the cloudless blue blinded her. Just the kind of day on which she would have married. It would have been. She hadn't thought of that horrible blight in her life in a long time. Dwayne had overshadowed that nightmare by a long shot.

"That bad?" Max walked up with two steaming cups in his hands.

"I forgot my sunglasses, is all." She looked back at the church and released a sigh. "Yes, part of it. I haven't set foot in there since ..." She looked back at Pastor Brooks and pointed. "He knows how to get you, doesn't he?"

"Yes, I'm afraid so. But like he said, there's joy in sorrow."

He should know. Philippa had been gone for quite a while now. She nodded as Max pulled a nicely folded handkerchief from his blue jeans. It struck her as funny. *Who still carried a cloth hanky?*

"The joy is there. We have to trust Him for it." Max interrupted her thoughts.

"I don't know how to do that. Just being in that building made me think of him."

"Come with me." Max took her elbow and led her toward the old Pecan trees. A boy stood on a chair, his arms hanging from a thick branch. The children below squealed as he shook down pecans and they gathered them. Max redirected Roxanne to the wooden bench beneath the Sycamore. Even in the shade, the unbearable heat hung heavy.

"I saw him," Max said.

Roxanne stared back. She knew he meant Spencer. Her ex-fiancé.

She closed her eyes, but instead of blocking out his face, all the past flooded her mind. He'd been a mistake from the start. A rebound after her first serious boyfriend, Gregory. A stab hit her heart. She didn't know which memory hurt more. The shock of being left at the altar, figuratively, or the tragedy of her first love.

She'd met Gregory, a Marine, at a college Bible study group. Someone had brought him, and they fell in love fast. After dating for a few months, he got deployed but promised to return for her. He never did. When she got news of his being killed in a training accident, she felt her life ended. Worse than any book rejection.

"Roxy?" Max touched her shoulder.

"I'm sorry. What did you say?"

"I saw Spencer," Max repeated.

Might as well get this over with. But her anger, mixed with curiosity, propelled her. Still, it could bring her some closure. "He doesn't live around here, does he?"

"Waveland."

Just great. The next small town over.

"I counseled him."

"Yup. He told me so. And for a year after he dumped me, he hounded me."

"Hounded?" Max raised his brows.

"Called. Asked me to forgive him. Wanted me to take him back. Max, he left me. He caused my father's heart attack, you know." No one but her believed it.

"I'm sorry. Hurt lingers, doesn't it? And clearly, you've had your share, but he's still got a hold on you, doesn't he?"

"No, he doesn't." She shook her head, her hair swishing over her shoulders. "He didn't just hurt me. My broken heart broke Daddy's heart. I blame Spencer for that."

Max's blue eyes glistened. "Your father loved you deeply, but he had a medical condition."

Roxanne turned away. Sweat dripped down her temples. "Daddy couldn't stand seeing me hurt. Crying all the time. I even quit my job. But it wasn't just Spencer. Maybe I used him as an excuse. God made me so angry when he took Gregory away from me." There, she'd said it.

"Gregory?"

Her voice lowered. "A man I fell in love with in college. He died in a military training accident. I thought I could forget him if I married Spencer. But I never could. Daddy didn't know it, but I still mourned for Gregory when it all happened."

"I'm so sorry. I had no idea."

"I guess I didn't know it, either. I've never met anyone like him." Roxanne glanced at Max. *Except maybe you.* "Gregory loved God, and he loved me. Oh boy, did he love me. And I felt the same. We spent every minute we could together. But I lived in the dorm, and he lived on base. Still, he even introduced me to his family over the phone."

Tears fell, and Max took the hankie and wiped them.

Roxanne smiled. "He asked me to marry him, you know. Unofficially, of course, because of his deployment. We talked and dreamed about all the details. I hated that he had to leave, and I couldn't wait for his return. That's all I thought about until I got the news of his death."

Silence hung before Max quietly spoke. He took her hand. "You'll find your heart will open once more. You're young."

Roxanne laughed. "Young? Young back then. Not anymore. And I did open my heart. Look where it got me."

"I don't pretend to understand God's ways, nor the hurt you've lived. But instead of trying to understand, perhaps you might surrender. Seek Him in all things. You haven't experienced joy in sorrow, but it's there. Let God take care of it. He'll give you the grace."

She sniffed and rolled her eyes, but his words softened her heart.

"When I spoke with him, Spencer showed true repentance. He knew he'd made a mistake," Max said.

Roxanne gaped. "A mistake? I found him making out with another girl downtown the night before our wedding. Who knows where that led to?"

"It led nowhere. A foolish boy's prank. They shouldn't have done it, but his friends got him drunk. You know he didn't drink." Max raised his hands. "I know, I know, what kind of friends would do that? But no matter."

"No matter?" Her mouth gaped and her eyes rounded. "Seriously?"

"Wrong choice of words, but it doesn't matter now, does it? Truth be told, the girl agreed to take part in their tease. He never saw her again. Roxanne, he is truly repentant."

"Well, he couldn't repent from my daddy's death, could he?"

"I think that was the hardest for him to overcome."

"I can't believe you are on his side." She stood.

Max stood and reached for her hand. Congregants gawked. She didn't care. Allowing the hurt to envelop her again, she stared back. At this point, she wouldn't return to

Bay Town Community or any church. What kind of God would put her through this wreck of a life?

"Roxy, I'm on God's side first. And being on His side means I love you enough to tell you the truth. Unless you forgive this man, you're bound to live a life of bondage."

It hurt. His words stung because that's exactly what she felt like. Bondage. Bondage to Gregory and then to Spencer. Even to the memory of her deceased father. She swallowed hard. And now bondage to Dwayne.

She couldn't speak, but when he squeezed her hand, she felt the love. He loved her. Max always had. He and Philippa loved her, nurtured her, and had been there when her father died. And when she moved to Meridian, they'd been there for her mother. When she couldn't be.

His gaze held hers, and like the blue in God's beautiful creation, his eyes soothed her soul. Yes, Max had always been there for her. Would he? Could he, forever?

"Thank you." She wanted to express more but couldn't. "Can you give my mama a ride home? She'll want to stay for Sunday School." Roxanne raised her eyes. Sadness gripped every part of her. It stifled her more than the heat of the day.

"Of course, love."

He dropped her hand, and she walked to her car. Roxanne drove the short distance home and cried the entire way. She parked the car but left it running. The air conditioning cooled her bleeding heart. Pulling out her phone, she scrolled, looking for Spencer on social media. Her eyes widened as she clicked on a profile, but she quickly clicked off when pictures arose. He had a family. A happy family.

The tears turned to anger, and she threw her phone in her purse, shut off the car, and raged into the house. The heat assaulted her like a furnace, and she griped about the lack of air conditioning. Stomping through the house, she pushed open the windows and clicked on every fan. Her pulse raced, and she stormed to the kitchen sink. Flipping on the faucet, she slapped cold water on her face. She'd heard somewhere that was a surefire way to ward off an impending anxiety attack. She held more anger than anxiety. Still, the cool liquid helped.

Wiping her face, she looked up, gazing through the window. She watched birds flitting back and forth, rustling the trees. Her eyes slipped to a little plaque on the wall beside the window. *"Let the fields be jubilant, and everything in them; let all the trees of the forest sing for joy." Psalm 96:11-12.* She chuckled. Funny how God worked. Shrugging, she offered a silent prayer. "I'm sorry, Lord," and her heart lifted. It actually helped more than the cold water.

The doorbell rang.

CHAPTER 23

R oxanne opened the door to Melanie Brooks' smiling face.

"Hello, Roxanne."

She gulped but pushed open the screen door waving Melanie in. "I'm sorry, the air-conditioning is out. Come in if you'd like."

Melanie stepped in

"Would you like some sweet tea?" Roxanne asked.

"Yes, I'd love a glass, thank you. I'm sorry to intrude."

"Not at all." Roxanne poured two glasses in the kitchen and returned. She waved to the sofa, offered the tea, and sat opposite. "So, what can I do for you?"

"Max asked me to come by. He said you might need someone to talk to." She hunched her shoulders. "He cares an awful lot for you. You're blessed to have a friend like that."

"I know."

"It takes a lot of courage to seek after someone who is hurting so deeply."

"He told you?" Roxanne placed her glass on the side table.

"No, he wouldn't do that." She shrugged. "But your mother would. When you first returned, she worried about you and spoke to Pastor Brooks and me. She asked then if we could help, but we hoped you'd come ask if you needed it."

Roxanne rolled her eyes. "Oh, Mama."

"Please, don't be upset with her. I know what a mom feels."

You're younger than me. How could she possibly relate? Roxanne hurried to open another window. "Lacey, right? Your daughter?"

"Yes. I'm afraid I've been a bit of a helicopter mom, especially with all this wedding planning, and it doesn't help that it's my business."

"Well, with a wedding soon, there's a lot of tension. Especially between mothers and daughters." Although, she and her mom had nothing but sweetness until Spencer.

"You have that right. Anyway, we moms can't help it. Sometimes our children become our idols, and we have difficulty trusting them to God."

"Idols?" Roxanne frowned.

"Well, I guess that's a modern-day idol. Not wood or metal." She chuckled. "Although some men have metal idols, cars, sports, or anything we put before God or can't give to him."

"You mean, like my writing?"

"I don't know. Only you know that. But it would be something that has a hold on you, and either causes great distress, envy, or pride. It can be anything."

She had many things that distressed her, and this day reminded her of them all. And now her writing, or her failure of it. She looked back at Melanie and pondered her wise words. *Okay. First things first.*

First Gregory. Still hidden in her heart. The profound loss lessened now, but the memories remained. But then, Spencer. Roxanne wiped the condensation dripping on her glass and cleared her throat. "So, how can I forgive someone who left me and killed my father?"

Melanie sighed. "Oh my. That's a big one, but you can't. At least not on your own. But it's for God's glory and your benefit if you do. I know I went through a time when I couldn't forgive, and ultimately, I blamed it all on God. Both my parents died within a short period. One after another. My daughter got attacked, I was abducted, and just a few years ago, my daughter was taken at gunpoint as well."

Roxanne's eyes widened. "That's horrible. I thought Bay Town was safe."

"It is, but outside influences find their way anywhere," Melanie said.

"How did you handle it all? You're so joyful."

"Oh, there's more. I met Desmond and fell hard for him. I couldn't believe God brought such an amazing man into my life, and we started getting close. I thought maybe true love and happiness were within my grasp."

Roxanne thought of the strikingly handsome man. A godly man at that. Almost too good to be true. But no man was.

"It was. Look at you now."

"Yes, well it was a long rough road to get here. At one point, my ex-husband wanted to re-enter my life, but I wanted nothing to do with him. Desmond thought differently. He pulled back to give my ex a chance. Infuriating, right? Then the police found my ex-husband murdered. And I checked out."

"You? You gave up on God?"

"I did. I didn't feel like going on, but I had Lacey, so I couldn't get too far off the rails. I felt crazy, though, and I wanted no part of God or church. But this town." Melanie smiled. "They loved me enough to confront my guilt, pride, and anger. I had no joy until I found my way back to God, and there He waited for me." Melanie took a sip of her tea.

But you don't know what I've done. Taking beatings from Dwayne wasn't the worst of it anymore. She had an intimate relationship with him for over a year. They weren't married. *In the church's eyes, wasn't that the worst?*

"What if God doesn't want me back? What if people find out who I've been? What I've done?" Roxanne swiped the sweat off her brow and fanned herself with her hand.

"It's none of their business," said Melanie. "God loves you, Roxanne, and He's already forgiven you. Confess it and believe in His love. Just like Max, your mother, and many others. We've all sinned."

"But —"

"No buts. Whatever you've done is between you and God, and none of us has to know what you don't want to tell us. Just give us a chance. You don't have to do this alone." She touched Roxanne's hand. "From what I've heard, you're fitting back into Bay Town nicely."

Finally, a breeze blew. Though warm, it cooled Roxanne's flushing face. "What have you heard?"

"Well, not to gossip, but Mrs. Hancock said you've been the best addition to her library volunteer staff in a very long time. She said the kids love you, and so do the seniors. Seems God might be using those writing skills."

"My idol?" Roxanne chuckled.

"If you're letting Him use it, I wouldn't call it that." Melanie winked. "And a little bird told me we may have an Olde Book Shoppe reopening in town."

"Now, that might be a bit of gossip."

Making a zipping motion to her lips, Melanie smiled. She looked at her watch and stood. "On that little juicy morsel, I better go. My daughter and I have some wedding details to attend to." She reached, pulling Roxanne in a hug.

"Oh, I'm so sorry, I'm all sticky." Roxanne pulled her dress away from her skin.

"Aren't we all? Listen, I'll leave you alone now, but you are coming to the wedding, right?"

A whoosh of air gushed from her lungs, and Roxanne

nodded. "Yes, thank you. Please let me know if I can help with anything. Anything at all."

"You're a writer … maybe you can write my speech for the toast. I'll be a blubbering mess."

"Any way I can help." Roxanne followed Melanie out and stood at the door, gazing at the ideally imperfect woman walking to her car.

The heat grew sweltering just standing there, and Roxanne propped the door open and reached for the screen. Maybe hope waited for her too.

CHAPTER 24

"Good morning, dear. What's on the agenda for today?"
"I should ask you that. Your calendar is booked more than mine." Roxanne squeezed her mother's shoulders.

"Well, I understand you have a project to get started on?"

Roxanne poured orange juice and leaned against the counter, crossing her ankles. Taking a sip, she hummed. "Fresh squeezed?"

"Max brought it over this morning."

"He came here?" Roxanne couldn't hide her disappointment. She felt she owed him an apology and even a thank you for his care after church yesterday.

"He has a tree in his backyard. Lemons and limes too. Maybe you should ask to pick some, and I'll make us both some lemon limeade." Her mother winked.

Roxanne walked to the living room and peeked out. No truck sat in his driveway. Her shoulders slumped, and she joined her mother at the kitchen table, scooting onto the window bench behind.

"Gone, eh?" Bethie Cook sipped a cup of tea.

"Who? What?" asked Roxanne.

"I can tell from that frown on your face." Bethie waved a hand. "Never mind. How about the project?"

"What project?"

"I spoke with Sally Trotman. She mentioned The Olde Book Shoppe." Bethie winked.

"Seriously. She's thinking about reopening?"

Her mother nodded. "Thinking about it? She practically asked me for money from our foundation to reopen."

"Wow. You ladies don't waste time around here."

"Don't undervalue the women at Bay Town." Her mother pointed upwards. "Most important, don't underestimate God."

"Yes, I'm getting that lesson hammered into my brain."

"Well, don't be such a hard piece of wood, dear." Her mother laughed.

Finding inspiration in those around her, Roxanne wrote for a few hours before leaving for the library for her afterschool class with the children. She left early, drove through town, and parked outside The Pink Rosette.

The doorbells jingled, and the familiar, "Be right there!" rang from the back.

When Max emerged, Roxanne had pulled a pink rosette from the galvanized bucket on the counter.

"Shall I put that on your bill?" He winked as he wiped his hands on his apron.

"That and the counseling session yesterday." Roxanne smiled. "Thank you."

"What are friends for?" he said.

"Tough love, I guess." Roxanne chuckled. "Max, I'm so sorry for my rudeness at church."

"Not to worry. You've been hurt, my love. You've been hurt deeply." His hand covered hers, and he squeezed, but not before his sparkling eyes locked with hers. His grip, his gaze, she wanted it to never end.

Roxanne smiled and stared down, relishing his touch. She traced the scratches on his hands with a single finger.

"Well, then." Clearing his throat, he pulled his hand away.

"Yes, but I want to get over it."

"Excuse me?" Max cleared his throat and shuffled some stems.

"You were right. I've been hurt, but not without fault." She bit her lip. "Oh, Max, you don't know what I've done."

He raised his hand to stop her. Removing the pink rosette she held, he pulled a sprig of baby's breath and a handful of white peonies from his work counter. He retrieved a short square vase from a shelf, placed the nosegay within, and filled it with water.

"Here. Just for you."

"It's so beautiful. I can't believe how quickly you did that. Thank you." She reached for them, but Max's hands wrapped around the vase.

"Whenever you start blaming yourself, whenever you feel less than worthy, look at these and be reminded how much you are loved." He snipped a few grape leaves and added them. "And when they wilt and begin to look less than—" he chuckled, "—bring them back here, and I'll remind you, myself."

Roxanne flushed. Being in the shop felt like old times. Her fingers touched his, and his warmth filled an empty ache in her heart. She pulled the vase to her chest. "Thank you, Max. For everything."

Arriving in time for her children's creative writing class, Roxanne hugged and gave fist bumps to all the kids. Their sweet, innocent faces smiled back at her, and her heart swelled with gratitude that parents took an interest in their children's passion for stories by bringing them to the library's free service. After reading a short picture book, she taught a simple writing lesson and let the children's creative juices flow. She walked around encouraging them as they wrote and illustrated their stories.

One dark-haired boy tugged at her arm as she passed. She stopped, and he stared up at her with wide brown eyes.

"Nice work," Roxanne said, pointing to his scribbled pages.

He beamed.

"Do you have a computer at home?"

The boy shook his head.

"Well, we'll get you started using the library's computers. They're free."

She felt another tug, and a smiling girl with slick dark hair stared up at her. Roxanne's heart sank. She looked so much like the little girl in Meridian. The one that had been bullied in her class. How could she have left her? But what more could she have done? Sunday's message and Max's and Melanie's words filled her head. She said a short, silent prayer and asked God to care for the little one she couldn't.

"What can I do for you?" She asked the girl and felt a weight fall off her shoulders. *Here's my start. I'm giving it up to God.*

"I'm stuck." The child blew a breath straight up, and her bangs flew upward.

"Let me see here." Roxanne took her pages and chuckled. The pages were filled with drawings. Beautiful drawings. Although the sketches weren't connected, they each told a story.

Roxanne knelt down. "It doesn't look to me like you're stuck. You don't need written words for these stories. Tell me about them."

She lifted the child onto a chair next to her, and the imagination of innocence exploded in verbiage, describing every scene, shape, and color. "The end," the girl exclaimed.

Roxanne clapped her hands and placed the sheets in a

folder. "I'll tell you what. You keep drawing, and I'll record your stories on my phone at our next meeting. Then I can write them out for you."

The child grinned from ear to ear.

Parents soon arrived to pick up their kids, and the girl saw her mother and turned to run but stopped. Returning to Roxanne, she hugged her tight, then ran to her waiting mother, her stories pouring from her mouth. *Thank you*, the mother mouthed back, as she left with a child much happier than when she came.

Roxanne said goodbye to each child and pushed in all the chairs.

"You're a natural." Mrs. Hancock spoke from the doorway.

"I've always loved teaching."

"Why don't you go back to it? I don't want you to leave, but Bay Town needs good teachers as much as any place."

Visions of the principal's office and the mother yelling and taunting her played across her mind. "Maybe. But for now, I'm more than happy here." As much as she meant it, she realized how fear permeated every aspect of her life.

"Good. Now, come on. I'm putting you back to work."

CHAPTER 25

"I'm home," Roxanne called as she entered the house. She wondered at the absence of a delicious aroma. Not that she expected her mother to cook for her, but Mama had always cooked a delicious meal every night since she'd arrived home.

"Mama?" Roxanne strolled into the kitchen.

"Oh, good. Can you make a salad, dear? I'm a bit late getting dinner on." Bethie turned down the flame on a pot of boiling green beans.

There didn't seem to be anything cooking but the beans. "Sure, Mama. I'll make a nice, refreshing salad." Roxanne retrieved a red onion, cucumber, lettuce, and tomatoes from the fridge and rummaged through the shelves. "Do you have any feta?"

"What's that?" Bethie frowned.

"Feta cheese?"

"Cheese. Why didn't you say so? Just get the shredded cheddar in the bag there."

So much for a Mediterranean salad with olives and garbanzo beans. Roxanne glanced at the small kitchen table, and her brows furrowed.

"Mama, why are there three places set?"

The doorbell rang, and Bethie shuffled off to answer it. She returned with Max.

Roxanne nodded. "What a nice surprise." Her heart swelled, and everything about him standing there felt right. He didn't always come for dinner, but each writing meeting with him filled her with anticipation of seeing him again. Enjoying his company relaxed her, and affection for the man had multiplied faster than she cared to admit.

"Even nicer that I've brought some grilled beef and baked potatoes," Max said.

"So that's why nothing is cooking here. Your house must be sweltering if you heated it up for those." She pointed at the plate of foil-wrapped potatoes.

"Not at all. I baked these on the grill as well. Philippa loved baked potatoes, and I found a way to cook them outside in the summertime."

Philippa, again? Roxanne's shoulders sagged. Would he ever be over her? Guilt hit her heart. Of course, Philippa, and why not? She and Max had married young, and they were so in love. Roxanne sighed as she looked back at him.

"Shall we eat, now? I'm quite hungry," Max said.

"We shall," Bethie said. "Sit, sit. And Max, please bless our food."

Roxanne closed her eyes, savoring each heartfelt word he expressed. She couldn't help but dream what it might be like if he always sat here with them.

"Amen," Bethie said too loudly.

Roxanne jumped a little, and the three enjoyed their meal. Well, two did. Roxanne tried to control her rising angst but sulked guiltily, feeling like a scorned schoolgirl. Stabbing at her green beans, she shoved them into her full mouth. Her head swiveled between her mother and Max, discussing flowers and gardening like she wasn't there. Yet her angst dissipated when Max slipped her a smile, and even when she looked down, she felt his gaze. Roxanne swallowed, relaxed in her chair, and stared back.

"Well, thank you for the delicious steak. Cooked perfectly," Bethie said.

Max shook his head as if waking up from a dream.

Roxanne grinned.

"Yes, well, beef on the grill is hard to beat," he said.

He swiped a napkin across his lips. His sweet, soft lips. Roxanne parted hers. He stopped mid-motion, the white linen napkin resting right there. His light blue eyes gazing.

Bethie Cook chuckled, stood, and picked up her plate. Max did the same and offered to take Roxanne's.

"Oh, please, Max. I'll do the dishes. You two young people, go sit and have a nice chat."

Bethie wore a sly grin.

"Young people? Oh, come now, Bethie. " Max's tanned face flushed bright red.

"You're both much younger than me. Go on, now. I'll dish up the pie. I picked it up at Bubba's Crab Shack."

Roxanne wrinkled her nose. "When did Hank start baking?"

"I don't know, but he may outdo the Mockingbird's pastry chef. Go on now. Shoo."

Max reached for a platter on the table.

Bethie slapped his hand away. "Don't you have work to do in there?" She pointed to the living room.

Roxanne giggled. Bethie Cook loved to see their heads together, pouring over her manuscript. She'd commented more than once how she found pleasure in seeing Roxanne happy again. Her mama connived to get them alone, and with the fluttering in Roxanne's stomach since the moment Max walked in the door she took advantage.

"Come, Max. You can't argue with Mama."

The night hung uncomfortably hot, but Roxanne didn't

care. She headed for the front door and pushed open the screen. He hovered behind her, and she heard him draw a deep breath. The heat rose within her, but just as quickly, he stepped back.

"Where are you off to?" Max asked.

Roxanne tilted her head. "The porch. It's a bit cooler out there, and the crickets are serenading." She flushed a little at the words she'd chosen.

"Don't we have work to do?" He threw a nod toward Bethie's desk.

"How about we let our food digest first? It's so lovely out here."

He cleared his throat again. "Philippa always said work first, play later." He turned towards the computer desk.

Philippa, Philippa, Philippa. Roxanne rolled her eyes and let the screen door slam shut. *Cool off,* she told herself. She'd only been in Bay Town a little over a month and the Dwayne mess still hovered. Even thinking about romantic notions with another man made her shiver. She sighed. Except for with Max.

Sucking it up, she sat, distancing the chair a bit. He pulled up her manuscript and read. Between listening and staring at his lips move, she imagined Max as the love interest in her story. Settling into a blissful calm, the romantic notions loomed with every word he spoke.

"He pulled off his glasses. Their eyes locked, and she tilted her chin upwards. Her lips parted. Their plump softness longed to be kissed, and how he wanted to... The door flew open. A silhouette filled the doorway, ending their moment. His body went rigid, and he walked casually towards an open window where a cool breeze blew."

Max stopped reading. He pulled off his glasses, and his eyes held hers. She had rolled her chair closer. So close their arms touched. With an open mouth, he sighed, and she leaned forward.

Max suddenly stood. Replacing his glasses, he nodded.

"Well, now, perhaps that's a good place to stop."

She felt like a delicious chocolate had melted on her lips but never touched her tongue. She wanted to scream. Roxanne stood, but Max walked toward the front door before she could speak. Did her love scene repulse him? Or was it her? She cringed inside.

Roxanne trotted after him like a love-sick puppy. "What's wrong? Can't we talk about it? I can rewrite the love scene. I know Philippa would have written it much better, but you can help me."

He moaned a heavy sigh. "You did a beautiful job, Roxy. I'm afraid perhaps it caught me off guard." He took her hand and squeezed. "It reminded me much of when I'd read the scenes with Philippa."

"Oh," she quietly groaned. And thoughts of romantic kisses enveloped her mind. Roxanne had been foolish enough to think he wanted to kiss her. Yet he must have been thinking of his departed wife throughout the entire reading. Roxanne scrunched her eyes. *Stupid me!*

Max looked past her and called out. "Thanks so much, Bethie. Delightful evening." He glanced back at Roxanne. "Truly," he whispered.

Roxanne squeezed his hand back. Delightful evening? Now she was thoroughly confused.

"Max?"

"I'm sorry, Roxy. I need to clear my head a bit. Good evening." He turned and crossed the street.

CHAPTER 26

The nightly readings after that were never the same. Max remained guarded. As much as it dismayed her, it played out for the best. Roxanne felt foolish for dreaming. She hadn't given her heart away yet, but it saddened her of the impossibility of a relationship with Max. A relationship with a man shouldn't always be the answer to her problems. Although it hadn't stopped her before.

Not this time. Instead, she hoped to relish and enjoy the friendship they had. The weeks turned into a month, and the hot July summer found Roxanne settling into a comfortable, though not entirely satisfied, routine. She'd been so preoccupied with Max, volunteering at the library, and helping Sally Trotman to reopen the bookstore that she no longer waited for the bomb to drop. Dwayne.

She got into a writing groove, but every time she sat at the computer, something nagged her to call the Meridian Police just to make sure. Like all the things that popped into her head, she wrote them down on a pad for later. She fixed herself to the writing task, and by the time hours passed, she'd talked herself out of doing anything that had to do with Dwayne. Besides, the Meridian Police would call her if there were any concerns.

This morning, she'd picked up Sally, and they got an early jump working at the bookstore. Max owned the building Sally had rented for The Olde Book Shoppe, which had remained empty since she'd vacated. He'd never given her an eviction notice, but when she couldn't pay total rent, he tried reducing it. She wouldn't have it. That's when she closed the shop.

It seemed provident that Max had never rented the shop again, until now, to Sally. A challenging tenant, but when Max refused to give her a lease at his agreed-upon price, she relented. He insisted on charging her less-than-market value for the rented shops on Main Street.

When he refused to collect rent until opening day, Sally hit the roof. But it would be months before reopening, and until then, she had no income other than her social security. Inventory needed to be reordered, and the shop needed some sprucing up. Thanks to Bethie Cook's foundation grant, all that wasn't a problem.

Roxanne and Sally were about done arranging furniture when Max walked in, pushing a dolly that held a huge potted palm.

"Look, lovely ladies. Where should I put this?"

"That's beautiful, but how much is it costing me?" Sally furrowed her brow.

"It's a housewarming gift." He pushed his hands into his front pockets and rocked back on his heels.

"Thank you, Max." Sally's eyes softened briefly, but the natural cynical nature took over. "But where do you expect me to put something that big?" Sally huffed as she walked to the back of the store.

Max looked at Roxanne and chuckled. She pointed to a corner.

"Over there is fine for now." She watched as he wheeled it effortlessly but struggled to tug it off the dolly. Roxanne rushed over to help. The fronds tickled her nose as she peeked around, looking at Max.

"One, two, three," he counted.

They pulled and pushed the green, lush tropic flora into the corner, and Max glanced around. Roxanne followed his gaze. The floor-to-ceiling shelving on one wall, custom-built by a local woodworker, gleamed. Shoulder-high self-standing shelves lined the center of the floor.

"Now, if only we could fill the shelves."

"All in God's timing." Max smiled. "Now, I best be off." But he didn't move, and his eyes held Roxanne's gaze.

Hanging on to every second, she never wanted it to end, but the roller coaster drove her crazy. Wondering how deeply he still cared for Philippa, she hoped their time together had lessened his feelings. Dare she dream? Contentment. Perhaps that should be the goal for now, at least with Max.

Roxanne marveled at the turn her life had taken. She hadn't felt this calm and content in a long time. *Is this your timing, Lord?*

CHAPTER 27

S ally interrupted the moment and called it quits for the day. Max said his goodbyes and quickly left, taking Sally with him. Roxanne had no library volunteering today, so she had plenty of time to write. Once home, she sat at the computer. Words flowed from her head to her fingers.

By dinner time, she quit. Rubbing her neck, she glanced at the words she'd written. Satisfied. Today had been a productive one. The pleasant morning had inspired her, and her story had flown from her brain. Clicking save, she looked around. She'd been writing all this time without a thought to back it up, and she didn't trust the Cloud. She decided to buy a flash drive tomorrow and start backing everything up.

The evening went much like many others of late. A simple dinner with her mother and Max. Roxanne smiled, relishing the peaceful nights of pleasant conversation, followed by Max's help with her manuscript. Although she longed for more intimate moments with Max, she resigned herself to contentment for now. Hope remained.

One evening, Bethie had already turned in for the night, and Max left early too. Roxanne went upstairs, showered, and changed for bed. Picking up a book, she read for a bit and fell asleep but awoke to a car rumbling to a stop outside her house.

Drawing her curtain aside, she saw an unfamiliar vehicle. The driver sat still. Her heart raced. Quickly shutting and locking her window, she groaned. Why hadn't she called to have the air-conditioning fixed, yet? Even the hot evening breeze moved the stuffy, stifling inside air. The fans just blew the indoor humidity around the rooms. A door slammed, and Roxanne jumped. Fear gripped her, and she dared not look out again, but ran down the stairs, praying as she went.

Please, God, please bring Chief Bert by for patrol. Her eyes widened as she thought of her mother. Running straight to her room, she peeked in. Mama lay sound asleep, snoring. She quickly closed and locked the bedroom window.

Roxanne ran to the living room and stopped short. Her phone rang faintly, but she'd left it upstairs in her room. She stared at the front door, afraid to move in either direction. The ringing stopped. Then, a light knock followed.

Panic set in as her heart beat faster, and she twirled around, not knowing what to do. Looking for something, she didn't know what. Her eyes rested on a wall cross hanging over the fireplace mantle. Another knock, a little louder this time.

It couldn't be Dwayne, she thought. He wouldn't knock. He'd break the door down. A nervous smile inched, and she felt grateful for the temporary calm. Still, she needed to answer the door. As she tiptoed across the floor, she looked out the peephole and yanked open the door.

"Lucy?" She dragged her friend inside and peeked out before shutting the door.

"I didn't know where else to go." Her eyes were red, but the mascara and liner were perfectly intact thanks to water-proof makeup. Tears stained her cheeks. "He got out. I don't know how, but he got out."

Roxanne checked every window downstairs, making sure they were locked. Lucy followed her around before sinking onto the sofa. Roxanne sat next to her.

"What do you mean he's out?"

Lucy's hands shook as she raked her nails one against another. The bright red, long acrylics clicking annoyed Roxanne, and she reached out a hand, silencing them.

"Dwayne came to my apartment. I was already outside going to the store when I saw him pull up in front of the building. He didn't see me, so I watched him run up to my door. He banged and yelled like a madman, and I left. I drove as fast as I could."

The knot in Roxanne's throat returned, and she couldn't swallow. The familiar choking sensation gripped her, one she hadn't felt in weeks. Roxanne couldn't find words, and the hot room stifled her even more. Both women dripped with sweat.

"Don't you have air-conditioning? It's awful in here." Lucy stood and walked to the oscillating fan. She swayed as it swept the room. "I don't know what to do."

Finally, Roxanne spoke. "Did he follow you?"

"No." She pulled at her hair. Now short and plastered to her head, her long locks gone. "I don't think so. I kept looking in my mirror, but —" She stopped.

"But what?"

"I don't know what he drove. I just wanted to get away. I didn't think to write down the license plate or even identify the car." Lucy cried. "I'm sorry, I'm sorry."

Roxanne felt like crying too, but for someone else more terrified than her, and because of her. *I'm responsible. Responsible to anyone who comes near me. No one's safe with him out there.* She had to take care of Lucy.

"Lucy, go shower. You can sleep with me, and we'll figure this out in the morning." Roxanne led Lucy upstairs to her room.

A glance at the bed, and Lucy shook her head. "I'm sorry, honey, but that bed is too small for the both of us. It's too hot tonight to snuggle." Lucy giggled.

Roxanne nodded, thankful for the brief levity. "Do you want the guest room down the hall?"

"And sleep by myself? No way!"

"Fine. I'll get some extra quilts for the floor. You take the bed," Roxanne offered.

"Oh, no, sweetie. I'm fine on the floor. Just give me a light sheet, and I'm good. I won't sleep anyway." Lucy stared at Roxanne. "Hey, maybe we should pray? I mean, I've been praying the whole way here. I haven't even called my boyfriend yet. I begged God to protect me." Lucy's big brown eyes welled. "And he did."

She reached out her hands, and Roxanne took them. Lucy prayed. Her sweet, lyrical prayers bathed Roxanne in peace.

When the dawn finally broke, Roxanne crept downstairs intending to open all the windows, but her mother beat her to it. Breathing deeply, Roxanne smelled the rich coffee aroma already brewing. When she walked into the kitchen, her mother's back was turned, staring out the window.

"Land sakes, those crows are back. I thought Max got rid of them." She turned. "Oh, my. Someone didn't sleep well." She looked past Roxanne.

Lucy stood in the kitchen entrance.

"A late-night visitor? Come, come in, my dear." Bethie waved at the kitchen doorway.

Lucy inched forward, tugging on the short pajama bottoms. "Sorry, I borrowed Roxy's pj's. She's a bit shorter than me." She crossed her arms, trying to cover the thin white cami.

"Well, I'm sure Roxanne can find you a nice sundress or something."

"Mama, this is my friend, Lucy, from Meridian."

Bethie pulled out a chair. "Nice to meet you. Would you like some fresh blueberry scones? Their my specialty."

Roxanne smiled at her mama, wondering when the questions would come. But ever the southern hostess, she waited till they finished breakfast, and Lucy had gone to shower again.

"Mama, I'm going to call the air-conditioner man today."

"Done."

"What?"

The doorbell rang, and Bethie stood. "He's here. Now go get dressed, and we'll talk."

The women dressed, as her mama suggested, in light sundresses. Lucy had come with nothing but the clothes on her back. Roxanne's mama remained quiet as Lucy retold the story. Roxanne looked down and felt a warm hand covering her twisted grip on the table.

"Now, ladies. Why don't you go see Chief Bert first? You should call him rather than be out and about."

Lucy's eyes widened. "Why? Do you think Dwayne is out there?" Her eyes darted to an open window.

"Well, I certainly hope not. No, I believe the good Lord brought you safely here. You ladies, just be smart and call the police first." She stood. "Never mind, I'll call him."

"But, Mama, please."

Bethie silenced her daughter and walked to the wall phone. Lucy pointed at the little beige box and giggled.

"Chief? This is Bethie Cook. Could you come over to the house? It's not an emergency, but my daughter needs to make a report...Chief? Are you still there...Yes, how did you know? ... Oh, all right, then. I'll tell them." She hung up and turned.

"Mama, what's going on?"

"Chief Bert said he'd been waiting for you to come by. He's sending Officer Blaine to escort you ladies to the station." Bethie nodded as if she'd thought of the idea.

Riding in the back of the squad car, Lucy kept glancing forward. She nudged Roxanne. "He's cute," she whispered.

"He's married."

"I didn't say I was interested. Besides, I have Jason."

"How are things going with him?" Roxanne asked.

Lucy bounced her head side-to-side. "Oh, you know. He's nice enough. Treats me good and all." She sighed.

"But?"

"I get this funny feeling every time I go to church alone. I'm always asking him to come, but he makes excuses not to."

Roxanne recalled all the funny feelings she'd gotten over the years. Ignoring them for so long had been responsible for her life now. *Choices.* She turned and smiled at Lucy. "Stay with me, Lucy. I just started back to church, and maybe we can do that Ladies' Bible Study thing together."

"Oh, I don't know, sweetie."

"Where else are you going to go?"

"Ladies, we're here." Officer Blaine pulled in front of a small, stand-alone brick building. He jumped out and opened their doors.

Lucy giggled. "I feel like we're in that old TV show, Gunsmoke or something. This looks like the sheriff's office."

When they walked in, the bells jingled, and Lucy smirked.

The chief stood. "Well, howdy, ladies."

Both women laughed.

"I'm glad you have something to be happy about because I thought you had some awful news." He motioned for them to come through the little wooden gate that separated his and Officer Blaine's desks from the rest of the room.

Roxanne's smile faded as she and Lucy sat in front of his desk.

"Blaine, get your fingers ready to take a report." He glanced over, pointed to a computer, and then looked at the women. "So, what's the story, Miss Cook?"

Lucy squeezed Roxanne's arm. "I'll go first, Sheriff."

"It's Chief."

"Okay, Chief. I left my apartment in Meridian to go shopping and to meet my boyfriend at Leroy's. Have you heard of it? It's the coolest Sports Bar but more like a restaurant. My boyfriend plays pool there with Dwayne all the time." She bit her lip. "Well, not anymore. Not for a while now. You know, 'cause Dwayne was in jail?"

The chief looked at Roxanne. "Whose Dwayne again? The guy in your restraining order?"

"Who's Dwayne?" Lucy stared wide-eyed at Roxanne. "Didn't you tell him? Why, I thought for sure you would."

"I did. But he was still in jail then."

"And now he's not?" The chief pointed a finger at Blaine. "Any notice come across the wire?"

Officer Blaine rolled his eyes. "No, sir. The internet went down for a while this morning."

"So this Dwayne came looking for you where?" the chief asked.

"Well, first at Leroy's."

"The bar?"

"Yes. It's a restaurant too. Me and Roxy went there every Sunday with the guys. Oh, my they have the best bar-b-cue. Do you like bar-b-cue?"

The chief cupped a palm over his eyes and groaned.

"Anyway, he scared me to death. Well, he actually threatened me."

"And did you report him?" asked the chief.

"Well, I called the police. But then I called Roxanne."

The chief closed his eyes and leaned back in his creaky

office chair. Gripping the handles, he leaned forward. "Ladies, just make a full report. File an official complaint. That's all. We're here to help, but we can't if you don't let us know what's happening."

"I finally did," Roxanne spoke up. "I went to Meridian awhile back when he was in jail there. I filed a restraining order. I gave you a copy, remember?" She dug through her purse and found Officer Chen's card from Meridian. "Here's who helped me. She probably knows what's going on. How he got out."

"I'll give her a call. And you, Miss Lucy, you need to file a report too."

"For both incidents?"

"Both?" Chief Bert rolled his eyes and glanced at Officer Blaine whose fingers poised over his keyboard. Officer Blaine shrugged.

"What other incident? I thought he accosted you at the bar."

Lucy frowned. "Accosted?" She glanced at Roxanne.

"Confronted you," Roxanne said.

"Why, he grabbed me! And my boyfriend and the guys pulled him off me."

"So you have witnesses," Chief Bert said.

"Yes!"

"And they'll confirm the altercation?"

"Whatever that is. Yes." Lucy giggled.

"A fight, a quarrel." Roxanne felt like a translator.

"Thank you, Miss Cook," Chief Bert said. "All right then. And the other time?"

"Yes. Late yesterday afternoon, he came to my apartment and pounded at my front door. So I hightailed it out here to Roxy's."

"Yesterday?" The chief's eyes widened.

"Well, by the time I got to Roxanne's house it was night-time. Like really late, but I feared for my life, and I didn't know where to go. I couldn't go to my boyfriend's. That's probably the first place he'd look for me." Lucy's voice cracked.

"Listen, you step over to Officer Blaine's desk and finish filing both reports. I'll contact the Meridian police and find out what happened."

Officer Blaine walked around and pulled out two chairs. "Please, have a seat. Can I get you some water or a cup of coffee?"

Lucy smiled. "What a gentleman." She winked at Roxanne.

Officer Blaine turned scarlet, and the color rose from his neck to his strawberry-blonde hair resting on his neckline. He nodded. "Water?"

"Yes, please," the women said in unison.

By the time Lucy finished giving her report, with every unnecessary detail, Chief Bert had the bad news. Legally out, Dwayne had posted bail.

Roxanne seethed. She was sure it was the money he had taken from her checking account that posted bail. "Now what?" she asked sternly but feeling like Jell-O on the inside.

"Meridian PD is sending over his mugshot," Chief Bert said. "They're expecting Lucy's report, and I'll keep an eye out for him here. Miss Lucy, what vehicle did he drive yesterday?"

"I don't know. I just took off."

"He previously drove an ostentatious Ford F-100." Roxanne sighed.

"Every redneck in Mississippi drives a F-100." Lucy let out a nervous laugh.

"But he drove a neon green one. Lifted and all souped up. But the last time I saw him, he drove a black beat-up old car."

"He's probably not still driving that one, either." Chief Bert tapped a pen on the desk. "He probably switched vehicles if he's out looking to cause trouble."

"He's not that smart," Roxanne mumbled.

"Excuse me?" Chief Bert narrowed his eyes.

"She said he's not that smart." Lucy threaded her fingers through her hair. "Honestly, Roxy, I don't know what you saw in the guy. He is hot, though. I'll give him that." Lucy shook her head. "But he is just plain evil."

"I see." He nodded at Officer Blaine, and their eyes connected. "We dealt with the likes of someone like that here in Bay Town before. I'm not going to let this Dwayne wreak havoc here. We'll set up extra patrols on your street." He looked at Blaine. "You get out there and show his mug to all the shop owners downtown, as well as all Miss Roxanne's neighbors."

"I'm on it."

"Miss Roxanne, you need to warn everyone you know."

Oh, God, no. Shaking her head, she sighed. "Do I have to? I mean, can't we just be careful?"

"If this guy is as nuts as you claim he is—" he glanced at Lucy, "—he won't stop with her. Your mother and friends are all in danger. I don't want anyone to panic. Just make sure they know what he looks like and tell them to call 911 if they see him. Just tell the dispatcher to contact me immediately."

Roxanne felt her life unraveling once again. *How could she have let this happen? Why did she let it happen?* Her shoulders drooped, but she stood. "Yes, sir. I will."

He stood and extended a hand. "Miss Roxanne, we'll get him. Stupid men don't last long out there. Bay Town is a good community. We'll protect you and your loved ones, I promise. And we got a fairly good Pastor in town. I sometimes think he has a direct line." He giggled an unfitting laugh for a man his size. "I know. He helped get the last bad guy."

A direct line. That's what Roxanne needed, and she smiled. A bit of the burden lifted.

Lucy and Roxanne stepped out of the police station. They

looked up. Clouds blocked the burning ball of fire, but the humidity hung thick. Fanning herself, Lucy waved vigorously.

"I do declare, being close to the Gulf here in Bay Town is lovely, but we don't have quite the stifling humidity at Meridian. Still, I can see why the tourists gather here," Lucy said.

"Excuse me?" A man's voice spoke.

Roxanne froze at the sound of a familiar tone behind her.

CHAPTER 28

"Do you know where the Mardi Gras Museum is?" the man asked.

A child tugged on the man's arm. "Come on, Dad, do we have to go? Can't we just go to the beach?"

Roxanne turned slowly, raising her eyes, fixing them on the voice. "It's in the train station downstairs. Near the Bayou Bar. You're familiar with that, right, Spencer?" Her tone was harsh.

Lucy stared at Roxanne. Her brows furrowed.

The man's eyes widened, and he quickly dropped the hand of the younger boy.

"Uh, listen, kids." He pulled out his wallet, handing them a fifty-dollar bill.

"Whoa. Thanks, Dad. What's this for?"

"Go get that shaved ice from the food truck." He nodded over his shoulder to the colorful food truck parked a half-block away.

The two children grabbed the money and ran.

"Roxanne?"

She didn't answer.

After too much silence, Lucy stuck out her hand. "Hello there. I'm Lucy. A good friend of Roxanne's."

His lips pursed, and he shifted his weight. Still tall and slender but with a bit of a paunch. His hair greyed at the sides. Nervously, he turned to check on his children, and Roxanne saw a thinning patch on his crown. He turned back around, and a corner of her lip lifted in a sly smile. His eyes widened, and Roxanne chuckled when his Adam's apple bobbed. She waited, wishing she could enjoy his discomfort more, but anger seethed inside.

Finally, he took Lucy's hand. "Nice to meet you, Rox..." He rolled his eyes. "I mean...."

"Lucy. My name is Lucy. So, how do you know Roxanne?" She elbowed her friend. "I think I have an idea." She sang out the words quietly.

He stared at Roxanne, his eyes pleading for her to speak. She didn't give him the satisfaction but tipped her head and crossed her arms.

"Well, we...I used to know... we're friends...uh, I'm from Meridian...college," he blurted.

"Oh. College sweethearts, huh?" Lucy squealed. "That's cute." She elbowed Roxanne again. "I take it didn't end well."

"Spencer is my ex-fiancé." Roxanne glared.

"Oh, my." Lucy's large eyes grew wider. She gave a sideways glance at Spencer. "Ex-fiancé.' You didn't cheat on her, did you? Because you look like a nice guy with great kids."

As if something suddenly registered, Roxanne looked around him at the teens getting shaved ice. She narrowed her eyes at Spencer. "Are those yours?"

He nodded. "Yes."

"Where's your wife? Still working at the Bayou Bar?" She felt a knife twist in her heart, both for the mean comment and the painful memory.

"The Bayou Bar?" Lucy stared at Roxanne. "Maybe we should check it out?" She giggled.

Spencer straightened. "I met my wife in Jackson at work.

She's a nice girl. Like you, Roxanne. I don't know how she picked me."

"Oh, honey, I don't think you should go there." Lucy smiled pathetically.

"No, please, Spencer. Go there. Because I don't know why anyone would pick you, either."

"Roxy, we need to go." Lucy took hold of Roxanne's arm and tried steering her away.

Roxanne stood like her feet were set in concrete. "Go on, Spencer."

"Roxanne, I'm sorry. You know that. I paid for my stupid mistake. It messed me up for years."

"Join the club, Spencer. But it seems like you've moved on."

"I've tried."

"Yes, you did. After you went wild for...what, a year? I heard you were quite the partier." Roxanne crossed her arms, nails digging in.

"I stopped. You know I did. I repented."

"Oh, are you a Christian now? 'Cause we are." Lucy pointed between herself and Roxanne.

"Roxanne, yes," Spencer said. "Me too. I am, but I just screwed up."

"You can say that again." The words soured in Roxanne's mouth. She wished she hadn't said that. She screwed up too. Big time.

"Don't we all," Lucy said.

Roxanne lowered her arms. *Maybe we should end this now.* Afraid that if he kept talking, she would hit him or start crying and run away. Something tugged at her heart, and she didn't like the rising bit of compassion.

Forgive him.

Roxanne looked around, thinking she heard a voice. She stared at Spencer but didn't glare anymore. Her eyes watered, and she swallowed hard, trying to think of something to say.

"I did. I screwed up, and I lost you in the process. Roxanne, I know I can never make it up to you."

"Hey, Dad? Can we spend the rest of this down at the beach? Maybe rent a wave runner or something?" One of the children interrupted.

Lucy giggled. "Kids, you better get another fifty from Daddy here if you want to do that."

The kids laughed, and the boy raised a palm for a high-five. Lucy slapped him back. "Cool," he said. "Yeah, Dad, how about it?"

Roxanne and Spencer continued to stare at one another, but their expressions and body language couldn't be more different. Roxanne stood rigid, lips pursed, and brows furrowed. Spencer's shoulders slumped as if defeated, and his sad eyes sagged.

A phone rang, and Spencer blew out a breath. He reached into his pocket, pulling out a cell. "I have to get this." He turned. "Yeah, babe?" He raised his head and waved to a slender woman standing a couple blocks down. "Sure, be there in a sec."

"Kids, go meet your mama." He pointed and waved again. "I'll join you in a minute."

As they jogged down the street, Spencer returned the cell to his front jeans pocket and left his hands in. "Listen, Roxanne. I have to go. Please forgive me? I'm so sorry. You never deserved what I did. I'm a stupid idiot, and I'm so sorry for hurting you."

Roxanne's eyes filled, and she fought back the waterworks about to burst. Gulping for air, she cleared her throat. She nodded. "Okay, sure." She turned and walked in the opposite direction, hearing Lucy behind her.

"Well, Spencer, I'd say, nice meeting you, but..." She lowered her voice, but not low enough. "Give her time. Bye."

Lucy hooked arms with Roxanne, but Roxanne yanked her arm away, picking up her pace.

"Give me time?" Roxanne whispered.

"Please, Roxy. You got to forgive him. It's eating you up."

"He has a wife. He's happily married with children. Look at me? What do I have?"

"Honey, don't look at it that way." She tugged at Roxanne's wrist.

Roxanne flinched. The pain from one of Dwayne's tirades still hurt, and a tear fell.

"Roxy, are you okay?" Lucy looked down at Roxanne's arm, cradled against her body.

"I do forgive him. I'd be a hypocrite not to, but I have no other way to look at it, Lucy. I can't get away from the memories. In my mind, in my body, in my heart, and now in front of me."

Lucy nodded, brushing the short, dark bangs that hung in her eyes aside. "I know. Life is not fair. But we just have to trust, right? I mean, doesn't the Bible say, love the Lord your God with all your heart, mind, soul, and body? Or something like that? You have to give all that to Him." Lucy looked across the street, and she pointed.

Roxanne's eyes followed, and a plethora of stained glass and metal crosses hung in the window. A beautiful display of colored prisms and shiny silver. The light shed rays that glittered, much like fairy dust in the movies.

"See? God's giving us a sign." Lucy giggled. "At least he's giving me one. I don't know about you, but I think I'm going to get more serious."

"Serious about what?" Roxanne continued to stare at the window of light.

"My faith. My sister's been bugging me to quit fooling around with God, and she's right." Putting her arm around Roxanne's shoulders, she hugged her tightly. "Come on. Didn't you say there's a Women's Bible Study we can go to?"

Roxanne closed her eyes. Her gut wrenched, and her heart hurt. Spencer's sad face rose up. So did Max's, and she thought of his words at church. Forgiveness. How could she ever forget? Pictures of the joyful teens and Spencer's happy wife saddened her.

A truck drove by, and the roar of the engine startled Roxanne. She snatched Lucy's arm and pulled her into the nearest doorway.

"What are you doing?" Lucy squealed.

"May I help you?" A sweet young voice spoke. "Do you have an appointment?"

The small clinic had a few patients waiting in the sparsely furnished office. Roxanne looked around. Her eyes locked on a woman with blackened eyes, holding her wrist.

"Roxy, a woman drove that truck out there." Lucy waved to the receptionist. "Sorry, we're in the wrong place." She tugged at Roxanne.

The injured woman looked up and slowly turned her gaze away. Roxanne's sadness gave way to rising nausea. *Why, God? Why?*

Lucy pulled her across the street, ignoring the crosswalk. She stood on the sidewalk, gazing at wispy white clouds blowing by before the sun blinded her. They slipped into a little gift shop. Bells rang, but no one seemed present. Soft music lulled through speakers somewhere, the shop smelled of fresh lemons, and trickling water bubbled from a fountain in the corner. Two small but overstuffed chairs sat on either side.

"Wow. This is so cool." Lucy picked up a plaque and smiled. "God is definitely calling me back."

A woman stepped out. "Well, hi y'all. Welcome. I's Lyla."

A slow smile spread across Roxanne's lips, and she nodded. "Hey there." She recognized the woman from church.

Her brows furrowed. "Say, are you Bethie Cook's daughter?"

"Yes, I'm Roxanne."

"Nice to meet you. Bethie told us you was coming into town. I hear ya' know my husband. Big Joe?"

"You're married to Big Joe? Do they still call him that?" Roxanne said.

"They shore do. And he's bigger than ever!" Lyla's whole body jiggled as she laughed.

"Yes, we were in high school together."

"Wow! What a cozy town you live in." Lucy clasped her hands.

"Lyla, this is my friend, Lucy."

Lucy beamed. "Hey there. I sure love your shop."

"Go on then. Take a look around." She smiled at Roxanne. "Your mama is so proud of you. I's sorry I didn't meet you at church. You were busy with Max out under the Magnolia tree."

Lyla winked, and her boisterous laugh shook her large, curvy body again. Roxanne blushed and didn't feel judged but loved. Lyla's perfectly lined purple-red lips smiled back at her. Her eyes fluttered behind long lashes, and her whole face exuded joy. She enveloped Roxanne in a bear-hug embrace.

"Max? And who is Max?" Lucy punched Roxanne, giving her a sideways glance.

"Oh, honey. Max is one of the most eligible widowers in town." Lyla flashed a sly smile. "When Roxanne first came home, we ladies at Bible Study thought she and Max might be a match."

Lucy's eyes went round as saucers. "Girl! Why didn't you say something?" Lucy danced a little jig. "Whoo hoo."

But Lyla's bright smile faded. "Wait a minute." She turned toward the register counter, walked back, and picked up a flyer. "Officer Blaine came by earlier. Is this the man that's bothering you two?"

Roxanne's shoulders dropped, and she covered her eyes.

Lucy gulped. "Uh, huh." She turned to Roxanne. "Roxy, your police are on it. The words out, he'll never touch us here." Lucy pulled out her phone.

"Who are you calling?" Roxanne stared incredulously.

"Jason. I'll tell him I'm staying in Bay Town for a while." She paused. "I mean, if it's okay with you? And I have to call my work too."

"Of course, it's okay." Roxanne's smile grew stern quickly. "I'm sorry, Miz Lyla. I didn't mean to bring any danger to the decent people in Bay Town. We'll be leaving now." She pulled at Lucy.

Lyla stepped not so lightly towards the women. Her thick, stacked heels pounded the wooden floor. "Now listen up. We's all family in Bay Town. Ain't nobody going to hurt you. We've rallied before when evil rises, and we'll rally again. When God's on your side, we fear no evil."

"Amen." Lucy raised a palm high. "See, Roxy, I told you."

Lyla laughed and rested her hands on her hips. She lowered her chin and stared intently.

"Now listen up. Ladies' Bible Study is every week. So next Wednesday, you come to Miz Melanie's house at six o'clock, ya' hear? She serves supper, and I bring dessert." Lyla winked. "You shorely don't want to miss that. Pecan Pie. Mmm, mmm."

"We'll be there," said Lucy. "Wait, who is Miz Melanie?"

"The pastor's wife," said Roxanne.

"That's right, girl. You bring yo' mama, and I'll see you there." Lyla raised a finger. "Just wait a minute." She moved quickly and retrieved two cellophane-wrapped packages secured with red ribbon. "Homemade Praline Pecan Candy." Handing them one each, she beamed.

"Thank you." Roxanne reached inside her purse. "How much do we owe you?"

Lyla threw her hands at them. "My gift. I's makes them, so I can give them to whoever I please."

Before the girls left, Lyla reminded them of the Bible Study and made Roxanne promise to come. Lucy pledged to go for them both. Outside on the curb, Lucy ripped open the package and took a bite of the caramelized sugar pecan sweetness.

"Oh, my goodness, this is heaven," she mumbled, then swallowed. "It really is, Roxy. God can turn everything around."

Roxanne didn't know whether to cry, scream, or give up. She felt like doing all three, but instead, she unwrapped her candy and took a scrumptious bite.

CHAPTER 29

Lucy stayed in Bay Town for another day. Waking up the next morning, she joined Roxanne at the kitchen table for coffee and announced she was leaving to see her sister in Idaho.

Roxanne stared back at her, coffee mug poised in midair. "But we were going to get serious about our faith. Attend the women's Bible Study together?"

"Yes, well, I still plan on the serious thing. But I need to see my sis. I owe it to her. She's about the most faithful person I know."

"I thought you didn't want to get her involved. What about Dwayne?"

Lucy took her hand. Her large, round eyes sparkled. "God will take care of me. He brought me safely here, and I love your town and the people. I love how they look after each other. But she's my family. I've stayed away too long. Besides, we know Dwayne's not here, so I can go safely, right? And when I get back, I can meet this Max." Lucy winked.

Roxanne ignored the Max statement and thought about Dwayne. She didn't have confidence that Dwayne wouldn't reach her, but logic set in. If he had followed Lucy to Bay Town, he would have acted by now. The fact that she and

Lucy had enjoyed the last few days of peaceful reconnection proved evidence of his absence.

"You're right. I could learn a little about trust from you. I could have learned much more about life if I'd listened to you before when we used to talk at Leroy's," Roxanne said.

"Stop it. I'm not proud of me either, but things will change."

"But you were doing better than me." Roxanne wrapped her hands around her mug. "When you told me that you were going to church, it uncovered something I'd buried."

"What are you talking about? I attended church in the morning and the bar afterward for a good time. I never much thought about God after I left church."

"At least you didn't quit going. And you didn't leave God somewhere behind like I did. But when you mentioned attending church, it felt like my faith peeked up from the grave."

"Oh, my. That's the spooky writer in you." Lucy stood. "Well, shake off that dirt, girl. Faith is about to revive both of us." She pulled Roxanne to standing. "Don't you just feel like praying again?"

"Sure. But you pray."

Lucy giggled. "Sweet Jesus, thank you. Thank you. Thank you for saving us, for protecting us, for bringing us back. Bless Roxanne, and keep her safe. In your holy name, I pray. Amen and hallelujah." Lucy squeezed Roxanne's hands, then threw her arms around her.

Spinning around the room like a lyrical dancer, Lucy broke out in song. Her sweet voice filled the room with choruses of praise. Some that Roxanne had never heard before. Had she been away that long?

Lucy made swift plans to leave. She'd called her work and got an emergency leave. With the flight booked, Roxanne drove her to the airport that afternoon. It all happened so fast that Roxanne still felt a spiritual high when she returned home and saw Lucy's car parked in front of her house. Lucy promised to come back in a week. Her joy sparked fireworks in Roxanne, and she couldn't let it stop.

After writing all afternoon, Roxanne stretched. Glancing at her watch and then outside, she finally noticed the darkness in the room. Dinner time and her rumbling stomach proved it. Pulling off the headphones that streamed her romance playlist, she laid them aside and heard humming emitting from the kitchen.

Standing at the stove, stirring a pot, Bethie sang. Roxanne stopped in the doorway and stared at her mother. She sang the same praise song that Lucy sang. Wow. She had been out of touch. Roxanne chuckled, thinking she'd definitely been left behind when her mama and Lucy shared the same music. She stepped forward. *But not anymore.*

"What's for dinner?" She kissed her mama.

"Just soup. Chicken, vegetable, and rice."

"Mmm. You make the best. What's your secret, Mama?"

"You mean, you don't know after all these years?" Bethie shrugged. "I guess you never paid much attention to my cooking, did you?"

"That and other things. But I will now. Really, what's the secret?"

"Sauté and soften the veggies first. Add two cups of chopped cooked chicken and a couple quarts of broth. Then put a teaspoon and a half of just about every savory spice I can find in my cupboard."

"That's it?"

"Bring it to a boil, lower it to a simmer for forty-five minutes, then turn off the heat and add a splash of vinegar."

Roxanne turned up her nose. "What's that for?"

"Brings out all the flavors. A little tartness sometimes

shocks the life into a bland dish. Much like our lives." Her mother winked.

Lucy shocked the life back into me. Tart and sassy. "I know exactly what you mean."

"Good, now go set the table. Max will be here soon."

Roxanne clapped her hands. "Right!" Just as quickly, thoughts of Dwayne threatened to darken her mind, but she pushed them out. For now, tonight, Max brought the end to a good day, and dinner with him was the beginning of a great evening. She laid out the plates, napkins, and silverware and gazed at the table. *Something's missing.* She snapped her fingers. *Flowers!*

A lovely bouquet for the table would be perfect. Her mother's pruning shears lay in a bucket just inside the front door.

"I'll be right back, Mama," Roxanne called as she sailed through the living room, grabbed the shears, and flung open the door. A brilliant blue and white bouquet of hydrangeas greeted her. Some simple twigs, large green leaves and a few pink roses poked out in between the large blooms. Roxanne gasped, pruning shears raised.

"Put those down, dear. I beat you to it." Max handed her the bouquet.

Heat rose on her neck. He'd been coming to dinner for weeks but never brought her flowers. *Did he mean something by it?*

"I don't know what to say. They're gorgeous," Roxanne whispered.

"They are, aren't they." Max smiled. "For your mum."

Roxanne touched her face and felt the heat. "Oh, yes, of course. Come in, Max. Mama's waiting. I'll find a vase."

He patted her shoulder as he slipped by, and her mother peeked into the living room.

"Right on time, as usual, Max," said Bethie. She glanced at Roxanne. "Dear, don't you think those need some water?" She reached for the bouquet. "These are absolutely beautiful."

Shaking herself, Roxanne found a vase and promptly filled it with water. She sniffed the bouquet, feeling silly, giddy, and foolish. *Of course, they're for Mama.*

After dinner, Max and Roxanne retreated to the computer, where Max sat reading, finishing the final chapters of Roxanne's book. He pushed back the hair that flopped across his forehead and removed his glasses, rubbing the space between his eyes. The pale blue color sparkled as he looked at her. He smiled.

"The End. And with that, we're about ready to submit. Would you let me call Philippa's agent?"

Roxanne gasped. "Do you really think I'm ready?"

"I do." He chuckled. "We'll first send it to Philippa's editor for proofing. But in the meantime, I'll call her agent and ask her to expect it."

"All right, then." Roxanne smiled and locked her gaze with Max's.

He stared at her for a moment too long, and her stomach fluttered. Her face flushed as heat arose. Max immediately lowered his gaze and turned back to face the computer. But the exchange between them fueled her courage, and she stepped to his side, placing a hand on his shoulder. It felt so natural.

"Whatever you think," she said quietly.

He reached up and patted her hand but didn't turn. Replacing his glasses, he said, "Let's do it. This is as clean as they come."

He stood, faced her, and drew a deep breath.

She didn't wait for him to welcome a hug but stepped in and hugged him tightly, wrapping her arms around his waist. He stroked her back. She thought she even felt a soft kiss on her head. But she definitely felt the warmth of his snug embrace. His arms didn't release her as quickly as they usually did, and she didn't mind.

"Roxy?" His voice was almost breathless. "I need to speak with you."

"Well, well. I wondered when something might happen between you too. Won't this be some clean gossip for this old town?" Bethie Cook stood in the doorway. Wrinkles spread across her face, accompanied by a broad grin.

Roxanne and Max immediately broke apart.

"We're celebrating," Max blurted.

"Yes. All finished," Roxanne said.

"Philippa would be so proud," Max said.

That ugly feeling arose in Roxanne's heart. She'd forgotten all about contentment. She wanted more. She gazed at Max. *What about you? What do you feel?*

Bethie laughed and raised a hand. "Yes, Philippa would be proud, but so are you. I wasn't born yesterday." She frowned. "Well, maybe so, but for Pete's sake, you have my approval."

Max turned the brightest shade of red that Roxanne had ever seen on a person. The contrast of his beautiful white hair accentuated the flush.

"Mama. He's just helping me with my manuscript. You know that."

"Yes, dear, and maybe some other things in your heart too." She winked.

Max shifted his stance. "Come now, Bethie."

"Quit acting like you're still an old married man," Bethie said.

Roxanne's heart hurt, and her body stiffened. "Well, Mama, it's as if Philippa is always with us." She nodded at Max without smiling. "Isn't that right, Max?"

"Well…a bit so, yes." His brow furrowed.

"A bit? I'd say every step of the way." Roxanne forced a smile. "So, I'll leave you two to finish up for me. I really appreciate it, though, and thanks." She traipsed to the door and flung it open. "It's late. I think you better go."

"Roxanne?" Bethie squealed. "Where are your manners?"

"I'm sure Max has a routine to attend to." Roxanne's mind went wild. Thoughts of old movies when a surviving spouse lit candles, embraced a photograph, and talked to their deceased loved one filled her brain.

Max tried to smile but hurt rendered in his eyes. "Perhaps so. Either way, this old man needs to head home. Roxy, I am so very proud of you."

Roxanne stifled a scream.

He raised the pages once more. "This is progress, my dear." His smile showed approval, but it didn't mask a dejected tone. "Good night, then."

Roxanne wanted to rip the pages from his hands. Rejection. Always rejection. Why had she let her heart feel for him?

Withholding the urge to slam the front door, Roxanne closed it quietly and leaned against it.

"And what was that all about?" her mother asked.

"It's about all the good ones being taken, Mama. Taken away from me."

"Are you talking about Gregory?"

Roxanne bit her lip. "Or Spencer? I don't want to talk about them. You don't understand. You had Daddy all your life."

"Yes, I did. And perhaps Philippa might be the same for Max."

"Gee, thanks for the painful reminder." Roxanne started for the stairs.

"But I don't think so. Give Max time to figure this out."

Roxanne stopped.

"God's ways are not for us to question. Yes, people come into our lives and toil with our hearts. Sometimes, he means them to be with us forever, sometimes not. But you can't even discern what's happening with all the baggage you're carrying. You have to let it go. But in the meantime, count your blessings, daughter, and wait on Him."

"Mama, I try to do that every day. It's just that Max *is* my biggest blessing."

"Have you asked God what Max is doing in your life?"

Roxanne shook her head. "Good night, Mama."

Mama's right. The baggage she lugged around caused confusion, and she didn't know how to reconcile her regretful past. Did anyone know how far she'd wandered? Shame laced her hesitation holding her back from any future joy. Why would a good man desire someone like her? She turned.

"Mama, thank you. Thank you for always praying for me."

"We'll get through this, Roxanne. Just trust the Lord. He uses all things for good."

Her mother took her hand. "Honey, I don't know what you're thinking, but remember, God's a good God. We may not know why He does what He does, but He is righteous, good, and just. And we're not. Trust Him. That's the answer. No matter what. Trust Him."

"Yes, Mama. I'll try."

Her mother hugged her and pulled back. "Roxanne, have you given any more thought to meeting the people at The Refuge?"

Stiffening her spine, Roxanne reached behind and rested her hand there. "Mama, I'm fine. I am not a battered woman anymore." But all the people who had instructed her to get help flooded her mind.

"I know you're not, sweetheart. But the scars are still there. You made some unsound decisions in the past, and you should figure out why. They could help."

Roxanne relaxed a little. Was this what it meant to trust God? "Maybe, Mama. Maybe."

"Pray about that, too, will you? For me?"

"Yes, Mama, I will." Her words weren't as affirmative as the thoughts in her spirit.

CHAPTER 30

The summer grew hotter still. With June past and a sweltering July hitting Bay Town, sluggish days lingered on. Roxanne settled into a routine without Max, now that he had her manuscript. She opened the front door and stared out. What else could she do? As she stroked her arm, loneliness set in, and she longed for a friendly touch.

Lucy had extended her visit with her sister, and Max no longer came for dinner. She peeked out the window at Max's house every morning before she sat down to write. Waiting. Hoping to catch a glimpse, but finally retreating to the computer, writing for a few hours before leaving to help Sally with the bookshop. Volunteering at the library in the afternoons kept her busy, too, but coming home in the evening brought disappointment.

He just started declining the invitations, making her feel horrible for the way she'd treated him. Each evening, the absence of Max at dinner time between her and her mother loomed. Roxanne slipped into a melancholy rhetoric as they talked of her library work and the Old Book Shoppe. Small talk, accompanied by the uncomfortable avoidance of the mention of him. Her stomach churned.

One evening, as Roxanne cleared dishes with her mother, Bethie unnaturally cleared her throat. "Ahem," she said.

Roxanne said nothing, hoping to escape. She washed, rinsed, and dried every plate and utensil.

"Maybe you should apologize," Bethie blurted.

A long sigh escaped, and Roxanne nodded, welcoming her mother's prodding. No one could sweep away the guilt. It lingered and festered like a gnawing sensation and ate away at her stomach, or in this case, her heart.

"I know. What I did…" Roxanne pinched the bridge between her eyes. "Just ugly, and he didn't deserve it."

"No, he didn't. So go on over there." Bethie picked up a two-layer coconut crème cake from the counter. "Here, take this. I just baked it today." Her sweet smile looked as yummy as the cake.

"Thanks, Mom. But not tonight. I'll stop by and see him in the morning."

Bethie Cook's pursed lips evidenced her protest, but it didn't deter Roxanne's determination, and she'd do it her way. Handling an apology swiftly had advantages, but she wanted to make it extra special. Because Max was extra special.

On Saturday morning, Roxanne had forgotten how Main Street traffic crawled with the weekend crowds. Tourists came in droves to shop, walk, and fish on the pier, and they filled the Mockingbird and other eating establishments. Roxanne stopped at Second Chance.

"Hey, there." Virginia ran to greet her. "Lacey's getting married next weekend." She grabbed Roxanne's hands, jumping like a child at Disneyland.

"Yes. I'm sorry that I haven't met her yet."

"Well, you will, right? I mean, you're coming to the

wedding." Virginia twisted a curl around her finger. "I'm a bridesmaid, and my husband is a groomsman."

Roxanne had forgotten about the big event. Sadly, she'd been so preoccupied with everything in her own life it slipped her mind. And a bittersweet taste arose. A wedding.

"Hey, you're bringing a plus one, right? Surely, you don't want to sit with your mama," Virginia said.

Frowning, Roxanne suddenly felt like an old maid.

"I mean, no one goes to a wedding without a date."

Virginia wasn't intentionally mean-spirited, but clueless. Roxanne swallowed. She hadn't even thought of taking a date. Local Bay Town weddings were practically a community event. Still, a wedding is where people ditch the person they brought and meet their soul mates, at least in the movies.

"Yes. You're right." Roxanne tried to giggle, but it came out flat. "I'm working on it." She moved toward the door, anxious to get out of this conversation. She stepped through the threshold and turned to a swooshing sound down the side-walk. Her eyes found Max sweeping outside the Pink Rosette. Virginia came up behind her.

"Hey, why don't you and Max go together? He's kinda cute for an older guy." Virginia giggled. "I mean, not too old for you, right?"

"Right." Roxanne turned. "Hey, I'd like to get a little gift for Max. He's helped me so much with my writing." Roxanne winced at the partial truth. In reality, she needed a peace offering.

"Sure." Virginia walked through the store, touching items, and stopped. "Food. They say that's the way to a man's heart, right? I'm afraid all I have is Lyla's Homemade Pecan Pralines."

"Perfect. I can't go wrong with that."

Roxanne made her purchase and stepped out.

"Good luck," Virginia called. "I hope he says yes."

Roxanne frowned.

"To being your plus one at the wedding," Virginia said.

Roxanne walked toward the Pink Rosette, but when Max saw her, he nodded and slipped back into his shop, definitely avoiding her. Still, she owed him. Count your blessings, her mama said. Maybe she needed to tell him. Roxanne stared at The Pink Rosette and forced her feet to move.

Good, the shop was empty, and Roxanne walked in.

"Be right there," Max called from behind the counter.

Wiping his hands on his apron left yellow streaks from the pollen of the lilies he arranged. He looked up.

"Hello, Roxy." He sounded so natural and casual. "What brings you in here?"

"I know, it's been a while. I haven't seen you."

"Right. I've been so busy. It's the wedding season, you know." He went back to arranging.

Oh, for goodness sake, she thought and rushed forward. "Here, I brought these for you." She pushed Lyla's candy towards him.

He smiled and took them. "Why, thank you. I do love Lyla's treats."

Apologize. Now. But her resolve faded. She should start with the plus-one thing. A little buffer first. "So, Max. I have a proposition for you," she blurted.

"Sure. You've not already finished another manuscript, have you?"

"No. I want to ask if you'd be my plus-one to Lacey Thompson's wedding." She held her breath.

Bending over a bucket of lilies, Max paused momentarily, then straightened. "Well, thank you, Roxy. But I'm already going."

Her mouth gaped. A hot flash arose, and perspiration beaded. She hadn't thought that he might have a date already. She swiped her fingertips across her forehead than down her dress. "Oh, good. Perfect. Wonderful. I guess I'll see you there." She turned and left abruptly, not waiting for a reply.

After Roxanne shut the Dutch doors, Max walked quickly to the bay window and peeked out. He squeezed the roses so tightly he jerked back his hand from a thorn puncture in his finger. Laying aside the pink rose, he squeezed his finger tightly, and it felt like his heart did the same.

Roxanne's light-yellow polka dot sundress blew in the hot breeze, but he sensed a burden with the hunch in her shoulders as she crossed the street. Did he do that? Burden her? She grabbed the hair off her neck and held it up, and Max couldn't help but wish he could hold her lovely locks in his hands, cooling her neck and kissing it as well.

He stared as a stronger longing for Roxanne filled him, but his confusion over remaining feelings for Philippa lingered. He'd felt the attraction for Roxanne coming on from the first day she returned to Bay Town but ignored it and refused to even recognize it. And until he knew what to do with these feelings, he decided it best to guard his heart and hers. The poor child. No. She was a woman now who had suffered so much. He only wanted to bring her joy and peace and possibly love. But still, he wondered what Roxy wanted.

Embarrassed and rejected, Roxanne drove straight home. She hadn't spent much time downtown, but early afternoon had already set in. She threw her keys on the foyer table and found her mother drinking a cup of tea in the kitchen. Roxanne dropped in a ladder-back chair. The lovely coconut crème cake sat in the center of the table with cut-glass plates and forks beside it. Roxanne stared at the delicious, white concoction. Beautiful, and she should have taken it to Max last night. Roxanne cut a huge slice and commenced stuffing her mouth.

"Shouldn't you have lunch first?"

"I am," Roxanne mumbled.

"Oh, my. Not a good day, dear?"

"It's Max."

"I thought as much. Did you talk to him?" Her mother's thumb and forefinger held the China teacup, and she sipped.

"I made an idiot of myself. I asked him to take me to Lacey Thompson's wedding."

"Oh, dear. Why ever would you do that? Didn't you apologize?"

"I wanted to, but I stopped in at Second Chance, and Virginia talked me into asking him to take me as a plus-one," Roxanne rambled. "Why did I ever listen to her?"

"A plus what?" Bethie asked.

"A date."

"A date? I'm sure he's going. So you didn't apologize."

"No. I didn't. But who cares now because he's taking someone else to the wedding." Roxanne took two more bites.

"Slow down. I'm sure you're mistaken. Who would he take?"

"I don't know. But it's not me." With an eye roll, Roxanne licked her lips.

"Why don't you go back and start over? Apologize."

"No. Not now." Roxanne let her mind stew. Too late. Max had a date. She assumed he did anyway. He didn't accept her invitation. A dark cloud brewed, and she wondered who it was. Taking one last bite, she stood. *If he had a date, she'd try and get one too.* She frowned. *Well, maybe at least take a friend.* Lucy popped into her head.

"Thanks, Mama." Roxanne grabbed her cell and stepped outside the front door.

"Where are you going?"

"Nowhere. I need some privacy."

Roxanne closed the front door and stood in the shade of the porch. She dialed Lucy's number.

"Hey, Roxy. Miss me?"

"Sure do. When are you coming back?"

"I'm extending my visit some more. It's really different here, And I'm loving my sister's kids."

"You're a professional Auntie, eh?" Roxanne teased. "Do you still have your job in Meridian?"

"Yeah. My boss loves me. I got a leave of absence. So listen, I'm not sure when I'll be back." She paused. "How are things there?" Her voice lowered a notch.

"Good." Roxanne scrunched her nose. "Not that good."

Young screams and laughter came through the phone. "Listen, I better go. Hold down the fort. I'll let you know when I make plans to return."

"Fine. Text me the flight info. Have fun." Roxanne rushed to click off.

"Wait, why'd you call?"

She huffed out a breath. "Oh, I got this wedding to attend and wondered if you wanted to go, but no worries."

"When is it?"

"Next weekend." Roxanne's voice squeaked a little. More of a question than an answer.

"Oh, I get it." Lucy giggled. "You need a plus one. Don't you hate that? At our age, we should be fine flying solo. But I hate going to friends' weddings alone. That's why I always drag my boyfriend, who hates it."

At least you have one.

"Hey, what about that Max guy? He's cute."

Roxanne pulled her cell away and stared. She hit the speaker. "He's just a friend. Besides, the guy is still in love with his deceased wife."

"How long has it been?"

"She passed years and years ago."

"Then he's over her. I'm sure of it, and you're just scared. Invite him to go with you and call me with all the juicy details."

"Seriously? You're talking like we're in high school or something."

"Sometimes romance feels like that."

Roxanne could almost see the wink on Lucy's face. Finally, she blurted. "He's going with someone else."

"Oh." Silence. "Well, maybe he got tired of waiting. Honey, you can't drag him along forever."

"What on earth are you talking about? I never…"

"Roxy, you spend more time with him than anyone else. At least that's what you told me. It's hard for women and men to be just friends for that long."

"Lucy, I have to go now."

"Love you." She paused. "Roxy? Just pray about it, okay. If I've learned anything from spending time with my sister, it's to pray. About everything. Bye."

Roxanne clicked off. *I'm not praying about Max.* Glancing at the old pecan tree in her front yard didn't bring her comfort, nor did Max's perfectly manicured lawn across the street.

Who could she invite? Anyone from her critique group? Definitely not. They were all women, most of them. Glancing down at her phone, she looked at her own messages. She noticed some unchecked ones from Travis. She smiled and punched his number.

CHAPTER 31

"Hello?" Travis answered.

"Hey, it's Roxanne." She paused, trying to find common ground before asking him to be her date. "I wondered if you took my manuscript and got famous somewhere. I mean, I haven't heard from you in months." She chuckled, but he didn't laugh.

Finally, he spoke slowly. "Well, really, Roxanne, it lacks something. A lot, actually."

She froze. How could it not be good? The librarian and those in her critique group gushed over it. Max assured her how good it was. Even her mother loved it. Well, of course, her mother would. Still, how dare he?

"I'm sorry to break the news, but you're missing the mark. I thoroughly reviewed it, and the bones are there. Maybe put it aside for a while and come back to it later. If you have another manuscript, I'd happily look it over."

She bristled, and she knew her voice took on the tone. *Seriously!* She blew out a cleansing breath. "Thanks, Travis. I'm afraid you took too long to respond. I've actually reworked it, and an agent has it now. In fact, I'm editing another book that's a sequel."

She heard him draw a breath, and he stuttered a bit, and

then what sounded like a fake laugh followed. "Well, I guess you're finally calling yourself a writer now. Good for you. I knew you could do it."

Roxanne felt a bit guilty at her harsh answer. After all, he pushed her to take the next step. Even if it did cause Dwayne to go off the deep end. "Well, I guess I have you to thank for that."

"So, where are you writing now? I'm serious. I'd love to read your new work. Maybe I missed something. Probably your new confidence. I knew you could do it."

Roxanne felt like a sucker for soaking in the praises. "I did join a critique group here." "Bravo. Good for you. I'm sure it shows. How long has the agent had your manuscript?"

She wondered why he asked. "Not long."

"Ahhh. So, you won't get the first edits back anytime soon, eh?"

He talked about the process of agents, editors, and publishers, and the more he spoke, the more comfortable she felt. Finally, she blurted out, "Hey, listen. I'm invited to a wedding, and I wondered if you'd like to be my plus one."

"Where?"

"Bay Town. Three hours south of Meridian. It's this weekend."

"This weekend huh? Hmmm."

"Yes. I know it's short notice." Roxanne bit the tip of her fingernail.

He paused for too long. "Yes, it is."

"We could talk books." Roxanne hoped she didn't sound desperate.

"I'm busy on Sunday afternoon."

"Great. The wedding is on Saturday," Roxanne said. She closed her eyes tight. *Please.*

"Sure. I'd love to come. Text me the time and place. And bring your new book."

"I'll have to think about that. Not sure if I can take your rejection again."

He laughed. "I promise I won't be as harsh. I'll see you on Saturday. Don't forget to text me the info. It's a date."

"A date it is." Roxanne hung up and opened the front door. She grabbed her purse and called out, "Mama? I'm going downtown to buy a new dress for the wedding. Want to join me?"

"Sure do. It's about time you bought some new clothes."

Saturday arrived, and relief flooded Roxanne when she saw Travis at the church. She waved from to him across the lawn but dropped her arm and wrung her hands together. The evening breeze hadn't entirely cooled her jitters. Her stomach fluttered. It had been so long since she'd dated. But this wasn't really one. Still, she felt giddy and nervous.

He joined her on the church steps, but most guests were already inside.

"Oh, good. You're here." Roxanne smiled.

Travis looked sharp as he pushed his hair behind his ears. The tan suit, white shirt, and no tie gave him a casual, trendy look. He smiled back at her.

"You look great. Love the dress." He took her hand and spun her around.

Her navy chiffon dress flared out, and she laughed as a few tendrils fell from her messy bun. The wrap dress tie loosened at her side, and she secured the bow. When she looked up, Travis smiled. He reached out and lifted a loose strand of her hair and tucked it behind her ear. The soft touch felt nice. Just lovely, and all the actions soothed her anxiety.

He offered his arm. "Your escort, at your service." He winked as she grasped his crooked elbow.

When they walked in, the packed church made her

stomach lurch. She felt light-headed. Her wedding would have been here. Roxanne closed her eyes and felt Travis squeeze her hand.

"Everything okay?"

"Fine," Roxanne said. *On the outside.*

An usher led them to the last two available seats, right in front of her mother and Max. Roxanne removed her hand from the crook of Travis's elbow. Her mother's mouth gaped, and she wore a nervous expression. Roxanne wanted to assure her of Travis's credibility, but she didn't want to meet Max's gaze. *Is he gazing?* The jumble of anxious feelings toiled inside.

The pianist effortlessly transitioned, and Pastor Brooks, the Groom, and an older gentleman entered from a side entrance. As the bridesmaids floated down the aisle on the arms of the groomsmen and took their places up front, Roxanne recalled all the weddings she'd been in. A pang hit her heart. Suddenly, she felt Travis squeeze her hand. She looked up, and he smiled.

"You're more beautiful than all of them," he whispered a little too loudly.

From her peripheral vision, she thought she saw Max roll his eyes. But Max never rolled his eyes.

Roxanne somehow managed to make it through the wedding. Much like an out-of-body experience, and she hoped no one would ask her what she thought. But that was easy. *Just lovely. A perfect ceremony, and the bride is gorgeous and so happy. Happy.* Simple words that left a knife in her heart.

After the ceremony, everyone drove to The Grand Terrace Hotel, where the reception was held in the stunning ballroom. Recently built and owned by Lacey Thompson's new husband's family. The Gardners. She'd learned that the groom's great-grandfather, Mr. Gardner, stood up front as his best man.

There were so many lights Roxanne imagined it resembling Disneyland at night. White drapery hung around the room, and Roxanne couldn't take her eyes off the massive crystal chandelier. As her eyes perused the room, roses, magnolias, hydrangeas, and peonies delightfully greeted her. Each table centerpiece vied for the most beautiful. Each uniquely infused with swirly, thin twigs and a variety of ribbons. Roxanne guessed Max had a hand in the arrangements. His creative inspiration shined in each one. His creative flair inspired them all, if not his actual hands

The scent of roses and night-blooming jasmine filled the air, and the tinkling of glasses with toasts rang out throughout the evening. Roxanne drunk in the magical romance, and couldn't help wishing she were with Max.

Thankfully, Max sat across the room with Bethie Cook and a few others from the church. Roxanne searched for his date, but he didn't seem to be with anyone. Her heart sank into her stomach, and she second-guessed her motive for inviting Travis.

They discussed her manuscript, though her heart wasn't in it. "I just finished it," she said. "It's still filed on my mama's computer, in rough draft."

Travis shifted in his seat. "Well, tell me about this new one. I'm curious. What's it about?" He touched her hand.

She pulled her fingers away and teased. "I'm not so sure I trust you."

His eyes widened. "Me? Why not?"

"Oh, you know. What if you steal my book and publish it? I just heard an author tell us all about self-publishing. You never know."

He pulled at his unbuttoned collar and cleared his throat. "Wow. This is a big wedding. Is everyone from this town in attendance?"

She wondered why he changed the subject. "Probably. Lacey is the town's sweetheart." Roxanne owned that title once, and everyone in town had been invited to her wedding too.

"How could they afford this place?" Travis wiped a white linen napkin across his brow.

"The groom comes from a wealthy family in New Orleans," said Roxanne. "They own a string of hotels, and this is their newest. The first outside of New Orleans, I heard. So yes. I imagine pretty much everyone is here."

"How small is Bay Town?" His eyes roamed the room as if looking for someone.

"Pretty small."

He seemed to relax, and their conversation turned to where Roxanne lived in Bay Town and whom she lived with. Her mother came over, not too pleased that Roxanne had a date she didn't know, but Travis charmed her. He even kissed her hand in a Southern gentlemanly way.

"Nice to meet you, Miz Cook. You must be happy to have Roxanne home with the family."

"With the family? Why, there's just the two of us living over on Magnolia Lane."

He nodded, and before he could ask another question, Roxanne interrupted.

"Mama, they're getting ready to cut the cake."

"Oh, I better go help serve. Nice meeting you. Be nice to my Roxanne." She pointed a finger and left.

"Of course." He smiled and started to sit, but another woman approached. He remained standing.

"Hello, Roxanne." Mrs. Hancock, the young librarian, stood next to her.

"Hello. Beautiful wedding, isn't it?"

"Yes. I'm so honored to be invited. I tutored Lacey a little when she homeschooled after the incident." she looked around. "After all that's happened to her." her voice lowered to a whisper.

Roxanne nodded.

"Anyway, I'm just thrilled how things worked out for her." Mrs. Hancock stared at Travis.

"Do I know you?"

He smiled back confidently. "I'm sure we've never met. This is my first time in Bay Town."

Her brows wrinkled.

"Oh, this is my friend Travis. He's a writer too," Roxanne said.

He seemed to stammer something, but the librarian interrupted.

"That's it. I've seen your picture on the fly-leaf in a new book at the bookstore chain in Biloxi."

Roxanne's eyes widened, but Travis's widened even bigger.

"Oh, no, ma'am. That couldn't be me. I'm not published."

She stared intently. "You know, my mistake. Now that I remember, I'm sure the author's name wasn't Travis. But my goodness, if you wore different glasses and had a mustache, you'd be the spitting image of him."

"The title of the book?" Roxanne asked bluntly.

Travis stood. "Punch anyone?"

"No, thanks. The book?" Roxanne asked again.

Mrs. Hancock continued staring after him as he practically ran for the drink table.

"Dissertations in Dirt." Mrs. Hancock chuckled. "I only read the synopsis. But it's a sweet romance about a gardener and an author who met during World War II. It sounded very intriguing."

Roxanne tipped her head, relieved that it couldn't be her story. Although her romance with a gardener had similarities. Still, hers wasn't set in World War II. As she sat pondering, she looked across the room, and her eyes rested on Max, dancing with Virginia. They laughed together and he spun her around. Roxanne admired his dancing, and apparently so did Virginia. They seemed to be having way too much fun. He never looked in her direction, and all thoughts of her book left her mind.

"Well, that will annoy me till I can remember the author." Mrs. Hancock excused herself.

Roxanne broke her gaze from Max and searched the punch table. Travis had vanished. Had he ditched her? He did say he had an appointment tomorrow, and she wondered if he'd already left for Meridian. *What a jerk.*

The music slowed, and she stared at the dance floor. Travis didn't even dance with her before he left. Maybe he just came for the food. Roxanne turned around and downed her glass of sparkling cider.

∼

Max gazed at her from across the room. Roxanne looked absolutely lovely. Her tousled hair fell around her shoulders in rolling waves, and the pouty expression added to the attraction. He chuckled as she coughed a little after polishing off her drink. *Her date? Where had he gone?* Max stood, casually placed his hand in his pocket, and strolled the room. Checking for Roxanne's date, he couldn't find the lean man with the glasses and longish hair. Funny how the man reminded him much of himself when he was younger.

He stopped by the drink fountain and retrieved a glass of sparkling cider. He downed it just as Roxanne had. As if fueling his courage, he stepped forward but halted. If he came to her rescue, would he be her knight in shining armor and commit to something deeper? Philippa. Thoughts of her flooded back, and a pang gripped his heart. *Lord, what shall I do? I'll always love her.* But as he patted his chest, a sweet release seemed to relax his body, and he decided right then and there that he'd pursue a relationship with Roxy. If she'd have him.

With each step, his resolve strengthened, and he hoped she felt as deeply for him as he did for her. Her eyes confirmed it as a smile lit up her face when he approached her table.

～

"Oh, hey, Max." Roxanne gripped her hands, quelling her excitement.

"What happened to your date?"

"He wasn't feeling well?" She didn't mean for it to be a question.

"I'm so sorry."

"And what about your date?" Roxanne asked.

"I don't have one."

"But you said…"

"I said I was already going." Max's eyes shined. "All right then. Miss Cooke, may I have this dance?"

Her heart fluttered, and Roxanne swallowed a breath. "I'd love to dance, Mr. Tippet."

He led her to the center of the floor, and his palm touched the space between her shoulder blades. With the other, he held her hand firmly out to the side. Her spine tingled, and as she placed her hand on his shoulder, the sensation spread. His arm braced under hers like they were joined as one.

Roxanne's father had taught her all the old dances, and as she lifted her face towards Max, thoughts of her father floated away. Every dip and turn syncopated perfectly. He held her so effortlessly and led her so perfectly. Couples parted, and some even clapped as they twirled. She let her head slip to one side, and he gazed at her like never before. As they swept around the dance floor, she felt as if her feet never touched the ground. One song after another, they never ceased to swirl and sway, the music bringing them closer and closer together.

Dancing in Max's arms made Roxanne forget everything else. When the song ended, Max didn't let go but pulled her even closer. Their eyes locked on one another, and her heart pounded as she stared into his sparkling blue pools. Smiling, he took a deep breath, squeezed her hand, and let go, making a chivalrous deep bow.

"Well, love, we best be saying goodbye to the bride and groom." He nodded across the room at the couple trying to make their escape.

Max pulled her outside, and the hot evening wind rushed through her hair. Everyone cheered Lacey and Wade off. Strings of bulb lights looped along the covered walkway, framing the magical night. The crowd cheered as the couple ran through a tunnel of bubbles the guests blew. All except Max and Roxanne, whose intertwined hands rested in a perfect fit.

Amidst the crowd cheering, Max reached up, swept a loose strand of hair from her brow, and smiled. The sweet night-blooming jasmine scented the air, and the crowds dissipated. Roxanne's heart beat so fast, she feared he'd hear it. He took her hand and hooked it under his elbow, securing it safely by his side. He led her toward the darkness under an old Magnolia tree. His tender touch and soft breathing made her light-headed. She walked so closely to his side that their thighs brushed against one another with each step.

When he stopped under the tree, Roxanne leaned her head against his shoulder. She'd never noticed the definition of his muscled arm before. Her stomach fluttered when he turned toward her. She looked up, and he lifted her chin to his slightly parted lips. Staring into her eyes, he bent his head toward hers, and she tiptoed up. A slight brush of his lips against hers created a lingering tingle.

"Roxanne?" Her mother's shrill voice rang from the venue.

Max released his hold but took Roxanne's hand and gently pulled her behind the tree. She stumbled, but he caught her in his arms, and with a fast swoop, he kissed her so completely her arms fell to her sides. She could barely breathe, and all she could think of was, where did he learn to kiss like that? He pulled away once more. Taking her shoulders, he turned her toward her mother. As he pressed her shoulders from behind, she felt another sweet kiss, this time on her cheek, as exhilarating as the one she'd just tasted. "Go, love. I'll follow later."

She turned, searching his eyes. He smiled, and the assurance she felt wasn't one of safety or security but something more meaningful.

"Coming, Mama."

"What, in land's sake, are you doing out here alone?" Bethie covered her brows with a cupped hand, peering past Roxanne, who sauntered towards her, swinging her arms without a care in the world.

Bethie narrowed her eyes, then burst out laughing. "I don't see him, but I bet he's out there."

Roxanne strolled on past her, a silly grin on her face. "Come on, Mama. Time to go home."

"Nice wedding," Bethie said.

"Like a dream, Mama. Like a dream."

CHAPTER 32

On the short drive home, Roxanne's mother prattled on about the wedding, and Roxanne half listened as if her voice came from far away. Everything changed tonight. She touched her mouth, still relishing the gentleness of Max's lips on hers. Exhilaration permeated her like a magical dream.

It all shattered at the sight in front of Mama's house.

Red and blue lights flashed, and a Sherrif's SUV blocked her driveway. Pulling to the curb, Roxanne walked quickly toward a uniformed officer. It wasn't Chief Bert but the Hancock County Sheriffs.

"What's going on?" Roxanne asked.

"Everything is fine, ma'am. A neighbor walking their dog noticed the broken window here and called." He pointed. "One panel aside the big bay window is broken, and the door is unlocked."

"Did you go in? Is anyone in there?" *A stupid question.*

"Yes, ma'am, we checked thoroughly. No one is inside. The house looks pretty much undisturbed. But I'd like to walk through with you, just to make sure."

"Sheriff, did you catch the intruder?" Bethie asked from behind Roxanne.

"No, ma'am. We guess he broke the window, went in, and left through the front door. No one actually saw him."

Roxanne stood frozen but somewhat relieved. "Are you saying they left everything intact?"

"As far as we can tell. Ma'am, I suggest we go in, and you can assess the situation. Any idea who might have broken in?" the sheriff asked.

A shiver went up Roxanne's spine. "Yes, but it doesn't match up."

She took a deep breath and stepped forward. No more hesitation. The gripping fear of Dwayne's wrath wasn't present. Somehow, she knew Dwayne wasn't here.

"Roxy?"

The whisper in her ear caused her to jump, stumbling backward into a body behind her.

"I'm sorry I frightened you." Max enveloped her so tightly. She relished the brief embrace, but he pulled away.

She turned to the sheriff. "I'm ready to look around."

The sheriff led them through the living room, and the roving beam of his flashlight illuminated the dark corners where the lamps didn't. Max held Roxanne's hand as they searched. Together, they examined each room, ensuring things were undisturbed. The sheriff handed his card to Roxanne and asked her to report if they found anything missing.

Max squeezed her hand.

"Lock your doors, ladies. I'll keep a patrol on the street."

Bethie closed the door. "Do you think it was him? Why would he break in and not take anything?"

"Mama, please." Roxanne slanted her eyes toward Max, not wanting to mention Dwayne in front of him. She recalled telling him a little, but not the sordid details.

"Maybe he's hiding somewhere," Bethie whispered. "I don't think we should stay here."

"I'll stay," Max said.

"Oh, no. I'm afraid we can't have that." Bethie clasped the

pearls around her neck. "Max, I know this is the new millennium, but I can't have a man staying in my house. Not a single man."

Roxanne rolled her eyes. "Oh, Mama. For Pete's sake." She turned to Max. "Could you?"

"Roxanne." Bethie stared at her daughter. "If the neighbors saw your embrace out there and are watching. Well, you know people talk."

"I beg your pardon, Bethie, but nothing inappropriate has transpired." Max dropped Roxanne's hand.

"Seriously, Mama. Is that all you're worried about?"

"Of course not."

"Good. Thank you, Max," Roxanne said.

"We need to have a little trust in our neighbors, don't we? If we can't think the best of them, how can they possibly reciprocate?" Max said.

"I guess you're right." Bethie narrowed her eyes at Roxanne and pointed. "Maybe you better sleep in my room, just in case."

"Mama!"

Max laughed and stepped away from Roxanne. His hands lifted in surrender. "You have my promise, Bethie." He stared at Roxanne and sighed. "I'm unsure what's happening between us or how to navigate it. Perhaps we'll talk tomorrow?"

"Well, isn't that something? The Lord works in mysterious ways. You pray for a situation to happen, and when it does, you don't know what to do with it. Well, I'm off to bed now." She turned towards the hallway. "Roxanne? Are you coming?"

"Yes. I'll be along shortly."

Bethie narrowed her eyes.

"Oh, please, Mama."

Bethie shuffled down the hallway. "Well, praise the Lord. It's about time," she mumbled.

Max loosened his tie and removed his jacket laying it across a chair. "I'll just sleep on your sofa tonight."

"Yes. I'll get you a blanket and a pillow," Roxanne said.

Chuckling, he said, "I won't be needing a blanket in this heat." He gazed at her and sighed.

They stood staring at one another, and Roxanne wanted nothing more in this moment than to experience another sweet, lingering kiss. A deep longing in her heart seemed to match the contented expression on his face. But he stepped back and crossed the room putting distance between them.

"You know, perhaps your mother is quite wise to be concerned. Tonight is not the time for us to be acting on impulse."

Roxanne's brow furrowed. *Impulse?* Everything about the evening from their first dance felt smooth and intentional, and nothing had felt so right in her life for a very long time. She took a step forward.

Max turned, fluffing up the sofa cushions. "Until tomorrow then. It's best we get some rest. I think the night will do us good."

Roxanne nodded. *Maybe he was right. What was she thinking?* Barely out of an abusive relationship, she shouldn't take Max's friendship lightly. But right now, she desired more than his friendship. Much more. She hung her head nodded.

But Max rushed to her, as if he couldn't help himself, and threw his arms around her, pulling her close, ignoring every-thing he'd just said. She pressed into his chest feeling the strength of his heartbeat. She clung on as if for dear life. A fulfilling tiredness overcame her, and she felt safe. He kissed her forehead, her cheeks, and gazed into her eyes, but stopped and pulled her to the sofa. They sat, but he scooted a foot away, still holding one of her hands.

"Only God knows what's going on. With you, with me." He drew a breath. "With Him. We don't have the answers, but we can believe that God has our best interests at heart."

"You are my best interest, Max." The words tumbled from her mouth, and she couldn't stop them. "You always have been. My life is perfect with you." She feared her heart might explode.

He smiled. "I'd like it to be. But let's take it a bit slow, shall we? This is new territory for me too." He kissed the palm of her hand. "By the way, you are a charming dancer, my love."

Although she'd heard the colloquialism since girlhood, the word felt fresh, deep, and unique this time.

"My father taught me. And you're quite light on your feet yourself there, sir."

"Thank you." He let go of her hand and rested his arm across the back of the sofa. "Did you know Philippa and I used to go ballroom dancing all the time? I almost felt as if I had her in my arms again."

The magic faded.

Max looked at her. "You are an extraordinary woman. Much like my Philippa. You need to know that God has blessed you in many ways."

"I don't feel so special." *Not like Philippa. Pure as the driven snow.* She shook her head, a creepiness crawling inside. Roxanne had messed around with Dwayne for over a year. A year, and they had never married. *Everyone does it nowadays,* she'd reasoned. But she knew better then, and she knew better now. "You don't know what I've done."

Max moved to her side. "But the Lord does, and that's all that matters."

"But..." *You need to know.* Her hands started to shake. *How could she ever tell him?*

Wrapping his hands around hers, he squeezed them. "Come on, now. It can't be all that bad. We're all sinners. We've all gone astray, right?"

"Some of us more so than others," she whispered.

"And yet, the Lord forgives us all. All we need do is confess, and repent. I dare say, I believe you've done that. And it won't be the last time. Not for me either." He touched her chin, tipping it up to him. "Roxy, all in due time. Just look to the Lord and count your blessings for now, you'll find Him working all around you. And recognizing those things will increase your trust in Him."

"Like what?"

"Like your work with the children and the seniors. You inspire them. And the re-opening of Sally's bookstore, you're responsible for her joy in that. And me." Max's blue eyes shone. "You've stirred something in this heart that's been long tucked away."

Roxanne's stomach knotted like a gut punch. *Dare she hope?*

"Your writing too. I've missed working with Philippa, but reading and editing your work has given me purpose again."

Her throat knotted. "I see." Even in the heat, a chill shivered her heart. "I guess we make a good team then, don't we?"

The rhetorical question didn't need an answer. Roxanne pulled her hands away. Maybe a working relationship was all that was meant to be. The thought caused mild nausea. Right now, she wanted him, and not just a writing mentor. How would she ever sleep tonight? "You're right. I have much to be thankful for. Especially my writing."

Max leaned back onto the sofa. "Maybe I should read some of your new pages while I'm here tonight." He nodded at the computer.

Roxanne followed his gaze and stood. A bittersweetness filled her. She loved listening to him read, and it certainly would help her sleep. No. She didn't want to hear his soothing voice. Not now. Yet how she longed to hear it forever one day. She shook her head as if dismissing the thought.

Walking toward the computer, she stared. Something seemed amiss. Peering closer, she noticed that the PC power button was off. Roxanne had a terrible habit of always leaving it on. She hadn't remembered shutting it down, but a soft rushing sound came from behind her, making her forget her concern. She turned.

Max's head rested on the back of the sofa, and he had the sweetest little snore she'd ever heard. His peaceful hands clasped on his chest, and his long legs spread before him. The slight part of his lips let out the whisper whoosh as his chest rose and fell. Like her emotions rising and falling as well.

Roxanne touched her lips and blew a kiss, imagining it landing on his lips. "Good night...my love...I wish." She trudged back to her room, trying to forget the whole magical but not-so-fairy tale ending to an almost perfect evening.

CHAPTER 33

Roxanne slept restlessly. She awoke with the sheets twisted between her fingers and her nightgown damp. Dwayne…Somewhere here…hiding in the house. But the chirping birds heralded a happy dawn as last night bloomed in her brain. She chose to recall the wedding, not the break-in. Max, not Dwayne, rested downstairs in the house. She smiled but wondered if last night had been just a dream?

Throwing on her robe, she skipped for her door and caught her reflection in the dresser mirror. She scrunched her face. She hadn't even bothered to wash up before bed. Grabbing a comb, she smiled as she swept it through her hair. Replacing it, she noticed an aged paper tucked under a tray. Pulling it out, the ivory notecard had a P scrolled in the corner.

"My dear Roxanne, Never forget how talented you are. Devote yourself to the craft. God has indeed gifted you. I'm here to help in any way I can. Carry on, Philippa."

Roxanne's skin tingled. *Was this a sign? How long had that been there? She'd forgotten that Philippa had even written it to her.* She stood, staring at herself in the mirror. *What now?* She tied her robe tightly, washed up in the bathroom, and walked down the stairs.

Max sat at her computer, and Roxanne's heart didn't flutter. It hurt. She stood, watching him. His wrinkled white shirt evidenced that he had indeed spent the night. His dotted yellow tie and blue suit jacket slung over his arm.

"Good morning, love."

Please don't say that. "Good morning, Max."

"I was leaving you a note. I must get to the shop."

He looked at her with sparkling eyes and moved toward her. She stepped back, and he stopped.

"Breakfast," Bethie called from the kitchen.

"No, thank you, Bethie. I best be off." He called out and winked at Roxanne. Reaching out, he touched her arm. "Let's talk tonight, shall we?"

His touch tingled her with warmth. "Yes." She closed her eyes and stepped away. "Actually, no, I'm busy this evening."

He frowned. Confusion creased his brow.

Everything in her wanted that to happen. Another warm embrace, another sweet kiss, but she didn't trust the Philippa thing. It could only lead to heartache, and she'd experienced enough of that. She didn't want another fiasco like Gregory, Spencer, or Dwayne. Roxanne's throat tightened. Too many men, but still, she wanted Max badly.

"All right, then." Max leaned in to hug her, but she stepped back again, cinching her belt. "I need to wash up. Thanks so much for staying. That was such a crazy night."

"I understand. Perhaps you can stop by the Pink Rosette for lunch, then?" His brows raised.

What about Philippa? She wanted to ask. "No, I really can't today."

His puzzled expression gave way to his sweet smile. "Listen, Roxy. Perhaps I stepped out of the bounds of a gentleman last night."

She gazed back at him, and her eyes burned. "No, you didn't. Maybe we both just got caught up in the moment." *And what a moment it was.*

His lips parted, but he didn't speak. A painful pause followed, and he nodded, pointed to the door, and left quietly.

Roxanne felt her heart crack. She trudged toward the kitchen. The coffee smelled wonderful, the bacon divine, and outside the kitchen window, birds flitted about, but nothing could lift her spirits. She sighed while lightly banging her head against the door jamb.

"Didn't sleep well, eh?" Her mother sat at the kitchen table. "Me neither. I worried about that break-in."

Roxanne had almost forgotten. "I'm so sorry." *Poor Mama.*

"Come sit." She patted a chair. "Was it him, Roxanne? Did he come here?"

"I don't think so. If he had, the place would have been trashed. It's bizarre. I just don't know."

The toaster popped, and Bethie stood. "Well, on a better note, would you like to explain?" Her mother winked.

"About what?"

"Max." Bethie buttered toast, and plated scrambled eggs. She placed them before Roxanne and sat.

A heaviness hung on her shoulders. "No, Mama. Nothing to explain. You know, weddings do crazy stuff to people." Her heart twisted.

Bethie kissed her daughter's cheek. "Well, I, for one, hope it's more than just that. You deserve a joyful life."

Wouldn't that be nice? But why get her hopes up now. Roxanne shoved food around her plate, hoping her mother wouldn't notice. After showering and getting ready for the day, she sat down to write, anxious to tidy up her manuscript. She recalled Max's encouraging words. She sighed. And Philippa's. The woman reigned ever present, but Roxanne didn't draw strength from her. The realization of her dependence on yet another man rose. It had gotten her into the mess with Dwayne and Spencer. Both rebounds. And Max? Perhaps he played the rebound from Dwayne. She shivered. No rebounds. No more.

Sitting at her computer, Roxanne hit the monitor button. She booted up the PC and logged into her docs. She glanced down at the incomplete note that Max had started to write. Mixed feelings flooded her body. Pushing them away, she looked at her computer screen and gasped. Her manuscripts were gone. She hit the search bar and combed through her Recycle Bin. Anywhere she knew to check, she tried. All her documents were gone. She opened her emails, thankful they'd still be there, but no. After saving them in docs, she'd deleted them.

Rolling her chair back across the floor, she swiveled and stood. Her pages couldn't just disappear. Narrowing her eyes, she glanced down at Max's note. *He wouldn't have done anything, would he?*

She shuddered at the flashbacks of Dwayne destroying her thumb drive in the garbage disposal. For a split second, she wondered if Max could even think of such a thing. *No, of course not.* But maybe he accidentally erased her manuscripts. But he'd gone to bed before her. Perhaps a power outage or something. A glitch?

Nothing sounded right, and the more she thought about it, the sicker she felt. She couldn't possibly rewrite everything. Roxanne closed her eyes. No one had her new pages. But what about her finished book? Max had a copy. He had given it to Philippa's agent. Travis had a copy, too, but he didn't like it. She shuddered, remembering his harsh critique. Her cell rang jarring her to the present.

"Hi, Roxanne. This is Mrs. Hancock."

"Good morning."

"Listen, I looked up that book I told you about at the wedding last night. *Dissertations in Dirt.*"

"The one you thought Travis wrote?"

"Yes. It sounded so much like your story. I remember when you read a few chapters in our critique group. They were outstanding and stuck with me."

Roxanne's stomach soured. "Go on."

"Well, I thought you might get a copy of Dissertations in Dirt and read it. You could order it online, but it's just a short drive to Biloxi. To the big chain store."

"Why would I do that?"

"I checked, and they carry the book there." Mrs. Hancock huffed, and a long pause followed. "It doesn't happen often, but sometimes manuscripts are stolen, changed a bit, and printed under a false name."

"Do you really think it's my book?" Her heart sank at her own question.

"It's awfully similar. Other than the historical setting, it could easily be the same story."

"Thank you. I'll check into it."

Roxanne sat on her bed. How could she be so stupid? If only she'd heeded the warning. She'd second-guessed giving her manuscript to Travis in the very beginning. Balling her fists, she felt like hitting something. Instead, she grabbed her keys and headed for Biloxi.

Within fifty minutes, she stood next to a display. *Dissertations in Dirt.* What a lousy title. But the cover was beautiful. A stunning woman in an intelligent forties style suit enveloped in the arms of a handsome man in coveralls. The backdrop of a cemetery outlined in flowers on gravestones, and behind it all, bombs exploding in the dark night sky. She opened the book and began reading. Her eyes widened at every line, lifted right from the pages of her manuscript with the setting tweaked. She quickly flipped to the back flyleaf. A white-haired man with a mustache and dark-rimmed glasses. A good disguise, but it didn't look like Travis at all. She peered closer. It looked like Max.

She threw the book down. *How dare he?* She grunted loudly,

and a few people around her turned. "I'm sorry," she said quietly. She took the book to the register. "Excuse me, how long has this book been released?"

"Brand new. That's why it's on the circular table out front. Usually, the publisher pays for that, but this author independently published it and paid for the table. He's having a book signing today."

Heat surged up her neck. "Really. What time?"

"This evening. Around six o'clock. We're expecting a crowd. For a new book, it's gotten lots of good reviews."

"Oh, really?"

"Uh, huh."

"Have you read it?" Roxanne asked.

"No, ma'am. Romance is not my genre." The thin young man pushed up his glasses, and grinned. "But most of the girls here have read it, and they loved it. It's selling pretty well."

Her mouth went dry, and Roxanne didn't know if she could control a scream ready to escape. She cleared her throat. "Okay, thanks. Six o'clock?"

He gave her a thumbs up as she paid for the book and stormed to her car. She drove home weaving in and out of traffic. A horn honked, and Roxanne yanked her steering wheel and swerved nearly missing the vintage VW bug in the next lane. Without looking, she waved a sheepish apology and continued home. Her disturbing thoughts returned, and she tried to fathom how everything had suddenly turned south. Travis ditched her at the wedding. Max possibly had published her book under a pseudonym. How could it get worse? Someone had deleted all her manuscripts. No. They'd been stolen.

Roxanne rubbed her temple. Why when things were going so well? But a sober thought stopped her and her heart beat faster. Things hadn't been going so well. Dwayne had been free too long, and no one knew his whereabouts. She'd let herself forget him while forging this new life. But she couldn't anymore. Life had definitely turned. Going from bad to worse. It only made sense he'd come back. Murphy's law, right? But she didn't believe in that. The hair rose on her arm and the power of Dwayne's terror returned.

That evening, Roxanne skipped dinner and shut herself in her room. She gazed at herself in the oversize, oval, antique mirror hanging over her dresser. The gilded gold piece her mother had chosen for her long ago.

"So, you'll always know you're God's princess," Mama had said.

Roxanne took a makeup remover pad and wiped off the foundation around her eyes. She peered closely. If she really concentrated, she could still see faint bruising. She swept aside her bangs and touched the faded scar over her brow. Glancing at her raised wrist, she twisted it until she winced. The break had healed, but a residual ache remained. Just like the searing pain deep in her heart.

Roxanne lay on her bed and stared at the ceiling. When Bethie came up to check on her, she closed her eyes, feigning sleep. Her mother left a tray of food and retreated quietly. Roxanne had no appetite and couldn't force herself to move. Tears slipped down the side of her face.

Dwayne now paralyzed her actions, and Roxanne missed the book signing. But he wasn't the only reason. She couldn't face Max and could hardly believe he had stolen her story. As much as she wanted to believe it was Travis, the picture on the flyleaf was Max. Why did Mrs. Hancock see Travis? Her eyes widened. Because Travis resembled a younger Max. Just a little. Her mind swirled, imagining scenarios that didn't really make sense.

Philippa. Max couldn't let her go, and he'd turned Roxy's story into a WWII historical romance. Phillipa wrote historical romance. Without reading the book, she knew the love story between him, and his deceased wife had unfolded. The back blurb synopsis painted a lovely story of a Royal Airforce Airman turned gardener in love with a British writer.

Her heart raced, and she found it hard to breathe. God had blessed her with so much here in Bay Town. *Why would He take it away now?* Her mom was wrong. She didn't deserve joy. Roxanne rolled over and sobbed into her pillow.

CHAPTER 34

Roxanne went through the motions of living her normal routine. Out of body experience described her interactions with everyone, and by the end of the week her motivation to keep pretending that everything was okay waned. She chose to isolate herself. Her mind played scenarios of what her future might be as her world crumbled around her. All those years writing, and for what? The man she trusted most had betrayed her, and the monster she feared returned to haunt her once more. Not physically, not yet. But Dwayne invaded her thoughts. Maybe her life should end with him.

She ignored a knock at her bedroom door.

"Roxanne, sweetheart. I'm coming in."

Her mother padded softly to her dresser, setting down a tray of food. She approached Roxanne's bed where she lay curled up drenched in sweat. Bethie pulled back the sheets and sat next to her. She stroked Roxanne's damp hair.

"The Lord is my shepherd, I shall not want..." Bethie proceeded to recite all of Psalms Twenty-three, and though it registered in Roxanne's brain, the words filtered out of her head.

"I know you can hear me, and only God's Word can heal

that heart of yours. But I'm not going to let your body waste away. Now daughter, get up."

Roxanne stared straight ahead. Her eyes fixed on nothing.

"It's Saturday, and you've been in here since Thursday." Her mother glanced at a large glass of water. Half empty. "Well, I'm glad to see you at least had the sense to get some liquid in you. You don't smell so good, and you're going to wash up if I have to douse you myself."

Wrapping her arms under Roxanne's, Bethie pulled. She complied and sat up but slumped back against the padded headboard.

"Today, you're going to get downstairs and write. Enough is enough. Mrs. Hancock over at the Library called. You missed your writing classes yesterday, but she wanted to know if you were all right." Bethie cleared her throat. "She also told me about the book."

Roxanne closed her eyes and sighed.

"Phew! Girl, you need to brush your teeth. Come on." Bethie tugged.

Scooting to the end of the bed, she finally looked at her mother. "It's no use. I can't write anymore. I tried. My fingers won't move."

"Nonsense. You know Max has been over. He wanted to talk to you about your manuscript."

Roxanne's eyes flew wide open. Heat rushed to her face. "How dare he."

Bethie pulled her shoulders back. "Well, that got a rise. But what do you mean?"

Roxanne's cell buzzed on her nightstand, and she glanced over, but didn't move.

Bethie reached for it.

"What's your password?"

Roxanne shook her head.

"Give me your password," Bethie said.

Roxanne seethed out four numbers and closed her eyes.

"Well, you got lots of messages, but this one is from Lucy."

"Lucy?" Roxanne said in a loud but hoarse voice. "What does it say? Is she coming back?"

Bethie squinted at the screen. "Yes. She texted flight info. Let's see. She'll be here in two hours."

For the first time in days, Roxanne's heart lifted. She'd forgotten all about Lucy, yet Lucy was all about hope. Shoving herself to stand, she wobbled and quickly dropped back down. The room seemed to spin around, and her empty stomach growled loudly. Bethie trotted to the dresser, retrieving the food tray. "Here, drink this orange juice and eat this toast. Now," she said forcefully.

Roxanne did so with eyes closed. She felt her blood flow again, giving rise to strength. "I'm picking Lucy up today." She nodded, and a smile edged the corner of her lips.

"Not until you eat and shower. And I'm driving. You're in no condition."

"I'm fine. I'll be fine." Roxanne kissed her mother's cheek.

Bethie's eyes held water, and she smiled at her daughter. "I was almost afraid I'd lost you dear."

"Thanks, Mama."

Bethie left, but not until she'd warned her to finish her toast and juice. "And take a bite of that boiled egg. You need some protein."

"Yes, Mama."

Roxanne took a bite of toast and egg and downed the small glass of juice. It amazed her how energized she felt. The food and Lucy's impending return.

How could she have forgotten her only friend? Here she'd ignored all nudges in her soul to call Melanie and Pastor Brooks. To seek counsel, and even to read her Bible. But Lucy's upbeat spirit inspired her.

Roxanne showered, dressed, and grabbed her keys. Giddy with excitement, she ran outside and yanked open her car door. She caught Max's wave as he crossed the street.

Roxanne wanted to run back inside, but her feet cemented. Her palms sweated, and she wiped them down her dress. She couldn't avoid him forever.

"Roxy, are you all right? Your mum said you've not been feeling well."

"I'm fine," she lied.

"Right then. So you've been avoiding me?" He chuckled.

Roxanne rolled her eyes.

Max tugged at his ear. "Look, I apologize if you think I took advantage of you at the wedding. Perhaps that evening got the best of me." He shoved his hands into his front pockets.

"Maybe. You know, weddings and all," Roxanne waved a flippant hand in the air.

He gazed into her eyes, but she wouldn't give him anything. She glanced away.

"Well, then." He sighed. "I guess we have no need to discuss the evening?"

Was he seriously asking her? "Nope, not at all." She shook her head. Calculated, and slow. Her head moved back and forth.

He swiped strands of his loose hair back and gazed at her. Waiting. If her anger over the book hadn't hovered, she might have weakened. Yet recalling the note from Philippa that she'd found on her dresser, fueled a strong defense.

"But, hey, I appreciate your help with my book. Yours's and Philippa's." She said the latter a little too forcefully.

His eyes narrowed. "Well, yes then. I'm guessing you're also a little perturbed about the progress of your book?"

Her jaw dropped. *A little perturbed?*

"I spoke with the publisher again, and they're very interested. It's just that —"

"Let me guess, there's another story just like it out there," Roxanne said.

"How did you know?" He looked genuinely puzzled. "I told them there's nothing new under the sun but that your book read much differently. The depth of your main character is rich and unique in a way that only you could have written it. Not even Philippa —"

"Never mind." Roxanne stopped him. "I get it."

"Get what?"

She didn't want to go there but couldn't stop herself. She gripped her keys so tightly they hurt her palms. "Philippa. Always Philippa. I know you'll forever love her, but she's not here, Max. You are, and I am. She didn't help me with my story. You did." There, she'd said it, and she hated herself for it. "I have to go."

Lines creased his brow. "Is that what you think? We need to talk. Roxy, you mean an awful lot to me."

"I know because I remind you of her."

"No, that's not why." His voice changed.

She'd never heard a harsh tone from him, but this was close. Still, she couldn't let her guard down. He was a thief! Of her heart and her story.

"Of course, it is. Besides, it doesn't matter. My story is not going anywhere, is it? Maybe you and Phillipa can enjoy the love story. I'm done with it."

"You don't know what you're saying. I'm sorry if I've misled you."

Misled? *Or here it comes. He's dumping me before I stand a chance.*

"But about your book. Apparently, this other book is selling quite well in its first week out. Although the premise is extremely similar, your manuscript is still with the acquisition team. I checked. It hasn't hit the slush pile."

Roxanne faked a chuckle. "I don't care."

He continued. "Just be patient. It's a good sign, and they'll see how much better yours is. This other book may not stand the test of time."

"Excuse me if I don't have much patience. I have to pick up Lucy now." She brushed past him and slipped into her car.

He took hold of her door. She stared back at him in disbe-lief, then tried yanking the door closed. He held it firmly open.

"Why are you being so unreasonable?" Max asked.

"Me, unreasonable?" she shouted back. *He's living a lie. That's all it could be.* She just didn't know him anymore. Her jaw clenched, and she yanked at the door again. This time he released his hold.

She didn't immediately pull out, and he didn't saunter, but stormed back across the street. She watched him in the rear-view-mirror, his head shaking. Roxanne drove away. Tears blinded her at the finality of his gait.

~

Roxanne drove to the Louis Armstrong Airport in New Orleans. Thankful for the hour drive, it still brought no answers. She toiled over Max's actions and his words, but not for long as she approached the curb, she saw Lucy hopping and waving her arms. Pulling up, Roxanne jumped out and hugged her friend. Oh, how she'd missed her. She loaded Lucy's suitcase and started the drive back to Bay Town.

"Hey, Roxy, thanks for picking me up. Oh my, I just couldn't take those noisy kids at my sisters' anymore. They're cute as buttons, and I loved reconnecting with my sis, but it's the first time in a long time that I've been happy with my life and not hers." Lucy laughed. "I can't wait to see Jason. Mind if I call him?"

Roxy nodded as she drove, thankful for Lucy's babbling.

"I really haven't had a minute to spare this last week. My sis and her kids kept me so busy." She fumbled in her bag and pulled out her cell and called. She waited. "That's really weird. His voicemail box is full." Lucy's brows furrowed. "Come to think of it, he hasn't called me in the last week either." Her voice cracked a little. "But his voicemail is never full."

"Maybe work has been crazy busy for him," Roxanne offered.

"Which is why he always answers the phone. He's a general contractor. The construction business, you know. He gets calls all day. Lots of them." Lucy took out a wrapper and spit out her gum. "You don't think Dwayne got to him, do you?"

Pounding rose from behind Roxanne's eyes. Lucy's words echoed in her brain.

"What did you say?"

"Dwayne. You don't think —"

"No." Pinching the bridge of her nose, Roxanne forced her brain. Suddenly, her eyes popped open.

"Lucy, call one of the other guys."

"Good idea. Why didn't I think of that?" She scrolled on her phone. "Got one."

Roxanne held her breath.

"Hey, it's Lucy. Can you call me back? Bye." She shrugged.

"I'm sure he'll call back soon." Roxanne bit her lip

But she wasn't sure, and she turned up the radio as they drove quietly until they reached Bay Town. Roxanne headed down Main Street towards the Community Pier, remembering the fun activities from days long ago. Maybe it would help keep their minds off of Jason and Dwayne.

Roxanne gazed around. So much had changed. *But this was still her home. Wasn't it?*

"Did you know Bay Town has Art Walks displaying regional artists?" Roxanne tried to sound cheery. "When I was young they used to have sidewalk sales, but now they have nighttime street markets."

Lucy gazed out the window. "We should go sometime. I wonder why no one is calling me back?"

Roxanne tapped her steering wheel and glanced at Lucy

who tapped on her phone. "Yes we should. I hear the food is great, and the local artisans have beautiful handcrafts."

"Sounds like a plan. If I stay awhile. I have to get back to work. And to Jason." Lucy forced a giggle.

"Did you know that Bay Town also has a Mardi Gras parade?"

"You sound like a tour guide." Lucy patted Roxanne's elbow. "But keep going. I love your town."

Roxanne gripped the wheel tightly. "The Mardi Gras parade has been running fifty years or more. Mama says it gets better every year, floats, and all."

"Guess I'll have to wait till next year to hit that one." Lucy's voice trailed.

Roxanne ran out of small talk as she passed the Mockingbird Café. She shivered remembering the incident her first week back. That fighting couple on the street. She turned up the air-conditioning.

When they reached the end of Main Street and stopped just short of the pier, Lucy let out a breathy sigh.

"Wow. What an amazing view." Lucy pulled down her oversized sunglasses and squinted, staring at the shining bay waters. The blinding rays bounced around, and ripples from a few kayaks disturbed the otherwise calm waters.

Roxanne turned and drove along Beach Road. "Let's do lunch."

She headed to Bubba's. Glancing over at Lucy, she smiled. Thankful for girl friendships. Once she and Dwayne became a *thing*, her co-workers and old college buddies slowly drifted away. But she was sure Lucy was here to stay. *Thank you, Jesus*, she whispered to herself. Her first utterance to God in days.

CHAPTER 35

Roxanne's shoulders eased down while Lucy chatted about her sweet family visit. Her heart lifted when she listened to Lucy share her sister's faith. Coupled with the beautiful view, Roxanne's angst all but disappeared as she drove.

"I even went to her church while I was there. It's so cool." Lucy turned to face Roxanne. "So can we go to your church tomorrow? Oh! Does that Max guy go there?"

Roxanne sighed. "Yes. He does." She hoped Lucy wouldn't press it.

Breathing a sigh of relief, Roxanne pointed. "We're here. That's Bubba's Catch Shack."

She parked her car and quickly stepped out.

The aroma of fried food filled the air. The savory smell mingling with the gulf breeze somehow relaxed Roxanne's battered soul. White seagulls screeched over Bubba's little shed. Distressed wood planking and aged tin roofing shaped the walls of the quaint structure. Nostalgic iron tables and chairs with large umbrellas dotted the gravel in front of the shed, and sauntering movements of people young and old seem to boast of leisurely days long gone by. Despite the heat, the tourists and locals alike relished the intermittent misters that sprayed light rain out over the front of the shed, cooling the immediate area.

Bubba waved from the window. A line had already formed outside. The yellow metal tables and chairs were claimed, but others stood by the rails of the boardwalk, enjoying lunches in the old-fashioned, red and white checkered paper trays. "This is so cool." Lucy squealed.

"Sure is, isn't it?" Roxanne waved at Bubba. "We went to school together."

"Roxy, you are so lucky. What a great life you have here."

Not lucky at all. Blessed. Or used to be.

Lucy's phone rang. "Hello?...What?...No. That's why I called you." She looked at Roxanne and whispered. "The guys haven't seen Jason."

Roxanne's hands shook. "Tell them to go to his house," she said, her voice quivering.

"Did you check his house? Or call the police? … Just do that, will you?" She drew in a deep breath. "Hey, has anyone seen Dwayne?...Oh, okay. Please check on Jason and call me, please?... Bye." Lucy sat quietly. Tears slipped down her cheeks, and she dabbed at her face with a paper napkin. "Now I'm really worried," she whispered.

Oh, God. Please help. The words flowed silently from Roxanne's heart, and she wished she could pray out loud with Lucy. But she couldn't bring herself to do it. "How about a sweet tea?" Roxanne laid a hand on Lucy's arm.

"Sure."

Roxanne retrieved two drinks from Bubba and handed one to Lucy. The blazing sun overhead and scorching heat from the sidewalk caused fear to rise again. But she had to help. This was her fault.

"Lucy, I'll go with you back to Meridian." She hoped her voice spoke confidence. "If you want to check on Jason."

"You'd do that?" Lucy blew her nose.

"Of course." Roxanne tucked a loose strand of hair behind her ear.

"I just don't know," Lucy cried. "What if he's …" Lucy's body shook with sobs.

"He's not." The words rushed so easily from Roxanne's lips. "Let's believe that God's protected him. It could be anything. Maybe he just got really sick and had to go to the hospital." Roxanne's heart raced, and she grasped at excuses and found herself silently pleading with God again. Again. *Was he still there?* Hope lingered like a thread.

"Yes. You're right. We have to trust God and give it up to Him." Lucy swiped her cheek.

"We do, don't we? But I've been running my own life for so long," Roxanne whispered.

"Me too. But that's what's so cool about God. He's always there for us. It's not like he's a genie in a bottle." Lucy sniffed and blew her nose into a napkin. She smiled. "But girl, we're turning back to Him, aren't we?"

Are we? We tried, didn't we?

Lucy glanced at her phone again as if she'd missed a call in the last ten minutes. The girls stood and turned for the car. They waved goodbye to Bubba, and then Roxanne froze. Max walked down the boardwalk towards them. She took Lucy's arm and nudged her towards the parking lot.

"Hey, Max!" Bubba called from the shack.

Lucy turned. "Max? That's your Max?" She wrenched free of Roxanne. "Oh my. He's cute." Lucy walked towards him. "Hi, Max. I'm Lucy. Roxanne's friend from Meridian." She stuck out her hand.

Max's gaze rested on Roxanne.

Lucy giggled and took his hand and shook. "Hi, nice to meet you."

"Lucy, we have to go," Roxanne said, avoiding Max's eyes.

Max blinked and turned to look at Lucy. "So very nice to meet you…uh, I'm so sorry." He leaned forward.

"Lucy. My name's Lucy." She giggled. "I can't believe we haven't met yet."

"Yes. Well, I've been busy of late."

Roxanne grabbed Lucy's hand and pulled her towards the car. "Gotta go."

"Well, I hope to see you again, Max." Lucy smiled. "Oh, hey, what time is church tomorrow?"

Max pointed at Roxanne. "She knows."

Roxanne left Lucy standing and walked to her car.

"Okay, thanks." Lucy joined Roxanne. "What's the deal? Rude, don't you think?"

"Please get in." Roxanne waited for Lucy to buckle up. She finished the short drive home before speaking. "I'm a little miffed at him. It's a long story. Listen, maybe we should wait before going to Meridian. Make some calls first."

"Maybe," Lucy said quietly. "Or perhaps the guys will check and call me. I guess we could pray and then make some decisions tomorrow. Oh, Lord, please be with Jason."

Roxanne wished her prayers would come as effortlessly.

They awoke Sunday morning and dressed for church. Lucy said she hadn't heard back from anyone, and Roxanne received no word about Dwayne either. Not from the police in Bay Town or Meridian.

"Good morning, girls," Bethie Cook called from the kitchen. Dressed and ready to go. "Lucy, I'm so glad you'll be joining us for church. Everyone is so nice and will love to meet Roxanne's friend."

Lucy's non-stop babble made the drive to church palatable. Roxanne couldn't blame the nervous laughter hiding Lucy's concern for Jason. At least, her mother seemed amused. She didn't add her two cents for once but seemed to enjoy Lucy's gregarious chatter.

Turning into the parking lot, Roxy pulled up close.

"This is it? This is your church?" Lucy asked. "Look at all those people outside. All milling about. It's like out of a movie. You know those old southern churches, where everybody is so nice, but deep inside, they're not?"

Roxanne remained quiet as the women exited the car.

"Well, that's not Bay Town." Bethie Cook had finally spoken. "Oh, we have our problems, but we try to follow Christ as best we can. And that means being kind to one another." She gave a sideways glance at Roxanne. "Inside and out."

When the women reached the front steps, they followed in a queue as all the parishioners waited to greet Pastor Brooks.

"Oh, my." Lucy cooed. "Is he gorgeous or what? He looks like Superman!"

"Shhh." Roxanne hushed her friend. "He's the pastor, and he's married."

"All the good ones are."

Roxanne rolled her eyes.

Stopping on the steps, Roxanne's feet wouldn't move. Max stood before her, looking better than ever, but his blue eyes didn't sparkle, and he looked at Lucy, not Roxanne.

"Good morning, ladies."

"I just love your accent. Irish, right?" Lucy cooed.

"British. But 'tis been an exceptionally long time since I've been back."

"How long have you been here?" Lucy asked.

"Max is our neighbor. And an old, old friend. Very old." Roxanne glared.

"Old?" Lucy frowned. "Why you're not that old. You're too cute to be —"

"Old enough, love. But young at heart."

"Don't you pay no mind to him. He's not even old enough to be in our seniors' group yet." Bethie Cook gave Max a big hug. "Roxanne, where's your manners?"

The guy's a user, she thought, *just like all men.* As a love-struck teenager, she'd admired him. But now, as an experienced, wiser woman, she recognized the game. Maybe worn, but not much wiser. She fanned herself with the church program and glared at him. She could never forgive him for stealing her manuscript. She hadn't the courage to confront him, but one day she would. Roxanne stared at the church.

"He's adorable." Lucy whispered. "I love your long hair, Max." She reached out and touched it.

"Oh, for goodness sakes." Roxanne crossed her arms failing to hide her annoyance at Lucy.

Lucy's phone rang.

"Honey, you should silence that before we go in." Bethie Cook spoke, but not unkindly.

Lucy grabbed for her phone. Looking at the screen, she held up a finger and left the steps. Roxanne watched as she walked swiftly to the Sycamore tree. Lucy dropped on the bench. She lowered her head and leaned forward on her knees.

"I'll be right back." Roxanne started down the steps. "You go on in, Mama."

"Can I help?" asked Max.

"No." Not wanting him to know their dilemma, she ran to Lucy's side. Lucy had clicked off, and sobs came in waves. Her shoulders shook, and Roxanne waited. *No, God, please.*

"He's in the hospital." Lucy looked up, her eyes already red. "Roxy, he's not dead, thank God. They think he'll pull through."

Think? "What happened?"

"He was beaten up pretty badly." She sniffed. "Probably Dwayne. One of the guys went to his apartment. The smashed coffee table had blood on it." Lucy dabbed her eyes. "He called the hospital in Meridian and found that Jason had been admitted a couple days ago with a bad concussion. They're monitoring him."

"Oh, Lucy. I'm so sorry." Roxanne tried to hold back the tears.

Lucy's flowed. "I have to go there, Roxy. Now."

Roxanne froze. She didn't like the rising fear gripping her again. She glanced around the parking lot as if Dwayne were waiting for her. She couldn't feel safe at church anymore and could hear his mocking laughter.

"Lucy, let's just call the hospital first." Roxanne's voice shook, and she forgot her offer to go to Meridian.

"No. He needs me. It's my fault he's in there."

Roxanne's throat went dry. "It's not your fault, it's mine, but Lucy, you can't go. What if Dwayne finds you?"

Lucy straightened. "Well, I guess it's time to trust God, right? Jason needs me." She stood. "And he needs God too. Maybe now he'll listen to me and come to church." She stared at the white clapboard structure with the bell hanging below the steeple. It rang out, and Lucy smiled. "I guess we better get in there first."

CHAPTER 36

I surrender all. I surrender all.
    All to Jesus, I surrender, I surrender all.

Roxanne and Lucy gripped hands together and sang. Lucy's sweet voice rang out melodiously. Her face turned upward, and tears trickled out the corners of her eyes. Roxanne turned her head slightly, watching her friend. It was as if that foundation that Lucy's missionary parents had instilled in her returned. Roxanne glanced at her mother. Bethie had planted the same in Roxanne. They both praised God with sweet voices. Roxanne closed her eyes, her voice soft but just as genuine in praise.

Pastor Brooks finished his message, and communion followed. Roxanne hesitated. How could she take it with the hardness she felt for so many? So much baggage. But wasn't that what communion was for? Confessing, repenting? Giving it all to Jesus and being grateful for his sacrifice? Grateful. Deep inside, she knew the truth. His sacrifice. It was meant for her too. No matter what her sin. She took the small piece of bread, laid it on her tongue, and soon followed with the cup.

As the congregation filed out and the ladies stood in the pew, waiting to exit the aisle, Bethie Cook handed Lucy a small, embroidered hanky. Lucy smiled and dabbed her eyes. Black streaked the dainty cloth.

"I'll wash it for you. Sorry." Lucy shrugged.

Bethie patted her shoulder. "Keep it, dear. Please, keep it."

Exiting the pew and heading outside, Lucy pushed past people and rushed to the car. Roxanne followed, making apologies, but stopped. She searched the crowd for Max. Spotting him near a clutch of men, she ran over.

She approached the group of men and tapped Max's elbow. He turned, and smiled, but it didn't reach his eyes. He looked past her. "Is Lucy all right? Anything I can help with?"

Just like Max. Putting aside his own hurt. The hurt she'd caused. She frowned. She didn't cause anything. It was he that was at fault. Still, she laid it aside. Right now Jason was most important. "Yes. I mean, no. But yes."

Max touched her shoulder. "Take a breath. What do you need?"

Roxanne breathed and nodded. "Can you take Mama home?"

"Of course, I can. But what of you?"

"I'm fine." But Roxanne knew her white lie glared brightly. "I'm taking Lucy back to Meridian."

"Now?"

"Yes, her boyfriend is in the hospital." Roxanne's voice wavered. *And it's all my fault.*

"Oh dear. May I please pray for him?"

Roxanne nodded, and tears slipped down her cheeks as he prayed for Jason's healing, for her safety and for her peace.

Dwayne threw the hunting knife, and it stuck between the logs. Methodically, he stomped across the floor and yanked it out. He'd been doing this all Sunday morning. The fishing cabin smelled of decay and fresh earth, but he had to hide.

Luckily, he'd come across this rotting cabin the last time he'd ran from the Highway Patrol.

What a lucky break that he'd gotten out of jail. He never thought they'd let him post bail. If they had found the guy at the campground, and connected him, he would still be in the cell. But he blew it again and they'd chase him once more. He hadn't meant to hurt Jason so badly. Dwayne kicked at nothing. Swinging his foot into the air. Too many beers, too much built-up anger. If Jason had only told him where Lucy had gone. She knew where Roxy went, but Jason protected his girl. They'd been best friends forever. Closer friends than any girl until now.

Pulling the knife from the log, he threw it again. The weak throw didn't reach the wall and clattered to the floor. A low growl came from outside, and Dwayne turned toward the open front door. A slight breeze floated in, but the sunshine blinded him, and he shaded his eyes. He'd grown accustomed to the darkness without electricity in the fishing hut. He walked to the front door, and a small alligator crawled out of the bayou alongside the short dock that extended a few yards from the front of the hut.

Dwayne slammed the heavy log door and threw himself on the cot. Grabbing a beer from the cooler, he chugged it and threw it against the wall. These fishing huts were good hangouts. No one ever checked them, but the police would be looking for him again. Or not. Maybe he hadn't hurt Jason that bad. He drew a hand through his hair. Of course, he'd injured him. He'd followed the ambulance to the hospital in Meridian, and Lucy never showed. A thought made him straighten. She didn't know. Not yet, but she might arrive at the hospital anytime.

Glancing at his watch, he decided to hit the hospital again. His hair had grown long, his beard full, and since he hadn't worked out in over a month, his muscles were not as toned. He'd also lost a lot of weight. So far, no one had seemed to recognize him. *Were they even looking for him?* Beating people up didn't warrant a manhunt. It wasn't like he killed anyone. But he always wondered about the old man at the campsite.

Thoughts of his mom and sister filled his mind, and his heart sank. The headaches were getting worse, and memories of them only made his head hurt more. If Roxy had just behaved. Life would be much different if his mom could just get out of jail and his sister would just give him a break. If, if, if. His only plan now was to get Roxy back. *Then what?*

Dwayne rose from the bed. He pulled the flak jacket from the peg on the wall and headed outside. Searching for the gator first, he half-ran, half-hobbled to the truck. His leg still banged up from the accident. He jumped in Jason's truck, hoping it hadn't been reported stolen. Driving it was a stupid move, but he had no choice since crashing the last car. Mud spun from the wheel flaps as he drove off.

His stomach growled. How long had it been since he'd eaten? No matter. He'd get Roxy if he could force Lucy to her car without incident. Dwayne slammed the steering wheel. Just the thought of her caused his head to crush as if she had a vise grip on him. She did. He had to find her.

Dwayne parked in the hospital's employee lot, grabbing the bottle of pain reliever from the glove box. He crunched the last four pills and downed another beer. Throwing the empty bottle in the bushes, he searched the lot and strode to the hospital entrance. He parked himself on a bench and waited. At first, he watched people come in and out. A group of young people spoke in hushed tones. An old guy using a walker with a nurse in scrubs holding his elbow strolled by.

One visitor caught his eye. She was young, even pretty. But without makeup and messy hair, she looked like she hadn't slept in days like him. She carried bags stuffed with junk and a Bible in one hand. She looked in his direction, and he stared.

She looked back, and a smile spread across her dry lips. "Hey, did you need a water or something?"

Dwayne looked around. He was the only one there. *Did he look that bad?* He nodded.

"I have an extra. My daddy likes Fiji water, so I always bring some when I come." She chuckled. "Anything to make him happy."

Boy, did Dwayne know that feeling. Only nothing he ever did made his daddy happy. "He's lucky to have you." It wasn't like Dwayne to make small talk, but he hadn't spoken to anyone in a week or so. And before that, it was just before he beat the daylights out of Jason. Dwayne closed his eyes.

"I know." She smiled. "Mind if I sit a spell? I have to take a breather before spending the day with Daddy."

Dwayne stood and offered the bench. "Go ahead. I'm leaving anyway."

"Oh, no, please. I didn't mean to intrude. You were here first." She tucked a loose strand behind her ear.

Like Roxy. Dwayne sighed. The girl seemed so nice, just like Roxy. Dwayne rubbed his forehead. The pounding started again. "I'm leaving anyway."

"No, you stay. I'll just go to the chapel for a bit." She patted her Bible.

He cringed. His mom had one. Heck, so did Roxy, and what good did it do any of them? "Does your daddy treat you right?"

The girl pushed back her wavy, brown hair. "He does. He's a little grouchy because he's sick, but he does now."

"Now?"

"He didn't always." She tilted her head way back, looking up at the hospital windows. "But he's trying. He drove Mama away, so it's just us."

Dwayne cleared his throat, wishing he hadn't pried.

The woman chuckled. "I don't know why I'm telling you this. Except that, if it wasn't for Jesus, I might be gone like mama too." Her voice wavered. "But everyone deserves a second chance at a peaceful life. That's what Jesus offers." She looked at him. "Know what I mean?"

A peaceful life? He couldn't even imagine what that looked like. Didn't know if he'd ever experienced it. But maybe with Roxy, he could have. "Yeah. Whatever." Dwayne shrugged.

"Okay. I gotta go. But I'll be praying for you."

Before he could answer, she walked through the hospital doors. As they parted, she turned and smiled. Her shoulders were hunched, and her feet dragged, but that peace. She had it.

Roxanne joined Lucy as she drove her car back to Meridian. Dwayne wouldn't recognize it, as he hadn't followed her here yet. Roxanne would figure out a way to get back to Bay Town later.

They remained silent most of the drive as they headed out of town. Roxanne even managed to doze, as Lucy sped up the highway. Though the nap was fitful. At one point, Roxanne's eyes fluttered open, and she broke out in a sweat despite the air conditioning. It was as if she sensed danger drawing close. She hadn't returned to Meridian since she'd filed the report with the Meridian Police.

Lucy pulled off the highway and waited at a light until it changed. She gunned the engine a little too hard and shot through the intersection faster than anyone else. She hugged a corner, making a right turn. The light turned red before she completed it, then she sped down the street. A siren blared.

"Oh, shoot." Lucy huffed and pulled over.

Pulling out her license, she slid down her window. "Hey, Officer. My boyfriend is in the hospital, and I need to get there ASAP."

He took her license and peeked in. He looked in the backseat. "If you don't slow down, ma'am, you might be joining him via the ER." He tipped his hat. "I'll be right back."

Roxanne's fisted hands soaked wet with perspiration. She glanced at Lucy, whose eyes were closed, and her lips moved.

"Lord, please get us to the hospital," Lucy whispered.

The officer appeared at Lucy's side. "You're all clear. Why don't you follow me, and I'll get you there, safely."

"Thank you, Jesus!" Lucy raised her hands.

"You can call me Officer." He winked.

Arriving at the hospital, Roxanne hesitated before exiting the car. She searched the parking lot but had yet to learn what Dwayne was driving. She glanced around, eyeing anyone who had the slightest resemblance to him.

Checking in at the registration desk, the women retrieved name badges and went up the elevator to the fourth floor. Roxanne glanced nervously around, taking a breath. She tried to calm herself. She passed the restrooms and heard a door open. Something made her turn before entering Jason's room.

The men's bathroom door closed, and a tall, thin man wearing a hunting jacket and ball cap exited and walked in the opposite direction. *Why would anyone wear a jacket in this weather?* Roxanne backed away as he trudged on. He had a slight limp.

Sucking in a breath, she blew it out through her mouth. Cleansing breaths. It couldn't be Dwayne. The man was too thin. Besides, Dwayne wasn't so stupid to come back here. But he was crazy. She couldn't begin to guess what he would do, but she was sure of his violent intentions. She waited until the man entered a room a few doors down. A gravelly voice called, "Mama, I'm here." A friendly voice that didn't sound the least bit familiar.

Roxanne sighed loudly and swiped at her forehead. Sweat practically dripped off her fingers. Squealing jarred her, and she turned. The sound came from Jason's room.

"Oh, sweetie. I'm so sorry, I'm so sorry," Lucy cried.

Roxanne stepped inside. She gasped at the sight of Jason's beat-up body lying on the stark white bed.

"Hey, baby? Are you all right? I was so worried about you." Jason smiled, his eyes heavy.

Lucy kissed his face everywhere and laid her head on his chest. He stroked her hair softly. His eyes connected with Roxanne, and he waved before she could lower hers. "I'm glad you're okay too. Dwayne's gone nuts."

"I know." Roxanne's voice shook. Any peace and calm that church had infused her with this morning disappeared. She knew she should keep trusting, but her chest heaved, and she couldn't breathe.

A police officer walked in and looked at Jason. "Mind if I ask you a few more questions? Just want to finish this report. You weren't too lucid when I first took it."

"I've told you everything I can remember, but my friend here can probably fill in more about the guy."

Roxanne put up her hands and backed away. She slowly slipped out of the room. Leaning against the wall, just beside the door, she lowered her head. Gulping air, she whispered a silent prayer for help. Panic rose as she flinched, remembering Dwayne's blows to her head and her body. The unpredictable monster tormented her once more. *Help. I need help.* Roxanne rubbed her forehead, and Max popped into her head. It didn't matter what he'd done or how she'd left things. He would help her. A hint of calm settled a piece of her heart, and she called.

Pulling out her cell, she tapped his number. *Pick up. Please pick up.* She shuffled her feet, hung up, and called again, but he didn't answer. Fear gripped her. She needed him. Needed him now. Her hands shook. Her sensibilities slipped away, and she rushed to the nurse's station.

"Excuse me, is there a waiting area nearby?"

"Just past the elevators." The nurse pointed down the hall.

Roxanne had to escape. She just didn't feel safe and

needed someone who could help. But who? She sensed danger and ran back to Jason's room.

"Lucy, can I have your car keys?"

"Sure, sweetie."

"Ma'am, can you answer some questions now?" the Meridian Police officer asked.

She shook her head no. "I know where the police station is. Can I come down there later?"

He handed her his card. "Sure. Or just call me, please."

Raising the car keys, she mouthed thank you to Lucy and left.

Roxanne ran to Lucy's car, jumped in, and locked the doors. She drove out of the hospital parking lot as quickly as she could. Her heart pounded. *Oh God, help.* She pulled into a nearby coffee shop. Before heading inside, she walked with her head down while hitting redial for Max. It went to voice mail.

"Hey, Max. It's Roxy. Listen, I'm at the Coffee Clutch in Meridian. Can you meet me here?"

She hung up, ordered, and sat for a long time. Too long. *It takes hours to drive here.* She got a refill and stared out the window, watching people come and go. Glancing at her watch, a panic arose. She couldn't stay here forever. Texting Lucy, Roxy gave her whereabouts, and Lucy told her not to worry. She planned on staying with Jason as long as they'd let her. Visiting hours were over at eight. Roxanne stared at her watch. Four o'clock.

"Mind if I join you?" The voice startled her.

A handsome man stood in front of her. Fit, young looking, but gray laced lightly throughout his dark, wavy hair. Much like Dwayne. She shivered and looked around at all the full tables.

"I'm waiting for someone."

"No worries." He smiled and left.

Roxanne finished another cup and retrieved a water. Sipping it slowly, she scrolled her emails, then looked at her watch. *Max isn't coming.* She forced herself to stand and walked to the exit. The handsome man stood at a high table and nodded. She looked down and shoved open the door.

She took one step and slammed into a rigid body. She stumbled and stared at the boots. Without looking up, she mumbled, "I'm sorry," and turned for the coffee shop door.

A hand squeezed her shoulder.

"Please, God," she whispered.

"You too? Seems everyone's got religion these days. Come on, baby. Let's go for a walk."

Dwayne shoved her, and she stumbled. Righting herself, she heard the coffee shop door swing open.

"Is everything all right?" The man who'd spoken to her in the shop asked.

Dwayne glared at him. And Roxanne felt his hot breath on her neck. "Fine. I'm a little late meeting my lady here. That's all. Have a nice day."

Roxanne tried to plead with the man with her eyes, but Dwayne squeezed her arm. She thought he might break it.

"Ain't that right, Roxy?"

For a split second, she thought of screaming, of running. But Dwayne's erratic behavior frightened her, and she feared he might hurt someone else besides her. Again. This had to stop.

"Roxy?" Dwayne growled.

"Listen, why don't you guys come back in." The handsome man shrugged. "I'll buy you a sweet tea. It's hot out here."

Just his kind voice fueled Roxanne. Kindness. Her mama spoke of kindness. *It's your kindness that leads to repentance, O Lord.*

"Mind your own business," Dwayne said.

Roxanne straightened. "We're good. Thank you so much."

"You sure?" the man questioned.

"I'm sure. God bless you," Roxanne called out. "Have a wonderful day." Her voice grew stronger despite Dwayne's grip.

He yanked her and strode down the sidewalk. Roxanne let him. Perhaps the man would call 9-1-1. Either way, she chose to trust.

"I can't believe you. You're flirting right in front of me. And using God to do it." Dwayne gave her a shove.

Roxanne's phone buzzed in her hand, and a muffled voice followed. Before she could turn it off, Dwayne grabbed it. He looked at the screen, and his face contorted, turning red. "Max? Is that the book geek?" He put the phone to his ear. "Hey, Max? Get lost." He shoved the phone in his pocket.

Dwayne's hold didn't feel as tight as the shame ripping in her heart. Dwayne pulled her to Lucy's car. "Give me the keys." She hesitated, and he slapped her so hard it made her lip bleed. She handed over the keys. "I thought we could start over, but here you are cheating on me already."

He pulled out so quickly that a car honked, and he cursed, and the berating began. Just like it used to. He stopped only to glance in the rearview mirror. Roxanne turned and thought she recognized the car behind them. So did Dwayne.

"It's the detective. I know it. I'll lose him," he said, pressing down the accelerator.

He made a sudden turn into a giant mall parking lot. He swerved through the covered structure and jerked into an empty spot next to someone getting in their car. He jumped out and ran around to get Roxanne. Dragging her from the car, he pulled a gun from his back and waved it at the driver.

"Leave the keys and get," Dwayne yelled.

Roxanne tripped, but he dragged her, and her sandals provided no protection. Her toes bloodied as he threw her in the passenger seat.

Not this time, Dwayne. God, help me.

He scrambled into the driver's seat, but Roxanne yanked her door open, thrusting her foot out. His long arms grabbed her, but struggling free, she turned and ran around the back of the car. She spotted the stairwell, and ignoring her broken toenails causing blood and pain, she ran. Grabbing the rail, she swung forward.

Her body smashed against the wall, and Dwayne's arm around her waist kept her from tumbling down the stairs.

"You're stupider than I thought." He dragged her back to the car, threw her in, and slammed the door.

Before he reached the driver's side, she had the her door open.

He jumped in. "Shut the door," he screamed.

"No!" Strength grew inside her, and fear gave way to courage. She stepped out again but shrieked.

Dwayne's long arm gripped her elbow, twisting it backward. He growled, "Give it up, Roxy."

"No!" she screamed once more.

He slammed the steering wheel and then slugged her. Her head flew sideways, and the world spun around her, her body falling limp. Hitting her square on the jaw, he cursed obscenities, but the words clouded her head. Dwayne continued cussing at her, but a deep fog swirled inside her brain. Roxanne struggled to stay coherent. The engine roared, and without waiting for the door to shut, Dwayne gunned the engine and raced out.

Nasty bile arose from her throat, and Roxanne knew she would wretch. But as she glanced out, she heard yelling. Peering out the window, she made out shapes of figures running toward the car. But they were so far away. Trying to focus, she narrowed her eyes and vaguely made out men in uniform and plain clothes. If she could lunge, she might be able to fall out of the car. Roxanne lurched without thinking, and her body half fell out.

Dwayne's hand gripped her arm, and he yanked her back

so harshly she felt her shoulder pop. The pain seared her body, and she fell back against the seat. Her head rolled sideways, and she watched as the men ran towards her, guns drawn. So surreal, like a movie, and her stomach roiled.

Swerving around a car backing out caused the passenger door to finally latch shut. Roxanne flew forward and retched violently. The contents of her stomach landed on her legs, shoes, and Dwayne's arm that still held her. He let go, yelling profanities again, and sped through the parking structure. Roxanne managed to sit straight and stared at a lowered parking barrier blocking their exit. *He'd have to slow wouldn't he?*

He gunned the engine, and Roxanne grew dizzy again. She thought she might black out, but resolve rose within. The song from church, *I Surrender All*, rang through her aching head. *I surrender all to you, Lord. Not to Dwayne.* As the car approached the gate, Roxanne grabbed the door handle and pushed against the door. She lunged out, and her body bounced across the concrete.

Shots fired out.

Everything went black.

CHAPTER 37

Her eyes fluttered open, but her head pounded with uncontrollable pain. She leaned forward and retched again. His muffled voice screamed at her. *Where was she? It couldn't be. She couldn't be back in his car. It had to be a nightmare. Oh, God, help me.* Roxanne blacked out again.

When she came to, the air smelled dank and stuffy. Opening her eyes didn't work. They jittered back and forth, making the room spin. Room? She wasn't in the car anymore. Suddenly, cold water hit her face, and she sputtered, trying to sit, but nothing in her body cooperated. She fell back.

"Get up."

That voice. *No, it couldn't be.* Roxanne couldn't remember anything after falling out of the car. "Where am I? How did I get here?"

"You're an idiot. You jumped from the car, but I got you, but not until after they shot me first."

"Who shot you?" Roxanne couldn't remember, but only thought she'd gotten away.

"Get up, I said. I need help," Dwayne screamed at her. "You gotta help me get this bullet out of my shoulder."

Roxanne sucked in a breath. "Are you crazy?" Her heart of stone filled with hate, and she started to cry. The tears burned, and she tried to lift an arm to wipe them. She cried out. Her shoulder hurt so badly that she thought she might lose consciousness again. "I'm not helping you with anything." She tried to shout, but it came out as barely a whisper.

"I bet your shoulder is dislocated. I did it all the time in basketball. Let me look."

"Don't touch me." Roxanne tried to yank away.

"Sorry, baby."

Dwayne pressed a hand into her shoulder and shoved down. She screamed, but the loud pop brought instant relief. *Why? Why would he help her?* The pain immediately subsided, and she forced her eyes open. He hovered over her. Anguish distorted his face. The room spun again, and she closed her eyes.

"I can't help you. Dwayne. I can't even open my eyes."

Quiet sobs and sniffling sounded above her. Dwayne pushed her hip aside, and she winced. Every bone in her body felt broken. The bed, or cot, or whatever she sat on, depressed as he sat.

"Why did you have to leave me, Roxy? We wouldn't be in this mess." Dwayne's voice was soft and whined like a hurt puppy.

An unfamiliar voice, for sure. Roxanne had never heard it like that before, and she cringed. His sorrow steeped in his pain, not hers. If only he could feel some regret. But he never did. Only regrets for getting in trouble, not for his actions. Roxanne thought of the Sunday sermon. Amazed that it popped into her head. She recalled Pastor Brooks reading the scriptures in Second Samuel about Saul's regret. All for self. No remorse, just like Dwayne.

"Dwayne, we need help. Both of us." She swallowed. Her throat felt thick and hoarse. "You'll die of infection, and I'm sure I have a concussion."

Dwayne ignored her and got up. A scraping sound grated, and a hot night breeze blew in. She heard his footsteps fading. *Was he leaving her here to die?* She heard a car door slam. Lying in silence, she took a breath and smelled the fresh earth. There were no noises. No city sounds, cars, or people walking or talking. It smelled like rotting decay. The pungent odor burned her nostrils. They were in the bayou. Sure of it, she listened and heard water swirling. Almost soothingly.

Using what strength she had left, she searched her brain for a logical assessment. He must have returned to Bayou La Croix. Like a dog returns to its own vomit. That's what the bible said. She shivered, remembering the last incident out here. And God had saved her then.

Wouldn't someone have followed him by now? An ounce of hope gripped her, and she felt around for her cell phone. Frantically, her fingers searched into the pockets of her dress. The one she'd worn to church. *Was it still Sunday?* Her sigh was almost audible as both pockets turned up empty. But if they were anywhere close, she had hope of being tracked. Maybe.

Dwayne stomped through the doorway and came near. He shoved her body toward the wall, and she cowered at his touch, but he offered her a bottle of water.

"Here." He opened it for her and another for himself, taking a long swig.

"Dwayne, what are you going to do?"

She saw his biceps twitch, then he turned his gaze on her. "Did I ever tell you, you remind me of my sister?"

Roxanne frowned. He'd never once spoken of his family after he'd taken her to meet them that one time, shortly after they'd started dating. Before he became violent with her.

"No," Roxanne said. "We look nothing alike."

"Not looks, but a nice person." His brows knit tightly. "But I saw her a couple weeks ago, and she wasn't nice no more. She wouldn't help me."

"What kind of help do you want?" Maybe if she kept him talking, he wouldn't hit her.

"I want to start over, Roxy. I want to get far away from here with you."

Roxanne's stomach rolled, and she felt like vomiting again. He couldn't possibly be serious.

"No. You hurt me."

"I'm sorry. Really, I am."

She'd heard it all before.

"I'll stop drinking. I'll get a job. We'll get a new home in Idaho or something."

Roxanne shook her head. "You're wanted, Dwayne. There's a manhunt out for you."

"But if you'll just do what I say and quit fighting me, we can get away."

"I should have fought you a long time ago." She half expected him to backhand her, but his shoulder bled, and she hoped the gunshot wound rendered his arm useless.

Still, he pushed her again and crawled onto the cot beside her. His damp body touching hers. Roxanne lay on her side, stiff and scared. She scrunched closer to the wall. Not even he would think of doing anything in their conditions. Would he?

"I'm so tired, Roxy. I'm really wiped."

An arm reached around her waist, his hand resting on her stomach. Roxanne prayed. She prayed like she'd never prayed before. Silent words rolled out, and she didn't know how long, but soon, she heard snoring and felt the heavy rise and fall of Dwayne's chest against her back. "Thank you, Jesus," she whispered. Soon, she rested too.

Chirp. Chirp.

Click. Click. Click.

And croaking. Nightlife in the Bayou woke Roxanne. She welcomed the sweet sounds but couldn't appreciate the peaceful gift with Dwayne still pressed against her. She didn't know if all the wetness came from his sweat-drenched body or hers. Either way, her dress wrung wet, sticking to her legs. Yet a mere inconvenience compared to the surmounting obstacles she faced.

The dark room assured her that dusk had passed. The sleep had helped her head, so she slowly peeked one eye open and stared at the wall. At least it wasn't spinning. The headache still pounded, but she had a lull in the dizziness. Not knowing how long it would last, she dared to move.

Stifling moans from the stabbing pains in her feet, legs, and head, she tried to roll on her back. Dwayne lay too close. She shifted back to the wall, but suddenly, he moved just a smidge. His arm flopped off of her, and Roxanne slowly tried again. She made it. Now, lying on her other side, she faced the room. She dared not lift her head but opened both eyes to look at Dwayne.

She stared at his sharp jawline. His cheeks covered with more than stubble, he looked tired and worn. His furrowed brow indicated a painful sleep. *Maybe it's not sleep*, thought Roxanne, and hope arose. *Maybe he's passed out.*

Rising on one elbow, she paused. He didn't move. Peering around the room, her eyes adjusted, and she thought it must be a fishing cabin. A rugged frame with crude walls. Not even finished on the inside. The floor was made of rough, unfinished wood planks, and nothing but this bed, a few chairs, and a table furnished the grim place. Yet somehow calm rested on her in the dark room lit only by the beautiful moonlight shining through the window.

Roxanne moved slowly. She had to. Her body wouldn't do otherwise. Not sure if her legs would hold her, she scooted to the end of the bed and slipped off. Her bare feet touched the slimy, rough wood. Quickly, she pulled her feet back up. Dwayne snorted and let out a moan. She waited. Lack of movement for several minutes spurred her on. She pushed off the bed and rested her feet once again. Trying to imagine the slime as algae and not fish guts, she tried standing. Wobbling, she placed a hand on the wall to brace herself. Everything but her mind wanted to drop back down on the bed. She couldn't. Not now.

Roxanne tried to step lightly, but her feet dragged, and her footsteps were audible shuffles. Halfway to the door, she glanced at Dwayne, and he moaned again. His blood-soaked arm lay across his stomach. It looked like he'd stuck a wad of fabric atop his shoulder underneath a dirty white tank. When he breathed, his chest heaved. She stared. How could she possibly feel sorry for him? But something stirred. Roxanne couldn't believe it, but she said a prayer for the poor, wretched man. A weight lifted from her heart. *Lord, reach him.* She padded to the doorway and struggled to open the door. Yanking hard, it swung wide, but she screamed.

An alligator blocked the path outside. She stumbled backward, but the monstrous reptile moved slowly towards her. One foot crossed the threshold, then, the other. Roxanne's head began to spin again. She tried to breathe, but as the creature made its way slowly toward her, she slumped. It felt like slow motion, but her body almost hit the floor before she felt Dwayne's arm around her. He dragged her back to the bed and threw her on it. He pulled a gun from his back pocket.

Roxanne froze, horrified that he could have used it on her at any time. Instead, he aimed it at the creature and pulled the trigger.

Click, nothing.

He stepped backward and cocked it again.

Click, nothing. Dwayne threw the gun down. The gator slithered more quickly now.

"Dwayne. Get up here, now," Roxanne screamed.

But the creature grabbed Dwayne's boot. Roxanne muscled all the strength she could and reached for Dwayne, pulling him back on the bed. She tugged, he kicked, and finally, his boot slipped off. Scrambling up, he pushed Roxanne behind him against the wall.

"We got to get out of here." Dwayne stared at the table.

Roxanne followed his gaze, where a butcher block filled with big knives sat with assorted fishing tackle. *He'd never make it.*

"But he can't get up here."

"They can climb trees. You don't think he'll get up here?"

Dwayne jumped off the bed, screeching loudly. He ran.

Roxanne screamed, pressing herself as far as she could to the wall, the alligator approaching the edge of the low cot. He raised one foot. Roxanne grabbed a pillow, guarding herself. She couldn't believe Dwayne left her.

But he didn't. He rushed forward with a huge knife. Raising it high, he plunged it into the back of the gator's neck, just above his spine.

The thick skin resisted, but finally, the knife stuck. The gator roared, and Dwayne yanked hard, stumbling backward, and landing on his gunshot shoulder. The gator spread his jaws wide going for Dwayne's legs.

Crack. Crack. Crack.

Gunshots shattered the air around them, and the gator went limp. His elongated head landed on Dwayne's thighs. Dwayne fell back.

Roxanne stood horrified, gun in her hand, but relief flooded her. She did it. Suddenly, she glanced at Dwayne, who lay still. Did she kill him too? She slid off the bed and struggled to his side.

"Dwayne? Are you okay? Dwayne, please. Come on." The words flooded out, and God graciously allowed her to think of a loving Savior who saved them not only from this world but for all eternity. She shivered. *Please, God, give him a second chance.*

A deep, throaty laugh bubbled from Dwayne. He opened his eyes. Staring at Roxanne, he pulled her head down and kissed her.

She pulled back, wiping her lips harshly. "You're a

madman! What's the matter with you? How can you think I'd possibly…" She scooted backward.

Dwayne tried to right himself but couldn't. He lay still. "I knew you'd never get over me. Come on, babe. We'll start over." He opened his eyes and stared at the animal, now bleeding from multiple holes in his thick skin, as well as the knife in his neck.

Roxanne felt sick, and not just because of the deadly creature. Without food or water, she swallowed the ensuing wretch rising. She stared at Dwayne, trying to gather back the compassion she had earlier. For his soul, nothing else.

"No, Dwayne. A new life is in Christ, not with us. You have to turn yourself in."

"Yeah, that ain't happening." Dwayne kicked at the dead animal. He strained to stand but grabbed her. "But you're right about the new life. I'm running, and you're coming with me."

Dwayne gripped her arm and pulled her toward the door. Slowly, they shuffled outside.

CHAPTER 38

Roxanne blinked at the bright full moon. She couldn't stare at the massive white ball for long. She closed her eyes, and her feet faltered.

"Ouch. Dwayne, please. I have no shoes." Opening her eyes a slit, she glanced down.

Mud oozed between her toes, and she cringed, guessing more than just wet dirt squished around her foot. She saw that Dwayne had only one boot on himself, and his ankle bled. The alligator had bitten through the thick leather, his sharp teeth leaving shredded, flapping skin. How did they even escape that monster? She knew without a doubt.

He slowed but pressed forward. She saw the car. The front fender hung off, and the windshield cracked. Suddenly, the memory of crashing through the parking gate returned. She'd fallen from the vehicle, hit her head. But what of the men chasing them? Her eyes widened as she saw a gun gripped in the hand of Dwayne's hanging arm. Had he shot them and then dragged her back into the car? She feared for their lives, as well as her own.

Approaching the vehicle, he let go of her to open the passenger door with his uninjured arm. Too weak to run, she'd take her chances with Dwayne rather than the bayou.

Perhaps because she'd never seen him so fragile, so vulnerable. If only his heart would break, and he could surrender. The odds would definitely be in her favor.

The pain surging through her body welcomed a seat in a somewhat clean car. She watched as he trudged to the driver's side, and she tried to think up a plan. Nothing came, but she heard whining sounds in the distance. Sirens.

Dwayne heard them too. He yanked her once more, dragging her to the low dock where a small, aluminum rowboat anchored.

"No!" Roxanne screamed.

He pulled her toward the dinghy tied up to the dock. She kicked as best she could, her feet bleeding. Fearing the swamp, she screamed until her voice gave out.

Police cars, Ranger Trucks, and a Swat van pulled up. Men jumped out, and lights flooded the scene.

"Stop! Police. Throw down your gun!"

The blinding glare hurt her eyes, and Roxanne shut them tightly. Scorching aches racked her body, but the relief that accompanied the pain filled her with momentary joy. Still, Dwayne yanked her towards the end of the dock. Gripping her arm, he pulled her up in front of him.

"You shoot me, you'll hit her. I'm not going anywhere without her," Dwayne yelled.

She squinted, forcing her eyes to focus on him. She not only saw a hopeless, crazy creature, but she also saw a broken sinner. Hope trickled from her, but something replaced it. Pity, empathy. *Poor Dwayne.* He wobbled, barely able to stand but waving his gun in all directions. So lost. Her heart actually wrenched. He honestly had no hope. If they killed him now, his pain and sorrow would torment him forever.

"Dwayne, I'll go with you." Her voice rasped. Only God's strength gave her the courage to say such things.

His grip loosened for a moment but tightened. "Tell it to them."

She coughed. "I can't. You're strangling me."

His arm dropped to his side, but he held a gun in her back.

She slowly raised her hands. "Let us go, please. I'm going with him."

In the far distance, she heard someone yell. "Nooo!"

Peering into the darkness, she saw a struggle, but the voice silenced.

"We can't let you go. Throw the gun down and put your hands up." A voice from a loudspeaker pierced the calm bayou.

A low groan escaped from Dwayne. "Why would you do that, Roxy?" he whispered.

Somehow, fear didn't grip her anymore. Her heart turmoiled, feeling not only her pain, but his. All those months of abuse, of battering, and somehow Christ gave her compassion for this poor soul.

"Because God loves you, too, Dwayne."

"You heard her." His gravelly voice screamed. "Let us go." Dwayne grabbed her once more and shuffled backward. "No, he doesn't," Dwayne whispered. "God don't give a lick about me."

"But he does. Give him a chance."

"It's too late."

"It's never too late." Her voice gained strength. "He's here, Dwayne, for you, and so am I. Please, they'll kill you if you try and leave. God will work this out."

Roxanne peered up at him. A laser red spot dotted his forehead. Before she could yell, a thud crashed on the dock. Water splashed, and Dwayne's stance buckled. He cried out, thrusting her forward.

"I'm sorry, Roxy," he screamed. "For everything."

She tumbled forward and turned. Her eyes grew round at the horrific sight at the end of the dock.

"Help!" she screamed.

A massive alligator gripped Dwayne between his jaws, pulling him into the swamp. It rolled too many times. Each time, she caught a glimpse of Dwayne's flailing arms pounding the animals snout. But the monster continued thrashing and rolling until Dwayne's body went limp.

Uniformed men ran forward, shooting into the swamp after the slithering gator. Roxanne covered her eyes.

"Medic!" someone yelled.

CHAPTER 39

A month had passed since the horrific incident, and Roxanne sat in the window seat of her mother's kitchen. Night again, and the full moon phase had long since passed, but she gazed at the sliver of crescent hanging in the darkness. Every few seconds, her hair fluttered around her face. The counter fan oscillated back and forth. The headaches were fewer, and the rest of her injuries were healing. Some physical therapy helped her body, but her heart ached.

There were moments when she felt calm, even peace. Knowing Dwayne would never hurt her again held little consolation with the horror of his death. His "I'm sorry" haunted her too. She'd heard it many times, but not like his last words.

His last words.

She heard a quiet knock at the kitchen screen door and looked up.

"Max?"

They hadn't spoken since she'd suspected him of stealing her story. She'd never actually confronted him, and since the book tanked, it didn't seem to matter, except that their relationship had suffered. But it was all too strange. It just wasn't consistent with his character. Her mind reeled. But she was no judge of character, especially of men.

Even still, Max had never visited her at the hospital after the horrific ordeal. It spoke volumes about him. *Didn't it?* Pastor Brooks, Melanie, practically the whole town came, but not Max.

"Hello, Roxy."

The accented words sprayed her like sweet cologne, but they floated by her like drugstore scents. Potent, but not lasting. Not like his flowers.

"Hello, Max."

"Your mum says you're moving soon."

"Yes. Back to Meridian."

"Ahhh. Well, right-o. Is there anything I could help with before you leave?"

Her brows furrowed, and it intensified the headache behind her eyes. "You never came to the hospital."

Rocking back on his heels, he shoved his hands in his front jean pockets. "Yes, well, there were many people by your side. I do my best praying in private."

"I imagine you do." Roxane breathed deep and held it. When she finally breathed out, she asked, "Max, did you publish my book?"

He frowned. "What do you mean, publish it? You know that I submitted it to Philippa's agent. We spoke of it, and I'm sorry it didn't get picked up."

"No. Did you self-publish it under a pen name?"

Taking his hands from his pockets, he braced himself in the doorjamb. Leaning forward, he stepped out on one foot. "Roxanne, if you need to ask me that…" A quiet groan emitted from his throat. "Is that why you created a chasm between us?"

"A chasm? It's not like this is a little rift or something. Someone took my story, changed it, and self-published it. I saw your picture on the back fly-leaf."

"My picture? Are you serious? Why didn't you talk to me about this before?"

Roxanne looked out the window. "All this stuff with Dwayne exploded before I could ask if you did it." Birds chirped outside, and silence hung inside. She turned back to face him. "Deny it, please? Say something."

He dropped his hands, straightened, and turned. "I wish we'd had that conversation, but perhaps the chasm has widened too far."

"Can't we have it now? I just need to know."

"Search your heart, Roxanne. I thought you knew me better than that. I'll always pray for you, and I hope you find what you're searching for back in Meridian." He left.

For an instant, she thought of going after him. How could she have ever doubted him? But the book. His picture. He must have published it, and if he didn't, why wouldn't he deny it? Or did he? Perhaps her accusation had hurt him too deeply. And yet, that's precisely where she was.

She cared for him too much and giving her heart away once more proved fatal.

Roxanne shifted off the seat too swiftly and felt as if a knife shot through her hip. Lying back against the wall, she wondered what she kept searching for. Joy, happiness, peace? She thought she'd found it in Bay Town. Perfect little Bay Town. But nothing was perfect because people weren't. Nothing on this earth was. She glanced out the window again. Clouds covered the crescent moon, and the darkness shrouded her mind and heart.

Bethie Cook shuffled into the kitchen, her robe cinched around her waist. "Mind if I make some tea?" her mother asked.

"Mama, it's too hot for a robe." Roxanne brushed back the strands fluttering around her face.

Her mother turned off the fan. "We have air-conditioning, you know."

Roxanne smiled. "Yes, but I can leave the windows open now." The smile faded.

She watched her mother put the kettle on and dig through her cupboards for her favorite mug. She set it on the counter and reached for the basket filled with a mix of various flavored tea bags.

"Well, now, shall I have chamomile or peppermint?"

Roxanne didn't answer.

"I'll have both." Bethie turned to her daughter. "Sometimes, we need more than one remedy to treat our ailments." She paused. "Did Max come by?"

Turning, Roxanne gazed at her mama as a smirk crossed her face. "You know he did. I imagine that's why you didn't come in here."

"Yes, dear." Her mother sat. "Did you work things out?"

Work things out. Since Dwayne's violent death, making up with Max seemed inconsequential. Everything in life seemed trivial. She wanted Dwayne out of her life. She just never expected it to be this way. Writing remained her only joy, and even that paled now. Now, Max couldn't be a part of it.

"There's nothing to work out. All value I found in him is gone."

"Nonsense. First of all, he didn't steal your manuscript. Get a lawyer, point your finger at someone else, but not Max. Second, he helped save your life."

Roxanne frowned. "What are you talking about?"

"He took me home after church when you and Lucy left for Meridian. We talked a bit, then he decided to drive to Meridian. He wanted to make sure you were safe."

"But I called him, he never answered."

"I don't know about that. Maybe he went to the wrong hospital. But he finally found you outside the coffee shop." Bethie shook her head. "He said he couldn't get to you before Dwayne did." Her mother choked back a sob. She cleared her throat and continued. "But he alerted the police and followed you to that parking structure. Do you remember any men chasing you and Dwayne?"

Her mouth gaped. "Max?" Roxanne closed her eyes and envisioned it. One of the men ran toward her. The one without a uniform.

Her mother continued. "He followed the police to the Bayou, too, and he rode with you in the ambulance, but you had passed out."

"Why didn't anyone tell me?"

"Would it have made a difference?"

"Of course, he saved my life." She stared back out the window. "But it doesn't change what he did, does it?"

"You are a fool, girl. You're so blinded by what you want."

"What do I want, Mama? Because I really don't know."

"It seems the focus on publishing your book somehow took precedence over all that's important."

"And what's important, Mama? Tell me."

"Well, first of all, God."

Roxanne looked out the window. A tear fell, and she swiped it harshly away. "I know that now. I know I could never have survived without Him. I know He saved me." Another tear fell. "I just don't know why he didn't save Dwayne."

"Oh my. I've heard of victim's remorse, but honey, that man." Bethie sucked in a breath.

"That man's a sinner like all of us. But who knows, maybe he asked the Lord's forgiveness in his dying breath."

Roxanne stared at her mother, eyes wide. "He did, Mama."

"What?" Bethie asked quietly.

"He said, I'm sorry. He directed it to me, but I think he might have meant it to God too."

Roxanne felt a hand covering hers. Her mother squeezed. "That's the hope we have, then. Only God knows. God is good, righteous, and just. What we don't know, we don't need to speculate."

"Thank you, Mama."

"Now, back to Max."

"No. That chapter is closed for now. I love Max and appreciate what he's done for me in the past, but this is unforgivable."

"Nothing is unforgivable. Not that he's done anything, but Roxanne, if you can forgive Dwayne, you can forgive Max."

Slumping back against the wall, she closed her eyes, hearing a chair scrape.

"Now, see there, my tea has gone cold. Roxanne, I dare say if you're trusting in God again and truly renewing your faith, you'll be back home before you know it. But be forewarned, Max might not be here, then."

"Mama, it's time for me to depend on me for a change, not on Max or anybody else."

"Seems you've done that before, and why then are you moving back to Meridian with that Travis? I have my doubts about him."

Her mother's words stung. "I'm not moving back with him. My house is there. I'm going to fix it up and start over. Travis just happens to live there, and he's helping me." Suddenly, her brow furrowed. "What do you mean Max might not be here? Did you mean physically? Is he going somewhere?"

"He's going on a long-extended vacation."

"How long? Where?"

Bethie shrugged. "Open-ended. Booked a pile of cruises all over the world. He's been quiet about the details, but he's leaving tonight."

Roxanne's heart lurched. Bay Town would never be the same if Max left. He was her rock. Even if she never forgave him, the security of knowing he'd always be here brought comfort. But the sureness of life shook her foundation. She stared back at her mother.

"It shouldn't matter, should it? I mean if you're depending

only on yourself. Daughter, you are not a selfish person, but somewhere, you've got off on the wrong track."

Roxanne stared out the window, but Bethie cupped her daughter's hand again. "Oh, I don't blame you for going there. With all that's happened to you. Just don't stay there, Roxanne. Set your feet firmly back on the solid foundation. And your feet won't find it in you or Max."

She stood and kissed the top of her daughter's head. "Goodnight, sweetie."

CHAPTER 40

One Year Later

Roxanne stroked the spine of the pink book sitting on the New Release shelf in the Hancock Library.

"Well deserved," Mrs. Hancock said.

"I don't know about that. But thank you, Mrs. Hancock."

"Gardenia."

Roxanne's eyes widened. "Excuse me?"

"My name is Gardenia. I think we can forgo southern formalities, don't you? I know it's a mouthful, so people call me Dena. Please do."

"Dena." Roxanne nodded. "Thanks so much for all your help and support. I just can't believe this has all happened."

"I just can't believe that man stole your manuscript! But God works in mysterious ways. What providence that the acquisition editor finally read your story and realized how marvelous it was."

Roxanne sighed. "Yes, well, I suspect that Max Tippet might have pushed for it."

"Still, if it weren't a wonderfully written story, you wouldn't be published. You did it, Roxanne."

"Thank you. And for putting my book in the library."

"Like I said, well-deserved. I can't keep it on the shelf. It's always checked out, and most everyone else has bought copies anyway."

"I sure appreciate it." Roxanne picked up her purse and headed for the exit. "Will I see you at the signing?"

"I wouldn't miss it."

Roxanne drove to Main Street, parking a ways down from The Old Book Shoppe. She wanted to take a longer walk, relishing all the gifts that God had given her. Bay Town hosting all of them of late. Still, a piece of her heart ached.

Virginia stepped out and locked her shop. She placed a sign on the door, and Roxanne stopped to read it.

Go to the Ole Book Shoppe! Local Author Signing Event.

Roxanne laughed. "Seriously? You'll lose business if you close in the middle of the day."

Virginia jumped as she twirled around. "Oh, my goodness. You scared me to death. Hey, you fancy author, you." She squealed. "I ain't losing business. I'm selling your books here, and they're going out like hotcakes."

Tears welled, and Roxanne hugged Virginia. The book released a month ago, but the book signing had been delayed due to her mother's unfortunate accident. A bad fall had immobilized her, but she agreed to a walker for the time being.

Virginia hooked her arm into Roxanne's elbow, and they strolled down the street together.

"Hey there, Pastor and Melanie," Virginia called out and continued to do so to everyone entering The Ole' Book Shoppe.

Roxanne's dream, and Sally's, too, unfurled before her. Everyone had pitched in to finish the store for its grand opening six months before, and today celebrated The Ole' Book Shoppe's first event. Roxanne Cook, Featured Author, and Book Signing. She and Virginia stayed outside the bookstore in front of the bay window, gazing at all Roxanne's copies.

"It's so beautiful. I'm telling you, I could decorate my bedroom walls with that cover," Virginia said.

Roxanne couldn't be more pleased with the cover of "Pages in Bloom." Various shades of pink peonies appeared scattered across vintage book pages fixed on the romantic cover. Roxanne touched the window. Scrolled across the bottom of the book, her name spelled out in fluid calligraphy. Every time she read the title, she said a prayer of thanks.

"Come on. They're waiting." Virginia pulled her in. "She's here!" she sang.

The Old Book Shoppe' hummed with excitement and thundered with applause. All her friends and then more attended. Chief Bert and Officer Blaine were in uniform, holding Roxanne's book and pointing proudly.

"Yup, I know her," Chief Bert said.

Pastor Brooks and Melanie hugged her. "I'm so proud of you," Melanie whispered.

"We all are. God will use this for His glory," Pastor Brooks said.

"Not too preachy?" Roxanne asked.

Pastor Brooks pinched his fingers together. "I'm not complaining. I think some of my sermons were in here."

Roxanne laughed. "Well, you've taught me a lot." She glanced around the room. "Y'all have."

"Come now. Let's set you down and get going here." Sally tugged at Roxanne, pulling her into a chair behind a small desk piled high with copies of *Pages in Bloom*.

She signed and chatted all day, but she stretched her neck to check every time the front doorbell rang. At the end of the day, Bethie Cook plopped into an overstuffed chair beside the desk. The crowd dwindled, and Sally brought them all a cup of tea.

"Thank you, Sally. This is more wonderful than I could ever imagine." Roxanne smiled, but a bittersweet remorse lingered in her eyes. Bethie didn't miss it, and Roxanne watched her mother's eyes mist.

"You are very welcome, my dear. Why, if not for you, none of this would be here." Sally sipped, and her cup tinked as she set it down. "But I half-expected Max to show up."

Bethie cleared her throat, shifted her eyes, and nodded toward Roxanne.

Sally frowned. "What?"

The doorbells jingled.

"You're late," Sally called out.

Roxanne's heart raced so fast she thought it would burst from her chest. Like a racehorse stamping at the gates, she waited.

"Sorry, we're late." A deep voice resounded.

We? Roxanne gulped. It couldn't be. She didn't recognize the voice. And why would he say *we?*

Bethie reached over and squeezed Roxanne's hand.

"Hey, Roxy. The traffic on the Bay Bridge is jammed. There must have been an accident. But I'm here, sweetie!" Lucy ran to her friend.

Jason grinned and bounced on his heels. "Congratulations, Roxanne. We got a little celebration to share too. Tell her. Go on, tell her." He kissed Lucy's cheek.

Roxanne pushed aside her disappointment and gazed at Lucy. "Don't tell me you're engaged?"

Lucy giggled. "Better than that. Jason loves Jesus, now! And yes, we are engaged." She wiggled a ring finger in the air. Overhead, lights flashed on the sparkling diamond. Lucy and Jason embraced.

"Now that calls for a celebration." Sally walked to the back room and returned with bottles of sparkling cider. A few clean glasses remained on the refreshment table.

"I'm so happy for you both," Roxanne said.

"Yeah, us too. The Lord saved us, and not just from Dwayne ..." Lucy gasped. "Oh, I'm so sorry."

The room went silent. Roxanne hadn't heard Dwayne's name mentioned aloud in so long. Every once in a while, the night terrors returned, but her sessions with The Refuge and Pastor Brooks had done their job. They always pointed her to God's Word, and the Bible had become her best friend.

"It's okay. God saves us all from this life. And He blesses us more than we can ever dream or imagine," Roxanne said.

"Ain't that right?" Lucy leaned into Jason.

"How long are y'all in town?" Roxanne asked. "It's been so long."

"Just overnight. It's crazy, ain't it. We're just a few hours apart, and other than phone calls, we can't seem to make the time." Lucy glanced at the book display. "That is so cool. I'm so proud of you." She frowned. "Say, whatever happened to ___"

"Cider anyone?" Bethie shouted. "Come on now, Sally's pouring it over there." Bethie stood, and Jason helped her with her walker.

"Travis? I thought I told you." Roxanne frowned. "I can't believe I didn't see it. That creep stole my book. Actually, I gave it to him."

"Well, we've all learned a lot of lessons, haven't we? Is he writing at all?"

"No. I don't think he ever did. *Dissertations in Dirt* just kind of blew away. You know how the Bible says, the grass withers, and the flowers fade. Or something like that."

"I've heard that." Lucy's eyes widened. "In Psalms, right?"

Roxanne raised a hand for a high five. "You got that."

"You know it, girl. Jason and I are in a Bible study. In fact, we been in biblical pre-marital counseling too."

"Nothing could make me happier." Roxanne meant it. Sort of.

Lucy stooped close to Roxanne's ear. "Have you heard from Max?" she whispered. "I mean, you haven't talked about him in ages. Did he never come back from his trip?"

Roxanne shook her head.

"Oh, sweetie. I'm so sorry. Is he okay? Has anyone heard from him?"

Biting her lip, she hoped she could hold back the deluge. "Some people have. He's sent notes to Sally, even Mama. Just postcards saying he's fine." She waved a hand in the air. "Having a grand time, he is." She couldn't laugh.

Lucy took a deep breath and grabbed Roxanne's hand. "Do you still love him?"

Roxanne's eyes widened. "I never said I loved him."

"But you do. And he felt the same. I just know it. You could see it in his eyes."

"I'm afraid I hurt him. Badly. I actually believed he stole my manuscript. And it was Travis all along." Roxanne shivered. "I've never had a chance to say I'm sorry."

"Well, sweetie. You had a lot going on. You just weren't thinking straight." She forced a smile. "And God's a God of second chances. Come on now. This is a celebration. Hey, Miz Sally, can I buy ten copies of Roxy's book so she can sign them for me?" Lucy asked.

"Drink your cider, girl, and come back tomorrow. It's late, and I'm locking up."

Lucy frowned. "Okay. What time do you open?"

"Nine in the morning. Jason, can you lock the front door and help us back to our cars?"

"Sure thing, Miz Sally." Jason bounded over to help.

"Oh, I'm parked out front." Roxanne dangled a set of keys. "I'll lock up, and I can open in the morning if you'd like."

"That would be nice, dear," Sally said.

"Sally, could you give me a ride home so Roxanne can visit with her friends a little more?" Bethie smiled.

Sweet Mama. Roxanne could use some time with Lucy. They'd been through so much together, and tonight, she longed for the special people in her life.

"Oh, we'll help you, Miz Cook," said Lucy. "We have to check into our hotel, anyway. We'll chat tomorrow, Roxy. How about we meet at the Mockingbird at eight for breakfast?"

"Sure." Roxanne smiled sheepishly and straightened. She really didn't want to be alone tonight. She feared having a lonely crying jag. This celebration just wasn't the same without Max.

The entourage left out the back door, and Roxanne bid them all goodbye. She picked up her purse, touched the pile of books still on the desk, and trudged to the front door. Placing her hand on the knob, she pulled, and simultaneously, it thrust open.

Max toppled into her, grabbing her, and protecting her from a fall.

Roxanne's eyes widened. She gulped. Choking back cries, she covered her mouth. But uncontrollably, tears flooded, and sobs came in waves. He held her at arm's length.

"I'm so sorry, Roxy. I tried to get here for the celebration. But they delayed the flight, and then the accident on the Bay Bridge."

"Where have you been?" Roxanne cried. "It's been a year. One whole year." She stepped away from him, hiding her face. She hadn't seen him since that night in her mother's kitchen and hadn't meant these to be her first words. She had so much to say. "I'm so sorry, Max," Roxanne whispered. "I'm so very sorry."

Knock. Knock.

An exotic-looking woman with long black hair in a smart black suit stood before her. Roxanne's mouth gaped. The most stunning creature she'd ever seen stepped in next to Max. Glancing at him, Roxanne thought she might wretch. No, it couldn't be.

"I'm so sorry to bother you." The woman spoke in the most beautiful British accent, yet nothing about her said United Kingdom.

Roxanne closed her eyes. This could not be happening. She didn't even look like Philippa. Her silky hair fell over her shoulders, and her almond-shaped eyes shined. Absolutely gorgeous. With all the strength she could muster, Roxanne buried her hurt. *Better get this over with.*

"Hello, I'm Roxanne, please come in."

"Oh, no. I must be going." The woman raised her dark lashes at Max.

"Right-o," he said and reached into his pocket.

Roxanne gulped. She deserved it. The way she'd treated him. *Oh, God, give me strength.* "Thank you for coming by, Max. I appreciate you making the effort. Nice to meet you, uh…"

"Kasumi Kato." She pulled out a business card from her tight pencil skirt pocket. "Kato Limousine Service." She handed Roxanne a card.

Max peeled off some bills and handed them to her. "Thank you so much, Kasumi."

"My pleasure. Anytime." She winked.

She closed the door behind her, and Roxanne's jaw clenched.

Max chuckled. He reached out a hand toward her but pulled it back. Shoving both hands in his pants pockets, he rocked back on his heels. "You wouldn't believe how crowded the airport had become. She had the last available vehicle."

A bubble of nervous laughter escaped, and Roxanne hunched her shoulders. "So, nothing between you two?"

Max's brows raised. "Oh, my goodness. Of course not."

"But she's English."

He frowned. "She's Japanese but raised in the UK." He took a deep breath. "Besides, my heart is set in America. In Bay town, to be exact. Always has been." Those blue eyes melted her heart, but she knew the words weren't meant for her.

Roxanne rolled her eyes. "Yes, I know." Not only had Max returned, but so had Philippa. But she'd long since learned to keep short accounts and listen to the gentle nudging. *Let it go. Apologize.*

"Max, I'm so sorry for accusing you. I'm such an idiot. I just tried to handle everything on my own. I left you out, God out."

"Shhh. Not to worry anymore."

"But I'm finally learning to trust God no matter what. I'm so sorry it took me so long. What I did to you was horrible."

"I know. Your mum wrote me."

"She apologized for me?" Roxanne's mouth gaped.

He chuckled. "No. But she explained plenty. But I'd forgiven you before I even left."

"Then why'd you leave?" She swallowed, and her eyes puddled. "I missed you so much. I mean, you and Philippa have meant so much to me."

"That's a conversation we should have had long ago. She'll always be a part of me, and I'll always love her, but since I've been away, I've let her go. I decided that before I left but never had the chance to tell you."

Roxanne's tears fell. "Because I never let you."

Max's blue eyes sparkled, and he took her hands in his and rested them on his chest. Encircling her trembling frame, he pulled her close. She gazed as his face grew closer, and she tasted his sweet, soft lips covering hers. Old Spice, mixed with the aroma of books, filled her with a dream-like euphoria. Roxanne pressed her lips onto his, thinking she might float to the top of the bookshelves. Max kissed her chin. He slid his mouth to her cheeks and brushed her forehead with his lips.

"A year is indeed too long," he whispered. "I love you, Roxy."

Roxanne tucked a sliver of hair behind his ear. "I love you too, Max. I always have."

THE END

ABOUT THE AUTHOR

Kathleen J. Robison is an Okinawan-American. Born in Okinawa, raised in California, Florida, Mississippi, and Singapore. Her travels are the inspirational settings for her stories. She and her Pastor husband have eight adult children. Seven are married, blessing them with fourteen grandchildren and counting. The diversity of their 31 family members provide the inspiration for more lively characters than can be imagined. Her husband grew up in the streets of Los Angeles raised by a single working mom, and that life provides fodder for many of the conflicts of her characters.

Tackling difficult life's trials with God's strength are the central theme of Kathleen's stories. She hopes to inspire her readers to trust God and with His strength, weather through and rise above trials and tragedies. If you like suspenseful stories with a thread of romance, you will enjoy Kathleen's Bay Town Series!

facebook.com/kathleenjrobisonauthor

instagram.com/kathleenjrobison

bookbub.com/profile/3794692396

ALSO BY KATHLEEN J ROBISON

Bay Town Series

Shattered Guilt (Book One)

Revived Hope (Novella)

Restored Grace (Book Two)

Let Them Eat Fruitcake (Christmas Novella)

Shadowed Doubt (Book Three)

Ransomed Doubt (Book Four)

HAVEN'S REST

RANSOMED PEACE BONUS SHORT STORY

KATHLEEN J. ROBISON

CHAPTER 1

A gunshot cracked, and Annie Greensprings ran outside. She reached the porch of Haven's Rest Gift Shop before the next shot rang out. *Was it a gun or a car backfiring?* This time, she ducked.

Across the street, in front of the newly opened café, a red-faced, wild-eyed man stood with a pistol raised high. Before he pulled back the hammer, Annie yelled.

"Are you crazy! Put that thing down." She held on to the porch post.

"Mind your own business, lady," he growled.

A strikingly handsome man in a tan suit stood next to a fancy sports car in front of the café entrance. "Hey, this isn't the Wild West. The little lady said to put the gun down."

Annie gazed at the man. *Did he seriously call her a little lady?* The wind blew around her face. Grabbing it, she twisted it into a messy bun atop her head. A movement down the street caught her eye. A young woman or girl stood with her hands up, head hung down, peering through poorly cut, thick bangs.

"Por favor!" she begged. "Please, don't shoot."

The looker in the tan suit stepped over and approached

the gun-toting man. "Give me that gun, or you'll be getting more than a bad Yelp review for your establishment."

His eyes widened, and the man holstered the gun and stuck out his hand. "I'm sorry, sir. My name's Luis Melendez. I'm not looking for trouble. It's just that …" he pulled at his dark mustache and pointed down the street. "That girl stole money from me—from the register."

Annie stepped off the porch and ran towards the girl. "Are you all right?"

The girl wiped at her mascara-streaked tears. She shook her head. "I steal nothing."

Slinging an arm around the girl's shoulder, Annie led her to Haven's Rest. Only then did she notice the half apron and the t-shirt that read Cocina Azul, the name of the newly opened restaurant across from Annie's gift shop.

"Hey, bring Leticia back here right now," Luis yelled.

"I think it's her break time," Annie called back.

She ushered the girl into her shop and took another look across the street. The man in the suit had a hand on Luis' shoulder. He stood a head taller than Luis. Annie's heart fluttered.

"You ought to take a break, too. Cool off." The stranger said to Luis but gazed at Annie. "So I don't have to call the police."

He flashed a gorgeous smile at her. It didn't help that his dark hair fell perfectly across his forehead, and the longish cut graced the top of his white-collared shirt. The tan suit, buttoned below a navy paisley tie, fit snugly across his chest— his massive chest.

Annie turned. Way out of my league, she thought. But before she stepped into the shop, Leticia brushed past her.

"Gracias, but I must return."

Annie's brow furrowed. "Return? Weren't you just running away?"

"Sí. But I have no place to go," Leticia said quietly.

"Stay here. I have room. You can stay with me," Annie blurted without a thought.

Leticia's mouth hung open, but her head lowered, and she shook it. "Gracias. No."

Running back across the two-lane road, she slowed when she reached the café. She stopped, turned, and waved to Annie. Leticia entered the restaurant just as the man in the suit walked back to a gleaming white two-seater vehicle. Annie stepped behind her screen door and watched. She had no idea of the make or model and didn't really care, but it screamed big bucks. Putting on sunglasses, he glanced back at Haven's Rest before pulling out and driving away.

Turning the "Be Back Soon" sign on her front door. Annie marched across the street to the Cocina Azul. Brightly painted terra-cotta pots filled with succulent-lined shelves and corners everywhere. Fast-moving ceiling fans added to the frigid air conditioning. The crisscrossed leather back bucket chairs surrounding small rustic wooden tables gave the feeling of old Tijuana. Though she'd never been there herself, she remembered her parents telling stories of visiting when it was still a sleepy little town.

"I have the right to refuse service." Luis glared at her.

"I guess you really are looking for a bad review. Didn't you just open up in town?"

"And you are?"

She stuck out her hand. "Annie Greensprings."

He frowned. "You don't look like a Greensprings."

Annie rolled her eyes. "I know. I'm half-Japanese. My dad was white. But I'm the owner of Haven's Rest Gift Shop. I'm your neighbor."

Luis gulped. "Look, we're just off to a bad start. I'm having some trouble with my help, that is all."

Annie looked around for Leticia. Something in her gut told her the help wasn't the trouble. Two other servers looked like whipped puppies as well.

"You know, Luis, there's a business owner's network here in town. We're a close group. Why don't you come to our meeting next week? Maybe someone there can help you out."

"No. I don't need any help." He glanced at Leticia and rattled off something in Spanish that Annie couldn't understand. Leticia rushed back to the kitchen. "Excuse me. I have customers to serve."

"Sure." Annie spun around and pointed to a table. "I'm ready for some lunch anyway."

Luis groaned quietly. "Fine. Have a seat."

Annie didn't have to wait long before she moaned with delight over the on-the-house sopapillas. The floury, airy pillows drizzled in honey were a big draw for Annie when she settled in New Mexico just five years ago. The chips and salsa traditionally served in every Mexican restaurant in Southern California, where she initially lived, had nothing over this sweet treat.

Ordering a to-go plate of rolled tacos, she paid her bill, took her order, and left. She'd hoped to speak with Leticia, but she never saw her again. Annie's heart bled for the girl. She wanted to help, but she also had to get back to tend to her gift shop. Although mid-week tourists were few and far between, she had a shipment to unpack, and she anticipated a busy Labor Day weekend.

Thankful for a six o'clock closing on weeknights, Annie had time to visit some of the other shops that stayed open an hour longer. Keeping in touch with other business owners helped her stay on top of their prayer needs, something God had put on her heart when she moved here. Besides, she needed to find out more about Cocina Azul and Luis Melendez. He'd only been there a month, and Annie felt this gun incident wasn't a fluke. She didn't trust the man.

After work, she got some of the inside scoop from the other shop owners. Some had nothing to report, but others felt things were amiss and had witnessed the young, frightened servers. One owner had also viewed Luis threatening a worker. Annie's first thought was an immigration violation. Perhaps he hired illegal immigrants and exploited them.

Later that evening, Annie sat by the window up above her shop. She lived all alone, although her Aunt Fumi lived just a thirty-minute drive north in Santa Fe. Annie's dream of opening a quaint gift shop along the Turquoise Trail came to fruition when she came of age to claim her parents' trust. The death of her mother, on the heels of her father succumbing to diabetes when she was a young child, left her an orphan, and she was passed around until Aunt Fumi took her in for good.

When she purchased an old house in the tiny artsy town of Madrid, not pronounced Mu-drid, but Ma-drid. Aunt Fumi and her cousins helped convert the home into her dream business.

The little one-bedroom apartment looked down on Cocina Azul. She took a bite of her rolled tacos, as tasty as the sopapillas. Annie closed her eyes and swooned with culinary delight. Luis had a good cook and would likely draw crowds here. But at whose expense?

Finishing her dinner, she opened her laptop but kept one eye out the window. She watched late into the night, and although the restaurant closed promptly at nine o'clock, the lights remained on long afterward. Girls shuffled back and forth, washing down tables, sweeping floors, and who knew what else. By eleven o'clock, Annie shut down her computer, stretched, and thought about going to bed. She couldn't. She huffed an exasperated sigh as she grabbed her purse, phone, and keys and crept down the outside backstairs to the alley where her red SUV was parked behind her shop.

Driving down the block of the one main street town, she crossed the street and moved into the alley behind Cocina Azul. Annie parked close, hidden behind a dumpster. She yawned and struggled to keep her eyes open. Shaking herself, she blinked, fearing if she stayed much longer, she might fall asleep.

Exiting the car, she trotted across the alleyway and walked along the building out of the moonlight toward the back door of the café. The door swung open. Annie froze. She side-stepped back to her car when barking startled her. A snarling, dirty mutt blocked her path. *Oh, Lord, please.* His yellow teeth bared as he reared back on his hind legs. Annie stooped to pick up a rock, and the animal pawed forward, barking.

"Knock it off!" A deep voice yelled.

"Luis, be nice. Come here, boy," a woman cooed.

The dog ran past Annie, and she could hear him chomping and lapping with his slobbering chops.

She didn't stop to watch but slid back against the wall and found a pile of cardboard boxes to hide behind. It had to be close to midnight when Luis and a middle-aged woman whom she assumed had fed the dog walked across the alley. Annie sucked in a breath.

Three teenage girls scrambled out the restaurant's back door. The dog snarled again, and the girls huddled together like scared sheep. Luis unlocked a black Cadillac Escalade, opened the front passenger side, and helped the woman in. He opened the back door, waved the girls over, and shoved them in, including Leticia. The dog whined, wagging his tail as if he wanted to go with them.

Annie waited until Luis got in and ran for her car. The dog took chase. Seconds before she reached her car, he bit the hem of her jeans. She kicked, trying not to scream but thankfully she wore her super-wide leg bottoms. One more swift kick shook him loose. Annie opened her door and jumped in. Her heartbeat pounded out of her temples, and she swiped her brow. She reached for a water bottle, sucked it dry, and wished she had more. The dog continued to bark, but Luis pulled away.

Tapping the steering wheel, she gulped. *Follow? Or*

not? With her finger poised above the ignition button, she stopped, said a quick prayer for guidance, and proceeded to follow the Escalade. The two-lane highway stretched out in the darkness as she stayed a safe distance behind. Checking her rearview mirror, as she descended a small hill, she noticed headlights coming up behind her.

Luis finally slowed and almost stopped. She hit her brakes, slowing as well. He turned onto an unmarked, unlit path, and Annie continued straight. She couldn't follow but glanced over her shoulder, trying to note where she was. No landmarks were present. But the action caused her to swerve off the road. She corrected quickly, but flashing red lights swirled behind her. It had to be the Sheriff, but still, her heart pounded as a shadow exited the car and came towards her. She blew out a breath of relief as the man in uniform knocked on the glass. She slid down her window.

"Are you okay, ma'am?"

"I am now." *Thank you, Jesus.*

"You seem to be driving a little erratically. Have you been drinking?"

"No, sir. I don't drink. I'm just tired, is all."

He flashed the light around the inside front and back of her car. "And what are you doing out here?"

"I'm a shop owner back in Madrid, and I thought I witnessed some suspicious activity this afternoon in town. I'm just following a hunch."

"Ma'am, you best be leaving that to us. I can escort you back to Madrid, and you can file a report with the police there tomorrow."

Annie sighed loudly. "Sure. I'll do that. Thanks."

She made a U-turn, and the sheriff followed. She slowed as she passed Luis' turnoff. Her heart skipped a beat. He stood next to a wide metal gate, locking a chain around it. He stared straight at her, and Annie hoped he didn't notice her in the dark. For the first time, she wished she didn't have a red car.

She noted her odometer reading so she could figure the distance from Luis's home to Madrid.

Thirty minutes later, Annie ran up her back stairs and slipped into her bathroom. Trudging out, she sighed, flipped off her sandals, and sunk into a wicker papasan chair. Her water bottle rested on the floor, and she gulped again. Right now, as tired as she was, it was easy to dismiss her irrational behavior as paranoia. But in her gut, she knew Leticia and the girls needed help. With thoughts of different scenarios of their possible terror rolling around, she slept fitfully in the chair.

It was still dark when yelling outside her window startled her. She'd forgotten to close and lock the windows again, an often-occurring occurrence in the summer heat. Even with air conditioning, she liked a little fresh air at night. Luckily, the apartment above her shop allowed her that luxury without fear of anyone breaking in. They'd have to scale the front of her wooden storefront. There was no balcony, no awning, nothing to aid a leg up.

Picking up her phone to check the time, it refused to light up. She'd forgotten to charge it last night. Along with neglecting to change her clothes and wash up, she already dreaded the day for lack of sleep. Still, the yelling continued. Very few people lived above or behind their shops, so the early morning noise might not affect anyone else. Most lived in scattered houses in the hills or at the edge of town.

Annie padded to the window. Sure enough, the lights were on in the cafe, and she could see the girls bustling about inside. She glanced at her illuminated wall clock. Five o'clock! She ran a hand through her untangled, straight hair. Why, she'd barely made it back by one o'clock in the morning. Those poor girls were being worked to death. She was sure of it. *How could she help?*

Showering and changing into a blue and white flowery peasant dress, she made a cup of matcha tea and sat down for her quiet time. While reading her bible and praying, she knew

God was prompting her, but to do what? Reading a devotional book, her eyes drooped shut, but the morning sleep brought ideas and resolution.

~

Haven's Rest opened at ten o'clock on weekdays, except Friday, today. She yawned and had exactly one hour to get downstairs. Her plan? Call Aunt Fumi and ask her to run the shop today. Annie would file a report with the Madrid police and do some more sleuthing over at the Cocina Azul.

"Hi, Annie. I'm glad you called." Aunt Fumi's cheery voice made Annie smile. "I was planning on coming out to help for Labor Day weekend anyway."

Within the hour, Aunt Fumi arrived. She bowed slightly, then hugged Annie. She pulled out a pink and red flowered print furoshiki-wrapped box. "I brought my lunch. Nigiri sushi, neh?"

Annie smiled. "Yum. I haven't had anything but Mexican food all week. Speaking of which, we have a new café across the street." She pointed but frowned.

Continuing to rifle through a large canvas bag, Aunt Fumi removed a navy and white cross-back Japanese apron and slipped it on. It covered her entire outfit. "What's going on?" she asked.

"I think the guy across the street is exploiting some women or girls."

Aunt Fumi's eyes went round. "You better come home and stay with me in Santa Fe. At least for a while. I knew it was just a matter of time before human trafficking showed up here."

"I think it's like domestic slavery." Annie bit her lip.

"*Nan desu ka?*" *What?*

"I think the owner of the Cocina Azul is using illegal immigrants to work for him." Annie's lips scrunched. "They arrive at five o'clock in the morning and work till midnight. Yesterday, the owner fired off a gun because one of the girls tried to run away."

"Did you call the police?"

"I didn't. He apologized, and this stranger in town calmed him down." Annie felt herself flush.

Aunt Fumi grinned. "What stranger?"

Fanning her face, Annie walked to turn on the AC. "I don't know. I've never seen him before."

"But you want to, neh?"

"Auntie!"

"So, what are you going to do?" Aunt Fumi asked.

"First, I'll file a police report for the gun incident and tell the police captain about my suspicions."

"Will he do anything?"

"I've lived here five years, and nothing like this has ever happened. I'm not sure what the captain will do. He comes in every once in a while to check on all the shops. He's a nice enough guy."

"Okay. Well, I'm here. You go do what you need to do, but be careful. Don't be impulsive. You can't save the world." Aunt Fumi nodded.

Tipping her head, Annie smiled. "Like you saved me?"

"Ah, so. That was Jesus. If I had known him sooner, I would have taken you in long before your years of heartache. *Gomenna sai*. I'm sorry." Aunt Fumi bowed more deeply this time.

Annie enveloped Aunt Fumi in a tight hug. "Please, if it wasn't for you…" She cleared her throat. "I love you, Aunt Fumi."

Blinking back tears, Aunt Fumi waved her off. "Be careful, whatever it is you're doing."

Annie didn't dare tell her about last night. "Thanks. First thing, I'm going over to the café. I need to buy something so I can snoop. How about some breakfast?"

"No, thanks. I ate miso soup and rice hours ago."

"Early lunch?"

"Annie, it's only nine o'clock."

"Okay, then say a prayer." Annie palmed her hands together and kissed her aunt's cheek.

"What exactly am I praying for?" Aunt Fumi asked.

"That I can help these girls somehow."

"You mean that the police will help them?"

Annie jabbed an index finger towards her aunt and smiled. "Right."

Fussing around her shop to pass some time so that she wasn't the first in the café, Annie swept the front porch. Plucked some dead blooms, hosed down the flower beds, and purposely sprayed her feet before she slipped on rubber sandals. The sweltering summer heat made gardening unbearable, but she managed to waste thirty minutes before heading over to the Cocina Azul.

"Hi, can I get some breakfast?" She called to the back of a server.

The girl turned, her eyes widened. She glanced around, shook her head, and pointed to the door.

"What? You don't serve breakfast?"

"Of course, we do," the woman from the alley last night called through the kitchen pass-through. "She doesn't speak much English." She walked out front and extended a hand to Annie. "Hola. I believe you met my husband yesterday. I'm Claudia."

Annie's mouth gaped, but she clapped it shut and smiled. "Yes," was all she could manage.

"I'm sorry about his hot temper. He really is harmless."

"He shot off a gun." Annie's eyes rounded.

"I know. Please forgive him. We're new in town, and we just came from Brownsville, Texas."

"Oh, my," Annie said. "I hear it's pretty rough there."

"It's terrible. So we brought our three girls and started all over." Claudia smiled and ran her hands down her ample stomach.

"Daughters? Those girls are yours?" Annie's suspicions went wild. Luis said his server stole from him yesterday. His server, not his daughter.

"Yes. And Leticia here, she's the wild one. Isn't that right, Leticia?" Claudia spoke rapidly in Spanish.

Leticia glanced down and retreated to the cash register. She picked up a menu and walked to a table far away from the kitchen.

"Please, have a seat," Claudia said. "Shall I make you some huevos rancheros?"

"That would be lovely. Oh, and some of your delicious sopapillas?"

Claudia laughed. "Those are my specialty. But I usually don't serve them until lunchtime." She winked. "For you, a morning treat. But it will take a while."

"Sure, no rush. My aunt's here helping me out today."

"You're fortunate to have good help." Claudia returned to the kitchen.

Annie sat, and Leticia offered the menu. When she turned to leave, Annie touched her hand. "Do you need help?" she whispered.

Leticia's eyes darted to the kitchen. Claudia was nowhere in sight. Leticia nodded.

"Are you illegal?"

Leticia gulped.

"It's okay. I can help." She didn't know how, but she'd find a way. "I can help get you some legal aid." Annie sighed, wishing she'd learned Spanish instead of Japanese. However, her limited skills in that language didn't help much, either.

"My sisters and came here years ago. We were just niñas."

Annie smiled. "You speak English?"

"*Sí. Un poquito*, just a little. Our parents brought us here illegally. A long time ago. But they died last year." Her eyes grew wet. "Luis and Claudia bought us."

"Bought you? Like paid for you?"

Leticia nodded.

"I knew it!" Annie bit her lip. "Listen, can you——"

"Leticia!" Claudia called.

She ran for the kitchen.

They're domestic slaves. Now Annie knew what to do. She needed to report Luis and Claudia and get Legal Aid for the girls. They were victims all the way around, and who knew what Luis and Claudia would do to them as they got older? Annie guessed Leticia to be sixteen or seventeen and the other two close in age.

Claudia brought out the huevos rancheros, beans, rice, and sopapillas. She smiled.

"Wow. You are one amazing cook. Did you have a restaurant in Brownsville, too?"

"We did, and quite a big clientele. But we couldn't get honest workers, and we needed a better life for our girls."

I bet. Annie almost snarled. Taking a bite of the sopapilla, she hummed. "Mmm. So, are you the only cook?"

"Oh, no. Luis cooks, too. Sometimes better than me."

"Oh, is he here today?"

Claudia narrowed her eyes. "No. Someone followed us home last night, and he wanted to guard our house this morning in case they returned while we were gone."

Annie gulped. Her hands shook, and she immediately dropped them in her lap, picking up her napkin. "That's really weird. It's usually pretty safe around here."

Claudia pursed her lips. "I have customers to serve. Thank you for coming in, Annie."

Annie flinched at the sound of her name. She hadn't given it. Had it registered with Luis?

Getting another to-go box, Annie took leftovers back to her shop, then headed to the Madrid Police Station. The three-man force occupied a newer building at the north end of town, near the one-truck fire station.

"I'd like to file a report," Annie said to the nearest officer sitting at a desk.

"Sure, have a seat. He picked up a pen. What happened?"

"The new owner of the Cocina Azul—"

"Luis Melendez? They make some mean sopapillas over there. Have you had their Chili Colorado?" The officer smacked his lips.

"The guy pulled a gun and shot it off yesterday. Didn't you hear it?" Annie said.

The dark-haired man leaned back. "We did. He came over later in the afternoon and told us everything. He apologized. The captain waived the fine. We're all good."

"No, we're not all good. Luis is holding illegal immigrants against their will."

"That's a big accusation."

"I can prove it. I talked to one of the servers."

"His daughters?"

"They're not his daughters. He bought them." Annie leaned forward.

He scratched his head. "Whoa. You got quite an imagination there. We're a peaceful community here. You know that. And we pride ourselves on watching out for one another, so let's give this guy a chance. I mean, teenage daughters can be a handful, and he's got three of them."

"I want to file a report," Annie said.

"All right then, if that's what you want. Go online with ICE, Immigrations and Customs Enforcement, and file a tip report." He sucked in a deep breath. "They'll take it from there. We don't handle immigration here."

"You're the law, and this is illegal immigration."

"Ma'am, just take the proper course of action."

"It's Annie. And I own Haven's Rest in town."

"That's right. You're a business owner. So why don't you

keep our town's best interests in mind? Folks won't take kindly to you stirring up trouble in Madrid, especially this weekend. We expect a lot of tourists, and it's the city's big money maker. You know that."

"So if I file online, then what?" Annie glared back at him.

"It all depends on whether ICE thinks it's a valid tip. If so, they'll get back to us in a month or two," he sneered.

"What if I file in Santa Fe, in person?"

"Now, why would you want to do that? Today's Friday. They won't do anything this weekend."

Annie stood, not believing he wouldn't help. But God willing, she'd find someone. Thirty minutes later, she reached Santa Fe and drove to the Mud Hut for coffee.

Pulling into the driveway, she spotted an empty parking space, but just before pulling in, a white sports car zipped in ahead of her.

"Seriously?" She yelled, but her mouth dropped when out stepped the gorgeous man from yesterday. Still, handsome, or not, she slid down her window and yelled again. "Rude!"

He stopped and turned. *And I thought he looked good yesterday.* His grey suit, navy shirt, and light blue striped tie set his eyes off. The blue hues practically matched the hot blue skies above. Annie gulped.

He slid down his glasses and gazed. "Hey, I'm so sorry. Were you waiting for that spot? My bad. I'll move." He flipped his key fob and returned to his car.

Annie shrunk down. "No, never mind." *What an idiot*, she thought. *Me, not him.*

"No, I insist."

But Annie pulled in a couple spaces down. He waited for her, and she watched him out of the corner of her eyes. The wind picked up as she rounded the front of her car. It caught her dress, and she struggled to tamp it down while managing to tame her swirling hair. She looked up and caught him smiling. Grinning actually.

Walking past him, she entered the Mud Hut. He followed.

"Can I at least buy you a coffee for taking your space?"

His deep voice resonated like a finely tuned bass guitar. Like smooth jazz soothing her soul. He waited. *Did he recognize her from yesterday?*

Annie cleared her throat. "No. That's not necessary. In fact, go ahead. I'm not sure what I want," Annie lied.

He approached the register and spoke quietly while placing his order. He tapped the counter, nodded, and took a seat.

"I'll take a medium latte." Annie pulled out her card.

"Oh, it's covered, miss," the server winked.

Annie let her head drop to her shoulder and spun around. Mr. Gorgeous waved. Mr. Way Out of Her League. Just another flirty guy playing with her.

She walked over. "That's very nice of you, thanks."

He offered a hand. "Hi, I'm Nicholas."

She looked at the well-manicured nails and wanted to hide hers. She'd let her gel nails go when she couldn't afford the thirty-five dollars every two weeks. Although short and clean, they didn't have a nice sheen like his.

"Annie. I'm Annie," she said, nodding and shrugging, feeling like a ridiculous schoolgirl.

"So what are you doing here? Don't you work in Madrid?"

He did remember. "Actually, I own the Haven's Rest Gift Shop there."

"Oh." He sighed. "A female entrepreneur."

Oh, a chauvinist.

"And you're a male, what …?"

He laughed.

"I'm an estate attorney."

"That makes sense." Annie glanced out the window at his fancy car.

"It goes with the job."

"Whatever it is."

The barista called out their orders, and Nicholas waved for Annie to sit. He picked up the drinks, but she still stood.

"Please, can you sit a minute?"

"Not really. I'm anxious to get to the immigration office."

His brows furrowed, and he unbuttoned finely tailored suit coat.

Annie stared down at her white, flat sandals. At least her toenails were polished.

"Why?"

"You know that incident yesterday?" Annie sat. "I found out that Luis guy, the owner, is harboring illegal immigrants."

"That's a big accusation. Do you have proof?"

Annie set her drink down and leaned forward. "I spoke with that girl. The one he fired a gun at."

"He fired it in the air."

"Did you not see how scared she was?"

"She stole money."

Rolling her eyes, Annie huffed. "Oh, please. You don't believe that. He worked those girls 'till midnight!"

"How do you know that?" He picked up his drink and sipped.

"I live across the street above my shop and watched them," she cleared her throat. "Then I followed them home."

He sputtered. "You what? At midnight? Where?"

"Down the highway about thirty minutes on the way to Albuquerque."

"You can't be serious. You don't even know if the girl's story is true, and you're risking your neck. Why not let the police handle it?"

"They won't. I tried this morning. That's why I'm going to ICE to file a tip, then I'm going to Legal Aid."

He smiled and flung out his hands. "Let me give you some advice—free of charge. Legal Aid is so backed up that they can't help—not anytime soon. File the report with ICE and give them time to look into it."

"You sound like the Madrid police. And in the meantime, I'm supposed to let those girls be exploited?"

"What's it to you?"

Annie stepped back, almost fell back. "Are you kidding me?"

Closing his eyes, Nicolas raised a hand. "Sorry. Wrong phrase. I mean, why you? And what can you do?"

Annie's eyes watered. "Because God calls us to care for the fatherless. Their parents died or were killed last year, and those girls are all alone." She patted her eye. "Someone's got to help."

Nicohlas sighed. "Fine. I'll help." He touched her hand. "You just have to promise me you won't go traipsing out in the desert after them at midnight."

His touch made the hair on her arms rise. The warmth of his fingers surged through her, and he gazed into her eyes, staring too long. He sighed, and his lips parted. *Did he feel it, too?*

"Promise me?" He squeezed her hand.

She drew a deep breath. "Why?"

The corner of his mouth lifted, and a dimple creased in his cheek. "Let's just say I like what you said about God and the fatherless."

Nicholas drove Annie to the ICE office. She filed the report, and they didn't give her the time of day until Nicolas asked to speak to someone in charge. He flashed his business card, and Annie wondered why an estate attorney would have clout. Still, he made progress. More than she could have done on her own. It irked her.

"They may send someone out this weekend, which means we have to work fast and smart." Nicholas placed a hand on her back, guiding her to his car.

"We? I don't understand?" Annie turned, well aware of the placement of his hand.

"I need to gather some information out there. So I'll take you back to Madrid."

"But I have my car," she said.

"I can bring you back when we're done," he reassured her.

"No. That's okay. Just take me back to my car, and you can follow me."

"Whatever you say." Nicholas shrugged.

When they arrived back at the Mud Hut, he stopped just behind her car. She walked out and stopped. Pulling down her glasses, she kicked her tire and spun back to Nicholas.

"I've got a flat!"

"Must be providence."

Annie's eyes widened. Her dad always said that.

"Hop in. I'll call a service and get it fixed." He peered out the window. "Wait a minute. Is the front one flat, too?"

Walking to the front of her car, Annie slammed a hand on the hood. "What in the world?" She looked around for glass. None. "That's so weird." *And how can I afford two new tires?*

She spun around to find Nicholas on his phone. *Think. Think.* And the solution was a credit card. The one she'd just paid off. Her shoulders drooped.

Nicholas waved her over. "Come on. I called a service. They'll take it to a tire shop, and we'll get you fixed up."

"I can't afford a tire shop. I need to get some discount tires somewhere."

Nicholas flashed those pearly whites. "Please, let me help. After all, I'm the one that made you leave your car here."

"No. I'll pay you back."

Annie stood arguing with him until a tow truck came. Nicholas did indeed take care of it and promised to get Annie back to her car by evening.

"Let's go," he said.

She complied, and a thread of excitement fluttered in her stomach as they walked back to his car. He opened the door for her, and the smell of new leather wafted out. She climbed in, her mouth gaping at the cockpit-like dashboard.

"What is this?" Annie asked, running a hand across the polished wood grain.

"A Lexus, LC 500."

Annie frowned. "How much?"

"About a hundred thousand dollars." He started the engine and pulled out.

Closing her eyes, Annie sighed. "I can't even..." Taking a deep, cleansing breath, she tried to sound casual. "So you said you needed to gather some information. What kind of information?"

Nicholas drove with one wrist hanging over the wheel. Expensive sunglasses perched on his perfect nose. *Could he be any more cool?*

"Somehow, we need to speak to Leticia without raising suspicion." He tipped his head in her direction. "If what she says is true, I can begin paperwork to legalize her status."

Annie's whole body warmed. He's like a knight in shining armor. But reality hit, and dollar signs rang before her eyes.

"How much will that cost?"

"Too much. More than they can afford. But lawyers always do pro-bono." He glanced at her. "And I'm overdue. Besides, we need to act before ICE comes and takes her away."

Annie sputtered. "What? Luis and Claudia are the criminals, not the girls."

"Right, and they'll get arrested but probably released. But Leticia and her sisters may get deported or detained unless I can expedite their paperwork and get them in a safe haven."

Annie smiled. Haven's Rest, her gift shop. *Providence?*

Nicholas cleared his throat. "So, Annie. Do you live alone?"

She turned her head, giving him a sly smile. For the first

time since she met him, she saw a softness in his eyes. Vulnerability. "Do you?"

Nicholas' deep laugh filled a void within her.

"I do. I have a place in Albuquerque. I was just taking care of some business in Santa Fe this morning." He glanced her way. "And I'm sure glad it was today."

Annie felt her skin flush.

He chuckled. "You're turning red."

Keeping her gaze on the road, she shook her head. "No, I'm not."

"Yes, you are." He reached over and touched her cheek with the back of his hand. "Definitely."

She yanked her head away. *Way too flirty.* But it felt so good.

"So, how come you're not married to some gorgeous trophy wife?" Annie teased while trying to protect her heart.

"Not my type."

"Oh, please. Look at this car."

"What about you? Where's your hippie, artsy fellow?"

"Not my type. I'm a church girl." She found this was the quickest answer to turn away a flirty guy. "I was raised that way and stayed that way for the most part."

"Oh. That's where the God and fatherless come from."

"That, and I am fatherless. My parents died when I was young. They were everything to me." Annie sighed. "As far as men go, Daddy is a hard act to follow."

"So you're looking for a church guy?"

"I'm not looking," Annie glanced at him. *Well, maybe, just looking...*

Nicholas remained quiet the rest of the ride. So did Annie. It surprised her how comfortable they felt as they enjoyed the scenery together. He'd put on a classical playlist, and her heart felt light—even fluttered a little. Riding in a fancy car with a gorgeous man, soothing music, and the painted desert flying by, it felt like a classic romance movie. But she was certain this couldn't be a happily ever after. There was an important missing element.

~

Arriving back in Madrid, Nicholas and Annie walked straight over to the Cocina Azul.

Luis walked in from the back of the café, opposite the kitchen. He frowned upon recognition.

"Back again?" He asked.

"Well, your food is pretty amazing," Annie said. She shrugged, not looking the least bit casual.

Nicholas frowned at her and huffed. "We're not here to eat."

"Then I'll ask you to leave."

"I'm an attorney, and I'd like to speak with the girls first."

"No. Leave my daughters out of this."

"Luis! It's about time you returned." Claudia called from the kitchen. "Did you go to Santa…" She stopped when her eyes connected with Annie.

"So, you were in Santa Fe today?" Annie tipped her head.

"I never said that."

Nicholas gazed at Annie. Her eyes went round as she thought of the two flat tires. He nodded slightly and grazed her hand with his fingertips.

"Look, a suspicious tip's been filed regarding illegal immigrant workers and this café. I'm a legal aid representative, and I need to talk with the girls. If they are indeed your daughters, you can stay while I have a chat. But I'll need to see their birth certificates."

"I'm not showing you anything. You need a warrant."

"I can get a subpoena for a hearing." Nicholas breathed deeply.

"I don't care what you do. You're not talking to my girls. Now, leave."

The girls huddled by the cash register, all holding menus. Nicholas called out to them in Spanish. Annie's eyes went wide as he spoke fluently and rapidly. "Understand?" He said in English.

Leticia glanced back and forth and opened her mouth, but Luis silenced her with his growl. Finally, she nodded and pointed to the girls. "Maria y Juanita Gonzalez," She said.

Luis's face grew red, and for a moment, Annie thought he might reach for his gun again, though she didn't see it anywhere. He spewed back in Spanish as well, and the girls ran to the kitchen. He turned back to Nicholas. "They won't listen to you. Now go."

"No. Not without the girls. You monster!" Annie gritted her teeth.

Nicholas took Annie's hand. "It's time to leave."

Pulling away, Annie glared. "You're crazy. We can't leave them."

"Now's not the time," Nicholas said quietly. "Let's go, Annie."

Annie's feet stood frozen, and she couldn't move. The front door of the café opened, and the police captain entered. The thick tension in the room escalated.

"What's going on here? I heard a lot of yelling from outside."

"Captain, I'd like to file a restraining order against these two." Luis raised his chin.

The captain nodded, resting his hands on his gun belt. "I heard Ms. Greensprings came by the station this morning. She still bothering you, huh?"

"Seriously?" Annie gaped.

"Luis, I'll have the paperwork filled out, and you can sign it. It's just temporary, but it'll keep her out this weekend. After that, you'll have to file one in Santa Fe with the judge."

"And him, too." Luis pointed to Nicholas.

"And you are?"

"I'm a Legal Aid representative. I practice law in Albuquerque."

"Did you bring him in?" The captain glared at Annie.

"I was here yesterday at the shooting, and we want to take action to protect these girls," Nicholas said.

Annie looked back and forth between the three men. Luis's red face was about to explode, and the captain fidgeted with his gun belt. But Nicholas stood cool, calm, and collected.

"This is what we'll do," the captain huffed. "It's Labor Day weekend. The crowds are already arriving. You two," he pointed to Annie and Nicholas, "just stay away from here until Monday, deal?"

"No," Annie said.

Nicholas took her hand. "We'll be back. And it may be before Monday."

"Not when I get the restraining order," Luis yelled.

Yanking her hand away, Annie stomped to her shop. Nicholas followed. Annie flung open the screen door. It bounced back, almost hitting her before Nicholas stopped it, and she swept by him.

"Aunt Fumi? I'm back," Annie called.

The petite, salt-and-peppered-haired lady emerged from around the register. She grinned broadly, and her wrinkled face shone with joy at the sight of Nicholas. "So this is your stranger from yesterday?" Aunt Fumi bowed. "*Arigato*. Thank you for taking care of my niece yesterday."

"Auntie! *Urasai!*" Annie immediately covered her mouth. She didn't mean to reprimand Aunt Fumi. "*Gomen na sai.* I'm sorry." And why was she reverting to Japanese?

Aunt Fumi flashed down a hand at Annie. "Introduce me, please. He's a looker." She laughed.

Nicholas chuckled and extended a hand. He towered over the small woman whose head barely reached above his waist. Placing both hands on her thighs, she bowed deeply.

He dropped his hand and reciprocated the motion.

"Aunt Fumi, we have to take care of some business. Can you—"

"Yes, of course. Go upstairs. I put the nigiri sushi in your refrigerator. Eat."

Upstairs, Nicholas gazed around. Annie rattled on about her little humble abode, but he didn't seem to be listening. Pulling out lunch and filling glasses with iced tea, she set everything on her tiny kitchen table. But Nicholas had stopped by the end table next to the papasan chair. He picked up one book after another.

"So you're a theology student?"

"Hardly," Annie said. "I'm just trying to understand the Word better."

"I see." He set down the books and joined her.

Annie groaned inwardly. That was an opportunity to share her faith, and she blew it. He dove right into his plan for the girls. His kind heart and desire to help still didn't override her disappointment at not talking about God with him. *Where did he stand?*

"I at least got her last name. Do you know where she's from?"

"Brownsville, Texas," Annie said.

"Good. How about Luis?"

Annie told him all she knew.

He pulled out his cell and punched a number. "Yeah, I need you to get all the information you can on Leticia Gonzalez from Brownsville, Texas. As far as we know, she's undocumented, has two sisters, Maria, and Juanita, and they're connected with Luis and Claudia Melendez. They owned a restaurant in Brownsville." He looked at Annie.

"What's the name of the restaurant in Texas?"

Annie shook her head.

"Okay. That's all we got." He chuckled. "You got that right. And I need the info today. Can you get the paperwork started for the three girls? And one more thing. I'll need some beds at The Nighhaven. Thanks."

She stared wide-eyed. "What's the Nighthaven, and what did you just do?"

Nicholas took a deep breath. "More time for that later. I have to get back to Albuquerque before the courts close. I know a judge I think will help."

"Who are you? I thought you were a rich people's lawyer?"

He laughed. "An Estate Attorney, yes. But I have connections." He reached out and touched her hand. "I'm sorry, I won't be able to get your car back tonight, but I'll have a driver bring it out tomorrow."

Her heart sank at the thought that this might be their last encounter. *Would his people take care of everything, and he'd walk out of her life forever? Of course, he would. Why wouldn't he?*

She chugged down her glass of tea and took a bite of the sushi. "Okay, then. I don't know how to thank you. I guess you're a God send."

He touched her hand again. "I think it's the other way around. I haven't been this involved in helping good people in a long time. I guess I got a little sidetracked by the rich people." He stroked the back of her hand with his thumb.

"Listen, Annie. When this is over …"

She pulled her hand away. "Yes. Well, hopefully, that'll be soon. And we can all get back to business—you with your fancy car and clothes." She stood. "I love your suits, by the way."

He looked down and grinned. "You're pretty sweet yourself in that blue floral," he said, pulling out his phone. "How about a selfie to commemorate our work this weekend? I think we look good together, don't you?"

She flushed. *Stop. Stop right now. This will never work,* she thought. She stood. "Oh, no. I don't think so. I have to get back to my shop, and you need to get back to your rich people."

He stood and took her hand. "Annie…"

He pulled her close and cupped his hand on her side, all the while gazing into her eyes.

Her heart beat so loudly, she felt it might pound from her chest. She gasped quietly for a breath.

The door flung open. "Annie…" Aunt Fumi froze. "Oh, gomen na sai! So sorry." Aunt Fumi closed the door and disappeared.

Annie stepped back, her heart fluttering and her mind spinning. She didn't know whether to be angry or thankful to Aunt Fumi. She walked to the window, opened it, and sucked in the hot air.

"Well, I better go." Nicholas paused as if waiting for her to stop him. She didn't. "Right then. I have a lot to do. I'll keep you posted. Bye, Annie."

She turned, searched his eyes, and whispered, "Good Bye."

When he closed the door, she sunk into the chair by the window. Glancing at the Bible sitting on the tiny table in front of her, she realized that letting him go was the right thing to do. A few moments later, she stood and planted her feet firmly. Shaking Nicholas from her mind, she headed down the stairs to the shop.

Aunt Fumi asked a million questions, which Annie struggled to deflect. It made the afternoon fly by, along with the incoming tourists for the big weekend. Any holiday in Madrid brought the flocks of day-trippers heading down the Turquoise Trail. She checked across the street at any lull in her business. As far as she could tell, the girls were still there.

Her biggest fear was that Luis might move them. But these next few days were a huge moneymaker for the town, and Cocina Azul had already gotten rave reviews. He and Claudia wouldn't do anything drastic now. But Tuesday, after the holiday, was another story, and Annie prayed that Nicolas could perform a miracle. Well, she trusted God to do that through him.

"So tell me why he's not good enough for you?" Aunt Fumi interrupted her thought.

Annie spun around. She coughed. "Did you see him? We're a terrible match."

"Nonsense. Because of his money?"

She leaned against the register counter, propping her chin on her fist. "I don't think he's a Christian, Auntie."

"Oh my. That's a big one. Didn't you ask?"

"I couldn't. I mean, I could. I guess I just got caught up in the moment, and by the time I realized how much I liked him, I didn't want to know."

Aunt Fumi's brow furrowed, wrinkling her face.

"Auntie, I knew he wasn't my type, but that gorgeous man paid so much attention to me. I think he just liked the idea of us working together to help someone." *Yet, he made it seem like more upstairs.* Annie shivered. "Anyway, I couldn't get my hopes up. So I let him go."

"He didn't kiss you?"

"Auntie!"

"But you were in his arms up there. You let that go?"

Annie laughed. "Thanks to you. And I mean that. I don't know what I would have done."

The front door bells jingled. "Welcome to Haven's Rest," Annie called out. A flock of women walked in, followed by one older gentleman. Annie pulled a bottle of water from the compact refrigerator under the sink and handed it to him. "We have a small sitting area over there for the men." She giggled.

"What a thoughtful idea," said the man. He mopped his brow with a handkerchief and sat.

And so the day went, then Saturday came with a force of tourists. The streets flooded with cars and pedestrians. Annie and Aunt Fumi had little time to eat or rest as the day rolled on, and still, she heard nothing from Nicholas. By dusk, she'd stepped out on the front porch for a breath of hot, fresh air and saw her SUV pull up, followed by a Mercedes sedan. Two beautiful women stepped out of each car. One blonde and the other redhead, both wearing sharp suits and high heels. They pulled open the little gate leading to Haven's Rest.

"Hello, you must be Annie," The svelte blonde offered her hand. "We work for Nicholas Nighhaven."

Annie frowned. She never knew his last name. *Nighthaven?*

The redhead with tumbling curled locks stepped forward. "Forgive her. By Nicholas's description, she just assumed that you were Annie Greensprings. Although the last name had us fooled."

"I'm half-Japanese. My father was born here."

"Well, you're every bit as gorgeous as Nick said you were." The blonde held up her key fob. "Here you go. Have a nice day."

Gorgeous? He said that? Annie grinned. "Thank you. And thanks so much for bringing my car."

"Our pleasure. It's a beautiful ride out here. Oh, was there any more news to report? Nick asked us to check."

Nick? Annie slouched, leaning against the porch post. "I'm afraid not."

"No worries. He'll come through—he always does." The redhead winked, and both women chuckled. "Bye," they said in unison.

Annie smiled, waved, and held back a gag as she walked back into the shop. Yup. She'd made the right decision. He was way out of her league, and the two models proved it.

By the end of the day, Aunt Fumi insisted Annie drive back to Santa Fe and spend the night. She wanted to take her niece to church but promised to bring her back before the store opened. Annie finally agreed.

Sunday morning, the sermon on seeking God's guidance was exactly what she needed. It may be too late for any hope with Nicholas, but if God chose to bring someone her way in the future, she'd be sure to apply James 1:5 and ask for wisdom. It all happened so fast with Nicholas that she'd forgotten to pray about him. Still, the evidence of faith wasn't there, *was it?*

After church, the women returned to Madrid, and Annie thanked God for the crowds. It had to be a record-breaking weekend. She and Aunt Fumi were exhausted by Sunday evening.

Tallying up the sales receipts, Aunt Fumi whistled. "If Monday is as good as this weekend, we can take the week off."

Aunt Fumi stayed the night, and it was a good thing. Monday proved to be even better. Annie had been so busy that she didn't have time to check what was going on across the street except to notice the lines. The Cocina Azul was doing well, too. Customers crowded every shop in town.

The day for Haven's Rest bustled to a close. Once again, Aunt Fumi did the books while Annie straightened up the shop. Thirty minutes later, she heard a loud ding from the register.

Aunt Fumi hit the button that opened the antique register and waved receipts in the air. "Let's go on a cruise!"

"How'd we do?" Annie asked.

"Better than ever. The best weekend yet." Aunt Fumi grinned, her eyes wrinkling shut.

"Let's close up and celebrate." Annie moved toward the front door.

She turned the sign to Closed, but a scuffle between patrons across the street caught her eye. The orderly line waiting to eat at Cocina Azul snaked down the street, but towards the front entrance, huddling groups parted. Leticia sneaked between them. Suddenly, she broke loose and darted across the street.

Annie's mouth gaped, and she flung open the door, ushering Leticia in.

In short gasps, Leticia tried to speak. Annie stared at the jagged cut welting on her cheek. The bruises on her wrist looked to be a few days old. She held the girl's hands, trying to calm the shaking.

"Please. I heard them talking." Leticia sobbed. "They will move us soon,"

"Move you? Where?" Annie whispered.

"No, se. I don't know." She looked up through watery eyes. "You must be careful."

Annie frowned. "Me?"

The front door flung open. "Leticia, come now!" Luis bellowed.

"Who hurt her? Annie stood in front of Leticia, arms outstretched aside her body. "What did you do?"

With wide eyes, Leticia shook her head. "No. Not him. Me. I fell. He didn't do it."

Annie didn't believe her.

"That's right, the clumsy girl hurt herself." Luis yanked her arm.

"You leave her alone," Annie wrapped a hand around Leticia's wrist, and a tug-of-war ensued. "She needs first aid."

Luis gazed at Leticia's face. Still red and bleeding. He glared at Annie. "You're not much of a nurse."

"Here!" Aunt Fumi rushed over with a First Aid kit in hand. She slapped Luis' hand away from the girl. "Give us a minute. You should take care of her better than this."

As if Luis was used to taking orders from women, he stepped aside. Aunt Fumi spoke Japanese as she worked. Her voice is sweet and soothing. Annie couldn't understand much of what she said, but she seemed to calm Leticia. Still, they worked together washing Leticia's cut, applying antibiotic gel, and bandaging the wound.

"I'm reporting this, you know." Annie crossed her arms.

Again, Leticia shook her head almost violently.

Luis laughed. "Go ahead. I'm closed tomorrow." He grabbed Leticia's arm and shoved her out the door.

Her last glance pleaded with Annie, who took it as a warning. But what did it mean?

"Perhaps I call your friend, Nicholas?" Aunt Fumi's furrowed brow meant it wasn't really a question.

"I don't even have his cell number. I'll go see the police or something. Go home, Auntie. It's been a long day. Don't worry." Annie tried to smile.

"We'll go to the police. And you come home with me." Aunt Fumi said.

"Oh, no. I'm not running from Luis or anybody. Besides, I have a lot of restocking to do tonight."

"I thought you were taking Tuesday off. We worked so hard."

"I changed my mind. Maybe the momentum will continue." Annie shrugged. "You go on. I'll call you in the morning." *Or before anything happens.*

Under protest, Aunt Fumi drove back to Santa Fe, and Annie unboxed trinkets, postcards, and wind chimes. Her mind troubled over the girls, but she imagined and hoped that ICE and Nicholas' actions to help the girls would all converge tomorrow. Her stomach flipped a little. Surely, Luis wouldn't act that quickly.

But Leticia said they were being moved. Maybe Annie couldn't wait until tomorrow. She had no choice but to stake out the Cocina tonight. Sitting by the open window once more, she watched the late-night crowds file in and out of Cocina Azul. A hot breeze blew in the window. The restaurant stayed open long past ten o'clock, and the crowds still came. The line outside diminished, but inside, the restaurant bustled with activity. Luis and Claudia must have had even better sales than Haven's Rest Gift Shop. They could do good business here, and it would be good for the community.

Why couldn't Luis and Claudia aid those girls instead of abusing them? Training good help would only benefit all their futures. And the girls obviously needed their help. Annie thought back on her past. People who took in children didn't often have their best interests in mind. Overwhelmed and strapped for finances, many parents made a quick buck fostering. Not an easy job and many meant well. But the children suffered, like Annie. The system was broken, and only God could fix it through changed hearts.

That's what happened to Aunt Fumi. At first, she fostered Annie for the money. She wanted nothing to do with her until God touched Fumi's heart, and her life changed. She quit fostering and lavished Jesus' love on Annie.

But some people were just plain selfish and evil, like Luis and Claudia. Annie shivered. Seeking God and trusting Him was the answer. Only God saw the whole picture, and she had to trust Him for His goodness.

Annie's eyes drooped, and she retired to the papasan chair for a little nap. As long as she heard the noise filtering in from across the street, she could rest easy. Somewhere, the noise ceased, and Annie fell fast asleep.

A sharp, needle-like pain pricked her neck. Annie sat upright to see men with ski masks pulling her off the chair where she'd fallen asleep. She flung her arms at them, but like wet noodles, they wouldn't cooperate. Drowsiness enveloped her, and everything went dark.

∽

Tuesday morning, Aunt Fumi stood outside Haven's Rest with the Police Captain and another officer.

"Hurry up," she said. "Annie was supposed to call this morning."

"All right, all right," the captain said. His large body fumbled with the keys Fumi had given him. "She's probably just taking Tuesday off. Lots of shops are open after the busy weekend.

"No. She said she was opening." Fumi said in a shaky voice.

"I'm sure she's fine," the officer said.

Pushing open the gift shop door, the captain yelled. "Anybody home? Ms. Greensprings?"

"Annie! Where are you?" Fumi called.

All three walked around the small shop, and then Fumi rushed toward the back door leading to the alley.

"Her car is gone," Fumi said.

"See. She took the day off."

"No. She would have told me," Fumi said. "Something happened to her. I think it was that Luis at Cocina Azul."

The officer went to the back stairs, searched, and returned. "Captain, there are a couple of muddy footprints on the stairs."

Taking off his broad-brimmed hat, the captain slapped it against his leg. "That doesn't mean anything."

"They look fresh, and they look like boot prints. Two sets."

"Fine, go patrol both exits from town and see if you find anything suspicious on the road."

"My niece drives a red SUV."

"Make and model?" asked the officer.

Fumi shrugged.

"Okay, Captain. I'll check it out." The officer left.

"See, it's that Luis," Fumi wagged a finger at the captain.

'Come on, now. Let's not go accusing the fine merchants of—" The captain paused and held up a hand. His head tipped to listening.

The sound of a caravan of vehicles lumbered up the main

road. He turned and reentered from the back of the shop, and Fumi followed. Both exited the front door to see three ICE SUVs pull up across the street. A Lexus sports car parked behind them and out stepped Nicolas Nighthaven.

Agents knocked on the cafe's front door. They pounded, shouting orders to open, and after a few seconds, a beefy, broad officer shoved his shoulder to the door, busting it open. Nicolas stood back and locked eyes with Fumi. She stepped off the porch, but he lifted a finger for her to stop.

"All clear," agents yelled from inside.

Nicholas turned to follow.

"Annie is missing!" Fumi yelled.

Stopping in his tracks, he crossed the street. "What did you say?"

"Hey, is all that necessary?" The captain asked. "We got a peaceful community here."

"You did, but we have evidence that the owner, Luis Melendez, trafficked his girls from Brownsville. He's also a suspect in the murders of their parents."

"How'd you find all that out so fast?" The captain scratched his head.

"Annie is gone," Fumi blurted. "You must find her. I think Luis took her."

Nicholas swallowed, and his Adam's apple bobbed. He loosened his tie and removed his jacket, slinging it over his arm. "Took her? Where?"

"Look, the woman probably just took the day off. Her car is gone, and the Closed sign was hung in her window," the captain rolled his eyes at Fumi.

"Captain, I know where Luis Melendez lives. Will you take me there?" Nicolas asked.

The captain shook his head. "Look, I got a town to look after. I can't be chasing every woman that decides to run off for the day."

"Fine, I'll take my car and go myself."

"What about ICE?" The captain asked.

"They'll go after they're finished here." Nicolas moved toward his car.

"I'll go with you," Aunt Fumi started down the steps.

The Captain stretched his arm in front of her. "Now, hold on. Why not let the Feds handle it?" He pointed across the street. "Those ICE agents know exactly what they're doing."

"So do I." Nicholas pulled his shoulders back. "They acted on a tip from Annie Greensprings, and my team checked into it."

"Your team?" The captain raised his brows and pointed to Nicholas' car. "How does an immigration lawyer make enough to drive a car like that?"

Fumi slapped the captain's arm. "Haven't you ever heard of pro-bono?" She smiled at Nicholas. "Right?"

"Somewhat. And I didn't say I'm an immigration attorney, but I have an organization, and I happen to personally know an ICE agent in Santa Fe. He got on it, and we have a valid case building against Luis Melendez."

"That was fast," the captain sighed.

"It helped that the Police in Brownsville had a file on him. Now, I'm headed for Melendez's home out a ways down the highway. Are you coming?"

Across the street, the ICE agents' SUVs roared to life.

Nicholas turned. "Never mind, I'm following them."

But he stopped at the sound of a siren and flashing lights atop a police SUV. It screeched toward them. The Madrid Police Officer pulled up and jumped out.

"What are you doing back so fast?" The captain frowned.

The officer sounded breathless. "I found it. A red SUV just a mile out of town and a half mile off the main road in the dirt. Tire tracks indicate two vehicles drove out there, but only one left. The red car is definitely abandoned."

Fumi gasped. She reached for a porch post and closed her eyes.

"The captain trotted to the police vehicle and called over his shoulder to the officer. "You keep an eye out here." He looked at Nicholas. "Are you coming?"

"The turnoff is about a mile out of town, going south. A couple of torn-up creosote bushes mark the path," the officer said.

Fumi sat on the porch swing and prayed in silence.

As they exited Madrid and hit the main highway, at almost the mile marker that the officer indicated, a red compact SUV pulled onto the main highway.

"There!" yelled Nicholas.

"I got it."

The captain hit the sirens and sped up. So did the red SUV. Nicholas reached up and clutched the grab handle above his door. The captain drew up so close that he almost rammed the bumper of Annie's car. He pulled out a microphone and spoke over the loudspeaker. One hand on the wheel.

"Pull over, now."

The car sped up.

"Oh, this ain't going to turn out good." The captain stepped on the accelerator, making chase.

"He's not stopping," Nicholas said.

"Nope. Doesn't look like it."

The captain called in for a roadblock from Albuquerque, and with the siren still screaming, he followed. Twenty minutes later, an ICE SUV blocked the road right about at the Melendez property turnoff. The red SUV turned off-road, and the ICE vehicle followed in pursuit. The captain slowed.

"What are you doing? She could be in there." Nicholas ran a hand through his hair.

"Or she could be in the home." The captain turned into the long dirt drive.

Another ICE vehicle barreled toward them and swerved around, obviously joining the pursuit. Pueblo-style structures loomed before them. One large building looked decent enough to inhabit, but three smaller ones were fairly run down. Windows were broken, and chunks of adobe brick were missing. They drove forward, and an ICE agent on foot approached them.

"We don't think they're here."

Nicholas gulped. He ran a hand through his damp hair. Sweat trickled down his temples.

"You check all the buildings?" The captain asked.

The agent nodded. "We'll make another pass through, but it looks like they've been gone a while. Beds are made, but there is no food on the stove. It looks like they've moved the girls already."

Nicholas punched the door with his fist. "We should have come last night."

"Sorry, Nick. We didn't have jurisdiction until this morning. You know that," an agent said.

The captain looked at Nicholas. "Why didn't you call me?"

"Because Annie said you didn't believe her." Nicholas shook his head. "I should have."

Nodding, the captain pursed his lips. "Yeah. Sometimes it's a hard call." He pushed open his door. "Did you look for underground bunkers? A lot of these old places have them."

"Yes. But we haven't uncovered any."

"Tunnels?" The captain covered his eyes, searching the desert beyond the structures.

"Nope."

"Tunnels? Aren't we a little far from the border for that?" Nicholas asked.

"Some folks sought refuge from aliens out here," the captain shrugged.

"Wasn't that in Nevada? Area 51?"

"Yeah, but we got our own myths, too. And you'd be surprised what you find out here."

The ICE agent spoke into a shoulder mic. He nodded. "They got the guy in the red SUV. They're bringing him back here now. But he insists he doesn't know anything. Said he was basically stealing the car after ditching it for the abductors."

She could hear them talking. Annie pushed herself to stand, straining to make out the voices overhead. A rumbling caused the earth to shake, and dirt broke loose, covering her head. The girls screamed through their gagged mouths. Annie joined them, but the duct tape pulled as she tried opening her mouth. Annie's eyes widened. If she could free their mouths, they might be heard. Not knowing when Luis or the others would return, she worked quickly. Turning around, she stumbled over stretched-out legs. Slowly, she backed up to one of the girls sitting on the ground. Assuming it was Leticia, she searched her face, fumbling to find Leticia's taped mouth with her zip-tied hands, Annie pinched her fingers and grabbed a corner of the tape. Leticia helped by yanking her head sideways. Annie spun around.

"*Ayudame!* Help me," Leticia yelled.

Another rumble and earth shake, and Leticia screamed. She sputtered and spit what Annie assumed was dirt. The girls managed to help each other by removing the tape from all their mouths.

"Follow my voice," Annie said.

The pitch dark prevented any visual communication, and Annie could only hope she crawled in the right direction. Leticia instructed the girls to follow on their knees.

"Keep yelling," Annie called. "Ouch!" She screamed. A sharp rock embedded in her knee. "And be careful."

Another rumbled overhead, and the girls dropped flat on the ground. Little dirt fell this time, but Annie's stomach roiled. It sounded like vehicles leaving. She listened. No voices anymore.

"Hurry!" Annie called as she edged forward.

Not sure how long they'd been scooting, Annie prayed and yelled the whole way, hoping someone would hear them. Finally, a shaft of light ahead. The girls squealed with delight. Reaching the end of the tunnel, a ladder stretched upward. Annie stared up, wondering how she'd make the climb. Turning her back to the ladder, she gripped the rungs with her hands and pushed down. Propelling her body upwards, she jumped atop each rung. Pain ripped through her shoulders, but finally she made it to the top. The trap door opened. More earth fell on her head, and her eyes stung between the dirt and blazing sunlight.

"You made my trip down there a whole lot easier," the voice of dread said.

Annie let herself slip back down, tumbling on top of the girls.

Luis jumped in and grabbed each one of them, hoisting them up the ladder.

When all four girls lay on the ground, gasping for breath, Annie kicked at Luis standing over her. He stepped back and laughed.

"Now, is that any way to greet your rescuer?" He sneered.

"Enough, Luis," Claudia bent over the girls, knife in hand.

Leticia gasped, but Claudia cut loose each of their feet. They stood as she spoke in Spanish. Luis grabbed the three girls and shoved them toward his Escalade.

Claudia narrowed her eyes at Annie. "Get up. We must leave now."

Annie shook her head. Long, loose, dark hair slipped from her ponytail. "I'm not going anywhere. Someone was here, and they knew we were, too."

Marching back, Luis slapped her hard. "See, Claudia. I told you. We should have taken them."

"No matter. Now we're free to leave. They'll not be back," Claudia said.

"I wouldn't be so sure of that," the captain emerged from behind one of the uninhabitable structures. His gun pointed at Luis. "Now step back. Move away from the girl, slowly."

Annie tried to focus. Luis's slap had landed too close to her eye. But she thought she saw Nicholas. Yes. He rushed over and grabbed the knife from a shocked Claudia. He cut Annie's hands free, but Luis leaped, grabbing Nicholas' arm, and wrestling the knife away. Nicholas pushed Annie out of the way, but Luis lunged, slicing Nicholas' bicep. Blood poured out, but he pulled back a fist. A crack sounded, and Luis fell before Nicholas could land a punch.

The captain stood with the gun pointed at Claudia. She immediately dropped to the ground, cradling Luis's limp body. The captain spoke in his shoulder mic, calling for backup and an ambulance. Luis moaned.

"You two okay?" The captain glanced at Annie and Nicholas.

Annie pulled off her belt and fastened it tightly above his wound.

"Hey!" he yelled. "A little easy, there."

She stared down at him and smiled. Her hero. At the moment she forgot everything else, grabbed his face and kissed him sweetly on the lips. She pulled back and giggled.

"I'm feeling better already. Got any more of that medicine?"

Annie punched his good arm lightly and glanced at the girls crying in the car. "Thanks so much. But what will happen to them, now?"

368 | KATHLEEN J. ROBISON

"We'll take good care of them."

"We?"

"Nighthaven Rescue." Nicholas smiled.

"Annie Greensprings, you got God on your side or something." The captain shook his head. "If it wasn't for that man, I'm not sure we could have saved you women."

"Not me. It was totally a God thing." Nicholas sighed loudly as if the wound was beginning to affect him.

God thing? Did he say that? Annie's heart leaped. "What's Nighthaven Rescue? Isn't your last name Nighthaven?"

"Yes, but it's a long story." Nicholas tried to stand but winced. "My grandfather helped some Japanese immigrants who were interned in Santa Fe during WWII."

"Interned?" Annie's eyes widened.

"An internment camp was just outside Santa Fe. It's all gone now, nothing but a boulder for a marker," the captain said.

"Aunt Fumi's mother was interned in one, way up in Wyoming." Annie swallowed. "I had no idea there was one in Santa Fe."

"Not many know about it. But it's about time everyone did." Nicholas sighed. "Some non-profit is building a museum dedicated to that blight on American history."

The captain walked over to Claudia and gazed at the tunnel opening. "Hey, I wonder if these tunnels have anything to do with it? Lots of bad stuff went on. Forced labor with the internees and stuff."

"I hope not," Nicholas said. "My grandfather used to teach Bible Studies to the Japanese POWs and then used his legal status to help stop the mistreatment." Nicholas smiled at Annie.

"And you? How did you get involved?" She asked.

"Before I graduated from law school, I did a lot of volunteer work for the organization. But when I graduated at the top of my class, offers from all kinds of top firms came in."

He rifled a hand through his hair. "You might say I got enticed by the world."

Annie nodded. "I'll say. Fancy clothes, fancy car—"

Nicholas touched a finger to her lips. He picked up a strand of her loose hair and tucked it behind her ear. "It doesn't mean anything anymore. Not since I met you, Annie."

Annie pulled back. "What did you mean when you said, 'A God thing'?"

He pointed to the Leticia and her sisters. "Everyone worked quickly, and we hit no obstacles in moving fast. I couldn't have done it alone. God definitely had his hand in this."

Annie held back tears.

"I've never walked away from Him. I just got a little luke-warm. But this weekend, when everything fell into place, I started praying more. I—"

"Wait a minute. You pray?"

He frowned. "Of course. But I've never prayed so hard as when Aunt Fumi said you'd gone missing," his blue eyes glistened.

"I prayed, too," Annie said. But she didn't tell him she prayed she could forget him. God's ways were so much better than hers. "Nighthaven's Rescue. Haven's Rest Gift Shop. I think there's a connection there." Annie hunched.

"I think so, too." Nicholas placed his hand behind her neck and gently pulled her forward. He kissed her softly. His lips lingered, filling her with exploding joy.

"I think Nighthaven rescued me, too," Annie said.

THE END